Of the Red

a novel

C.J. LONG

Page Solutions - Prowriters Network
541 Buttermilk Pike
Crescent Springs, KY 41017

Copyright © 2025 by C.J. Long.

ISBN 979-8-89633-040-0 (softcover)
ISBN 979-8-89633-041-7 (ebook)

This book is a work of fiction. Names, characters, places, and incidents are the product of the author's imagination or are used fictitiously. Any resemblance to actual locales, events, or persons, living or dead, is purely coincidental.

Printed in the United States of America.

To my wife Anna. Sweetheart I love you with all my heart. To Bella who always encouraged me to finish, and to Ben whose nap times I used to write this novel. I love you all!

…and to Kyle, I miss you.

Prologue

Waking up in this place, both scared and comforted Danny. It was dark all the time, and the dark is what scared him the most. You never knew what was in that darkness, whether it was the people, monsters or even just the stillness that remains with the uncertainty that something is waiting for you. To see you. To have you.

The people, if you would call them that, beat Danny for most of the day, while screaming questions that he couldn't understand. Even if by some miracle he understood whatever Arabic language that was being spat at his face, he knew nothing of what they wanted. That was where the comfort part came into effect. As long as he woke up to this place, this hole, he knew that he had hope that he wouldn't be taking out back of some woods and shot. That survival was still in his mind, and hope of escape was still possible. But even the chances of getting out alive were slim at best, and getting smaller by the day. Though his captives were not feeding him, they gave him water, but his body needed nutrition. Danny knew from survival courses that the human body can go twenty-one days without food, but even with the constant supply of water his captors were giving him, his body was getting weaker and weaker with each passing hour. Besides—this was day eighteen.

Trying to lift his head up was like lifting a barbell. The weakness was everywhere in his body, right along with the pain that enveloped his stomach from the hunger that engulfed him. Hunger was all he knew. The wanting, the needing of food. He missed food like an alcoholic misses the drink. This struggle has been happening for days now, and just like those days before he had to fight it. Fight this pain that felt like a rat burrowing inside him and eating him from the inside out. Fight the mere thought of having food, that maybe some insect might come through the bottom of the door and see it in the darkness and try to be quick enough to snatch it and put it his mouth, and crunch down on it with every savory bite. Danny knew now as he would until food actually came that he would lose this fight today, if the battle wasn't already lost at the moment.

Slowly Danny was trying to get up, move to the wall closest to him that was the opposite side of the door. Darkness still engulfed the chamber, but Danny had been so used to the darkness since being brought here that his eyes adjusted to where he could see the corners of the walls, the sand on the floor, even the cracks of the door that held him in. As he looked around the chamber he noticed nothing had changed in his settings. His water bottle that those sons of bitches usually filled was still empty by the door, where they told him to leave it every time he finished it. Normally, this wouldn't be so strange. Hours went by all the time before he would get a refill. Even though Danny had no sense of time in this place, (there was no clock of course and no windows to look outside) he felt that time had elapsed further than the other times when water was given to him. No, he didn't feel, he knew. Something was going on.

There was no noise, no voices, no curses, no sound. Just silence.

There was no light, no movement outside, no life. Just darkness.

Since being here there have been guards outside his chamber door, standing and shifting their weight from one foot to the other. The sounds that they make, breathing, talking, walking. All were absent now from the hallway outside the door. Silence that burned, silence that screamed through the darkness and into his empty, hungry stomach and outweighed the feeling of hunger to the feeling of dread.

"Hello?!" He yelled.

There was no answer.

"Is anyone there? Hello? HELLO!" He screamed.

He waited for an answer, any answer from the outside world that might come back to him. Washing away the fear that he was feeling now, that his captors would return, because even though his captors were nowhere near what you would call friends…Hell. You couldn't even call them human beings, they were all Danny had left to keep his survival going in this place. His water supply at least. Now, there was this feeling…This sinking feeling that they were gone. Leaving him here with no food, no more water, nothing but darkness and pain.

It wasn't suppose to be like this, he was supposed to be retired from the military. Into civilian life, like he had been enjoying for almost five years. The days of being locked up like a prisoner of war in some hole-in-the-ground bunker were over. Not that he had all that much time in concrete cells in his time in the military. There was only one time he was ever really locked up, and that was training purposes in the Army version of SERE school, or the Survive, Evade, Resist, Escape, training facility they had at the National Training Center in Fort Irwin, California. Two weeks of a hell on earth where they played mind-games, beat you daily, and subjected you to tortures, like water-boarding, with the soul purpose to break you. If you broke during the course, you failed and were rejected from the program, and sent home with your tail between your legs.

During the course they got intensely personal with the mind-games that they played on you. What they did with Daniel Staubach as he was tied to a chair was ask him if he knew where his wife Brittney was at that moment? At the time he did not know the answer to that, because from what he knew of the current day that he kept track of in his head, it was Saturday and for all he knew Brittney was having a girls day where she was getting her hair done, or nails colored. He didn't answer the man, who he guessed was some Sergeant or officer that was trained for this type of interrogation.

"No? Well I'm not going to waste my time telling you about where she is." He said.

What the hell does that mean? Danny thought. But he saw his interrogator pull out a smartphone from his pocket, pressed a couple of buttons on the screen, and then showed Danny the screen.

"Here." Said the interrogator as he slid him the phone on the table.

What Danny saw scared him and angered him so bad, that if he wasn't tied down he would have choked the life out of the little man in front of him, and watched his beady green eyes burst with red as the veins in them would burst. What was on the the smartphone screen was a video of his wife Brittney at home standing in front of the TV. She was wearing her pink and black workout clothes that she usually wore for when she went out running. Underneath where she was standing was a purple yoga mat, where she started to bend down and touch as she began a stretch that took to touch her calves behind on her legs. After about ten seconds she slowly lifted up her arms while simultaneously moved her left leg to the back of the mat. Finally she put her arms up above her head and interlocked her fingers together except for both index finger where she pointed them straight up into the air as if she were going to shoot holes in the ceiling with them.

"That's a live feed by the way. Just look at the way she stretches, you are a lucky, lucky man!" His interrogator said with a smile that said he would like to fuck her three ways from Sunday. "Since you have been here we've kept a close watch onto her. I mean, not all the other prisoners have either a wife or a girlfriend that can bend like that. A couple of the guys were comparing them altogether last night, and yours is by far the hottest. Tell me, is she that flexible in bed?"

Rage was all that Danny felt when he both saw and heard this. They went into his house and planted cameras in his living room, if not in other places of his house as well, so they can use his wife as a tool to get him to break. He felt more than rage as his thoughts gathered while watching the video, he felt…..felt….violated. Like nothing was safe, nothing was personal, nothing was off the table, so to speak. Everything in his life was fair game in this training, everything in his life could somehow be used against him so he could break and tell them anything they wanted to know. Danny was fighting all of these thoughts and emotions on the inside. On the outside, he showed no more emotion than a stone statue. Knowing that even giving his interrogator even a small wince was too much satisfaction than he deserved.

"Do you want to see the shower scene I previously recorded?" His interrogator asked.

Danny remembered this as a low point in his training as the closest he ever came to breaking in his training. Since being captive in this place, he replayed it in his mind to remind himself to try and remain strong. Even though his training never starved him the way he was being done now. Nor was he left to die, like he was now.

Danny tried to lift his body up off the hard stone floor. He didn't realize how far his body had fallen without any incoming nutrition. Moving around was harder now with his very weak muscles, but he managed to get to his feet with a hand holding him up against the wall. His right leg throbbed with pain as he put weight on it. His leg has been hurting about three beatings ago when one of the guards started to kick him repeatedly, making his way up and down Danny's body, kicking along the way. Until the guard stopped moving along his body and remained by his right leg, then engaged his leg with two kicks, and a stomp right down on Danny's kneecap with a nice pop sound that would almost sound as if someone opened a Tupperware container if the sound wasn't drowned out by Danny's screams, and the guards laughs.

Moving slowly along the wall, Danny tried to make his way to the doors' small window that slides open from time to time when the guards look in on him. After about two minutes of edging along the wall, he finally made it to the door. The view slider was closed so Danny lifted his hands to lift it. While doing this he put too much weight on his sore leg, and the pain shot up the right side of his body. Danny winced with the pain, he put his right arm down on his leg to try and hold it still and stop it from hurting too much. With his left hand he used his fingers to try and slide the piece of metal to look outside. Slowly it moved and was completely opened.

When Danny first arrived in his cell he tried to move the slider on the door, he was greeted with an angry face, and a butt stock of a rifle. Now, even with darkness in the hallway, there was no one to be seen on either his right or left. Silence was in the hallway. No echoes of distant voices, or that of closing doors, or of footsteps pounding on the ground. Nothing. No one.

Terror began to fill up inside him. His breathing started to become heavy as the panic took over. He tried to calm himself by working to control his breathing, making it his lungs take small breaths with quick exhales. Trying this four times to try and control his nerves, and come back to his senses. But a part of him that was still terrified took hold of his impulses and tried to grab for the locked doorknob, thinking there was no way the doorknob was going to budge. They locked him in here so he could starve or dehydrate alone in the dark. To Danny's surprise, the knob turned about a quarter of an inch, more than it had any other time he tried to open the door. He kept turning the knob, slowly. It continued to move. Danny couldn't believe what was happening, he kept moving the knob until it stopped at half turn. He then lightly pushed the door to open it and the door moved to reveal a small crack of opening that lead to the hallway.

What the fuck was going on? Why leave me here in my cell, only to leave the door unlocked? These questions flooded Danny's mind, but he remained on alert in case this was some sort of trap that got him shot in the back. Opening the door slowly, he entered the hallway. Looking both right and left and seeing only darkness both ways, Danny decided he was going right. His captors brought him in while he was unconscious, was woken up in this place with a hard thud and pain in his head. Going right somehow made sense in his mind, and if going right would somehow lead to a dead end, he would just come back and try the left. Moving slowly and painfully along the wall of the hallway, Danny thought about the pain that was in his stomach. How much he could eat almost anything at this point. He didn't think it was possible that his hunger pains could eclipse the pain in his leg, but it was and it was horrible. He could feel his stomach try and eat itself as if it were a worm in an apple slowly devour itself from the inside out. While moving down he felt a corner in the wall that lead to the left. Following for few feet ahead of him, he suddenly kicked a cold solid object that stubbed his big toe.

"Ahh! Dammit!" He cried out, hearing the echo through the darkness come back to him. Danny bent down trying to cope with the pain that his foot now brought him. While bending down with his left leg while trying to keep his right leg straight, he tried to feel what it was his foot hit. Moving his hand blindly along the ground he felt the object was apart of the ground and leveled off about six inches off the ground. Reaching along this plateau, his hand suddenly stopped at another object that moved up diagonally up.

"Stairs. Thank God!" He exclaimed in low breath. If there were stairs there was probably a door at the top that could lead him out of here.

Danny got back up, even his pain from his leg and stomach was muted some with the knowledge he might be able to get out of this cold, dark, hell hole. He had to take it easy up the steps, climbing up with one bad leg and be physically weak was no easy thing. Even though he was moving slow he thought he was moving faster up the stairs then he thought he ever had. He was getting out of here! The excitement ran through him like electricity. Going up the steps he had his hand on the wall balancing his...

Suddenly, Danny's left foot landed on something that felt odd and tripped forward onto the stairs. Getting as far up as the fifth step, his body landed on something that was both hard but soft, but his head made contact with one of the stairs ahead of him. Hitting his head hard enough to cause him to curse out in frustration, but not enough to where he could feel the trickle of blood coming out of an open cut.

While trying to get up, he put his hand down on one of the steps. Only when his hand made contact with the step it came on top of something that felt all to familiar. He released his weigh from the hand— the cold, dead hand.

Danny tried to get up quickly, muscling through his pain. He balanced himself on a single step, with his right hand holding onto the wall. A dead body? Was he another prisoner? Was he a guard? What the fuck's going on?

He bent down to try and feel if he could identify anything on the body he was able to recognize through touch. Feeling around and touching the skin of the hand was like feeling up ice, the cold still skin that wouldn't budge an inch due to the setting in of rigor mortis. Moving up on the arm he felt the clothes of the body. Moving up on the arm and made his way to the shoulder, he felt a hard band of cloth tightly pulled down across the chest of the guard. He followed the band of cloth, hoping the band of cloth is a sling to a gun. Suddenly, his hand felt something hard, and moved to try and feel around the butt stock of a AR-15 assault rifle. Danny pulled on the rifle hoping that it wouldn't be wrapped under the man's body, there was resistance from the pull. Danny decided to bend down again and try to feel were the sling was wrapped around the back of the man's head, while resting on his right shoulder. All he would have to do was pull the sling over the man's head and the rifle would be his. After doing this, the questions began to riddle Danny's mind.

How did this guard die? As far as he could see the man wasn't shot stabbed, or even hit with any blunt object. Feeling around on him he would have felt blood, cuts or gashes, or if he was hit with something, broken bones or a bashed in skull. He had none of those. Maybe he could have died of a heart attack or a stroke if the gods of luck were truly that kind. But even if that happened, it didn't explain why any of this bastards buddies didn't come down to help him if he was dying? Surely they would have noticed if one of their buddies was gone for long periods of time, especially if going down by a prisoner, wouldn't they?

Danny wasn't going to take a chance in case this guy just happened to bite the dust, he was going to be ready for his buddies coming down the stairs. Danny raised the rifle on his right arm to check for a magazine in place. He didn't know what happened and he didn't give a fuck about any of these pieces of shit. As far he knew, they deserved whatever death came to them times a hundred. What he did care about was getting the hell out of here as fast as he was able to move.

Moving past the body, he began once again to move up the stairs in his slow and staggered climb up. He kept to the far right side of the stairwell so he could lean against it to somewhat support his right side as he climbed up the stairs. Also to steer clear of anymore bodies that might be lying around on the stairs, if there were anymore lying around. He climbed the stairwell for about seven more steps when finally the barrel of his rifle banged up against something hard. It hit with a hard tap on what sounded like hard steel. Danny put a hand out in front of him and could feel the hard cold metal and knew this was a door. Moving his hand to the edge of the door, he tried and felt around for the doorknob and prayed that it wasn't locked. After a few seconds of trying to find the doorknob while maintaining his balance on the stairs with his bad leg, he found the doorknob and turned it. The door opened.

Cool air surrounded Danny's body and raised the hair on the back of his neck. His bare feet touched upon dirt and leaves. It was dark outside, but by the light of the moon he could see that he was in a woodland area by looking up and seeing their tall shadows up against the starry sky. He was cold, but warmth coursed through his body on a simple thought. He was free. How could this be happening? Where were the rest of the guards? If someone killed that guard, why not come and help him out of his cell? What the fuck was going around here? What? What?! WHAT?!

Danny moved forward a few steps then looked back at where he was being held for the last few days. All he saw was the door that he left open, surrounded by a concrete foundation. It was a bunker of some sort or other. Either that or a compound of some sort, but looking at it reminded him of the show *Doomsday Preppers.* Where entire family's dedicate their free time and money on these grandiose bunkers that can not only save them and their families, but pretty much prepare them for whatever else the elements would throw at them after the initial apocalypse ends.

Backing away from the bunker, he felt a genuine hatred toward the structure that held him for weeks, as well as the people who kept him there. Time was taken from him. A resource precious to most people, including him, was robbed from him so they could ask him fucking questions about the military that were probably out of date by now. What was worse is his captors made him feel they kidnapped him to another country. Like some desert in one of those marvelous countries that most of the military refer to as "The Stans", and for all he knew he still was, but he didn't seem likely. With the thick smell of pine in the air as well as the leaves he felt on his feet, if he were in "the Stans", he would be in the closest one to Russia. Chances are they fooled him by fly him around in a private plane for a few hours while keeping tied up, blindfolded, and drugged and saying they were in the middle of a desert. Chances were in was somewhere in the Midwest.

Danny's foot stepped onto something. He turned around and looked down and jumped back with surprise and horror. Down by his feet, a body looked up into the stars with a look of terror on his face, as if he saw that the sky was ready to fall on top of him. Looking around he saw there two…no, three more bodies laying around in the dirt, two laying facedown, one fell down onto his side, the last one face up like the one he was examining. Something strange was happening here.

"Why hello there! What's your name?" Said a voice that was high and shrill just like a very perky little girl.

Danny turned around to the direction of the voice, but all he saw was the bunker he just crawled out of. The voice was calm, energetic, and curious, as if the voice was was going to ask to play a game of some sort. What? This was all too strange for Danny. The situation was getting stranger and stranger as the minutes went on. Who was this now? And why were they so damn happy? Did she not see the bodies laying around on the ground? Unless….she caused these bodies to be here?

"Hello, who's there?" Danny asked with a nervousness in his voice.

"Na ah ah, I asked you first!" Said the voice. Danny looked around the woods frantically, trying to see if anyone was standing around him. Fear started to grip his insides and he started to raise his rifle and moved slowly around himself to scan his sectors.

"D…Danny. Danny Staubach."

"Well, D…Danny Staubach, I would put that away if I were you. You wouldn't want to get hurt, would you?" The voice sounded like it was coming from all around him, all throughout the woods.

"Where are you?"

"Over here handsome." Danny turned around and saw, leaning against the bunker, was a woman. She was tall with brunette hair that was done up in pig-tails, with big eyes that had a sour apple green to them. They were the greenest eyes Danny ever saw on a person. The biggest feature that stood out the most on this woman, was all the red. She presented herself in a dark red corset that was bottomed out with a just as red skirt that went down to her knees, and was almost greeted by the top of her tall boots that were of course in a shade of red that didn't exactly match the rest of her dress, but was still a shade of unmistakable red. Danny was also surprised to see that her shoulders and arms were exposed. He was freezing in his jeans and t-shirt he had on out here, his shivering arms were a tell-tale sign, but she wasn't shivering. She gave off a stance and look as if the cold wasn't there at all, what she did was give him a look as if he was the most fascinating person she ever saw.

"Why don't you put that gun down? I'm not going to hurt you."

"Says the only person around a bunch of dead bodies. What happened to them?"

"They were starving you, weren't they? I wanted to help you."

"I asked you, what happened to them?" Danny said raising his voice slightly, but without water for the past day to lubricant his vocal cords, it was the highest his voice would go.

She answered in a matter-of-factly tone. "They wanted to take something from you that you had stored up here." She pointed to her head in a gesture with her index finger and thumb like she was putting a gun up to her head. "But what I wanted from them, was all in here." Then with a smirk, she made a gesture with her arms and hands that curved the outline of her body.

Danny stood back and raised his rifle at the woman with fear. His arms were killing him from the weight of the rifle, but he had no choice. This woman was a threat to him if she openly admitted to killing the men that were now scattered around him on the ground.

These men though…these men were psychotic. They tortured him, starved him, all for what? To ask him questions that he didn't know the language in which it was spoken, let alone answer them. Didn't this woman technically save him in some way? There was nothing technical about it, she *did* in fact save his life from these monsters. Did he not owe this woman his trust, if not at least his respect? Maybe. Even if that was true, trust was not something he gave out for like free ice cream cones. If she did kill these men around her, then she would have no problems taking a life. *His* life.

"What are you doing here? Why *did* you help me?"

"I've been watching them for some time, ever since I saw them take you here over a week and a half ago. I wanted to see what they would do to you, and how you would get out." she started to move closer to him. "Then after a while, I saw they had no intention of letting you go. They were just going to leave you in there like a starving cat in a box, so then one thing lead to another and..." She waved her arm around to show what became of them, like a model on a game show.

"They have no marks on them. How did you do it, poison?"

"That's not important. What is important is what I want from you."

Danny stepped back. "You're not getting anything from me lady!" he snapped at her. "I just want to get out of here!"

"If you give me what I want I will take you away from here. If not, I leave you here. Right now you are in Canada, near a small town thats not far from the Ottawa river. I won't tell you which direction or how far."

"Why not?"

"You refuse to help me by giving me what I want when you have no idea what I want. You close yourself off from me, assume that you do not need anything from the likes of me, even after I saved you from these...these...fiends that would have left you here to starve. So in what way would I help you, when you offer nothing to me in return?"

Danny was taken aback by this. Save me only to leave me to die anyway? He knew by looking around and being in the woods he could survive out here on nature if he had to. Could he? His strength was so low, his stomach hurt so much from starvation, and his knee. Christ his knee. After doing this assessment on himself, he realized he didn't have a chance out here. One bear, or wolf would just have to look at him and think: "Oh a free lunch today!". He needed help to get out of here. He needed this woman to help him, if she was going to kill him she would have done it before when he wasn't looking or while he was asleep in his cell. Right? What could she really ask for anyway?

"Okay, ask me what it is you want."

She told him. It took two minutes for her to explain what she needed, his role and what it would mean for him. Danny thought about what she wanted, pondered for a little over five minutes, knowing that the woman was getting more and more restless. He knew it wasn't just going to effect what would happen in a few days if he got out of here, but also the rest of his life. But it was either this, or die out here. Sometimes when it came to survival you had to pick the only way that would lead you to life.

"I'm waiting...", said the woman.

"I'll do it." Danny said as he put the rifle onto the ground.

"Excellent!" exclaimed the woman in red. "Now lets get you something to eat."

"I don't even know your name?"

"I know, but we will get to that eventually."

They walked into the darkness of the woods.

Part I:
The Woman

"I see a red door and I want it painted black
No colors anymore, I want them to turn black
I see the girls walk by dressed in their summer clothes
I have to turn my head until my darkness goes."

—*Mick Jagger & Keith Richards*

Chapter 1

Two years later.

Tyler George Green laid awake in bed staring up at the ceiling with the biggest hangover he felt for at least the last year. Last nights alcohol intake while dealing with the notice that his wife Samantha was going to divorce hit him particularly hard. Leaving him that very day and saying she was going to stay at a friend's house, was just the language commonly known as bullshit for she was going to be staying at the guy she is fucking's house until she needed to retrieve the rest of her stuff from his apartment.

The windows in the apartment had their shades open, which caused a huge beam to steamroll through his eyeballs and into his skull that felt like it wanted to melt his brain to the point of complete agony. Squinting through his eyelids, he tried to move up on his bed to pull the line on the curtains to try and close them, but then there was a huge lurch that moved in his stomach that indicated that some of the Jack Daniels that was still in his stomach wanted to come up and say: "Hello and good morning!". Tyler pulled the covers off his bed and made a mad dash to the bathroom that was just next to his bedroom on the end of the hallway. He saw that the toilet seat was open still, started to assume the position and let the fireworks fly out of his mouth.

"Fuck." he said after he finished with his third heave into the toilet. The brown vomit that was now in the toilet made him think that he might not be done with he firework show just yet, so he went from a kneel to a sit right next to the porcelain throne.

While waiting to see if the fireworks would continue, he thought back to the conversation he had with Samantha. She never did liked being called by her full name, but with the hurt that she give out on him last night with just her words, he figured from this point on weather in his thoughts or directly into her face, the nickname "Sammy" would forever be gone and the bitch will be known as Samantha.

When Tyler came home to the apartment from work at 3:25 last night, first thing he thought was to hit the shower. Working outside with his road crew that put tar in the cracks on the roads, the black seal coating you see on the driveways and parking lots, then painting the striped lines for parking spaces was messy and made a mess out of you. He kicked his work boots off, and started to make his way to the bedroom to undress when he walked by the living room and saw Samantha sitting on the couch. She was staring at the corner of the wall with her thumb softly rubbing her bottom lip as if she were contemplating eating the wall. This Tyler knew was her thinking face, when she had something on her mind and was trying to find the right words to say it to him. Tyler also knew that when she had this face it never really meant anything good for him. It was always the first sign of change to him when she had this face on. She had it on when she said she wanted to move to another apartment, because the one they were currently in wasn't big enough. Or when she said she needed a different vehicle because it wasn't working right, so she traded up for a nicer Chevy Traverse that came with a nice car payment that Tyler had to pay as well.

He wondered what it was going to be this time around. Did their corgi Max need a companion? Did she need to find a new job because the people were not taking her personality all that well? She absolutely needed to take that course at the university for Underwater Basketweaving? What?

Tyler said "Hi."

"Hey." Samantha said. "We need to talk."

"Judging by the look on your face I say it is pretty serious. Did someone die?"

"No."

"Is Max okay?" Tyler said this as he made his way into the living room, careful not to sit on any of the couches because he knew he was still dirty.

"Yeah, he's fine. It's not about anyones health or even the stupid dogs." Tyler could tell something was wrong now. Samantha loved Max, she always hated it when he referred to the dog as stupid or worthless, or when he called him a little shit. But she never, ever, ever called the dog anything other than Max or sweetie. Even when Max was being anything but sweet.

"What's going on?"

There was a long pause before she decided to hit him with it cold and blunt. "Tyler, I'm seeing someone else."

Tyler's day went pretty well today. Though working on the road was hard, the people he worked with more than made up for it to help pass the time. Besides, today consisted mostly of striping lines so nothing was too strenuous. All that came to a nice an end in an instant as soon as the words came out of her lips.

"Wh…What?!" he exclaimed with the tension raising in his voice.

"Don't get upset, let me expl…"

"Don't get upset?! DON'T GET UPSET! That just might be the most stupidest thing anyone could say after hearing that his wife is seeing someone else!"

"I want us to talk about this like adults. Not give in to any rash feelings that we are going to regret having later." She said in a calm tone that was a little condescending.

"I'm pretty sure I'm not going to be regretting me reacting to the knowledge of my wife fucking around on me as being out of line, when I'm going to go completely out of my mind!"

"Yeah, understandable!" she said, now starting to raise her voice as if finally realizing the only way to fight fire was with fire. "But I want to talk about this like adults! You know like act our age and explain why things ended up this way!"

There was some underlining meaning in way she said the last part. Like saying he was responsible for her cheating. Almost at once most of Tyler's anger cleared away so it could make room for a defense from whatever bullshit story she was going to give about this being his fault.

"Alright then, talk." Tyler said. He moved over to the chair that was placed next to the couch on the far side from where she was sitting. He didn't give a damn about the couches or chairs now, and he didn't want to sit anywhere near her right now.

Samantha leaned forward in her seat with her hands up to her mouth as she was trying to choose her words carefully. She spoke calmly. "You know things have been hard on us from all sides. Finances haven't been great, all we seem to due is drown in our own bills. Ever since you been discharged, our jobs haven't been that great. Me working at the Barbershop hasn't been a picnic, with all the men that need there haircuts and stupid massages."

"Our financial troubles made you want to fuck another man?" Tyler said in a calm but tense voice.

"Will you let me finish?! Like I said it was from many things. I feel like you haven't give me enough attention when you are home. You seem distant always like your mind is always someplace else, and me being here isn't enough for me to be here." Such a clique. "You never let me into your thoughts for awhile, like if something is wrong, you don't say that it's wrong, you let it boil up inside and try to bury it deep down. Until one day you blow up in my face and tell me that it is wrong for me to do this certain thing in a certain way. Don't you understand it's like walking on a minefield in this house, and I am sick of it, and exhausted by it."

Tyler was getting sick to his stomach hearing all this bullshit. She wasn't doing this because of financial troubles that they were having, or that he got frustrated every time she broke a plate or something along those lines. They had financial trouble since they met, their first date was spent at his old apartment eating left-over Chinese food while watching movies because they were both too broke to do anything else. Even his temper has always been around their lives, he has been that way since joining the Army and learned the word discipline. It drove him nuts when he looked around and found out that nobody else seemed to know the meaning of the word. No, she did what she did, fucking some piece of shit barfly for one reason that can be explained all by one word: *boredom.*

She was bored with the way her life was, even though that's the life she wanted. Bored that she had a husband who rarely ever said no to her unless it would hurt the both of them financially (even then sometimes he would tried to pull some money magic to try and make her happy). Always did what she wanted when it came to the weekends, even if some of the events they went to like Farmer's Market and garage sale hopping drove him completely nuts. He always did what she wanted… always. Always tried to make her happy, always had it her way.
Now where did that take their marriage? Right here in this room, and hearing her confession and excuse of her sleeping around on him.

"Wow!" Tyler said in a sarcastic tone. "How long have you been practicing that speech in the mirror?"

"Don't condescend me!" Samantha said.

"Then don't feed me a mouthful of bullshit Samantha. You go and cheat on me, and somehow that's all because of me. I have giving you everything from the car that's in our driveway that you so desperately needed, to the food that's in our fridge. Is it the greatest or the best out there? No, but its the best that I could do for you giving our finances. You wanted something, I would bend over backwards to help you get it, or at least try to get it. When I would come home from work, my attention was on you when you were here. I would always give you my attention to try and make your day better, especially on rainy days because I know how much you hate those days. Now, all that doesn't matter anymore!"

"What do you mean?" Samantha said, with a heavy tone in her voice. Trying her best to fight back the tears that were coming. As she finished speaking one had overflowed from her eyelid, and made its way onto her cheek.

"You said that you ARE seeing someone else. I take it that it wasn't just a one-night stand?"

"No. His name is Drew, we met.."

"I don't care where you met him. I already hate him." Tyler got up from the chair and moved around the living room, pacing. He said in a calm voice. "When are you going to pick up your stuff?"

Samantha was taken aback by this. She got up from the couch and said. "You are throwing me out? We can't work on things under one roof? That's too hard for you to…"

"You're damn right its too hard for me! No matter what if I look at you, just like right now. If…If I look at you I know that it's over, and that is killing me right now." Tyler said with a grimace that brought him to the verge of tears. "So I think you need to leave right now." Then, he walked out of the living room.

Tyler didn't hear the words "I'm sorry." that Samantha spoke next. She didn't call them out to Tyler, just said them out loud to herself. But also Tyler felt he couldn't listen to another word she would say. So his selective hearing meter (Which Samantha always told him he had.) was switched on, and walked straight to the bathroom where he took his clothes off and stepped into the shower. He always did his thinking in the shower. His body was always on autopilot and went through the motions of washing his dark blonde hair, and lathering up his mild haired body with his Axe shampoo, body wash, and face scrub. Then his mind would go to things that would appear out of nowhere like: how the last conversation went with his brother, or what the best thing to say to his boss if he found another job elsewhere and wanted to go out in the blaze of glory and get fired, though he knew the latter would probably never happen.

This session of shower thinking, there would be no surprise topic that would pop into his head today. *How could she do this?* He thought to himself over and over. *I love her. I loved her ever since we went out on our date to go see* Alice in Wonderland. *The movie was great and we had great time at* The Great Dane *afterward, drinking and talking about the movie and all the special effects and how great Johnny Depp was in the movie. Four years of marriage, four years that at least I thought were wonderful. The vacations to the Dells, and walking the beaches of Lake Michigan. The times in bed. The wanting of children. The dreams of owning a house together and playing with our kids in the backyard together. All of it gone now. All of it. Kids, house, backyard…gone. At least with each other it is. What am I going to do now? I'm going to need a lawyer for sure, maybe Charlie knows one that he had from his divorce.*

Divorce? I guess no one ever thinks their marriage is going to fail, but shit. Whatever problems we were having, I thought we would be able to work them out together. Now it's just over…over.

The shower was warm, and would have felt great any normal day. Hot steam showers felt great during the summer. Right after you get out and feel the once hot sticky air, would feel cool and perfect for up to a half hour. It would give you a break from heat and humidity.

His anger didn't give him that relief today.

Tyler got out and was as hot after his shower as he was before. He didn't know if Samantha was still in the apartment, or if she left. Quite frankly, he didn't care.

He needed to get out of the apartment. Preferably to Marley's Bar with Charlie, and spill about the conversation that he had with his now soon-to-be-ex-wife, and see what can be done.

Charlie walked into Townies' Bar with a concerned look on his face. He saw Tyler sitting at the bar, staring into his drink as if the glass was somehow revealing Netflix on the front of the glass. He made his way toward Tyler and sat down next to him at the bar.

"You okay, Green?" Charlie said.

"How the fuck you think I'm doing?"

"About as well as I expected, I know you really love her buddy."

The bartender came over to them. "What can I get you?"

Charlie looked at the bartender "PBR, please."

While the bartender went to go fetch the beer, Charlie looked back at Tyler and said, "You had no clue?"

"Clue about what?"

"That she was sleeping around?"

"No, that's one of the things thats killing me. She hid it well. Got me fooled for God knows how long."

"You didn't ask her how long she's been with this guy?" normally, Charlie would use more vulgar language to describe Tyler's wife extra curricular activities, but he recognized that it was best to be delicate as possible.

"I didn't think it was particularly that important. She was fucking the guy. That was the only thing that seemed to stick out of my mind."

"Yeah, but for all you know it could have happened either last night, or since you've been married. I don't know about you, but *I* find that pretty important information."

"Would that effect the decision for the divorce?"

"Divorce? You sure you want to jump straight into a divorce? You two could be able to work it out if you sat down and talked about it with each other."

"We did talk about it. How do you think I found out she has been cheating on me? She told me as soon as I walked through the door of our apartment. Damn bitch barely let me take my boots off. I came into the living room, and saw her sitting there on the couch, asked her what's wrong, then she let the cat out of the bag."

Tyler took a drink from his glass of New Glarus beer, he always loved the local Wisconsin breweries. They sat there for a few seconds in silence before Charlie said, "You two could go and see someone. Like a marriage councilor or something."

Tyler gave Charlie a look as if he were offended by the mere mention of such a thing.

"For what? I know what she's done. There's nothing that any 'professional' is going to tell me that's going to erase what she did. Make me forgive her. I don't know if I ever could forgive her. It feels that she robbed time away from me. Four years are gone, Charlie. *Four years*! Feels like such a waste."

"It wasn't a waste Tyler." Charlie said. "You guys are good…sorry, *were* good together. You where in love and you did right by her in marrying her, and you two were happy. Happy times are never a waste."

Tyler thought about that for a while. He decided he was right. Those years weren't a waste, they were some pretty happy times.

"I guess thats why it hurts so much."

The night went on with drink after drink, after drink. If it was just beer, the hangover he felt the next morning would be minimal. He would grab some aspirin, wash it down with some water, thank you very much and have a good day. That was only if he only stopped with beer.

While the conversation continued through the night, he started taking shots of Fireballs, Bazooka Joe's, and of course Jaggerbombs.

Then he started to hit up the hard liquor. Jack Daniels, Captain Morgan, and finally ended the night with Johnny Walker Red Label. Even though the drinks that were going down the hatch felt good going down, Tyler didn't take into consideration of the aftermath,(which he usually does.) and the cost of the alcohol. The end cost of all the beer, shots, and liquor came to $53.72. For a man that makes only ten dollars an hour that seems pretty expensive, but to Tyler who was not in the right frame of mind physically and emotionally, he would have told you that was money well spent.

Up until he woke up.

After feeling like he wasn't going to shoot off anymore liquid fireworks in the toilet, he started to get up and move to the bedroom. When walking back to his bedroom to get dressed, he moved from side-to-side hitting the walls of the hallway with his shoulders. Since getting on his feet, the apartment started moving side-to-side. He wondered if he actually had a hangover or if he was still drunk. It felt like he was still drunk. The headache was where it confused him on which is which.

Tyler went to the dresser to get dressed. He put on his work jeans and his fluorescent work shirt, then he looked up onto his dresser to see his alarm clock. His clock read that it was 9:08 a.m. on Saturday the 12th of June. Tyler panicked for a few seconds, then felt immediate relief. He thought that he was late to work, since he was suppose to be at work by 7 o'clock. When the relief washed over him, he found out just yesterday that him and his crew were not going to work this weekend, due to the fact that there wasn't enough work for his crew to work the weekend. Tyler started to take off his work clothes and started to put on his regular street clothes. A worn out grey *Rolling Stones* t-shirt, and a fresh pair of cargo pants. While putting on his clothes, Tyler had a debate in his head weather or not to just go back to bed. After thinking about it for a few minutes, then decided against it. He had to get up and face the day, no matter how much it hurt him emotionally. Samantha was gone, probably staying at her new boy-toys' house or apartment, or cardboard box for all he knew. Walking around the apartment, everything reminded him of her. In the corner of the living room was the 10-speed mountain-bike that he received from her on his twenty-third birthday. She surprised him by riding up the street with it. He remembered that while she rode up the street, that she must have borrowed the bike from a friend. Then, jokingly thought to himself that she must have stolen the bike, because since they have been together, he has never seen her ride a bicycle. She rode up the driveway and presented it in a nice Ta-Daaa!! gesture that brought a smile to his face, along with lots of kisses going toward her.

All of the furniture they bought together with the money they received from their wedding day. The nice wide, blue couch that took up the center of the living room, facing the 40 inch television that was up against the wall. Placed on top of the entertainment center, that was made with a combination of both stained oak, and glass. Adjacent to that was both the lounge chair and end-table that connected to the couch. The chair matching the couch, while the table being made of stained oak. And in the center of all that was a nice large coffee table made of, you guessed it. Stained oak.

Tyler all of a sudden had the feeling he had to get out of there. He needed a distraction from what was going on, mostly what was going on in his own head. He thought about what he could do to pass the time. His favorite activity for passing time was to go for long walks. He would throw on his black Nike workout shirt, his loose-fit shorts, and his nice Nike running shoes, and go for a nice jog…ish sort of stroll around the next few blocks and back. Eventually, he would slow down to a nice brisk walk, and start to cool down. He enjoyed those cool-downs the most, because it gave him time to think about things like: *How is mom doing? What do the Packers need to do to get into the playoffs? What the hell were Sam and I really fighting about?*

That is exactly what he is trying to avoid.

Bicycling was out. Driving around was out. Shooting…not a bad idea. Yeah, shooting!

He had his Colt .45 up in his bedroom closet. He didn't do it often, but he liked to go down over to Rusty's Shooting Range and Gun Store, that was just off of Highway 29 to the west of Wausau. There was nothing better than when you had a lot of stress, than to shoot off a few clips of ammunition at a paper target. Especially with this stress. But Tyler never liked going to the gun range alone. He always had either Charlie, Matt, or even Tanya come and release some lead downrange with him.

Tyler knew Charlie wouldn't be able to go with him. Charlie was a Graphic Designer over at Sunrise Printing. Even though it was Saturday and the shop would be closed, he received requests from either family members or friends to help make either business cards, party invites, or flyers almost on a daily basis. He would save this work for his Saturday mornings. Sometimes, even his Saturday afternoons. After designing these type of miscellaneous projects, he was able to print them out. At an auction about two or three years back, he found an old offset printing press that was still in great condition and still worked halfway decent. He was able to purchase it, even after the price was pushed up to seventeen-hundred dollars, which bit his wallet hard. Charlie cleaned it up, purchased ink, paper and tools, then had a startup business right in his garage. He saved only for the weekends, and that helps bring a little extra cash into the household, and that can only make everyone happy. The downside was that it bit into all of his personal time. Startup, run-time, and clean-up sometimes took from three to five hours, which always kinda killed Charlie's weekend social life. He would tell you though no matter how much you thought differently about it that he enjoyed it and that it gave him something to do, as well as maybe become something bigger down the road.

Tyler thought about calling Matt and Tanya, they both loved to shoot off a few clips from time to time. He went over to his room and found his iPhone on his nightstand. He called Matt. the phone was ringing—ringing—ringing. Until it finally went to voice mail. Tyler spoke into the phone. "Hey Matt, it's Tyler. Just wanted to see if you wouldn't mind going over to Rusty's to throw around some lead with me. Just give me a—"

His phone started to vibrate. He was receiving another call. Tyler looked at his phone and saw that Matt was calling him back right away. Tyler ended the voicemail without another word, then answered the call.

"Hey Matt."

"Green! What the hell are you up too?" Matt said with excitement in his voice. It occurred to Tyler that Matt had not yet heard about

Samantha yet. Then it was confirmed with the next words he said. "How's the Mrs. Green doing? She still keeping you on your toes?"

"Yeah, she has got me on my feet alright. Listen, I was wondering if you would like to go on a date of sorts, that involves going to the indoor range?"

"Man I wish I could, Lord knows that with all the stress I've been dealing with, I would love to put some holes in some paper. Unfortunately, I have my hands full with what's been going on. I have to rain check."

Tyler seemed confused by this. "With what's been going on? I'm not following you?"

"You haven't heard? Don't you get the news on Facebook at all?"

"I haven't been on Facebook yet today, and most of the crap that people post I don't listen to anyways. It's mostly just hateful crap, or people just bitching about their lives."

"You might want to check it out today, or at least look at the news on T.V. I can't tell you over the phone, but I would defiantly take a look at it. Channel seven, or nine for sure."

"Wow. That big huh?"

"Big enough to let you know that I'm getting on scene soon. So no, shooting is out."

Tyler could understand that if Matt was about to be "on scene" somewhere—especially for a Wausau cop—phone calls were out for civilian use. "Okay man, I will let you get to work then. Talk to you later."

"See ya, man." said Matt.

Tyler pulled the phone down from his ear, and made his way over to the television. He turned to channel nine and saw something puzzling.

On the television, he saw that there were two big white sheets on the ground, or they looked like sheets. When you would see sheets like that on T.V. when the news was on, you knew that underneath those sheets—were bodies. The bottom caption read:

TWO DEAD IN BAR ALLEY, FOUL PLAY SUSPECTED.

There were cops and photographers around the area. Along with the typical I-wanna-see bystander that was always juicing for a good gossip story.

And nothing was juicier to talk about then dead bodies.

Bodies? In Wausau? Was there some serial killer running around that people had to start worrying about? If there was, Tyler thought they might wanna pick up and move to a new town. Hell, maybe even a different state. Conceal and carry laws passed a few years ago, and the redneck population wasn't high, but substantial enough to want to take some justice in their hands if the itch ever arises.

"Jeez, Matt is going to have his hands full today." Tyler said to himself. The story was only up for a few minutes and then moved on to politics. Where the governor was pushing to move to eliminate the remaining teacher's unions of the state. That lasted only about a minute, when it pushed back to the bodies under the sheets. Tyler turned up the T.V. to hear the male news anchor send the story to the scene. Where there was a young woman in about her thirties that looked Egyptian by heritage, but nevertheless beautiful. She looked directly into the camera.

"Thanks Brad. What we have here is a unique situation that involves these two young men. According to witnesses at the tavern where the young men where found, the deceased left the tavern at around 11:42 p.m. The bartender has stated that the men were not intoxicated when leaving the tavern. Both were speaking normally, and were in pleasant moods."

The image then showed the face of a blond woman in her mid-twenties doing an interview for the camera. She clearly looked tired, probably from being dragged out of bed after working so late.

"They both seemed fine…uh, you know. They had no signs or anything like that…that told me that they were sick, or were in any kind of trouble." Then the picture went back to the scene where the bodies where.

"Within five minutes, the two men were found in the back alley of the tavern, dead." the picture moved back to the bartender.

"It's just really s-sad that this happened to them. And we don't know what happened to them. Which makes all the w-worst."

Back to the anchor. "That is right. At first look at the deceased men, there appears to be no physical assault wounds that suggest a struggle has happened to them. Which could suggest poison or certain health problems the two men may have had. Right now both men are waiting to be identified, so next of kin may be informed.

"And now we will show you what is coming up in sports for today. Can D.C. Everest Girls Soccer take home the trophy in this weeks..."

Tyler thought that Matt was going to have his hands full today. Wausau was never so big as to wonder about looking over your shoulder when you walked down the street. People in this town were pretty trustworthy. Yes, you did have to deal with the occasional drug bust of a meth lab that happened in the outside the city in the middle of nowhere. Even the every so often tweaker that would roam down the street saying things like: *The ravens will never give them back!* Or some shit like that.

But ever since Tyler lived in Wausau, he couldn't ever recall a time where there were two people that mysteriously died from unknown causes. It was strange even for big cities, like Minneapolis, or Milwaukee. This story caught Tyler's attention for two reasons: One, one of his good friends had been on this case. And two, He had been out and about himself last night. It could have just as easy have been him sucking on pavement and being killed. Hell, he was even alone. No one would have known he was gone if he bit the dust from some killer running around. His friends wouldn't have notice. During his night of getting shitfaced, he noticed that his iPhone didn't go off once at the entire time he had been drinking. And he had been gone for almost eight hours, going up until bar close.

Shit. This was stupid. They didn't even know how those two guys died. The both could of had a heart attack—at the *same* time.

Was that even possible? It sounded far fetch even as he thought about it. The odds of having a heart attack weren't unreasonable, but to have one at the same time as your buddy while walking down an alley at night? Anything is possible I guess, but it was too strange to be true. Then again, people say that winning the lottery is impossible, and people win that thing everyday.

"I wonder what Sammy would think of it?" Tyler said.

That hurt him thinking about it. Samantha would have found it just as strange. Probably thrown some of her own theories into the air, and constantly obsess over them until it drove him crazy. Even when they would be in the car driving to where ever they were going, she would probably be filling his ears with theories after they would have nothing more to talk about.

Stop fucking thinking about her. She's gone, okay. She's fucking gone and sleeping with some other asshole.

Tyler got up and started to dial his phone again. Trying to get ahold of Tanya to see if she wanted to go shooting today. Hopefully she wasn't at work.

Chapter 2

Driving down the street to reach the crime scene, Matt got off his phone after finishing up talking to Tyler. Sorry buddy, looks like shooting was going to have to wait. Matt knew how much Tyler was hurting. Tyler's friend Charlie didn't see eye-to-eye on a lot of things, particularly the status that cops are nothing but pigs with badges. Just like he thought graphic designers never produced anything that really mattered in the world. But what they did agree on was Tyler's well-being, and having your wife leave you for another man never did any man much good at all.

The sky had some sunlight out but had heavy clouds moving their way. The sidewalks were mostly vacant of people with the exception of one or two couples that were either out for their regular jogs, or just getting out of the house for a nice walk. Traffic was minimal right now for a Saturday. Usually people would be getting into their cars to try to get to the mall or get ready to go to the various small waterparks that were around the city. Now, traffic was just scattered around in small areas.

Then Matt made his turn onto the street near the scene and saw why.

There was a gathering crowd around the bar looking onward toward the alley. The crowd had about forty, maybe even fifty people. Most of them probably thought it was the best piece of gossip they would see for years. Trying to see if they knew anyone of the victims, maybe learn some hidden agenda that the police might not know about. Or, which was more likely, they just wanted to be near the area where two people just died.

Matt parked his cruiser about a half a block from the bar(he had no choice but to do this with the jam packed cars that hogged up the street) got out of his car and made his way to the alleyway. He knew the bodies of the men wouldn't be there they were moved and taken to the city morgue that was over at Aspirus Hospital. No, he was here for the good ol' evidence hunt. Maybe there was some poison hidden in the bar, rat poison in the garbage, hell maybe even a recently discharged shotgun hidden under a dumpster.

He had to find something here because so far this case was becoming increasingly strange.

When the responding officer, named Drew Bowden reached the scene, he saw that the bodies had no marks that indicated a fight. It was strange because with his eight years on the force, usually you see anyone that is found in an alley, weather they had a pulse or not, were usually found with a black eye, bloody fist, or a new hole of some sort that has been freshly made by a pissed off person that wasn't far behind them. There were no marks. Not one on either of the men. Even if it *was* poison, there would be some sort of vomit or or foaming of the mouth, anyway for the body to try and expel the poison from the body. According to the accounts of some of the responding officers, there was nothing of the sort. Matt hoped the autopsy would bring some light to this dark mystery. The practicing doctor, said it would take a few more hours, so that would have to wait.

"I heard they were covered in blood." said a woman.

"No, no, they weren't covered in blood, but they were drunk out of there minds. How else could you jump from a building." said a nearby man.

"Poison, it's the only way. Most likely they drank something that defiantly didn't agree with them from that pit of a bar. I hope this causes them to shut down." Matt saw that that comment came from Todd Dodds. A bar owner that thought his place should rise to the clouds on how great of service you get from getting a drink at his place was.

Matt pushed his way through the crowd. When he reached the end, he flashed his badge at one of the three deputies that were in place protecting the scene from contamination.

What was at the scene was a black pavement alleyway that was wide enough to let at least a car through. Right next to the building there was a green dumpster that had two plastic recyclable trash bins next to it. The red brick building stretched about twenty-five yards to the back and stopped to have a small parking lot attached to it. It had four vehicles parked in it. At least from where he was standing. Two blue Chevys: a Malibu, and a nice Impala, a red Ford Focus, and a Black Pontiac Grand Am. On The other side of the alley was a long wooden fence that lasted until it reached the street down the end of the alley.

Right where the building met the parking lot, damn near touching the dumpster, is where the bodies were discovered.

Matt stood and looked at the area for a moment. He saw the pictures before he drove here and saw how the bodies were positioned. He started to walk toward the end of the building, moved slowly and cautiously to the area. Looking all over the area to see all of the scene to see if he could spot anything from an overall view from where he was standing.

Matt started to move closer to the area were the bodies were found, when Sgt. Don Gentle showed up next to him.

"Matt what are you doing approaching the scene? Stay by the tape." Sgt. Don Gentle wasn't Matt's biggest fan. Well, that was putting it too lightly, Gentle thought that Matt was too nosy when it came to his job, that he wanted to fly through the ranks at a young age so that one day he could shit can Gentle. None of this was true of course except in Gentles mind. Usually this line of thinking reflected in his police work, but Matt never said anything to anyone about it. Matt still had the thinking that no matter what bad police work was exposed and never excepted, and the truth would always show itself somehow.

"Sarge, I was just giving the scene another pair of eyes, that's all. No harm in getting a fresh perspective right?"

Sgt. Gentle gave a look that suggested that Matt must've been crazy. "Well consider that we have men that have been taking apart this scene most of the morning since it has been secured, and are not finding anything that consist of foul play, yes it could."

"Excuse me Sergeant?" Matt said incredulously.

"This is clearly nothing more than an accident, or a case of natural causes. There is no blood here at the scene or any wounds on the bodies other than those that have clearly been caused from when the so-called victims fell down to the ground. We won't find out anything more until the tox-screen comes back from the attending physician. But I'm guessing that there is nothing more in those two men's blood then some Spotted Cow or Miller Lite. Which is the beer the bartender a Miss…" He turned to his notes in his notepad. "Cathy Lange said she gave to both men before they moved out of their seats, gave Miss Lange a nice tip, said farewell then left. Once they left, one of the men must of had a heart attack in front of his friend. His buddy seeing that his buddy might die, gets himself overly excited, and he too, starts to have a heart attack. No one else heard them suffering. No one to help them. Only left to die together in this dark alley."

Matt looked around again at the scene. Sgt. Gentle saw this and snapped his fingers in front of his face as if to say *eyes on me.*

"You paying attention? Or is this too much for you?"

"I'm still listening." Sgt. Gentle was exemplary when it came to make small power plays at lower ranking police officers.

"Good. Then what have I said, makes this seem more than natural causes?"

This was all just to embarrass him, Matt knew. He could feel the eyes move across him. Not just from the crowd, but from the other officers that were around him. It was working to say the least. "Well…" Matt could feel his face heat up from the blood that was rushing there. The anger that he felt against Sgt. Gentle is what helped him speak up. "Well, what exactly are the odds that two physically fit men that, looking at their families medical history with no signs of heart disease, have heart attacks at the same time?"

"How do you know their family medical history?"

"The families released their files a little over two hours ago."

"And you looked at both men's medical history in that time? Who even authorized you to look at those files?" Gentle's own face was starting to get red but not of embarrassment.

"Chief Tippy gave me the go ahead. His exact words I do believe were: 'I need a fresh perspective on this to make sure I'm seeing this right." Chief Tippy always did like Matt more than Sgt. Gentle. What was once a mild shade of red on the Sergeant's face was now full blown rage red. "The men's medical files were so thin that the only thing that either men suffered from in their entire lives were broken bones. Nothing that indicates a heart attack."

Gentle's voice went down to a low growl of a whisper. "You and the Chief should know that heart disease can occur to anyone at anytime. The autopsy, if the families permit it, will show just that. Now get the hell out of my *sight!*" He said the word sight with a quick snap, and followed it with a glare that could melt ice.

Matt gave Gentle a look that suggested that he had also gone mad. Were they not on the same team? That was one of the points in trying to solve a case, getting different ideas with a team that will ultimately get to the truth of the crime? He stared at Sgt. Don Gentle for a little longer, then walked to make his way back to the crowd. All of a sudden he didn't want to be here. His help that he was offering wasn't wanted, nor his opinion of a logical problem with this so-called natural caused death. The problem was he couldn't leave the scene until he was relieved and everyone got the evidence that they needed.

He moved along the yellow police tape where it was tied off onto the building. He started to hear voices again after it had been so silent from the crowd. Everyone was eager to hear Matt guessed. He stood there staring and studying the faces of the crowd. Despite Sgt. Gentle's opinion, Matt knew there was something strange about these deaths. The odds alone on two heart attacks happening at the same time was astronomical. Most likely impossible. Especially from two fit men that had no history of smoking, or heart disease.

A few shovers got through to the front of the tape to try and get a better view, but mostly Matt's time by the tape had been uneventful. The *what happen?*s and the *are they alright?*s would just blend into the white noise after a while. Actions were all that Matt was looking at now.

Just actions. The sounds, and the voices that were being spoken were being lost throughout the blaring thoughts that were going through his head over and over again.

Can't be a heart attack. Not possible. They must be able to find something here. Anything that would show foul play. A syringe, a pill, fuck a goddamn sewing needle if that is the case. Something….SOMETHING!!!

Over and over his thoughts went like that.

About an hour later the investigators that were standing around like they worked for the highway department instead of law enforcement, started to pack up their items and there chemicals that would show any trace that this was more than a freak natural causes case. The head investigator told Sgt. Gentle that he could take down the tape, the scene was clear. Though if it had been up to Matt, the scene would remain as it was until every pebble was inspected.

He started taken down the police tape when he saw it, but didn't pay it any attention even after given it a few seconds glance.

Regardless of what Sgt. Gentle, the investigators, even what the city morgue would say in a few hours from now; this wasn't an accident. No. What happened here was indeed a crime. The only piece of evidence of this crime was hanging off the side of the dumpster. Never to be processed. Never to be noticed.

In the months to come Matt would think about this object that just danced by his field of vision and think to himself, "Why didn't I see it then? Why was I so *blind!?*" It was there, for everyone to see, yet no one saw.

Hanging of the side of the dumpster from a piece of jagged metal that some idiot must have used their car to hit in the side, was a piece of silk about an inch…maybe an inch an a half—that was dark red.

Chapter 3

BANG! BANG! BANG! BANG! BANG! BANG! Click. The sound of the gunshots echoed through Rusty's Indoor Shooting Range that Tyler and his very outdoorsy friend Tanya were firing their Colt .45 (which was Tyler's) and Saturday night Special. Tyler had more shots than Tanya because the Saturday Night Special was a revolver and had only six shots, whereas Tyler's Colt used a clip that could fit up to twenty shots. But Tyler believed on playing on an even ground, so he only filled up each of his four clips with six bullets.

Tyler's aim was pretty impeccable. His years in the Army helped see to that. Drilling into his head all the fundamentals of perfect sight aperture not only on a M-4 rifle, but also with a 9 mil., it made you feel like an elephant, and you'll never forget. Not only from the days of Basic Training where everything you did was wrong in those damn Drill Sergeants eyes, but the years after when you where with your unit and would practice, practice, and practice some more. Then when you got sick and tried of practicing, you practiced some more. Eventually just like at all things in life, when you practice so much you do it without even thinking about it. From reloading, to unloading into a target.

It was as easy as breathing.

"So what's the game plan?" said Tanya after a lull in the shooting came.

"Well, I figured we could throw a few rounds downrange, then grab something to eat over downtown. Sound good to you?" Tyler said.

"I didn't me—"

"I know what you meant. I don't know, I really don't know. This is only the second day since she told me. I'm not feeling a whole lot other than heartache and hunger. And maybe a little hate." Tanya gave him a look as if to say: *Really?*. "Okay, maybe a lot of hate."

"I wouldn't blame you if you did."

Tyler turned to her slightly from the firing line. He knew that Tanya knew Samantha well. He just didn't know how well she knew her for these last few months. "So, have you talked to Samantha lately?"

"Why do you call her by her full name? You have always referred to her as Sammy for God knows how many years. Now you want to call her by her full name?"

"I figured I don't need to give her anything more than a divorce from now on. She is just fortunate that I don't start referring her as The Bitch. Anyway, you didn't answer my question. Have you talked to her as of late?"

"Yes, but not since she dropped this whole big bomb on you. Why? Is she already asking to divide up the stuff and asking who will get Max?" Tanya said as she started pulling down her bunched up pink camouflage shirt down to her blue jeans.

"Did she mention this at all to you, that this was going to happen? That she was seeing someone else?"

Tanya gave him a look like he was on fire, but she made sure she looked him in the eye when she said the next words. "No. Absolutely not. She only told me about some rough patches that the two of you were going through, but other than that, she never said that she found someone else." She turned back to the firing line and got ready to fire her next shots. "Even though you two were having your problems, she thought the *both* of you would get through it."

Both her and Tyler raised up their weapons and began to fire.

BANG! Click. Click.

The guns once again fell silent in the shooting range. Tyler loved that they had the place practically to themselves. Other than Rusty himself, who was minding the store up front, the firing line was empty of people. Making this a nice private conversation.

Tanya continued, "I swear Tyler, I was just as blindsided by this as you were."

"Alright I believe you." Tyler said as he discharged the clip from his gun, then inspected the next one. "I guess I just can't believe I didn't see it coming from anywhere. I thought we were happy. Well, not happy as in everything was okay, but not so unhappy as this happening at all."

"I don't think anyone ever really expects to be cheated on Tyler. Not until it slaps you in the face when you either catch them, or in your case the person admits it."

There was a huge click that rang throughout the range as Tyler rammed his magazine home in his handgun. Tanya was still loading bullets into her revolver. On other occasions when Matt, Tyler, and herself would come to the range she could talk to the guys and reload within a matter of seconds. mostly they would bullshit and what they saw on the *Big Bang Theory*, or *The Blacklist*, even the nice deer that they had been seeing in Tanya's parents house which would be great to get some of that venison when hunting season began.

Not today. Today her friend was hurting. she could see it in his eyes. Like Samantha took the life out of him in a way she didn't think possible. Like a ghost that made its way into a room and put out a candle, then all you saw was the darkness and the emptiness that remained there. That was Tyler now. The loving and caring that he felt for Samantha wasn't completely gone, the only flame that would keep the marriage alive. All that remained was the embers and the smoke from that flame, and soon, very soon those would go away as well. Only would that ever really be true for a person you married? Because wasn't apart of your heart forever bonded with them?

Tanya and Tyler both finished reloading then began to fire.

BANG! BANG! BANG! BANG! BANG! BANG! BANG! BANG! BANG! BANG! BANG! BANG! BANG! BANG! BANG! BANG! BANG! BANG! Click. Click.

Tanya wanted to change the subject from Tyler as much as possible. This *was* suppose to make him feel better and take his mind off things, mostly his impending divorce. "So how many rounds are we gonna throw at these targets before we see what we did?"

Tyler summoned a little bit off a smile to his lips. "Well we already know how I am doing. Shooting wise that is. I know I hit center mass with my first twelve rounds I sent. Second clip I started aiming for the head, so I know this guy is as dead as dead can be. Now, I'm just fooling around and starting to aim for the ears."

Tanya gave him a smile back. "Whatever. I bet you twenty bucks you have about—oh…seven misses on that target."

"I am not going to take your money on that. Those targets are about thirty yards away and I can see that I have no more than three that just barely missed the outside of his head. And I know that's from just now trying to aim for those damn ears."

"How can you see *that*? Those holes aren't no more than a centimeter in diameter. There is no way in hell you can see that far. I call bullshit."

They both started to unload from the last firing session. The loading and unloading speeds were starting to feel normal again for the both of them now that they were starting to have a good time once again.

"Okay I'll tell you what." Tyler said. "I'm going to remove two rounds." As he said this he pulled back the charging chamber twice, each time a bullet flew into the air as if it were a bird that was set free, then came crashing to the ground. "The target has ten fingers am I right?"

"Yeah."

"If I shoot all the fingers with my remaining ten rounds, you have to buy the first round of beers."

All of a sudden Tanya was concerned again, and not because she was worried about spending a few dollars on what she thought of was the cow piss that was New Glarus beer. "Tyler, its not even three o'clock yet. Why don't we wait until tonight?"

"My mother has a saying, you can't drink all day if you don't start in the morning. But I guess that since it's the afternoon that doesn't really apply here."

"Well, how about we wait to go out later tonight?" she said with a shrug of her shoulders. "I mean we can have plenty to drink tonight when the Courtesy Cab service is available." Courtesy Cab was what the bars had for when someone had so much to drink that people were afraid their kids were gonna be born drunk. The cabs would come and give the inebriated person a ride home free of charge, so they wouldn't put themselves or anyone else in danger of driving home drunk. It was a great service, the only problem with this was it didn't start until about one a.m., and if they started drinking from this point on in the day up until one in the morning, driving home would be the farthest thing anyone could do. More like having problems just to stay breathing from all the alcohol poisoning.

Tyler just kept his smile. "Well then, that's the deal we can make. If I miss just one little finger, you can choose the time we hit the bars tonight, *and* I will buy the first round."

"And if you hit all ten, we hit the bars right now and I buy the first round?"

"That is *correct!*" Tyler said with a little bit of friendly yelling as he said correct.

Tanya thought about it for a few seconds. She didn't want to risk Tyler's health like this by betting on when to get drunk, but it was getting his mind off the problems he was having. Wait. No it wasn't. Either way he was going to get drunk tonight, she said so herself. Not that getting drunk was always a bad thing, but when you got drunk for the wrong reasons, especially with pain on the heart and mind, it was never good. Getting drunk for the wrong reasons?! That was stupid thinking. She already agreed that she would stay with him throughout the day and night tonight, so what was the big deal? She would just have to take it easy on the drinking herself.

"Alright you're on."

Tyler looked down range focused on the fingers of the target, aimed down his weapon and began to fire. BANG! BANG! BANG! BANG! BANG! BANG! BANG! BANG! BANG! BANG! Click!

At 8:12 p.m., Tanya and Tyler walked into Malarky's Pub. Tyler with a upset look on his face, because his drinking time got cut by five hours.

"Finally, should have been here hours ago." Tyler said. "I still say I didn't miss."

Tanya smiled at thinking about it this afternoon. "Hey there was one finger that was almost completely untouched."

"*Almost* is the key word in that sentence missy." Tanya hated being called that. "The target clearly had a rip in it from a bullet."

"Yeah but the rip was clearly from the shot of the other finger. How many times are we going to discuss this?"

Tyler ignored this question, "We never agreed that all the shots had to hit the fingers. If one took out two fingers so be it."

"Okay, but again the shot that was suppose to hit the finger that was *slightly* ripped, missed the finger entirely. So no dice big boss!" She knew Tyler hated being called this. "Even Rusty agreed with me."

"That man clearly just wants to get into your pants, of course he will take you side." Tyler always thought of Tanya as a beautiful woman. Any man would be lucky to have such a woman by his side. Or maybe it would be the other way around. Tanya was always strong-willed enough to where it would be hard to imagine anybody telling her what to do with her life that didn't co-inside with her plans.

"Ha, I wouldn't let that old man touch me with a yard stick. Fact is I won, you lost, get over it."

They made their way to the bar. Tanya ordered a Ol' Fashioned sweet, Tyler ordered a nice pint of beer. As soon as the beer touched Tyler's' hands, he had it to his lips and nearly had the glass half down when Tanya said.

"Hey, Hey! Slow down, there is still plenty of night left to get wasted. In the meantime, let's talk a bit."

Tyler pulled the glass away from his lips and just looked at his glass of half finished beer. "Why? I already know what you want to talk about. That seems to be the only conversation anyone wants to have with me and I'm sick of it. Goddamn it, its only the end of day two since she told me and I'm already sick of it."

"I know that Ty, but you have to face what is happening. You have to have a plan."

Tyler sat silent for a moment. He did have a plan he thought up earlier this afternoon. He just didn't know how Samantha would like it.

"I'm going to call her to come over to the house tomorrow so we can start dividing up the our stuff. The house, Max, furniture if she wants everything." He didn't like it. No, that wasn't accurate, he downright *hated* it. The fact that he had to give her anything after she took away everything made him sick to his stomach.

"Yeah? You just decided this?"

"No, earlier when you brought the subject up when we were shooting. When I said that I didn't know what I was going to do, the wheels in my head began to turn. It took a while to get the gas going, I'll give you that, but you were right on trying to have some sort of plan for what's to come. It's just going to be uncomfortable as hell, that's for sure."

"Well…" Tanya took a small sip from her drink. "…it's a start. Do you know what you want from your stuff?"

"Yeah. All of it if I truly had my way. But the nice guy in me says that that's just not going to happen. She did a terrible thing, but that doesn't mean she shouldn't get her table that her grandparents left for her. I know that for sure means the world to her."

"That's really nice of you, I know I wouldn't be that nice. I guess that just makes you a better man than me." She said this with a half grin.

Tyler laughed at her. "Yeah, just a man with different equipment downstairs."

"Hey don't knock the plumbing. I'm just better at manly things more than most men." They both laughed.

There was a little bit of silence between them. Mostly they spent it taking sips from there drinks. Tyler seemed a little more at ease now, and didn't have the need to slam his beer back. He realized that telling his plan to someone who was willing to listen, took some weight off his shoulders. Not completely, he didn't think that the weight would be completely off until everything was finalized. Maybe not even then. Right now though, it felt like he could breath a little bit again. Like he just came up for air after spending hours under a deep lake.

"So what's the game plan for tonight? Are we just staying here or are we bar hopping around?"

"I don't know. Maybe just keep it low key and just go with the flow."

"Hey, how are you doing tonight?" Tyler turned around to see where the voice was coming from, when he saw a man standing directly behind him. He had a scruffy face with a black t-shirt that said STOP PICTURING ME NAKED on the front of it. Along with blue jeans and a pint of beer in his hands.

"I'm doing fine, how are you doing?" Tyler said. The man looked at him with the same feeling as he would a bug that was moving into his face.

"I was talking to the lady." said the man.

"Hi." said Tanya. "I'm doing fine. I guess I will ask my friend's question. How are you?"

"Well I've been doing a lot better ever since you walked in here. You look like you haven't been having a nice conversation with this loser, so I figured I would come rescue you from him." He moved right up to the bar in-between Tanya and Tyler, giving his full attention to Tanya, while at the same time cutting out Tyler. One of the oldest bar moves in the book, Tyler didn't think anyone used that move anymore it was so worn out. Judging by the smell of Mr. Smooth-as-Pudding, he was already pretty drunk enough to think that if he pulled down his pants to his ankles and took a piss on the floor, all the woman in the joint would just come crawl up to him begging to take him home.

Mr. Smooth-as-Pudding didn't expect Tanya though. Surely in his drunken state he still was expecting some sort of resistance, then he would keep moving forward with his one-liners, and endless pursuit to get Tanya in the sack. But what most men forget—especially the drunk ones—is that woman have built up their defenses from the endless pursuits of men for all of their adult lives. Yes, the spider may catch the occasional fly in their web, but that didn't mean it would get the whole swarm. Especially the smart ones.

Tanya started by giving Smooth-as-Pudding a look like he was the rudest man she ever met. This was almost the truth, there was always a man more rude than the one before. Then she took her left arm and put up in front of the man so she could reach for Tyler, and slowly move him away from the bar.

"Excuse me, I like having a *nice* conversation with my husband. Leave us alone and go find some other girl you can charm the clothes off, or better yet go pay the girls at Chunky's, they always take their clothes off for a dollar bill."

This stopped the man in his tracks. Tyler could see the blood rushing up to his face. He got shot down by woman before, Tyler was sure of this; what guy didn't? The problem was that Tyler didn't think he was used to being embarrassed by a woman before; and that was a problem.

Smooth-as-Pudding went from putting his charm on, to being as pissed off and as deadly as a viper. He reached up and grabbed Tanya's hand and she gave a small sound of pain along with a look of disbelieving pain. The spider wasn't use to not getting what it wanted.

"Listen here bitch! You got a mouth on y—." That was as far as he got in his speech to her, when a glass pint of beer that was half full and in Tyler's hand, smashed into about a hundred pieces against the side of Smooth-as-Pudding's face. Blood and beer started to run down the man's face as he fell down to the floor. Glass was purtruding from the man's cheek and eyebrow, when a loud scream of agonizing pain escaped from his mouth. "AAAAAAAAAaaaaaagh!!!"

Tyler stared down at the man who was wreathing in pain on the ground. He turned to the bartender and was going to ask him for a towel and to call nine-one-one. What he saw when he turned back to the bar, was the bartender with a huge Louisville Slugger up into the classic hitting position, ready to knock Tyler's head clean off.

Tyler tried his best to ignore this, even though that was pretty hard. He didn't want anymore bloodshed tonight. "Call 9-1-1!"

"You make another move toward him or me and I will, right after I lay you out. The cops then can come pick up the pieces afterward."

The screams of the man were agonizing to the ears. One man that was a bystander started to kneel down with a bunch of napkins so he can do some sort of attempt to stop the bleeding from the man's face. "All the fight is out of me now. Please. Just give me a rag to help him try and stop the bleeding."

Tanya started to move to grab a towel from the bar, when all of a sudden the bat came slamming down onto the bar about two inches next to her hand. It made a loud CRACK when it made contact with the bar; leaving a nice dent into the finished wood.

"Either you get the fuck out of my bar now, or the cops are getting called, and you can spend the night in a cell. Or for however long it takes to bring up assault charges."

Tyler looked from the bartender, down to the man now gushing blood from his face. He started to back away from the bar. He wanted to help the man, he really did. This was something he caused even though the man started it by grabbing Tanya.

"He grabbed my friend. You saw that right?"

"Yeah, that's why I grabbed the bat in the first place. Until I realized I should have been preparing for you. Also why I'm letting you walk out of here instead of just hitting you in the skull. Get outta here, NOW!" And so they did.

Outside of Malarkey's was a large city block that was covered in grass, a huge cement X that was used as sidewalk through the area, and a giant cement stage on one end. If there was a roof over the entire area, one would confuse it for a concert arena right smack dab in the middle of Wausau. Only it was outside in full view for everyone to see. This was called the 400 block, one of the most popular places during the summer months. When there wasn't art shows that would put up tents to display their fine works(that were always for sale of course), or sidewalk chalk shows that were always the big hits of the summer, there would also be the Concerts on the Square. Bands that were usually small and starting out, or cover bands from all genres performing in front of everyone that could fit their lawn chair and their coolers were welcome free of charge. Every Wednesday night at seven, when the sun was just starting lift up its hand and wave good-bye to the day, the music would start.

Standing right next to the 400 Block would be the Wausau Grand Theatre. Showing all the professional broadway plays that would be traveling through, or a stand-up comedian that wanted to bring a little more substance along with laughter to a town that never really took itself too seriously.

Tonight there was a show of *Chicago* that was playing, which was incredibly exciting. Popular shows made their way to Wausau sure, but it always took a chant and a blue moon for them to get here; and when they did come, they always sold out within an hour of going on sale. Like most of the shows that would be playing at the Grand, tonights show started at 9:00 p.m., with a small pre-show party to enjoy a nice glass of wine, or two right before you took your seat. Or of course you could enjoy a nice stroll along the Block before making yourself comfortable to the show.

People were about to make their way inside The Grand, when they all of a sudden heard yelling on the other side of the 400 Block.

"What the fuck was that?!" yelled Tanya, as she made her way to the sidewalk from Marlakey's.

"The guy grabs you like he's going to take you in his hillbilly truck. What do you think I was doing? Stopping that motherfucker from doing just that." Tyler said with a voice that was starting raise granite.

Tanya rolled her eyes. "You think I couldn't handle it in a little less *insane* way? You slammed a glass into the man's face! What the fuck is wrong with you?! He may have been a forceful dick, but he sure as hell didn't deserve to picking shards out of his face for the rest of the night." Anger was raising in her face as she walked across the street to go on to the grass to walk to her car.

"Wait, Tanya I was just trying to help you out."

Tanya turned around to face him. People were starting to stare in their direction. "When have I ever needed help from you Tyler? Whenever has that happened?" She paused "Never has that happened, ever! You know me better than most that I can defend myself from anyone. I knew exactly what to do to him if he wouldn't stop. In no way did it involve sending him to the hospital!"

"Look, I'm sorry okay. I didn't mean for it to go that far. But Something in my head just snapped when he grabbed you like that. I don't know what it was, but I haven't felt rage like that in a long time." He toned down his voice. He knew he regretted what he did in the bar, just thinking about it caused him to be sick to his stomach. Sure the guy needed to be taught a lesson in manners, but he didn't need that. "He crossed a line, but what I did was way worse."

"You're damn right about that. Now cops are going to be called, or worse that guy is going to be looking for us whenever he goes to a bar, to get his sweet little revenge, whatever that might be. Bringing his batch of good ol' boys to teach not just you a lesson, but myself too. This is bad Tyler, and your temper is the one that got us into it."

"Christ, I know Tanya!" He was starting to get angry again, "You don't have to keep telling me this. I will try and fix it."

"You better, and while your at it, fix your temper. I know you are going through some shit times, but it's only day two of this shit storm you're going to getting through. You can't keep doing this throughout your whole divorce. You will end up either dead, in jail, or just another lonely drunk."

"Don't lecture me on getting a divorce Tanya, you haven't had a relationship for longer than three months, always ending up with you getting bored with them and moving onto something else. My wife left me for another guy! I wish I could be over it just after two days, but I can't. Sorry I'm trying to figure this out still, sorry I'm going to get mad at stupid people when they get in my face. I don't know what to do about it."

Tanya walked about ten feet up to Tyler. Then, give him a big slap across the face. "My suggestion to you now is this; call Sam, get everything separated with the whole who gets what process, and start moving past this. The only way through it, is going forward." She turned around, walk to her car and drove away. Leaving Tyler in the middle of the 400 Block in a dumbfounded stupor. Wishing he could have taking back what he had done tonight.

Chapter 4

Danny sat at a table and chair right next to the street on the 400 block, enjoying the drama that seemed to unfold before his eyes. He was relaxing a while waiting for a phone call, when he saw the scene unfold after a loud noise that sounded like glass shattering, followed by a loud commotion of people screams, and raised voices. About a minute or two went by, all of a sudden a loud crack followed the rest of the noise. Then, a minute later two people left, no, they seemed to be retreating with their backs facing the street. Moving slowly outside at first, then turned and started away from the pub. The woman all of sudden shouted at the man and had their little tif about how he smashed a glass against another man's face, Danny thought if she screamed a little louder there were going to be some police officers making their way into the area pretty soon to be making some arrests. If that was the case Danny was going to have to make himself scarce from this area, post-haste. So far though he figured he would just watch these two play out their argument about drinking, divorce, and anger. Three combinations, in Dan's mind that always went together like dynamite, a wick, and a lit flame. Something was always about to blow.

About five minutes of arguing, the woman decided she had said enough and left the man alone standing in the clearing of the block. Danny watched the man for a few minutes more before the man walked into the opposite direction. Danny thought the man looked familiar to him for a while, maybe he was from his Army days. Unfortunately the man was a little too far away to be a hundred percent sure that he could recognize him. He followed the man with his eyes until he turned right from the corner at the end of the block, and then disappeared from his view.

"Oh well," thought Danny, "maybe his name will ring a bell later, right now I might as well relax and wait till I have to work."

Danny sat there for a while to admire the area that was for the most part, the main attraction of Wausau. Looking up to try and look at the stars and thought about the last time he looked at at those stars. Right after he got out of the dank hole that he was kept prisoner in. He thought about that a lot, the confusion that followed, the bodies. Oh, the bodies.

A lot has happened since his so-called "liberation" that day two years ago. Since walking out of that woods…with her. She saved him. But sometimes he wondered what she saved him from. Most days it still felt like he was still in that fucking hole in the ground. Like he traded one prison for another.

When they walked out of those woods two years ago, they eventually came to a road like she said they would. When they walked about five-hundred yards down the road they came to a car. Not just any type of car, it was a smoking red hot Ferrari that was waiting for them.

"This is your car?" he asked her.

"Yeah, I had to get here as fast as I could." she said without looking at him. She reached into a small pocket that was sewn into her dress that was not noticeable to him before, but he thought that he really didn't notice anything about this woman other than her looks. How gorgeous this woman was gave him goosebumps all up and down his arms. It was incredible how this feeling would push out the pain that was in his knee and the hunger in his belly. "I have to get you to a hospital as soon as possible." she said. Though she said it without any sense of urgency, as if what she said was just a passing comment that we could get to if they had some spare time

As soon as this was said, the pain returned to him. "Yeah, whenever we get to the closest town would be nice." Then, they sped off through the dark woods, the headlights piercing the nighttime with high-brights. They drove for about an hour-an-a-half until they reached a town called Deep River, where they pulled into a hospital called Physio To Go.

The doctor took one look at him and saw that Danny was malnourished and had a cracked kneecap to his right knee. The doctor patched Danny up and put him in a room for the night so he could put fluids into him, and supervise his food intake.

The lady in red stayed with him the whole night. She told the doctor that she found him on the side of the road like this, while Danny told the doctor that he was lost in the woods when he walked around looking for a good fishing spot while on vacation from the states; so it could explain his sudden appearance on Canadian soil. Most of which was the truth, other than the whole fishing and vacation. Finding him was the truth, he guessed, as part of the story. Thomas Perkins; was the name that he used, the name came to him after he remembered the Perkins restaurant back home. Lady in Red wanted to keep his identity a secret for the time being, she didn't want to risk raising any unnecessary alarms that might get police involved. Danny was getting medical attention, and that was what really mattered. He couldn't go home anymore. Not after saying yes to her.

Once they were alone in the hospital room, he decided to finally ask her the question that has been on his mind since he first saw her. "What is your name? You are doing all this for me and I have no idea who you are."

The woman looked at Danny with a smile. "You can call me Charlotte, sorry I haven't told you it sooner. I wanted you to hear what I had to offer first before you heard my name."

"Because if I didn't agree to the terms, you would have killed me?" Danny asked.

Charlotte just smiled a little bit as she gave him an answer. "No. I wouldn't have killed you. But I would have left you there alone with no one to help you. Who knows how far you would have gotten before the inevitable would have happened."

Danny thought of their trip the hour an a half it took them to get to this hospital through Canadian forest and backroads. How many miles had it been? Seventy? Eighty? A hundred? A shutter went through his body at the thought of having to walk with his knee injured, and half starving to death. Having to travel almost a hundred miles to get to any kind of civilization. That was if he even traveled the right way. He could have gone an entirely different direction from where he should have been and gradually starve to death. Sure he would have lasted a few days with some of the survival skills he learned in the Army, but with a wounded leg, that would have only gone so far until infection set in, or starvation took him. Or worse a nice grizzly bear crossed his path looking for food. Canada had those right? Even if he played dead, the bear would still have smelled blood, then it would be game over for Danny. See ya next time.

"You would have left me there." he said this as a statement. "How could you do such a thing?"

"You would have proven that you are of no use to me." she said. Then went silent as if the discussion was over. Danny went silent for a few minutes and stared at her. He was absorbing every feature of her face, of her body. The beauty that radiated from her was stunning. Sure underneath all that beauty, beat the heart of an ice cold bitch. His conversations with her have proved that, he still wasn't so sure if she would have acted on her threats, but the tone or lack there of indicated that he didn't want to try and find out. He looked down her arms and seen how silky smooth that skin must be like a goddess. Right down to her hand—.

He then saw that she had a wedding ring on her finger and his heart sank just a little bit, drops of jealousy started to trickle into his heart. Like a leaky faucet into a sink.

"So, does your husband know about you picking up men in the woods, and how you get them by killing other men?" Usually when mention of a husband or marriage, the man or woman in question would look down at their finger in a: Oh gosh I forgot that I was still wearing this sort of attitude. A mixture of embarrassment and pride would occur. Especially when the two people experienced something as strange and personal as they just have. A murder rescue scenario.

Charlotte only turned her head slightly to face him, looked him in the eye and said. "He is not my husband, he is my King. Husbands come and go, just as wives do. One always leaves before the other. On very rare occasions they may leave at the same time, but more often than not, one always leaves before the other. By choice or not. My King and I are bound by more than that, as you will soon see for yourself. As to answer your question, the answer is yes. I share everything with him."

"This King approves of this?" Danny said with a hint of horror in his voice as he said it.

She turned back to face the wall, "He doesn't really have a choice."

The night dragged on. Danny's leg didn't have a lot of pain ever since they gave him some pain killers from a drug he had no idea what it was called. He thought he should ask the nurses if he could get a sedative to help him sleep, but he decided against it. There was too much on his mind, the way his life just turned on him. All his friends, and family would still have their lives, still go to school, work. Still have fun by going to concerts, bars, movies, car trips, waterparks, hell even with their own families. Just he was no longer going to be in them. He knew they would wonder where he went to, and if they would ever see him again. Only he knew that the answer was going to be no.

He looked around at Charlotte and saw that she was reading a magazine while having a closed book of *20,000 Leagues Under the Sea* on her lap. He wondered if she ever slept at all. Maybe she was a vampire and that's why there wasn't any blood on the bodies of his captures. Danny thought that might be just a little too extreme, and maybe even a tad juvenile to think that way. There was no such thing as vampires. Could there be? It was 12:43 a.m. right smack dab in the middle of the night and there was no sign that she was even the slightest bit tired. No, she just kept on reading the latest issues of *Canadian Living* that had a picture of some sort of food dish and read "FABULOUS EASTER BRUNCH" for the title. Danny's best guess was this issue was just a tad old. Then after she was done, he imagined she would start the book that was on her lap after she was done with the magazine.

He stirred in his bed and turned to her, "Listen, if you need to get some sleep as well it won't bother me at all."

Charlotte looked up from *Canadian Living* and gave Danny that classic signature smile that she had been given him all night. "What? Afraid I'm going to kill you in your sleep or something?"

"No, no. I just didn't know if you were tired that's all." Although the thought did cross his mind.

"I'll sleep when I'm ready. I usually stay up for a while on most nights. I'm what you would call a night owl. Being out at night is what I do best. Reading usually gets me to sleep most nights. Plus I need to see that they are taking good care of you, Danny." Then she picked up the magazine and continued to read as if that was the end of the conversation.

"Okay." Danny said. turning his head to look at the ceiling. if there was a T.V. in his room he would try to watch that to try and help *him* sleep. Most nights thats what did the trick for him. But even if he had one to try and fall asleep to, he didn't know if he could as long as she was here watching over him. They way she said that last sentence: *Plus, I need to see that they are taking good care of you…Danny.* For a man that didn't scare easily, that statement alone was enough to make him wonder. What exactly did he need to be healthy enough for?

Around 2 a.m. he was still awake. Still looking at the ceiling replaying the words that were spoken to him before leaving the bunker. Replaying, over, and over, and over. Remembering the promise he made. At the same time condemning himself for making the promise for something as simple as survival. Right then, at that moment, he hated himself for that.

He turned his head to look at Charlotte again. He hadn't looked at her since he talked to her the last time, he was too busy drowning in his thoughts to pay her any attention. Also he was a little afraid of her a little bit. When he turned to her he saw was that she was finally asleep. The magazine and the book were both laying on her lap, as she had her head back on the chair for support. He saw that the chair she was in was a lounger, and she had the footrest up to keep her feet off the ground, and have a more comfortable position to sleep.

As soon as he saw that she was asleep, he felt a little relief sweep within himself. It was good to know that she wasn't always on guard and watching his every move. Not many people have scared Danny throughout his life. Not the classic schoolyard bully named Justin Bower. Nor the drill instructors at Basic Training, hell even his captives that had him in that bunker. He knew how to play them all. By not giving into them. Charlotte though…that was a different story. She scared him right down into the blood that coursed through his veins that ran cold from her gaze back at him. A great weight of sleep fell upon him at once, his eyes started to flutter. In less than a minute, he fell asleep.

Danny's memories were whisked away when he finally heard the chirp that came from his phone. He looked down and saw that he had a text message: **Great dane brewery. fifteen minutes.** He knew early in this line of work that if you kept Charlotte waiting a minute longer than requested, someone was going to pay; and that someone was you. Danny got up from his chair, and started to make his way over to his car that was parked a few feet away from the curb. Before he got into his car he asked his phone for the directions to where Great Dane Brewery was. When the phone came back with a response it showed that the Brewery was no more than a ten minute drive, in which case Danny got into his Mercedes sedan on began making his way there. His thoughts turned to last night briefly from what happened. Wondering if Charlotte was going to be mad at him for the way things went last night with the two men over at The Glass Hat. Things didn't go quite as planned when the second man interfered with Charlotte. That was the man's mistake, not his. Now the man was dead. So be it.

The real problem that occurred to Danny was that the two men were left they way they were after Charlotte was finished with them. That Danny was sure that was going to be mentioned when they would meet in a little bit. Danny wasn't worried all that much about it, sometimes things happened, and he knew that he tried his best. Yeah, he tried his best. He just hoped that Charlotte would see that. The thought of him being fired made him shutter a little bit. He knew what would happen to him if that occurred; can we say *without a trace* ladies and gentlemen?

A few minutes later, Danny pulled into Great Dane Pub & Brewery and judged by all the cars in the parking lot that the place was packed for a Saturday night. Finding a parking spot was a little tense to find, even though he was technically at the brewery, it didn't matter to Charlotte until he showed up right next to her at the bar.

With a little bit of hard work he was able to find a parking spot, locked his car, and made his way into the brewery. When he walked in, his prediction that the place was going to be filled to the brim was spot on. The noise that hit him when he opened the doors was loud as people were shouting, and music was playing at a high volume from the digital jukebox. Being that this was a brewery restaurant, he could smell the different flavors of beer in the air, mixed with the Cherry wood that seemed to be everywhere. From the floors to the tables and booths, almost everything was made from the nicely stained polish wood. All including the bar area which was raised about three stairs above everything else in the area, with two large flatscreen T.V.'s at each end of the bar itself. Danny couldn't see much else from the gathering of people that flocked around the bar either waiting to get a drink from the bar, or deep in conversation with people that planted their asses right onto one of the many barstools that were gathered around the bar itself. Sitting in one of them, Danny could see without having to do a big scan of the place, was a brunette woman with slightly pale skin covered in red clothing sitting on the far end of the bar. She was sipping a white wine in front of her, and miraculously in a bar that was full of people, there was a empty chair right next to her that was only occupied by her nice red Coach purse. Danny made his way through the crowd to meet up with her, looking at his watch at the same time. He made it by a minute and a half. Breathing a sigh of relief, he gently touched Charlotte's left shoulder. She didn't move. She kept on looking at her glass of white wine.

"Where, and who tonight?" Danny asked.

"We need to talk about something first." she said without looking away from her glass. "Were there any complications that happened last night? Anything you didn't understand?"

Danny looked at her for a second, took a breath and said, "No."

"No, with the complications, or no to the not understanding?" she said with an annoyed tone in her voice.

"Both."

"Okay." she paused, then she turned to him and whispered in his ear with a fiery tone, "So then there really is no excuse that both men were found, in the middle of an alley, *right where I left them!*" Charlotte was close to almost screaming the last sentence in his ear, but decided at the last moment to just shrill it in his ear instead.

Danny backed away from the high shrill. His ear now in pain. Then looked around to see if anyone heard. Two people that were behind him that looked at him briefly, but otherwise there was no one that paid them any attention. Everyone was too absorbed by their own problems and stories to care about the two of them.

"If you recall what happened," he also said in a low voice to her. "the one man that we were waiting to come out, suddenly showed up with a friend." Charlotte closed her eyes. Danny knew that she didn't want to hear a recap of the previous night, but it was the only way he could think to explain himself. "Soon enough, the man I was trailing had his friend join him at the bar; drank for a little bit. Both men decided to leave at the same time. Weather to go hangout some where else, go to one of their houses, hell maybe going to go fuck each other. I don't know, and we didn't particularly care. One turned to two. Which I think that was pretty good for you wouldn't you say?"

"You will refrain from talking down to me Danny boy. I think you are forgetting who you are talking too."

"I'm talking to my employer, one who's interests I am looking out for. As soon as you…did what you did…I was to move the gentlemen somewhere else." He was suppose to bury them somewhere out into the woods where they wouldn't be found. At least for a while. When the two of them would be far from here. The fact that one turned to two didn't matter. It only meant more work for Danny to do when getting rid of the bodies. "And I was going to do just that as soon as you left. But I ran into a problem."

"Were you followed?"

"No."

"Was I followed?"

"Unless you didn't check to see if anyone was; I don't see how that's possible. You did che—?"

She finally turned and looked him square in the eye, with a glare that could set him on fire. Telling him that he could go to hell.

"Anyway that wasn't the problem. The problem was that right as I was about to pick up the bodies, a group of people walked out from the bar across the street. Four or five barflies making their way toward me and my two new friends. Before they got a chance to get a look at me, I decided to get the hell out of there." He looked remorseful toward Charlotte. "You have to understand, my lady, there was nothing I could do."

"Why didn't you just stay out of sight until they went into the bar?"

"I did that, and for about a minute I thought I was in the clear, but then one of the drunk bastards decided to use the side of the building to take a leak on, instead of the restroom. After that, it was all over. The guy freaked out, and ran inside. As soon as that happened, I was in the wind."

"You were in the wind you say? How convenient for you to just leave like that when you could have taken care of a fucking pisser as well."

"Risking two was already too much, isn't that one of the first things you told me when you wanted me to do this job? You wouldn't go more than two, because it could arouse suspicion for me to get rid of. So adding a third was out of the question. Hearing from the news, police think that they both suffered from heart failure."

"Do you know if they did an autopsy?" Charlotte asked.

"I know that's the protocol for what appears to be a double homicide. But to the police this looks like to them a case of double accidental death. I think they are hoping it will be drugs or something."

"Well let's hope they had something like that in their system. Or you might be in big trouble depending on their conclusion."

"What do you mean?"

"If they find anything suspicious with those two bodies, I'm telling you flat out that you are going to know what it means to be under my kind of unemployment. I hope I don't have to elaborate anymore than I have?"

Danny felt a cold shiver going down his spine. For a few minutes he sat there at the bar in silence. He tried to take in the noise that was around him, listen to other peoples conversations, try to get the tune from the jukebox in his head. Anything to get his mind off for the few seconds that unless luck changed in his favor, he might not be on this earth in he next couple of days.

Finally after a few minutes, the silence that was between them broke when Charlotte said, "All of that is for another time now, we will see what will happen. Right now I need more for the King. At his age he needs more substance, and I think this is the place to get it."

Danny was taken aback, "What, here? Now?"

"Yes. Why? Not that convenient for you is it?"

Danny said nothing to this. He knew there was no talking Charlotte out of anything. Once her mind was made up, that was the end of that. All Danny asked was, "You have someone in mind?"

Charlotte motioned her head down the bar. "The brown curly-haired woman in the middle of the bar. I think she would be perfect for my King."

Danny thought that was a load of bullshit on her part. The King, Danny was pretty sure didn't give a shit where he got his substance from. He was pretty sure that man, woman, fuck even a dog might just be as good. No, Danny was pretty sure that this woman was being chosen because Charlotte, the glorious bitch in red, knew that when woman were chosen, it bothered Danny a lot, not as much as children, but having this happen to a woman was still hitting a sore spot with him. He would often beg her to try and go after killers and rapists. God knew if anyone deserved this sort of thing, this travesty, it could be done on them. No, Danny was being punished for his failure last night. For not being able to dispose of the bodies in time. For possibly causing police heat catching wind of their presence. Charlotte was punishing Danny, by punishing this beautiful woman that couldn't have looked a day over twenty-two. No matter who was being punished, this young woman was going to die.

"When do you want to do this?" Danny asked.

Mindy Crass had a long day at the end of a long week and was happy to have some time to unwind with a nice glass of beer in her hand. Being a full time student with a full time job while being a full time mother to a five year old was not easy these days. Especially when the father of your daughter was a worthless womanizing piece of shit. Even though things were a little tough, she would thank God that man had signed his fatherly rights away. Dealing with his bullshit would have been the last thing she could have needed out of life. Trying to find some time with her daughter wasn't always easy, going to school full time to be a paralegal was also pretty hard, but at the end of the day she was happy with the path her life was going. Sure right now she took a job of flipping burgers at a fast food restaurant, so what it was only temporary, even though her boss has kept insisting that if she stayed on when she was finished with school she could have a nice management position waiting for her to just reach up and grab. Thanks, no thanks. Mindy never could understand that when people went to school for a profession that was different from their current job, why the employer would constantly think they would want to stay around? Not this girl, no sir! As soon as a new job would peek its head up after graduation, Mindy was going to be nothing but dust in the wind. With her daughter Harper by her side.

Mindy just finished her shift when she decided that right before she was going to go home and relieve her parents from their babysitting duties, that she was going to have one afterwork drink at her favorite place over at the Dane. Her parents didn't really approve of this, since it was their time that Mindy was taking up when having her drink, that in the past was never really more than one. Tonight was a little different for her, she was pretty beat, and still had some homework that she had to finish before class started on Monday. She would usually push it for tomorrow, but tomorrow was going to be her only day off from both work and summer classes at the UW. Mindy had every intention to spend every waking moment with Harper tomorrow. They were going to go over to the Aquatic Center in Weston and play for as long as they were able too play for. Swimming, going down those huge water slides, and splashing around sounded incredible to her after this long week she had.

When Mindy just arrived she found the place to be packed with people, but just like most of the bars that were around here, no matter how fancy, the people that were usually standing around at the bar were usually just the bull shooters that were giving their jaws a nice exercise before they realized that drink that they were holding onto for so long was empty and they needed a refill. Mindy started to make her way to the bar, pushing her way through the men and woman, mostly getting what she liked to call "Hey Bitch" stares as she was making her way toward the bartender. When she finally got to the bar, the bartender that had nice blonde hair and blue eyes asked her what she wanted.

"I'll have a Landmark, please." and she gave the man a five dollar bill. He took it and started to grab a glass, fill it up with beer, and gave it to her. She took a nice long sip and felt like she was in heaven. If heaven had the tasty aroma of beer that is. She was lucky enough to see that a man at a nearby table, got up from his chair. Quickly she made her way to the table, careful not to spill any of her beer, beating anyone that was making a mad dash toward the spot just like her. One of them was a man in a button-up flannel shirt that gave her the stink-eye as if she slapped him in the face instead of taking a vacant seat. She didn't give a damn.

She sat there and started to do some people watching all around the bar. Four people are playing pool over by the dance floor and one of them was scratching like crazy as if this was his very first night he held a pool stick before. As soon as his turn was over, a red-haired man picked up his stick and started to knock the balls in as if he was born to play pool. She turned and looked around and started to look at everyone else that was at their tables, wondering what they could be ta—.

"Hey, how are you doing tonight?"

Mindy turned and looked at the face where the voice was coming from and saw that there was a man in a suit standing in front of her and her table. Mindy was a little taken aback that this man wanted to strike conversation with her, but when the booze hounds were out, they will look everywhere. "Hi, I'm good, how are you?"

"I'm good, My name is Thomas, Thomas Perkins. What's yours?"

Mindy quickly thought about using a fake name, it wasn't unheard of, and it certainly wasn't the first time she would have done something like that, ultimately she decided against it. Even though she was in no mood to be looking for love tonight, didn't mean they couldn't be friends that ultimately lead to love, right? "I'm Mindy."

"Mindy, huh? That's a real nice name." said the man.

"Listen," Mindy said. She decided to try and put him down easy so she could finish her beer and go home. "you seem really sweet. But I'm only here for one drink and then I got to get home to my daughter."

The man's face lost a little bit of its twinkle as soon as she mentioned that she had a daughter. This wasn't uncommon when she talked to guys. As soon as the child card was played they were usually smoke in the wind, or would get the solemn look on their face, like they didn't even want to touch that responsibility yet. The look on this guys face was different. True the twinkle was dimming, but there seemed to be a touch of sadness there—maybe even dread. Mindy didn't think much of it, maybe this was the Thomas's default face when it came to being shot down.

"Oh. Well would you mind some company while you finish your drink then? It could make the time go by faster?"

Mindy was shocked that this guy stuck around. "Umm. Sure I guess. But there isn't another chair for you to sit on."

"That's okay I'll stand. I'm use to standing for my day job."

"Oh really!" she said with a small chuckle. "What is your day job?"

"I'm a lawyer. I work with Habush, Habush, & Roeteir." Thomas said.

Mindy's eyes widened as she was taken a sip from her beer. "No, way! I'm currently going to school to be a paralegal! Habush, Habush, & Roeteir are one of the firms I want to go work for!"

"Huh, you don't say! Well when do you graduate?" he asked while at the same time his eyes moved to something behind her. She felt a gentle touch on the back of her neck that she barely notice it at first. When she turned around there was a tall brunette woman walking past her all dressed in red trying to make her way out of the bar. She gave a polite "Excuse me" as she touched Mindy, then got out of the crowd of people and made her way to the exit when Mindy turned back to Thomas. He had his attention back onto her now.

"Well, I'm suppose to graduate in a year, if everything goes according to plan that is. School has been murder on the finances, and as I told you I have a daughter."

Thomas made that small little frown as she mentioned her daughter again, as if he didn't approve of them. "Yeah, kids defiantly need their mother. That takes precedent over everything." he said while keeping the look onto his face.

"Do you have kids Mr. Perkins?"

"Please, just call me Tom. No, but I knew how hard my mother worked for my brothers and I just to keep things afloat at home. So we could have all the nice things when we went to school. Taught us how to save our money for important things. I learned a lot from her."

Mindy grew a little smile on her face. She like this guy. Although Tom looked like he might not hesitate to flash around his money every now and then, he seemed like he had a sincere enough heart inside of him. Maybe this *was* an opportune time for love—or lust.

Tom looked down at her glass and said, "Looks like you finished your beer."

"Huh?" Mindy looked down and saw that there was a small quarter inch sliver at the bottom of her glass. "Oh looks like I have." She then slammed back the remaining alcohol and plopped the glass back down to the table. "Maybe one more won't hurt me."

"Don't you have to get back to your daughter?" Tom said.

Mindy looked at his eyes in a nice dreamy state. "Yeah but she will be asleep, besides one more won't hurt me."

"Actually it could if you have too much behind a wheel." Tom said

"Well all of a sudden I like the company I have." she said with a *come get me* look on her face. Then it started to turn to a small frown. "Why? You trying to get rid of me all of a sudden?"

"No ma'am. I just thought you were going to stay for one drink? Want to keep you honest you know, if you are going to be working for the legal system."

Mindy gave him an eye-roll. "Yeah…I suppose I should get going." she said with a little disappointment in her voice. She was hoping to at least get his number or something. As she got up and grabbed her purse, Tom cleared his throat.

"Umm, would it be too much to ask if I could have your number to call on you sometime?"

God, this guy was strange. "Uh yeah I guess."

"What?" asked Tom

"Well you kinda send mix signals there buddy. You want me to leave yet you want my number? Is this for business or could this be for personal use?"

"Well both is what I hope for." Tom smiled a *really* nice smile for her.

Mindy smiled. All the weird questions that stacked up in her head like dominos all of a sudden tumbled out of existence as soon as that smiled appeared. "Well alright then." she saw that he pulled out his phone and started typing in her number as she recited it to him.

"Great I will give you a call sometime tomorrow if that's okay?"

"Well tomorrow I will be spending the day with my daughter. So if you do please wait until around 8 p.m., that's usually her bedtime."

"Okay, sounds good to me. I will talk to you then."

Mindy smiled got up from her bar-chair and started making her way to the front door.

Mindy got outside with a big smile on her face. That went better than she thought it was going to go. Go in wanting a drink, go out with a possible date. Not that she has been on a date for a while, and she picked a good enough guy to start dating if she said so herself. Walking down the steps toward her car she thought about Tom, or Thomas. She liked the name Thomas better, thinking it was much more proper and gentlemanly than Tom. Hopefully he wouldn't forget to call her tomorrow night so maybe they could talk a little longer. Maybe even set up a date for them to meet up sometime next week. That was if she didn't have to work next weekend and if he was willing to do something with Harper as well. As much as she wanted to go on a nice date with him, she still thought time with Harper was more precious and needed to spend more time with her as well. She thought he would be okay with that, but of course ask him if she could bring her along. Who knows maybe he already thoug—.

Suddenly her left leg stood where it was in the middle of the parking lot as she was making her way through the cars. As if her whole leg decided right then she wasn't going to be needing to go anywhere. Or that it was just downright refusing to move anywhere, like she lost control of a part of her body.

"What the fuck?!" She said, in a terrified voice trying to move her leg an inch. It wouldn't budge, like being superglued to the pavement stuck. All of a sudden she started to lose the feeling in her toes, a tingling sensation that first felt as though her leg was starting to fall asleep but then quickly and furiously shifty to a shearing pain. Mindy let out a cry of pain as soon as this happened. *Was she having a stroke? Is this what it felt like to have a stroke?*

"Help me! He—." Her voice was instantly gone. She looked around the parking lot and seen that there was no one around to see this happening to her. To help her. She turned around and look to see the front door of the Dane, with her one good leg she turned and shifted her body to try and make her way to the front door, but the pain was excruciating and felt that she might collapse soon from the pain, but she didn't think her leg would let her collapse. She kept going, moving her right leg over to try to pull her left leg from its permanent state. She pulled and pulled, but realized that it was no use.

The door of the Great Dane opened and she saw that it was Tom. Her Tom that she just met, making his way down the stairs. Maybe to leave, maybe to get something from his car, who cares as long as he could see her that was all that mattered. He would see that she needed a doctor and could rush her over there in his car. Mindy started to wave her arms in the air, trying to get his attention, but he had his head down looking at the pavement. She wanted to scream so bad right now so she could get him to look up, but the fucking stroke or whatever it was that she was having right now wouldn't release her throat or her voice. she had a brief image of *The Little Mermaid* where Ariel's voice was taken by the sea witch and she was trying to describe to her prince how she washed up on shore. Only in this case her prince needed to look this way so she could at least show him what was happening. The pain was becoming too much as her throat started to turn numb then all at once feeling like it burst into flames.

She did see that he was starting to make his way over to her. Maybe somehow, hope against hope he parked near her car. Suddenly she had a quick idea and saw that there was a car arm distance away from her. She started pounding on the car to make loud BANGs to maybe get Tom's attention. He still didn't look up, and yet still made his way toward her. She pounded onto the car two more times when all of a sudden her right leg stopped in its place on her. *What? I thought a stroke only effects one side of your body? Am I having some sort of double stroke?* Mindy all of a sudden thought that this was something else. Instantly after her right leg decided to take suit with the left, the pain that took a little time to come skipped the lag time and the numbness and started pulsing with the exact amount of pain she felt with her left leg. She thought she was going to either pass out or die. No, that was foolish, she prayed for death. If the rest of her existence was going to feel like this, she hoped that she would just die. She saw Tom was about twenty-five feet from her and he still didn't look at her, even after all that noise that she was making to get his attention. Still didn't notice and still made his way over. Did he have something to do with this? Did he *do* this to her?

Finally she felt like she couldn't fight anymore, the pain, shearing horrible pain was too much for her to continue. She released all the tension in her body and let the pain take her, thinking she was going to collapse. Only, she didn't. She stayed there with her right arm raised, frozen in place like her legs were, and as for them spread shoulder width apart while her left arm dangled down by her side and her head drooping down to where she looked at the pavement. Only she didn't see the pavement. She didn't see anything, with her eyes other than Harper's face and how she was never going to enjoy kissing it. Never going to hug her again, or hear her voice. She knew nothing, she felt nothing. Only pain, and how it engulfed her.

Through the pain she saw a pair of feet in her vision. In her pain stricken memory she remembered a little bit that Tom was coming near her. She tried to look up but failed to make her head lift up when she heard him say: "I'm sorry about this. Really, I'm very sorry."

What? He did this to her?!

"I know what is happening to you Mindy. I know that the pain is unbearable. But soon it will all be over. Once you follow me."

Was that some kind of sick joke this fucker was trying to play on her? She couldn't move no matter what she did!

Thomas began to walk away, and as soon as he started walking her legs began to move all by themselves. Walking closely behind Tom. The way she was talking she realized was like a tangled puppet caught in its strings. The pain was still there but she felt that it wasn't so unbearable, as if something entered her body to take the slight edge off, but still very much present, and had no control of her own actions. Soon her right arm was lowering and fell by her side. Soon her legs started to walk normally as if there was nothing wrong with her. But there was plenty wrong with her. While all this was happening, since the pain was subsiding she was trying to run away, only her own body wasn't hers anymore. Something was controlling her. She was screaming, only there was no sound. A deafening scream that had no sound to the dark and terrible night.

As they started walking she saw that Tom wouldn't look back at her, as if she wasn't there at all. Without a doubt now she knew that he was part of whatever was happening to her. Even though he wouldn't look back and see her face, she knew that he was feeling guilt, no, more like down right shameful for what he was doing. Not looking at her when he approached her as she was going through the worst hell ever to imagine. Fuck his shame. Fuck him! She saw him as nothing more than scum now. When this was done, she was going to make sure that his ass was going to rot behind bars, and hoped he would be never be let out.

Both Tom and Mindy started to approach the wooded area that was near the river. She turned her eyes and saw the main highway 51 and the passing of cars with their headlights on. They were moving too fast to get their attention, even if she could move to signal them. They started to make their way down to the bank, when Mindy saw a figure standing by the water. There was very little moonlight on this cloudless night, but she was able to make out that it was indeed a woman that was standing by the river. Not just any woman either, it was the woman in red that made her way out of the bar. What the fuck was going on? Terror that seemed to have reached the brim of her sanity, was subsiding just a little bit to make way for a tiny ounce of curiosity.

"Hello, Mindy." said the woman in red standing by the river. "Yes, I know who you are. I know a lot about you now. You may not know how, that's okay because that no longer matters wouldn't you agree." The woman turned back and looked at Mindy.

Mindy couldn't speak, she opened her mouth like before, but still no words came out. But if she could speak she would have said, "What have you done to me?"

The woman looked at her as if she heard every word that was spoken and said, "What is necessary for me and my King. Unfortunately for you it requires a lot of pain on your part. I wish I could say that I'm sorry for that, but I don't believe in lying when I don't have to, so I'm really not." Tears were falling down Mindy's cheeks as she started to cry. "You will do nicely. I will try and make this as quick as possible."

The woman started to raise her arms and walk towards Mindy. Mindy's eyes widen as the hands made their way towards her. At the corner of her eye she saw that Tom started to walk away.

The woman stopped, turned towards him and said, "Where are you going? You stand right there and see this. Like always."

She continued to walk towards her until finally her hands made contact with her body, and instantly all the pain that subsided shot through her, and not only was felt in her legs, arm, and throat, but now her entire body was yelling, and screaming to die. Every cell, every hair was in gut wrenching, shearing agony. It lasted only ten seconds to the rest of the world, but to Mindy, it was a lifetime. There was a light orange mist that looked like it was being dragged away from every part of her body. From fingers, all the way down to her toes, the orange mist crept off of Mindy's body all the way into the woman hands where it faded away into the skin. Soon the mist was gone and Mindy feel down to the ground. Where she felt nothing, knew nothing, and became nothing.

Chapter 5

Matt Mullen walked into the station feeling good about himself. Even after having to work on Saturday, his weekend went pretty well and went by way too fast. He didn't have anyone at home to call his family, unless you counted his cat Mork as a steady contributor. Although Matt thought more of Mork as a blackhole of food, money, and sometimes time. Still he was a good cat, he stayed out of trouble and out of the way.

His weekend was good though because he spent most of it up at Cranberry Lake fishing off the side of his boat. He caught his fair share of Bluegills, but what he was pleased about catching the most was his nice twenty-four inch Walleye that he couldn't wait to clean and eat tonight when he got home. It was such a sweet catch after fighting with the fucker for a few minutes. The little bastard gave him a small blister on the inside of his palm that was starting to hurt a little bit.

What he enjoyed the most about yesterday was the silence. There were hardly any boats on Cranberry Lake, because there wasn't enough space for a lot of boats to be placed on it, and no one ever went on there to water ski, or water tubing for that matter. Nature was the only sound on the lake. The wind blowing across the water and the reeds. The squawks of the loons and morning doves that could be heard clear across the lake with the splashing of water against your boat. To him, there were no sounds that even compared to that.

That feeling carried with him all the way to this Monday morning, making it seem not so bad that he had to work. He still had his questions about the two men at The Glass Hat, but he would get to the autopsy report as soon as he had his coffee. Also he made a point to try to get ahold of Tyler to make sure that everything was going alright for him. He tried to get him to come along for fishing yesterday, but he said that he had some important business to take care of. Probably something to do with him and Samantha, that was okay. He needed to deal with that. Just like his dad always told him: *The best way to approach a problem was head on.* Tyler was indeed going to have to face this problem head on, and he might as well get it over with.

Matt got to his desk to see if there were any new documents on it, or reports that he might need to redo because he filled them out wrong. There were none. So after seeing this he decided to make his way to the coffee stand that was at the wall.

"Hey Matt!" an officer in passing said to him.

Matt gave a *Hey!* back just as he made it to the coffee pot. Matt heard someone approach him from behind with those heavy footsteps hitting the linoleum floor. He turned around saw that Lt. Jeff Coyer was making him way towards him. He had a rather big figure as if he fit the perfect description for a cop. The big gut, the waddle, and of course having a donut in his hand. His red hair gave off a little bit of glare, which told Matt that the L.T. had some product in his hair, and was probably going to try and impress some lady or ladies later if he could. Not that he ever could that he knew of. Lt. Coyer wasn't exactly a ladies man, he had a bit of a smart mouth on him that a lot of ladies didn't find impressive all that much. Even though it could get him to tell some pretty wicked jokes every now and again. Some clean ones, some dirty ones. It didn't really make a difference to him, but if there were ladies around at work, he would try and keep it professional as much as possible.

What he lacked in looks, and muscle he made up for in leadership skills. He was always fair to everyone. Made sure that when it came to good ideas, that even the lowest ranking guy could have some good ones, so he usually asked them what they thought. Nor was he one for beating around the bush. Told you exactly like it was, never going for many metaphors, always straight forward.

"Hey Matt. How has the weekend treated you?"

Matt gave him a grin. "Treated me pretty well. Even running the double homicide that was on Saturday. I did some fishing on Sunday to make up for it, and got some nice bluegills that should be nice to grill for breakfast one of these mornings. But the what was really nice was the twenty-four inch walleye that I caught that will look nice after the taxidermist gets finished with it."

"Wait, wait, whoa!" L.T. said with an astonished look on his face. "What do you mean the double homicide on Saturday? When you say it like that, it makes this city sound like New York, or L.A. where the gangs run around. This is Wausau, Wisconsin. Not so many *homicides* here." He said homicides by breaking it down to each syllable in a sarcastic tone.

Matt made a smile that told the L.T. that he saw his point. "Well whatever you want to call it, it was still two dead bodies that were murdered. I don't know what fancy name you want to give it. Like you said this is Wausau, Wisconsin. Not many murders happen in this city even with its size."

Lt. Jeffery Coyer took a look at Matt incredulously. "Maybe you're not hearing me here Matt. I'm saying that they weren't murders period. I don't know where you got the idea or who told you that they were murders, but its clear cut that they were heart attacks."

Matt just finished pouring coffee into his Brewers coffee mug and was making his way back to his desk when this bomb was dropped onto him and turned around to meet the L.T.'s eyes. How could anyone think it was a heart attack? Two heart attacks for fucks sakes! "Wait, what?! What did the autopsy report say?"

"Duel heart attacks, according to the coroner. Didn't think such a thing was possible for two guys under their forties, but that was one of the damnedest things I ever saw in my fifteen years patrolling this town. I guess things like that can happen every once in a while."

Matt was stunned. "The chances of that happening are astronomical. Any coroner would tell you that. Can I get a copy of the autopsy report?"

"There should be one that's on your desk already. If not you should be getting it soon. Just ask Sgt. Gentle for one if you don't have one."

He made sure that the Lt. Coyer didn't see, but Matt rolled his eyes at the mere thought that he had to ask Sgt. Gentle for anything. And it was an even fatter chance that he would get anything once he asked for it.

"Alright sounds good L.T."

"Don't get down about this Matt. We all thought that this was foul play at first glance."

"Yes, sir." Matt replied, he thought to himself how could the deaths be considered natural causes? Two people dying the exact same way, at the exact same time wasn't natural. It was anything but natural. They had to be poisoned, or drugged. Hell maybe they both were pushed from the top of the building headfirst, but to both have a heart-attack at the exact same time wasn't possible. There just was no way for that to be. Unless they both took a drug that would somehow induce a heart-attacks, but even if they had the right doses calibrated to their height, weight, body type, and ages, it would still take minutes after the first heart-attack to take effect. Plenty of time to get any sort of help inside of the bar before falling over dead to the same thing.

He was making his way to his desk to see if the autopsy report was going to be on his desk. He already anticipated that the file wasn't going to be there. Either Sgt. Gentle swiped it from his desk to try and get an *I fucking told you so rookie*, in on him. Or Sgt. Gentle was in charge of distributing the file and withheld it; so he can try and get an *I fucking told you so rookie*, in on him as well.

Just as he reached his desk, he saw that all that was on it was his computer and keyboard, were his desk calendar on the face of the desk, and his file holder. He sat down into his chair an turned on his computer. Maybe the autopsy report was emailed to him instead. Not likely, since autopsy reports and death certificates were usually hard copied to all police officers usually, but there was no harm in hoping against hope. After a few minutes waiting for his Dell to fire up, Ditzy Dell he liked to call it, he logged onto his police profile page and saw that he had two new emails. One for a benefit for a fellow officers child that had leukemia, the other was an email memo that stated that the Wausau Police summer picnic was going to take place on August 6th, please bring a dish to pass, and help clean up afterwards, family members are encouraged to attend, etc.etc. etc.. No autopsy report. Fucking great.

Matt stayed at his desk for about a minute, not because he was afraid of Sgt. Gentle. No, Matt knew that Gentle was more bark and little bite compared to some other officers that he has worked with at the academy. No, he just wasn't feeling anxious about being embarrassed in front of the other officers because his initial response to these bodies was that they were dealing with murder victims. A big part of him still felt that they were.

He finally got up from his desk, took a big swig of his coffee, and started to make his way over to Sgt.Gentle's desk, located all the way to the other side of the offices in the bullpen. Mentally preparing himself for the onslaught of verbal language that was going to be coming his way in about thirty-seconds. He decided that he wasn't going to say anything to set off Gentle any more than usual. Stay silent, and take it, otherwise he was just going to try and milk it out of him as mush as possible. He knew that he was going to try and do that anyways, that was what Sgt. Gentle liked to do with lower ranks, hold mistakes over other peoples heads until he was done laughing at them about it. That would take months for him to get over. Yep, hell was on the way.

He approached Gentle's desk and saw that he was working on something on his computer. Maybe a report or something that was going to take a while he hoped, maybe he would just give him the report in passing. Anything was possible.

"Hey, Sergeant. Do you have that autopsy report from the two bodies on Saturday?" he said it in a professional fashion that almost made it sound like the two men were friends and not hated co-workers.

"Yes I do." said Gentle, not looking away from his computer as he said it.

"May I have a look at it?"

"Why would *you* need to look at it? You've been promoted without me knowing it?", still looking at his computer as he said this.

"L.T. said that I could go to you to get a copy of the report. So I'm asking you, if I may have a copy."

"I guess I'm telling you that you don't need to see it then.", turning in his chair and facing his back to Matt so he could get something from his personal printer. "Being that the report pretty much says that your theory of a man going around and killing people in dark alleys, has been disproved, and for that fact that you are not a lead investigator of the so-called 'crime' in question.", he made imaginary quotations with his hands in the air as he said this while holding the piece of paper that was in the printer in one hand. "So I guess that means we are pretty much done here. Wouldn't you say?"

Matt was trying to keep calm, and not loose his temper. "No, actually we are not finished, the autopsy report is not a sealed record to other police officers. Even if the officer in question is not a lead investigator, as long as he was involved in the processing of the crime scene, the officer in question is able to look at all documents pertaining to the case." Trying not to loose his temper he decided it was best to quote textbook material as best as he could. He wasn't sure if any of this was right down to the letter, being that he only really skimmed the part of the police manual when it comes to rules and regulations of handled police paperwork.

One look at Sgt. Gentle's face and he knew that he must have swung and missed on quoting the regulations. He had a skeptical grin on his face that said he didn't believe a word that just plopped out of Matt's mouth.

Gentle began to laugh. It was almost a hardy *Ho ho ho* sort of laugh that little gasps of air in-between each ho. It always brought irritation and annoyance to anyone that heard it. Matt remained stone faced and stared at Sgt. Gentle as he was waiting for this God-awful fucking laughing fit to die down.

"I think maybe you need to check up on your regulations. That claus distinctly works between NCOs of the force. Go ahead and check it. It will give you something to do, now that you won't be reading the autopsy report." said Sgt. Gentle and turned back to his computer.

"Give him the fucking reports Sergeant!" Said a booming voice that was almost right behind Matt that caused him to turn around and made Sgt. Gentle snap up from both his computer and chair. "I'm sick of your shit that you keep dishing out to everyone in this department", Now everyone around them was looking at the men, probably the most excitement they have seen since the bodies on Saturday. That and Lt. Coyer never really yelled at anyone before unless it was to motivate you. Now he was yelling at a N.C.O., which was almost unheard of among police precincts. "You want to keep holding stupid shit over people's heads, I'm sure I can let you go and have someone else put up with that shit. Now give Mullen the fucking autopsy report like he asked."

Gentle's face was starting to turn red from his neck all the way up to his forehead where he was starting to loose some hair. "Sir, he isn't authorized to look at the report."

"You must be fucking deaf or something because I told you he was authorized. Besides your little quotes on the regulations was incorrect, *Sergeant.*" Putting special emphasis on the sergeant, like he was making a threat that if he kept it up, that was going to be the last time he was going to be called that. "Plant your nose back into those regulations and you will see that Officer Mullen here is correct. Every officer that is involved in the investigation has a chance to look at the autopsy reports, and all other special documents."

"But sir, he is only a rookie. He was only at the scene to stand guard at the tape." said Sgt. Gentle through clenched teeth. Lt. Coyer just gave him a stare that said only certain death was waiting for you if you don't listen to what I'm saying. It was about thirty seconds before anyone said anything. Finally it was the L.T. that made the first move.

Looking down at Sgt. Gentle's desk he saw a single file that was on the corner of his desk and picked it up. Gentle made a quick jerk reaction like he was going to stop the lieutenant, but then stopped halfway and put his arm back to his side. Doing something like grabbing the file away from the L.T. might not only look petty, and weak; it could get him a free and permanent trip to the curb with all of his belongs along with him. Lt. Coyer gave the file to Matt, which Matt took with a thank you and started making his way to his desk, embarrassed as all hell.

"You need to straighten your shit out Sergeant!" said the lieutenant as he was walking away.

Matt could've gone without the confrontation involving Lt. Coyer. Things were already pretty bad with Sgt. Gentle in his face all time, now after the confrontation with the L.T., things were only going to get worse. Only now Gentle had to be more careful, and make every hit towards Matt hurt.

When Matt Mullen got back to his desk to open the autopsy report that was won for him by Lt. Coyer. Looking it over up and down he saw that the bodies did have a body toxicity level of .011. Which told the coroner that the victims had about two drinks at the most. Not enough to even slur their speech a little bit. No signs of any type of drugs, except small traces of tenazapam on the first victim. "Tenazapam? What the hell was that?", thought Matt. He made a note on a small notepad on his desk to look into the name of the drug. Most likely it was something to do with a prescription that the man had with a pharmacy. There was nothing in the toxicity about blood thinners or blood-pressure medicine. At least not by what he could see.

In the report they took out both men's hearts, and found that they were a little fat and plague on them, no more than normal on the hearts. Yet under both reports the analysis for the cause of death was mido-cardular infarction. Though there was no trace of dead tissue on or around the heart, unless they were now considering the whole heart as dead tissue.

Matt closed the file, disappointed in the results. He might have to visit the coroner's office and see if he could get a more definitive answer to the report. Nothing really made a whole lot of sense. There was no reason these two men should be dead, without the cause of foul play. but there was no evidence to support this conclusion, that was the problem. The coroner's office probably saw this as well, but couldn't put anything in the report that could support it. Matt hated this more and more as this went on. Unfortunately, as far as the police were concerned, this case was closed.

Chapter 6

It is fucking hot out, that was for damn sure!

This thought slipped into Tyler's mind, as sweat mixed in with the dirt on his face. As the sweat made its way down his head it began to make its way into his eyes, and caused a sharp sting of pain as the salt filled liquid entered his eye. Dust was flying up in his as the wind blew dirt around onto Nelson Road. The heat raised up from the asphalt of the road as well as the heat from the tar that was being laid down onto the scorching road. With a high of 96 degrees out and a high humidity from last nights Wednesday rain fall and lightning show, this thought creeped into Tyler's mind a lot this morning. The key was to always stay hydrated. As long as water was in him, there was no need to stop.

Moving down the road, Tyler looked back at Justin Tanger following behind. Justin's job was to cover the tar with what amounted to as toilet paper, with a long painters roller at the end of a stick, so cars and trucks that were passing through wouldn't get their vehicles all splashed with fresh wet tar. Only this is what Tyler and the other guys on the crew called "Bitch Seat". Dealing with the toilet paper and the tar almost always lead to a mess that would leave burn marks on your fingers and tar stains on your shirt and pants. Justin had this done to him enough times that his work clothes and reflector vest, looked like someone decided to splash him with black ink.

"How are you doing there, Justin?" asked Tyler yelling over the machinery.

Justin looked at him with a smile and yelled back. "I'm fucking fantastic! Tar keeps getting on the side of the toilet paper roll. Which is always fun because it makes the roll stick to itself, and doesn't want to unroll."

"Yeah I've been there. Have you sprayed anymore of that water mixture crap on the side of the roll?"

"I tried to get as much as could from the bottom of the bottle, but until the Brian orders more of the shit, I'm gonna be dry rigging it for the time being. I would put some of my water on them but just straight up water makes the T.P. fall apart on itself."

"Yeah I know that, but you might want to try just a little bit on them because its better than what your doing now and struggling to get the thing unrolled, ya know?"

Justin look at his roll for a moment and nodded, saving his breath from yelling too much. He raised a fist high above him to signal to the driver named Gene, to stop the truck towing the tar melter. Once the vehicle stopped the GMC, Justin started to run up toward the cab of the truck and went back to his thoughts. Mostly about what happened this last Sunday and how Samantha took whatever she thought was hers.

Sunday morning started out almost the exact same way that Saturday morning started out for Tyler. Hangover, puking, hydrate, and repeat. Tyler kept the party going at home as soon as he parted ways with Tanya after their spat in the 400 Block. There was a whole lot of liquor at the apartment, but Tyler made sure there was plenty to last him the night so he could deal with the next day meeting with Samantha.

It occurred to Tyler sometime during the nights drinking events that he didn't even call Samantha to let her know that they should meet sometime on Sunday to talk about who gets what, and who gets to take responsibility for Max. So, at 12:34 a.m. he decided that the appropriate time had arrived to inform her and gave her a call. He thought that he would get her answering machine, so he was preparing himself to talk to a machine, because he was never any good at leaving voice messages. Instead Samantha picked up at about the third ring, in a tired and irritated voice that gave Tyler a little satisfaction to hear. He informed her that he would like to meet with her sometime tomorrow, but he guessed that he meant today, so they could have an adult conversation about separating their belongings. She agreed and told Tyler that she would try and make it at about one-in-the-afternoon at the apartment. Then said goodbye and hung-up the phone without another word.

After the morning liquid fireworks were completed, Tyler remembered trying to get some breakfast and had him a bowl of Frosted Flakes. Twenty minutes after he finished with his bowl, he made his way to the bathroom to continue the offering to the Porcelain Gods.

Samantha showed up like she said she would. At 1 p.m., she showed up in a truck that Tyler didn't recognize. Probably from her new boy toy, and she most likely was going to take what she got after they we through meeting each other, so she would need the truck to load all her crap.

When she entered the house she had clothes on that he never saw on her before. She had some Dead-Head shirt on that looked like it wasn't a day over from being bought, and denim jean-shorts that had some sort of cheap jewels on them. Tyler thought to himself that either she just bought those clothes, or that she already had some clothes that she bought for this guys place and hid them from him. He started to feel a sliver of anger that was trying to rise within him, but Tyler was going to try and keep this as civil as possible.

"Hey Ty." Samantha said, trying to sound friendly as possible by using the nickname she had given him when they first met.

"Hello, Samantha." Tyler was not going to use her nickname.

Max heard her voice and started to run toward her to get some licks in and to receive some belly rubs. "Hey Max! How are you doing?" she said as she started to rub his belly. Max's hind leg started to move up and down, telling Samantha that the belly rubs were hitting just the right spot. Samantha then turned to Tyler and asked, "How's the weekend?"

"Fantastic. What would you expect?"

She lost her smile on her face. "Yeah, I guess that was kind of a stupid question. So should we talk in the living room or in the kitchen?"

"Let's take it into the living room. I think we might need to be somewhat comfortable when we talk about this." said Tyler. Samantha nodded and started to make her way over to the couch in the living room. Tyler sat down in his lounger that was right next to the couch. He started off.

"So I guess the first question is what is it that you want?"

Samantha looked at him and said, "Well I guess the first thing I would like is Max. He was my birthday present from last year, and I care about him very much. He was pretty much like the child we never had."

Tyler gave her such and incredulous look and said, "Okay, if he means that much to you why didn't you take him with you when you left on Friday?" Tyler didn't really give a shit about the dog. He fed him when she left, but right now the dog would just want all this attention that he couldn't really give him. So he was happy to let Samantha have him. He just wanted her to feel a little guilty over *something* if she wasn't going to feel guilty for leaving him.

Samantha looked like she was starting to get a little angry now. "I didn't know if Tony's landlord would allow pets at the time. Now, he got confirmation that it is okay, so I would like to take him to live with me."

"I'm sorry, who's landlord?"

"Tony's. You know— the guy I'm living with."

"His name is Tony? Tony who?"

"Tony Yost, he's a really nice guy."

"Okay, I don't really care. I just wanted to know his name so I could stop referring him to the fucker that is nailing my wife." Tyler said with a straight face.

Samantha looked annoyed by this comment. "Can we continue with the topic at hand? Can I have Max or not?"

Tyler was thinking about saying no. Just out of spite. He knew that wasn't what he wanted out of this, to make Samantha sour at him and make the coming months ahead more trouble than they already were gonna be. Not to mention that he really didn't want to take care of Max anyway.

After a sigh, Tyler looked at Samantha and said, "Yes you can have him."

Samantha didn't smile, didn't make any emotion on her face. She said thank you and then moved on.

Samantha wanted to split the furniture, but Tyler made a polite argument that he was going to need the couch and lounger more than she was when his friends were going to come over. Also stating that he was sure Tony had furniture of his own that she could use. Then brought up that he was the one that purchased all the furniture with not only the funds from the wedding, but also out of his own pocket. Samantha relented on the furniture, but insisted that she take the vehicle that was bought for her. Tyler hated that, but let her have it because it would mean one less bill to pay for, and another Tony was going to have. Tyler also thought he only needed one vehicle anyway. Samantha took her clothes and some of the DVDs that Tyler didn't care too much about. They spoke and divided their belongings for about two hours when Samantha decided to drop a bomb on Tyler.

"Well I think this about covers everything." said Tyler as they divided the silverware that they received from their wedding.

"Well there is one more thing I would like to talk about." she said.

"What's that?"

"I would like this apartment." she said in a cold tone.

Tyler did a double take. "I'm sorry, say that again?"

"I said I would like this apartment as well. Tony's place is small and this place is way bigger. Besides, you won't need all this space anyways now that its just you. I will have Tony and Max to fit into a tiny one-bedroom. This is a three-bedroom that is in the perfect location."

"Nope, not going to happen. I work hard to get a place like this. I can afford the bills, the rent, all by myself now that I'm not wasting money on stupid crap for you. If you don't have enough room at Tony's place, then you never should have left. I already informed the landlord that you left, so he can start shaving off what I own each month. Besides, my name is on the lease like we agreed it to be because of your credit card debt. So as much as you want this place, Tough titty said the kitty."

"So you're going to keep this place out of spite then?"

"No. Not out of spite. I'm keeping it because it's fucking mine to rent." Tyler was starting to get angry, unable to hold it back. First Samantha wanted to leave him, now she wanted to take his home.

"I think your lying; you didn't call the landlord. If you did he would have called me to let me know about the change."

"You know what? You can believe whatever you want to believe. My name is on the lease, *solely* my name, and there is nothing you can do about it. If you want to get a new apartment with your fuck buddy *Tony*, then you can go and have fun with that. But I guarantee you, that you will not get this apartment as long as I'm in it."

Samantha didn't say anything. She didn't give him any kind of look, didn't get mad, or stomp out angrily. She got up, grabbed a few of the possessions that they agreed upon, like the tall living room lamp, and Max as well, dog food and all. Then she left without another word. Tyler didn't like the way she left with nothing but silence, in all the time he knew her she was never silent when she didn't get something she wanted. It was strange to see that in her. He thought he was justified in his reaction. She left him, then wants to have the place where he lived. That was messed up. He had to talk to his landlord now, he lied before when he said that he talked to him. Now he had to talk to him to see if she was going to try and have him evicted or something. He knew he was going to fucking hate this whole divorce process.

On Monday, he went to work and tried to get ahold of lawyers which was a far more difficult job when he was screaming at them over heavy machinery on busy roads that needed to be tarred or parking lots that needed to be seal coated. He found one named Jake Hendricks, he sounded like a really young pup in the game of lawyering, but it was all that Tyler could afford for the time being. Jake told him that he would meet with him on Wednesday when Tyler got off from work at 4. When Tyler went and met with him, he liked what he heard. Telling him that unless the landlord was willing to pay a heavy fine, he couldn't just evict Tyler and turn around and give it to Samantha. It was music to Tyler's ears.

Gene started to pull up again and move the melter slowly down the road. Cracks that were freshly cut out and heat lanced started to appear from under the melter. As soon as they got a little passed the melter, Tyler started to move his wand right at the beginning of the crack and start filling it up with tar. It didn't take long to do, maybe about five seconds for a crack that was about three feet in length. It was just God-awful hot work, in God-awful fucking temperature.

Justin came back and started to cover the freshly laid down tar with his roll of toilet paper. Tyler noticed it was rolling along a lot more smoothly now, and was glad to see that. Justine gave him a smile and a thumbs up saying things were good to go now.

The work day was starting to come to an end, but the heat sure had no end in sight. Tyler always thought that the sun from around four in the afternoon, till about seven were the hottest in the summer days. The sun giving its last bit of punishment for the day like a long distance sprinter giving it all the energy he has left to reach that finish line.

Tyler, Justin, and Gene were just finishing up with the crack sealing of their last road. Now they were starting to pack up and head back to the shop so they could prepare equipment and tar supplies for tomorrow. And tomorrow is Friday, one of the best days of the work week in Tyler's opinion. No more work for a couple of days, unless Saturday him and three other guys from the crew want to go and take the seal coater to get some overtime to put in. The chances of that happening were very slim because the guys didn't want to miss anymore time to get their drink on. Secondly, their wasn't very much work to spread out to the weekend. The company hasn't been getting a lot of jobs coming in because a lot of smaller companies have been taking the business away from them. There was still plenty of work, just not enough for overtime to kick in.

Tyler finished putting the hose and tar wand away in the melter when he spotted Justin and Gene grabbing a few tar blocks, and started to make their way to the melter.

"What are you guys doing?" asked Tyler.

Justin looked at him and said, "Well the melter is running low on tar. Shouldn't we put the remaining blocks in? There's only like ten of them."

Tyler looked at them for a few seconds then started to climb up on the melter, and pulled back the cover to the melter. A huge wave of heat slammed against his face. As smoke, steam, and the awful smell of burning, melting tar. Looking into the melter he could see that the tank was about three-quarters of the way full. Putting in the remaining ten might cause it to overflow. Spilling wet hot tar onto the roads wile they were driving home would be the very definition of bad news.

"Why don't we just hold off for the next job in the morning fellas. She's full enough already to where it will take a while for the tank to completely melt in the morning when we get ready. Besides, saving a little bit of money never hurt anyone. Hell it might even show off to the bosses in charge that we try to save as much as possible." Tyler gave a smile. Justin looked indifferent to the decision. Gene on the other hand was a little disappointed. Tyler knew that getting out of the vehicle to put some blocks into the melter was one of the highlights in Gene's job, because sitting in a vehicle listening to the radio all day and looking in the rearview mirror to see if you needed to hit the gas had the tendency to bring suicidal thoughts in a comical way.

"Goddamn it. Well can someone else drive back to the shop? I fucking sick of sitting in the drivers seat. It's about a half hours drive back to the shop, but I'm starting to really hate that seat." said Gene.

Tyler and Justin both laughed a little bit, until Justin said that he would. Tyler was just going to have to show him where to go. Tyler agreed, and then Gene scooted his big figure into the back seat of the cab so Tyler was able to get into the front passenger seat.

While driving back to the shop, Tyler's phone began to ring. He pulled out his iPhone and saw that it was Matt Mullen. He hadn't spoken with Matt for a while, not since last Saturday when he went shooting with Tanya, and invited him along for the fun. But there was some sort of case that Matt had to do that stopped him from tagging along. Something about two guys getting killed, but was then ruled natural causes. Which was strange even to Tyler's mind, and he had no knowledge of police work or how heart-attacks work for that matter. He slide his thumb on the answer key and responded "Hey Matt how's it going?"

"Hey buddy, its going okay at best. Things at work are a little slow as usual, but they are finding ways to keep me busy."

Tyler smiled, "Yeah but those bodies where pretty crazy, I bet that kept you busy for a while."

"It would have if there was something more than a heart-attack that happened. Personally I think that was just some of the weirdest shit I ever saw. Two men in the peak of perfect health just collapsing dead after a few drinks sounds too unbelievable to me."

"Sounds like you don't quite believe it at all by the sound of your voice." Tyler said with a little grin. He could tell that Matt really loved his work, and loved the fact that he was helping people. He was listening to that caring side right now and that was always something to hear. That's when you got to hear what he really felt about the cases he thought were all wrong. How someone else had an answer that was completely different from his own, and that answer was the one that was accepted over his. It drove him nuts, but it was fun to watch.

"No, I don't believe it for a minute. But I have to stop talking about it, or I will go off on an hour venting session on a case that is deader than the two stiffs we found. Besides most of our work is going into finding that missing single-mother that was missing since Saturday night."

"Oh yeah. I heard vaguely of that. I think the ex-boyfriend did it."

"No, I can't talk about it. But so no rumors get started, he was found clean and we will leave it at that. Believe it or not, I called you with a topic in mind."

"Oh, Holy shit. You didn't want to just want to talk to me. Crazy." Tyler pulled his mouth away from the phone and said, "Justin you want to make a right turn up here." Justin nodded.

"Huh?

"Sorry about that. We are just making our way back to the shop, and Justin is driving. So I'm helping us by making sure we don't get lost on the way there." Justin lifted up his right hand gave Tyler the bird. Tyler gave a kissing motion with his lips in a gesture that said, "Love you too."

"Okay, well the reason I'm calling is to see if you wanted to go to the bar tomorrow night. I have the weekend off, pending if no one gets murdered. And I know you have been having a hard time with things since Samantha left. So I willing to be either your DD or your shoulder to cry on or hell your drinking buddy. What do you say?"

"Well I'm not much for crying on shoulders, but I'm up for having a few drinks. When did you want to do this? I'm up for anytime this weekend."

"How about Saturday? Get drinking started at seven, seven thirty. I wouldn't want to go too early. Otherwise we might have to get dinner together."

"Hey, I only buy dinner for men who put out. Now that I'm not tied down thats not such a big leap for me." Tyler said with a chuckle.

Matt was laughing as well. "Good to see that you haven't lost your sense of humor you son-of-a-bitch."

"Yep thats still in one piece. I will see you on Saturday." They were only a half a mile away from the shop. The time was spent in silence.

From the time that Mindy Crass went out for her unfortunate after-work drink that lead her to become a missing person, up until Saturday morning, there were three more disappearances throughout the state of Wisconsin. On Monday a thirteen year old girl named Jordan Rothmeister was swimming at a beach on Lake Sacketts near the town of Medford. She was with her friend Jaimie Gaston and were always called J.J. whenever they were together, making it out that they were one person because generally they were connected at the hip. They were their waiting for their boyfriends that their parents had no clue they were seeing, named Gunner, and Austin. Gunner showed up for Jaimie, but Jordan was still waiting for Austin so she could take him out to the lake and possibly have some fun with her lips and her tongue. Maybe if he did that right, he could have some fun playing the bases. She knew what sex was about from her Health classes in school and decided that it was no big deal. Even though she was still a virgin it seemed like something that could be fun, and Austin might be someone she would want to do it with. Jaime had her eyes on Gunner ever since he arrived, and almost had her lips locked around his near the same moment as well. She never noticed the woman in the red bathing suit arrive.

Jaimie and Gunner went to the back end of the changing building and went over to the men's section. Jaimie wasn't quite ready for the "juicy stuff" yet. She was ready for the PG-13 stuff though. Which lead to the heavy petting.

When they got out of the changing room, Jaimie noticed that Jordan was gone. Her towel and her bike were also gone. They lived over on the other side of the lake, but she found it odd that Jordan wouldn't tell her that she was leaving. She thought that maybe Austin had arrived and that they might be off somewhere doing something more than heavy petting.

When Austin arrived at the beach with his clothes, towel and no sign of Jordan, she started to get worried and made her way over to Jordan's house and found out that she wasn't there either. About three hours later, after all Jordan's friends were contacted and all the neighbors around the lake were asked if they saw her, The police were called.

Johnny Krug liked to do endurance runs this time of year. Summer, especially June, was always green and beautiful to him. At least that was what he told his wife when he went out for his runs. Though it was true that he did run, (and he did want to someday do one of those Tough Mudder, or Spartan Warrior races) what he really spent his time doing instead of running was his twenty-five year old neighbor that was just a half a mile down the road from him in the town of Appleton. When he arrived at his girlfriends house they decided to explore some sheets together instead of exploring new running routes like they always said they were going to do. To be fair this was only their second month of their relationship since they met running on the same bike route together, so their sex drives were still set and possibly a little stuck on the high position. After about fifteen minutes of what Johnny would call a very strenuous workout, he gave Kirsten a kiss and grabbed his clothes, threw them back on and headed out the door.

That Wednesday night Kirsten started to make herself some dinner and was thinking about how and when she could get Johnny away from his fucking-cunt of a wife, and move in with her. Or better yet. She move in with him and kick that stupid bitch to the curb. She decided that she needed some background noise and decided that the six o'clock news on channel twelve was the perfect cure for that, until she heard something that made her head turn. She saw a picture of her Johnny and saw the word MISSING right underneath it. Her heart felt like it stopped in its place and she started to have a panic attack. The report said that Johnny Krug has been missing since his morning run today and didn't return, if anyone had any information about Johnny's whereabouts please contact the number below. Where was he? Did his wife find out about them? Was she going to be on her way here with police and arrest her for thinking that she was the one that made him go missing? What happened to her poor beautiful Johnny? Was he dead? She bet he was dead. If he was dead she didn't know how she would survive. After all she was in love with him. He might not be now but he is goi—*was* going to be in love with her. They were going to be together once he was going to divorce that stupid bitch of a slut he was attached to. What if she was responsible for this? She was, wasn't she? She must have followed him here this morning and saw that he was falling in love with her. Then when he returned home she must have confronted him and killed him. Now she was crying to the police that he was missing and that she had no idea were he was. Saying that he went for a run down such and such a trail and lead them right here and having her arrested.

All this scrambled through Kirsten's mind, like a lunatic on cocaine. She thought she needed to do something about this. She knew that it was too late for Johnny,(which was true) but she thought she could make that fucking cunt pay for doing this to Johnny. So she went to her attic where she kept her father's old handgun. She had no idea what it was called, but we would recognize it as 9mm Colt. She went and got dressed and put the gun in her purse, and started to make her way to Johnny's house.

She decided to walk until she started to see the police. They were probably plotting to make a break-in at her house, only they weren't going to find her at her house. Kirsten always found that the police were stupid, and incompetent. In this case especially, she figured out that the person responsible for Johnny's disappearance and his murder, if he was murdered, was sitting right next to them.

She waited two hours in the bushes that were right next to the house for the police to leave. By then it was quarter to ten when the last police cruiser left the house. As soon as it left Kirsten made her way to the front door where she knocked. She was in tears when she was knocking on the door, thinking about all of the times she took Johnny in her bed. Thinking about how she was doing this for him. How she was giving him justice.

The door opened and she could she that the stupid bitch wife had wet-teared-filled eyes as well. Only Kirsten thought that they must be tears of joy for getting away with murder. This thought filled her with rage. Without thinking she raised her purse with her hand firmly around the gun and pointed the purse at Jessica. She spoke in a soft tone that was barely audible. "For my love that you stole from me." and pulled the trigger.

The round hit right above Jessica's left eye, killing her instantly. Kirsten looked at her handy work and saw that there was no escaping from this. The police would be here and then at her house, and then blame her for everything. The bitches murder, Johnny's disappearance. She thought they could so that if they wanted, but they weren't going to have her to see them spread their lies about her. She she took the gun that was still smoking from the shot at Jessica, pulled it out of the purse and placed toward the right side of her temple— then blew her brains out.

Bobby Jo Wagner loved ice cream. Being five years old and summer starting to get really hot out, this surprised nobody. To her, the only thing better than playing on the monkey bars at daycare, was the ice cream the teachers gave when you come inside. If she knew that the teachers did this so the kids wouldn't suffer from dehydration, she probably wouldn't care, just as long as she got it. She thought that the playground was pretty special, she got to talk to a lady today that was asking to Miss Haley if her son Elliot could come and play with her and all her friends and daycare. Bobby Jo didn't think that everyone at daycare were mostly not her friends. Cole always thought that it was funny dump sand from the sand box in her hair. Bobby Jo hated that the most and told the lady that Elliot should stay away from Cole otherwise she might have some sand in his hair as well.

The lady smiled at Bobby Jo and said it was a deal. She then took her hand and shook it. After that, the lady that was wearing a lot of red started to talk to Miss Haley on what seemed like forever. Then she left in her car after they were done. Then Miss Haley rang the bell and sent everyone in for ice cream. Once ice cream was done Bobby Jo felt like she had to go potty and asked Miss Haley if she could go and take a tinkle. Miss Haley said yes but to be quick, her and her friends where going to start singing the Wheels on the Bus, which Bobby Jo always thought of as a babies song. Her parents told it to her so many times at home that she asked them to stop, she was turning six years old, not two. She laughed at the thought of that as she made her way to the hallway where the bathroom was.

No one saw her again.

Chapter 7

Over on the other side of Rib Mountain, from where the ski hills and the golf courses are, a series of houses that stand out from the rest of the houses that reside in the Wausau area. They have more elegance, square-footage, and scenery than most houses, because of the residents that reside in them. One resident of one of house, whos has heaters underneath the driveway so they have no need to shovel or plow snow in the winter, makes air conditioners for most of the midwest. Another that has a beautiful fountain in the front yard and looks as though Thomas Jefferson would reside, owns a well-run, well-earned window factory that makes all the windows in America for every house, and skyscraper.

Near the forest covered side of the hill with a mountain in it's name there is a house, that is not as elegant as most, but still needed a pretty penny to purchase. It's a one story with no pool and has wooden siding, because Charlotte always in her many years loved the look of trees. Inside the main bedroom Charlotte was putting on some blush onto her cheeks, because she always thought that her pale skin would always freak out other people. Naturally she was right after Bram Stroker came out with his book about *Dracula*, people were weary around that time of people who had pale skin, and attraction for such a thing was the last thing that she needed. People were crazy at the time for that stupid book, but than again she saw a resurgence of that sort of behavior from those *Twilight* books she could have done without. Although this sort of attention seemed to be more popular than of suspicion. Nonetheless it still annoyed her, profusely.

She knew that Danny was in the front living room most likely watching that stupid television box that she never liked or got use to. The bright lights and loud obnoxious noises she saw when they first came out really gave her a headache. She couldn't understand that when people had a limited amount of time on the earth as they did, would waste one minute of it watching such dribble. Even for information purposes it was always the same; a leader did this, a leader was caught with that, natural disaster killed so and such many people, sports team beat other sports team. Nothing was ever really different from the newspapers of old. It was people ways, with people problems.

Charlotte, (or so she called herself these days in Danny's presence) preferred the night life of everywhere. The middle of the woods, a small town or a big city was always her cup of tea, and discriminated against none. The world was filled with activities and people that could satisfy almost any of your needs. Having a lot of money to do these activities didn't hurt. From BASE jumping off of Angel Falls in South America, to climbing Mount Everest. Or going into a nice honky tonk bar and getting down with the so-called cowboy. Each one was a new adventure, and with her King by her side, making each one worth while.

Danny started to muffle something in the living room that was inaudible, but Charlotte didn't worry, she knew exactly what he was doing, and knew he couldn't really do anything rash against her. Even though she could feel it off of him that their were times that he really wanted to just beat the shit out of her, and make her suffer slowly. That was no matter for her, as long as he didn't say that to her face. Then that would be a problem for Danny. She never thought that it would come to that. She knew Danny was smart, that was why she picked him to work by her side, but when it came to standing up for yourself he was like all soldiers; followed all orders before emotions.

Even if those emotions made you sick.

She started to spray Chanel No. 5 on her left wrist and started to rub them together. Tonight she was going out on the town, and pain the town red. After all red was her favorite color, ever since she was giving that color so, so long ago. She wore it in the plague filled cities of Italy, that caused them to be emptied out. Except for the bodies that scattered the streets and the fear filled residents that remained. Those days were scary for the people, but not for her. She danced in the streets with her brother, wearing her red dress she made for herself. She loved that dress. She made it last as long as she could. But like most things, just like her, they never last. It lasted about five decades after the plagues decimated most of Europe.

The dress she wore tonight was an all dark maroon dress that had a cut in the cleavage that went down almost all the way to her bellybutton, but it stopped just short. on the sides of the cut, there were little diamonds that were placed about one inch apart from each other. It moved perfectly with the curves of her naked body underneath. The dress went down to her ankles matching her diamond studded shoes. If Jessica Rabbit was here, Charlotte could feed her her own heart. A man would think that she was going to the premiere of a hit Hollywood movie. To her this was the perfect dress-ware to hunt in.

She walked into the living room where she saw Danny sitting in the living room watching the local news. There was a story about missing people that seemed to interest Danny, and she knew why. He was checking to see if their recent activities that took place this week lead the police to them at all. It was his job to worry about such things and for Charlotte to not give a damn and carry on with her life. That was his job. That was what she paid him to do.

"You know that guys' disappearance lead to a murder suicide." Danny said.

"Really?" Charlotte said, vaguely interested.

"Yeah. His wife and some woman that lived a few blocks away. The way I figured was that the guy must have been sleeping around on his wife when he went on his morning runs. Once you took him, she must have flipped out and went over to the wife's house and shot her in the doorway. Then turned the gun on herself."

"Not the most crazy thing I've heard of." Charlotte said. She was busy pouring herself a little pre-night out drink of a Mimosa and keeping a little conversation going "There was a man that went and killed his entire family of four kids after I took their mother. He said at his trial that after the bitch left him, he didn't want to be stuck raising four kids by himself. There is a little crazy in all people. Sometimes it's just waiting to come out."

"Yeah I guess so." Danny was a little nervous talking about this. He suddenly thought that he must have been working for Charlotte for far too long, if he can talk about how she killed someone and was ultimately responsible for the murders of the entire family, and be so cavalier about it. It stuck him that he didn't really care about them and that stuck him as a little scary. How much longer would he be doing this job until all of a sudden he could start killing without feeling.

"Did my King get ahold of you today?" Charlotte asked Danny to get him to come back down to earth. She could see that he was in that place in his mind that he went to to escape some unpleasantness that was spoken. He did that a lot when he first started working for her, although nowadays she was noticing more and more that he was starting to get use to this new life. That was good. It was making him more reliable. Yes he messed up every once in while, like the two guys outside of the Glass Hat, but it worked itself out.

"Yes, ma'am. When he last spoke, he said that he was feeling a bit weak from some of the medicine he was receiving so he was going to retire early this evening."

Charlotte had a sad face on her now, "Oh, my poor darling. Well when we arrived back at Lake Geneva tomorrow, my darling King will feel all better when he gets the latest batch. Hopefully that will be all that he needs, being that our time is so close now."

"Yes, ma'am." Danny said.

"So do you have any suggestions on where to go tonight? Or are we just playing it by ear, as they say nowadays?"

"Well, on the night of that girl at the Dane,(he knew her name, he never forgot any of their names when he was used as bait, he just knew that she wouldn't care about them) I was over at the 400 block, and there is this theatre next to it called The Grand Theatre. I guess *Chicago* is playing all this weekend. Maybe do some hunting there?"

Charlotte thought about it. She had seen *Chicago*, both the city and the broadway musical about a billion times and thought that if she had it her way in the world, they would both be thrown away in the trash where they belonged. People and all. The only thing that was holding her off from saying no, was the simplicity of the hunt that can be done there. All that she would have to do was sit it a back row and wait for either the person in front of her or next to her and then make them go to the bathroom and then she could take from them right there, and even leave them there if she wanted to. People died from heart attacks all the time in theaters she found out. Mostly because these days the people that attended them were about a stones throw away from kicking over and seeing that great old broadway play in the sky. Then she could come home, relax, and fall asleep before she would make the three hour drive back to Lake Geneva to see her King. Getting him healthy for what was to come.

She had waited so, so, long for this to happen. Both her and her King had wanted ever since she liberated him from his prison so long ago. Back when the knights ruled the land an ocean away. It was magical back then, and it was magical now as she stood there and thought about it. She knew that she earned what was coming, they both did. The time for taking chances was over now.

"Yes. Let's do that. We can finish early enough and then grab something to eat on the way back. Then come back here and go to sleep so we are nice and refreshed for tomorrow. There won't be any need for clean up tonight Danny. So let's get going."

Danny was taking aback by this. "No need for clean up? Are you sure? Ma'am, we are so close to the end now I don't think we should take any chances."

Charlotte turned and look at Danny with a furious look on her face. "Am I sure? Why yes Danny. I am sure. I am sure that I most certainly know that we are nearing the end, and that we don't need to take any chances. That is why I agreed to do this sort of outing tonight, because its the one that is the least amount of fun, but produces the most results and is the safest for our getaway. I am sure that you will not need to clean up, because even if there weren't like a hundred people at the lobby or in the bathroom waiting to take a leak or just wondering around there, how would you explain the sack that contained a dead body on your shoulder as you were leaving the showing? The 400 Block always has something going on there, and people are always there. And

I most certainly don't plan on killing everyone in this fucking city, if you know what I mean."

Danny raised his hands in the air as if to surrender. "Alright. Calm down. I will do as you please, ma'am, I just don't want to see you get caught that is all."

"You worry about yourself and your job Danny. I will worry about myself and my King." Then she started to grab her purse and started to head for the door. "Are you coming?"

Scrubbing oil off your fingers was always seen as a pain in the ass. Even with that scented orange soap that big industrial factories and automotive shops had that was an ingredient away from being considered chemically unhealthy, still made the task difficult to get just a portion of it off. The way that Tyler had to do it was to rub one spot on his hands at a time. It made for a seemingly slow process, but eventually his patience paid off.

The oil was all over his shirt and jeans as well as his hands. While working on his truck to change the oil and the oil filters, there was a little pressure that lingered in the filters somehow and sprayed all over him as he was laying underneath the truck. The whole thing soaked him and turned him black like he was a pig in the mud.

Like all things that have been happening to him, his head was just not in it. His head was always on Samantha. Always on the divorce. He was sick of it. Sick of not only his time and his future income that was going to have to be invested in it in the future, but also brain space that she was taking up there, rent free. It was really fucking annoying once you thought about it. Everything had to stop until the divorce was final. Six months, six fucking months. According to the law of the land in great state of Wisconsin, you and your spouse had to be separated for at least six months, as well as go through counseling sessions to try and save the marriage before you were legally able to finalize.

Tyler looked at the clock and saw that it was 5:30. He had about a half hour to get ready and meet Matt Mullen over at Malarky's Pub and Grill. He looked down on himself and saw that he would need a miracle to get there in time.

It might have taken a miracle to get there on time, but it turned out that Tyler didn't need one. He arrived at the Pub about fifteen minutes late and saw that Matt was no where to be seen. Matt was running late as well, which was a little lucky for Tyler so he wouldn't have to make up some see-through story about why he was late, when Matt would be the one that was going to have to make it up. Neither man cared if the other was a little late. It was kind of a joke they had with each other to make up some lame story why they were late at their meeting spots. When it was first started about a year ago, they would say the obvious stories like needed to hop into the shower, or work ran late. Soon they started to get a little interesting and would say things like "I had to help some ducklings across the street.", "My mother wanted me to do some chores.", "Sammy was having me help her train pigeons to deliver messages and the one that was going to be sent to you got lost.".

Nowadays the stories would turn into this elaborate ballad of nonsense that would usually leave you in stitches as soon as it was over. It was always a great way to start the night. Laughing is always a great cure for the troubled reality.

Tonight however when Tyler was running late he was worried that he was going to have to think of some stupid elaborate story that was suppose to deliver the nights starting out laughs, only on the way there he couldn't think of anything. His mind was too troubled. He thought that if he couldn't think of anything that it would indeed show the sad state he was in. This thought made him feel troubled and tried harder to think of funny story. But he couldn't. When he saw that he was almost there he decided to hell with it and would give him a sad dose of the truth. That he was working on his truck and time ran away from him. It wouldn't cause any laughs, but it was the best he could do. Besides, there was plenty of time tonight to make some laughs happen tonight. Maybe if they called Chuck they could have even more fun. Chuck and Matt didn't get along very well, but who cares. When you were planning on getting drunk, you could all be friends right?

As he walked through the pub and saw that Matt wasn't there, Tyler blew a sigh of relief. Knowing he wasn't the one to supply the ridiculous story brought him some comfort. So he walked to the bar and saw that it was the same bartender that was here last Saturday. The bartender saw him and immediately his faced turned into a scowl. He walked over to the side of the bar where Tyler was approaching and said, "I think you know what I told you last Saturday when you were here with your little girlfriend, and caused all that shit to go down."

If he thought that Tanya was little in anything, he didn't really know her at all. "Listen I not here to make any trouble for anyone. All I want is to have a good time, and to have a drink in peace."

The bartenders face didn't change. "That maybe what you want sonny, but that doesn't mean that is what you are going to get. Seeing as I know how much trouble you can be, I'm extending my right to refuse service to you tonight."

Tyler's mouth gapped open. He couldn't believe what he was hearing. He went to this pub for a long time, at least three years. Now this prick bartender that was about a month into starting here was saying he couldn't have a drink because of an altercation that happened a week ago that wasn't even his fault. This was some bullshit.

"Listen I'm sorry about last week. Truly, I really am. But don't punish me forever over one stupid night. Come on."

The bartender started to straighten up and got an even more serious look on his face. Like he was about to tell Tyler a long scary story. "It won't be forever son. But I don't need to be a shrink to see that there is something that is bothering you. I don't know what that is and personally I don't give a flying fuck. That's between you and whoever its about, if I had to guess it was probably a woman. Like I said anyway: I don't care. But until you get it figured out you best not come back here until you get everything squared away. Understood?"

Tyler felt like he got punched in the gut. He nodded and started to head for the door. Bartenders were always good at seeing into a person. A complete stranger just spelled out everything for him. *Straighten up and get squared away*. All easier said than done.

He made his way outside and took a right toward the corner of the block. He pulled out his phone and started to dial Matt. All of a sudden he felt a hand on his shoulder.

He jumped up in the air a little and turned around as quickly as he could and started to make a grab for the collar of whoever had just grabbed him. To his horror he saw that it was Matt Mullen. He saw how fast Tyler was moving and started to raise his hands in the air to show that he was unarmed. Tyler relaxed instantly as soon as he recognized that it was Matt that was the one who touched him.

"Easy tiger!" said Matt. "I was just going to say that I'm here and why are we outside instead of having a drink right now?"

Tyler lowered his eyes to the ground. "We can't go in there."

Matt looked bewildered. "What? What not?"

"Last week I caused a scuffle in there when this guy was trying to put some rough moves on Tanya. I stood up for her and now I am considered to be too rough to be in there."

Matt gave a little grin. "What do you expect after you smashed a glass against the man's face?" Tyler gave him a look that said he didn't really want to talk about it, but Matt continued. "My buddies at the department, who are not as nice as me, could have been called to take care of it. You would have been spending the night in the drunk tank for sure with an aggravated assault charge attached to it."

"I don't know if you can't see it on my face right now, but I am really in no mood for a lecture. I agreed to come out tonight to get away from the things in my life for just a couple of hours. To forget that I had a wife that left me. To just hang out with my friend. I know that sounds like I'm running away from my problems. Well, I'm not, I've been dealing with everything that has been thrown at me. Last Sunday, Samantha and I started to separate our crap. Did you know she took the dog and then wanted to use the fact that she has the dog to try and get the apartment from me?"

"What? Why didn't you tell me?"

"Because you have been busy, and I didn't want to lay all that on you like that. You've been dealing with dead bodies and missing people, and I think a drug bust as well. Didn't you?"

Matt shifted from one foot the the other, as if he were uncomfortable about something. "Yeah, but you could still give me a call. I would like to know what I'm walking into when I'm going out with my best friend."

Tyler looked at Matt like he was starting to get offended. "What's that suppose to mean?"

"It means that I'm your friend. I may not be able to all the time, but I would like to try and help put out the fires every once in a while. Nights like this and seeing you this broke down from that stupid future ex-wife, makes me a little mad that you just didn't come to me in the first place. I mean for Christ's sakes, we are friends. So what I mean about helping you put out the fire, I would like to know if you need a fire extinguisher, or a God-damn fire hose."

Tyler laughed a little bit at that, and thought that Matt was right. Since he was told by Samantha, he thought that he was going to have to go through all the rough spots of the divorce by himself. There were parts of it were he would have to go in alone, but in the meantime he could try and be with his friends more. He tried to do that with Tanya last Saturday, and it was going well for a good portion of the day. Until he fucked it up by putting that glass into the shit-heads face.

Later on that night, hours after he left Tanya, he knew that he overreacted, but at the time he thought that it was the perfect response to what was going on. He supposed he could have just grabbed the guys arm until he let go of Tanya. But something rang clear in his head that he was suppose to really ring it through the guys head that he was unwanted by Tanya. He told himself that it was to protect Tanya, but there was something else inside of him that just really wanted to do what he did. That scared Tyler a bit.

Tyler turned and looked at Matt. "Well tonight let's get the fire hose out and try to put this fire out as much as possible." They both laughed.

"Well alright. Let's see if we can go back in. I'm sure the bartender will serve us once he knows that the buddy you brought in is a cop." said Matt as he started to go towards the pub.

Tyler just stood where he was. "No, don't bother. The guy was right. I do need to work through some personal shit, and I don't want to spread it around in that bar more than I already have. Let's go find somewhere else. Isn't there a Mexican restaurant in the building next door that has a nice bar? We could get tacos before we start drinking, so we won't get too torn up from the floor up."

Matt turned to Tyler so he would look at him. "Maybe you don't understand what tonight really is. You can have as many drinks as *you* can. That's fine with me, and hell I might even buy a few for you. But I am the designated driver. Only soda for me tonight with my tacos please."

Tyler was going to protest this because he felt that drinking alone was for no one but hippies and stew-bums. He thought about it for a second and thought that he wasn't going to be alone tonight after all. Matt was still going to be by his side, and maybe it wasn't that important to have a drink. You could still have fun without them. And the company of your friends did go a long way. Oh, what the hell.

"Okay. Sounds good to me." Tyler said as they made their way across the street to the Mexican restaurant. But something was bothering him. "Hey, who told you about last Saturday anyway?" Just as the question left his lips the answer popped out of both his and Matt's mouth at the same time.

"Tanya!"

Both Matt Mullen and Tyler Green ate some of the tacos that the restaurant had and thought that they were pretty good. Having never eaten at the place before they wondered why none of their co-workers of other acquaintances have ever eaten here and told them about it. After Matt had a soda, and Tyler had just one New Glares beer, they received their check. Almost instantly they realized why.

The prices were outrages for a small town restaurant. The food was good but not that great where they would make a continued run of the place for the night. They paid their bill and decided to make their way over to another bar that was about a half a block away from the 400 block called The Side Street. Once they got out of the building to the street, they saw that there were people in and around the 400 block, mostly gathered around the Grand.

"What the hell's on tonight?" Tyler asked.

"I think *Chicago* has been playing the whole week. *Want to get tickets?*" Matt said in a mock woman's voice. He gave Tyler a little raise of the eyebrows that said if he played his cards right, the night might lead to something more.

The were approaching and alley when Matt did this gesture. The gesture caused Tyler to burst out with laughter. Once he got himself under control again he answered Matt's question. "I think you need to get me a little more liquored up than I am now to make me sit in to watch a show about women murdering men."

Matt gave a little chuckle at that. Then he brought up a subject that hit a little sensitive spot in Tyler's gut. "Have you spoken to Tanya since last week?"

Tyler raised his head in a little surprise as if he just caught someone grabbing him from behind. "How did you think of that?"

"Why do you answer a question with another question? *Chicago* got me thinking that Tanya would love that show, and then I thought about why she wasn't here with us enjoying this night out. So when was the last time you two spoke to each other?"

Tyler lowered his head to look at the sidewalk. "Last time we talked was last Saturday. When she told me not to talk to her until I had my head out of my ass. I don't think it was those exact words, I'm just paraphrasing here. This was shortly after the whole—." Tyler made a gesture with his hand like he was holding something in his hand and swung down onto something.

Matt completed Tyler's thought by saying, "Glass to the face? Sure."

Tyler went on, "I mean, I guess I have no idea on how to go from here. What should I do?"

Matt was felt a little annoyed that he had to spell out the obvious for Tyler. To him it was crystal clear that he should just call up Tanya and apologize for what happened. Tanya was a human being just like every other person, and when her feelings get hurt, you need to apologize to try to move on from whatever happened.

This time was different. For one the incident didn't really happen to her. Sure, she was there and the guy that Tyler stood up against, was for her safety. Matt understood that. What he also understood, was that Tanya saw a side of Tyler that she probably never saw before in him. She got a glimpse of that soldier side that was buried before last week. That soldier side showed up every now and again through the way that Tyler spoke when he would answer someone by saying "Roger" or "Ten-four". Even the way he walked showed a little bit of his soldier side, when he would keep in step with a person he was walking with. Hell he even did it tonight while the two of them were walking down the street as they are speaking.

But the soldier side that Tanya got a real good look at last Saturday was one that was the ugly side. When push came to shove and you had to pull out the weapons to defend yourself. No matter what weapon it was: knife, gun, beer bottle. In a fight where there were no rules, everything was legal. She saw that, and it must have scared the shit out of her. Seeing that side of Tyler would scare almost anyone if you weren't used to it. Matt remembered his service in the Military Police. Remembered seeing that side of people with both the people he worked with and the assholes he would be going after. Once you saw it enough times on other people you could put up a good defense against it. Hell after a while it wouldn't even phase you anymore. Tanya saw that side, the soldier side, for the first time and thought what most people thought that weren't use to it: *Get them away from me!*

Matt thought about this and saw that there was a silence right now between him an Tyler. He looked at Tyler in the eye and told him. "Just give her a call and apologize to her. She knows that you are going through something right now Ty. She probably wants to help you out too. But last week I think that you scared her a lot. You have to make it clear that it wasn't directed at her in any way. See what she's doing tonight and see if she wants to hang out with us."

"You want me to call her right now?" Tyler asked

"Yes. You have had only one drink in you, so I know you are not going to slur your words." Then Matt cracked a smile. "Well at least not as much, you are a lightweight. And also, I will be right here with you on this call. Let her know I'm with you and that things are going good tonight. See if she wants to join us. After your done saying your sorry of course."

"I don't know, something tells me this might end badly." Tyler said.

Matt was getting impatient. "It's going to end badly for you if you don't call her. Now pick up your damn phone and say you're fucking sorry."

"Alright!" Tyler started to take the phone out of his pocket. "See. I am dialing her number and putting the phone to my ear." He did these things as he was saying them. He waited for an answer as he heard the tones from the ringback. There was a little part of him that hoped she wouldn't be able to answer. He knew that he hurt Tanya in some way, he just couldn't really understand. He was only trying to help her, why couldn't she see that at the time. Finally he heard the ringback tones end and heard her moment on the other end of the line.

"Hello?" Tanya said.

"Hey, Tanya? It's Ty."

There was a small silence on the other end of the phone, until Tanya spoke. "Hi Ty, How are you doing these days?"

Tyler didn't really want to go into small talk about how he was doing okay and how we have been getting great weather, and so on, and so fourth. He knew it was going to awkward for the both of them anyway, so he might as well rip off the preverbal Band-Aid and get it over with.

"Listen, Tanya. I'm s-sorry about last week, okay? You saw a side of me that I didn't really want you to see. I clearly overreacted in that situation and it was wrong. I-I'm sorry."

Once again there was that silence on the other end of the line. It made Tyler uncomfortable and thought right away that this wasn't going to work. Tanya broke her silence.

"Are you okay now?" she asked in a firm voice.

Okay now? Of course I'm not okay now. I still hurt from Samantha. He thought this over in his head before he answered her. "No, I am not okay. I don't know how long that will take. But I have Matt standing right next to me, and I have you as a friend, at least I hope we're still friends."

"Of course we are still friends." Tanya said. Tyler went on as if he didn't hear her.

"No, I'm not okay. And what I'm going to say next might be very corny but, oh well. I just need my friends to help me get through it and point me in the right direction. So I don't have what happened last weekend come around and take a big bite out of my ass again."

Tyler heard Tanya give a big sigh. Like she saw a big mountain in front of her that she had to climb in order for her to get to her destination on the other side.

"Okay, well you can count me in on helping you get through this. I never went through a divorce, and I'm sure its going to get ugly before it's going to be pretty again. But if you need me, just give me a call."

Tyler smiled. "Does this mean you forgive me for last weekend?"

Tanya could hear that smile on the other side of the line. "Yes this means I forgive you for last weekend." she also said with a smile.

"Awesome! Thank you Tanya. Like I said, I have Matt right next to me if you want to come out and join us, you are more than welcome. Don't worry, I'm taking it easy, and in worse case scenario, Matt has agreed to be my D.D. for the night."

Matt put his face close to the phone. "He's right. I'm right here if ya need me."

Tanya gave a small chuckle. "Naw, not tonight guys. I just want to take it easy tonight. Saving some money for the bills."

"Alright." Tyler said with a smile on his face. "Well you have a great night then! We will talk to you later."

"Okay, well you guys just be safe, and have a good night. Bye."

"Bye." Tyler said as he heard the click and the beeps from his phone that indicated that the call had ended.

Matt and Tyler started walking again. They started to approach the alley that was coming up on there left side. Matt was closest to the building when Matt asked him, "So how do you feel, now that that is taking care of?"

Tyler turned to look at Matt. The words he was going to say were that he felt great to bury that hatchet into the ground. But when he turned his head, the two men were just passing the dark alley. When Tyler looked toward Matt, briefly glanced at something. Something that was a little bit off. It didn't register right away in his mind, which caused his voice to break away in his speech and do a double take on the darkness of the alley. Once he did this his eyes focus and adjusted and what he saw what was off. And it horrified him.

It was blood. Blood everywhere.

Chapter 8

Charlotte was riding in the back of a black SUV around the time that Tyler and Matt were enjoying their overpriced Mexican food. Before they were going to go to the theatre, she asked Danny if he could grill her a nice New York Strip. She knew that he could cook when she first "discovered" him. One of his many duties. He did and while he was cooking this nicely cut piece of meat, she noticed that he wasn't making one for himself. She asked him if he wasn't hungry. He said he was, but he was going to make himself some buttered noodles. Just as he said this, she noticed that he was boiling water on the stovetop that was inputting her view a little. She told him not to be silly and to throw a steak, or ribeye, or whatever he felt like having, onto the grill as well. This was going to be their last night before they were going to return to the King, it was time to let hair down, so to speak. Danny gave a little nervous nod, and went over to the freezer and grabbed a New York Strip out for himself.

After they finished their dinner, that was complete with mashed potatoes with gravy, and asparagus, Charlotte noticed it was time to make their way over to the theatre. Danny took both the plates from his place on the table as well as Charlottes' and began to wash the dishes. Once they were completed they made their way over to the black GMC, and made their way over to The Grand Theatre.

We are almost done. Tomorrow I get to see my love and we can finally have what I always wanted. Our family. Our family. Our family. She repeated the words over and over in her mind. She couldn't wait for this night to be over. She was one away. One *soul* away.

She thought that about just fluffing Danny up and get him good and drunk before going out and just taking his. Only she grew quite fond of Danny. Like a master that grows fond of a pet that has learned all the new tricks that can be taught to such an animal. You didn't really want to start all over with a new pet. Even if the pet had what you needed. No, one last night to hunt around would be good for her. Who knows she might not be able to hunt for a while anyways. Who knew what kind of state she would be in when she was with child. Her mother would have known. If her mother were here she would be able to help her through what was to come.

Thoughts of sorrow and rage rang through her head as she thought of her mother. How men came after her and and her mother saying that they were both witches and that they needed to be punished by God for making their dealings with the devil. She never knew this God, or this devil that they were speaking of. In all her years of living she never really saw any proof that one or the other really existed. It was no problem for her anyways, it was what they say nowadays: not my circus, not my monkey. But in this Gods name, they caught her mother. Her father was able to get her and her brother out of that city as safety as possible, but by the time he went back to get her mother, she was already screaming on a burning stake. Enough to where she could hear her mothers screams from over five miles away. She never forgot that night. Always wishing that her power was strong enough then to go and free her mother. When her father returned, they ran.

She snapped away from her memories when the car stopped in a parking spot in a multi-leveled parking garage, that was about three blocks away from the theatre. She took her purse and got out of the SUV when Danny opened the door for her and took her hand. Always a gentlemen this Danny, even when doused in fear.

"Thank you Danny." she said.

"Yes, ma'am." Danny said as he shut the door behind her. "Is there anything else you want to get while we are out tonight ma'am?"

"No Danny, this night will be great once it is over with. We are just going to go to the theatre and go." Once she was adjusted with her purse on her left arm. she lifted up her right arm to Danny. "Will you joined me Danny? To celebrate?" She smiled at him with earnest.

Danny looked a little terrified. The fact that he might be the final victim in all of this didn't just cross his mind once. In fact, the thought seemed to plant itself right in the middle of his mind as if it were a redwood tree in the middle of a small town. When she told him to get a steak out of the freezer for himself, he had a vision in his head of an inmate before he went to the electric chair. His last meal. New York Strip that was slightly bloody, with mashed potatoes and gravy, with buttered asparagus. He didn't want to talk to Charlotte during dinner because he didn't want anything to trigger his early demise. Despite always being prepared in the military for the chance of death to knock on your doorstep, he never really wanted to die. Especially, in the way that Charlotte dealt death out. There was nothing Danny could think of worse than dying like that. He couldn't kill her, oh no. She had made sure of that a long time ago he knew. He thought that if he was going to die though, he was going to try to doing without showing fear. That was never easy. Fear engulfed him now. He decided if now was the time. Then now was the time.

He showed no emotion to her. That would have been unprofessional. He merely took a hold of her arm and interlocked it with his own and said, "Yes ma'am. To celebrate." And then he waited for it.

They began to walk across the parking garage over to an elevator. Danny parked on the third floor of the structure because all of the other levels were full. *Chicago* must be very popular around these parts because as far as he knew there was nothing else that was going on in this town. All the while walking he was waiting for it. Waiting to be taken. Each step felt like he was lifting lead boots on his feet. He felt that he was starting to perspire.

"Danny?" He jumped as soon as he heard her voice. That cold stone-like voice of hers. She took a step back a little as soon as this happened. "Whoa there. Easy Danny. What's wrong?"

Danny turned to meet her eyes. He couldn't take it he decided, he had to ask. Even it was a lie, he still had to ask. "Am I the last?"

Charlotte chuckled to herself. "What?"

"Am I the last one Charlotte? If I am please just get it over with. Right here, right now."

Charlotte rolled her eyes. "Don't be so dramatic. No, you are not the last one. You have kept your promise to me Danny. I will keep mine. Once this is done tonight, you will be done with all of it as well, and I don't mean in a dead sense either. You have served me well and I am going to reward you like I said."

"How do I know that this isn't just something to say to me so I will still go along with you and co-operate."

Once again there was a chuckle that came from Charlotte. "Oh, Danny. It's like when I first found you all over again, and I will give you the same answer like I did two years ago: Do you really think you have a choice? This isn't your first time around the block, you know better than to go against me. Unless that is what you want. Do you want to be me last?"

Danny shook his head. "No ma'am." Somehow his manners came back to him through this confrontation.

They reached the elevator. Danny didn't notice that while she was talking to him she took him lightly by the arm and continued to walk toward the elevator. She pushed the button that pointed down. "Then you have nothing to worry about. If I wanted you dead, well… You know what would have happened wouldn't you?" He nodded. He never would have left the house he finally realized. Lost control of his whole body and then be taken like the rest.

They walked into the elevator. Danny was feeling a wave of calmness wash over him. He knew that this maybe a lie. But right now, he had something to hope for once again. "Besides." Charlotte said as the elevator descended to the ground floor. "You're the best human I've ever been around." she said with a smile.

The doors opened and they were greeted by three men that were leaning against a cement parking post. The men looked over at Charlotte and Danny and instantly stopped whatever conversation it was that they were talking about. The tallest one looked at Charlotte and started to eye her up from the ground all the way to her wavy long hair. He had a pitch black t-shirt on that had a Metallica logo on the chest. He had black hair that looked like it had been colored to Charlotte, because she never saw black hair *that* black before and was called natural. Completing this image was a number of piercings that almost had his ear completely covered. The other two had piercings on their faces as well. One had a nose ring, the other had both of his eyebrows filled with what looked like big needles that were getting bigger as their length went on.

"Well hellllllooo, hottie!" said the tall one. "What brings you out to this little neck of the woods?"

Danny started to look at the tall one and briefly grazed his gun on the inside of his jacket just to make sure he had it. "Excuse us, gentlemen." he said. Although he thought to himself that calling these men gentlemen based on their appearance was stretching the word out to its maximum.

"Oh big man thinks he her protector." said needle in the eyebrow, that sounded like he just came from the backwoods and the only other person he ever talked to was himself. "He thinks he don't have to pay us no attention."

Charlotte and Danny walked past them and started to make their way to the street. Danny was thinking that if they got to the street. Maybe, just maybe. He could stop them from doing something stupid to them. Like getting themselves killed. Charlotte on the other hand had a smile on her face as she walked past them. She welcomed whatever they had in store for her. It was the smile of someone that knew they couldn't be touched. That nothing could hurt them. Tall one saw this smile and took it as an invitation. He signaled his two buddies with a nod of his head pointing in Danny and Charlottes direction, and started to move up on them in a light jog to catch up to them.

Danny heard the sound of the mens' footsteps. It sounded like they had some heavy worker boots on, with the sound of BLUM, BLUM, BLUM, BLUM, that was coming their way. Then Danny heard the tall one speak again, only it was loud enough that it sounded like they were right behind them. Danny turned his head and saw that all three men were less than ten feet away for him and Charlotte. Charlotte herself still had her smile on her face, that looked more like a grin than a smile, when she turned and faced the men.

"Hey I was talking to you you bitch!" said the tall one. "You better look at me when I talk to you."

Charlotte, not losing her smile said to him. "What are you going to do if I don't? Turn me around and spank me?" She gave out a loud taunting laugh that was directed at all three men. Danny had a worried look on his face. All he was thinking to himself as he looked around in the parking garage was: *No! Not here! Not now! We are too exposed! If anyone comes in here, she will chase after them and make more trouble for me from all ends!!*

"Why don't you teach her a lesson, Connor." said the nose ringed asshole, who until then was silent. He must have been speaking to the tall one, because all of a sudden he started to move forward about two steps. His two buddies started to slowly move their hands behind them as if they were going to stand in a military position of at ease.

"You hear that you bitch? Once we take care of your friend here, we're going to teach you a nice long lesson. Maybe show you what that mouth is meant for."

Danny let go of Charlottes right arm with his left suddenly and tried to make a move to retrieve his weapon from its holster with his right hand. Right as he tried to step back to pull it out he tried to yank it out and found it was caught in its holster. He looked down in his jacket to see what the obstruction was when there was a yell:

"HEY!" said a voice, and he looked up at the men and saw that Nose Ring and Needle Brow were holden guns up to both his and Charlotte's faces. Danny stopped what he was doing and pulled his hand out of his jacket. He saw that both men had the same gum a Colt 9mm. Not a big gun, but more than enough to kill the two of them.

Kill the two of them?

Maybe just her.

Danny thought about it and finally realized that this might be his ticket out of here. Only they would have to kill her now, and not try to get what they were wanting to get. If they could just skip thinking about trying to get their dicks wet by force for more than five seconds and maybe just skip to just trying to kill the both of them, it would all be over. He wasn't worried anymore about saving himself. He was more worried about saving these idiots more than anything. His thoughts were interrupted by the voice of Needle Brow. "Trying to get the jump on us huh? I think I will take that!" As he said it, Needle Brow came over to reach in his jacket and released the button-flap that was keeping the gun in place. "I don't want anymore surprises so…" With a quick arm movement he pulled the gun back and pistol-whipped Danny right across the forehead and knocked him out.

The last thought he had when everything started to turn black on him was: *Your all fucked now!*

Charlotte saw as the man hit Danny crosses the forehead and had no reaction. Still the same grin that was on her face. She thought that maybe she was going to have a fun time tonight after all.

"What the fuck are you smiling at?" the Tall One that went by the name Connor said.

"I was just thinking about what you boys want to do now?" Charlotte said. Smile remaining.

Connor came up and grabbed her by the shoulders and dug her fingers in deep into her shoulders. It hurt her a little but she could take it. "I think we are going to go someplace a little more private. Don't you think that would be nice?"

Needle Brow started to hop around, like he was excited for what was about to happen next, or it maybe the fact that he might be getting some pussy for himself. He would have to share, but that didn't seem to phase him at all. "Yeah, Connor! That sounds like a plan to me! Get her ins tha mood." he said with a chuckle.

Connor looked right into her green eyes. "Yeah. Get her in the mood. I like that. Guys make sure you hide her friend. Maybe behind some cars. And give him another hit on the back of the head too, so he won't disturb us any." The two guys pulled Danny behind one of the cars. A nice white Ford Taurus that looked brand new. Then Nose Ring lifted his arm and THUMP, hit Danny on the back of the head again so he wouldn't wake up. "You scream, I'm going to make sure we come back here and put two rounds in your boyfriend's head. With his own gun. You got that."

Charlotte nodded her head. "Crystal clear." Her grin remained.

Connor hated that grin. It made him think that she thought *she* was in control. He wanted to show right now just how wrong she was. No woman was ever in any control around him. "Get walking. Go over by that alley."

"What alley?" she replied.

Connor sighed to himself. "Jess." Needle Brow stepped forward. "Take her over by that alley next to the garage. Can you do that?"

"You ga it Connor." said Needle Brow, aka Jess.

"You be wise to forget the names missy. No one would believe you anyway."

Charlotte kept that smile on her face as she turned her head to the side and said, "I bet you tell that to all the girls."

Upon hearing this, Connor spun Charlotte around. Threw back his hand and slapped her right across the face. Charlotte's head rocked back to her right side, and stayed that way for a moment before she lifted her head. When she lifted her head, she had a nice red welt on the left side of her face.

Her smile still remained.

"You must like it rough you cunt. Well you are going to get it rough." Connor pushed her forward so she could continue walking toward the alley.

When they reached what the creeps called the alley, Charlotte could only see a small in-between space that was had a single dumpster on the back building. Seeing that the space was only about twenty yards long, she figured that these idiots weren't thinking about if anyone was going to spot them doing her. Classic sign of a man thinking with his little head than his big one. Maybe—she thought—she just had more experience at hiding forbidding acts, than these three assholes. On the others side of the alley where it opened out, she could see a parking lot that was jammed full of cars just like the parking garage was. She guessed that the viewing of *Chicago* was more popular than she imagined around these parts. Who would of thought?

Suddenly she felt both of her arms being grabbed by two of the assholes. She turned to her side and saw that it was both Jess, and Nose Ring. She never got Nose Rings name, and at this point she didn't care. None of these men were going to be worth anything soon enough.

"Alright you cunt, here is how it's going to go." Tall Man that was known as Connor started to approach her from behind and made his way to the front of Charlotte. One of the men all of a sudden pulled her hair back so she could watch what Tall Man was going to tell her. She felt that it was Nose Ring that had her hair. There was no real way for a normal person to know that, but she did. "I'm going to drop my pants and you are going to suck all of us off. Just to make sure you don't start any biting," He pulled out what looked like a buck knife out of his pants, it was hard to know for sure in this light. "I'm going to hold this up against your throat. As soon as I start feeling any teeth, I start cutting, you understand?" She nodded the best she could with her hair still being grabbed from behind, but she still had that smile on her face. "Yeah, keep smiling. She still smiling boys. I think we are going to fuck that smile right off of her." They other two agreed with Connor, Tall Man, The Man in Charge—The dead man. "And depending on how you are, I might just let you live." Connor started to unbuckle his belt and dropped his pants.

There was a foul odor that came from Connors crotch. Like he hadn't washed down there around his penis, since his parents did it at birth. The bastards all around her started to to drop trousers as well. They were laughing, all anxious to get a sweet taste of her. She was on her knees when Connor grabbed her and was just about to toss what little that he had down her throat when she said in a clear calm voice that was not frightened or excited. In fact it was void of all emotion, which would have caught them off guard if not for what happened next: "Stop."

The laughter stopped. Their movements stopped. The three men stayed right where they were. Their pants all touching the ground showing all of their cocks for all the world to see. Connor still had his left hand holding Charlottes head by the locks of her hair, but his grip was very loose. Jess was standing right behind Charlotte, right in front of Connor that made it look like he was about to give Charlotte a nice surprise through the backdoor. Instead he now stood there and looked on in terror. Wondering what happened to him and his friends that made them so still. Like an obscene statue. Nose Ring had his right hand on his cock when he found out he couldn't move. He must have thought that he was next after Connor was finished with her. He still had an erection. The little fucker still had that. Charlotte was making sure that they all had erections for what was about to come. Charlotte rose from her feet.

"Alright." She said with the biggest smile that she could greet them with when she stood up. As if the last ten minutes didn't happen and she was greeting the men for the first time. "How are we all doing right now? Huh?" She gave a twirl around to look at all the men. Jess and Nose Ring had looks of absolute terror on their faces. They had their mouths open and Charlotte could hear the two men blow out air from their mouths in large intervals. She was allowing that. The two men were trying to scream. Charlotte was stopping that. These men were not getting out of this by interference from someone on the street, oh no. She turned and saw Connor was not trying to scream. He had a look on his face like he was thinking very hard. He was trying to move. He was trying to escape. "Oh Connor, Connor, Connor! You can wear yourself out as much as you want, but you aren't moving. I know what you're thinking: How can I wear myself out if I can't move? Well excellent question Connor!" She had the most delightful voice like the men were guests invited over for tea. "Apparently the human body uses up more energy to stay in one spot, than it would take to run around for about two miles. Oooohh, I think that is always an interested fact that a lot of people nowadays overlook. So calm yourself Connor. Before I end the show early for you, and you don't want that. I want you *especially* to see this show. Since all of you stopped me and my date, which I will have to go retrieve, from our show that we were going to see."

Charlotte turned around and started to approach Jess. "So…. Jess is your name huh? I would tell you to answer, but I am never going to hear your voice again. You know how I know that Jess? Cause I'm making this happen. Oh yes! You boys picked the wrong cunt tonight. Calling me a cunt. Oh how I always hated that word. If there was a word Jess that had absolutely no class whatsoever, it is cunt. I hate it. I hate being called it. I hate hearing it, reading it, and saying it. Truly an awful word." She looked around at them again. "And you little boys called me it a few times in a span of a few minutes."

She got up right into Jess's face. Enough to smell the horrible bad breath that was spewing out of his mouth. Like a cross between spinach and curry that absolutely was revolting to the nostrils. Yet she endured the stench to ask him this. "Tell me Jess. Do you think I'm a cunt now?" Jess's face remained frozen, other than the blinking of his eyes. "Blink once for yes, twice for no. Okay?" Jess blinked his eyes twice in a fast flutter. "Wow. That was so fast I could have sworn that that was one blink. Is that what that was?" Jess blink twice again, only this time more slowly. Charlotte turned to Connor and Nose Ring in their frozen stances and took a half step away from Jess. "What do you think boys, yes or no?" Nose Ring blinked twice and was struggling to move. Connor had a look in his eyes of pure hate. He wasn't going to allow himself to be scared by this bitch. In his defiance he kept his eyes wide open. Charlotte saw this and responded. "Oh no Jess. Connor doesn't want to play my little game. So I'm going to take his answer as a yes. Don't worry I'm going to make sure you get off light." She maintained eye contact with Connor.

Suddenly her right arm lifted up from her side and in a quick motion that looked like a blur she drove her hand behind her into Jess's chest cavity. Blood instantly shot out of the wound as she dug deeper into his chest like a gothic oil drill. As she dug into his chest, Jess didn't make a noise but it was obvious that he was screaming in pain and horror. Keeping her eyes on Connor, she saw that his expression went from hate, to horror as soon as her hand made contact and a loud THUMP, followed by the cracking sound like she broke a branch from a tree inside his chest. Then the squishing around inside of his body while she was digging around inside of him. All while keeping those eyes locked onto Connor's face, and she smiled from what she saw there. Horror. The horror of a child from the bogeyman. The horror of the unexpected, and of death. After digging for what seemed like forever to the men—Jess most of all—there was another loud crack of breaking twigs that finally registered to Connor as the breaking of ribs, and Charlotte pulled out a large chunk of meat. She pulled it out, and showed it to Connor just inches from his face.

"What does this look to you Connor? How about you Mr. Nose Ring?" The men had looks of terror on their faces as she passed the piece of flesh between the two men. Making sure they both got a nice good look at the bloody meat that she tore out.

Jess, miraculously, was still standing. He was breathing very heavily like he was trying to find the right amount of breath. There was also a liquid rasp that came with all that breath as well. Charlotte than turned and faced Jess, and showed him the piece of flesh she just moments ago ripped out of his chest. "How about you Jess, is this your heart?" she paused as she looked at it for a moment and then she gave a small chuckle to herself. "Well, probably judging by the way you are breathing with such difficulty, this must be a nice big piece of your lung. So you must be feeling like you are going to be drowning on your own blood. and by looking at the rest of your body you are going to bleed out from that nice big hole I just put into you. Plus, an added bonus, Your lungs are probably going to collapse on themselves, due to the exposure of your chest cavity." She looked at the pale and pain ridden face that was Jess, and she saw that he had maybe seconds before he collapse so she decided to wrap up her time with him. So she went up to his ear and whispered ever so slightly, "Enjoy hell if it exists, can't say for sure your friends will meet you there. Like I said before. You got off easy." Halfway through this sentence Jess collapsed and died, but she held him up with her hands to finish speaking to him in his ear. Now with her right hand she let go of Jess, and let him fall into a pool of his own blood. Then she dropped the piece of lung at him so it landed on his face. It hit with a wet and sticky splash as it turned Jess's face from a pale white to an instant red bloody mess. His body laid down motionless just as much as he was when he was standing a few minutes ago. Blood oozed everywhere, from the hole in his chest all the way to his naked legs, and ran all the way to a drain that was just past Charlotte's feet. She then looked at her dress down by her feet and exclaimed, "Dammit! I got blood all over my dress. Oh well, I guess I know for sure there will be no show for me tonight. Well, a Broadway show that is." She then put her attention on the two remaining men when she heard a what sounded like a constant stream of water that was hitting the pavement. She looked from where the sound was coming from and saw that Connor was urinating all over the pavement and on his pants that were laying scrunched up around his ankles. Charlotte broke into small sinister chuckles as she saw this happen. She knew that if they weren't scared before, they were most defiantly scared now. Connor's eyes looked down on Jess on the pavement. Tears started to form, under his eyes. As if he finally grasped the trouble he was in now. He thought to himself over and over again that she said Jess was getting off easy. *EASY!!!* Then what the fuck was in store for him?!

"So, I see that I finally have your attention Connor. Now you can see what I can do. But I think that I will show a little more of what I can do." she went and leaned on the opposite wall of the two men. "You remember when you wanted to rape me?" she asked them. After the question left her lips Nose Rings eyes widened, as if what Charlotte said wasn't true. "Of course you do, it was only a few minutes ago, I guess that was a rhetorical question. Anyway, I can make it so you two can have some tail if you want." Her smile grew from cheek to cheek. "Just like this."

Connor began to turn to his right, involuntary, so that his back was facing his friend Nose Ring. Then he started to bend forward so he could touch his toes. Tears started to stream down Connor's face and dripped onto the alley pavement. His cry was silent. Charlotte saw this and felt instant pleasure throughout her body. She then made Nose Ring move right behind him with small, clumsy steps. Finally she made him rest his hands right onto the butt cheeks of Connor's ass. There they stood. Frozen like statues in a park. There wasn't any movement from the men other than the heavy inaudible screams from their heavy breathing, and the tears that fell from their faces. There was no insertion. They just stood there, waiting for Charlotte to make them do what they feared would come next. What they thought was a fate worse than her just killing them. She was going to make them violate each other. Just like they were going to violate her, only they felt that they could argue that this was much worse. She was controlling both of them to do this. Both of the men were victims this time. Both of their bodies were already being violated by taking what control they were supposed to have. She stole that control, already as a punishment. Now using that control to make them—fuck each other. Connor felt that was too much for his sanity to take. It was just too much for him to bear.

"I would have thought you would like this position the best. I wanted to show how you exposed me, to a certain degree. I'm not afraid of rapers. No, even if I didn't have these powers. They are cowards, all of them. They are the fucking scum of the world that throw up some sort of illusion that they are in control of their lives and of the lives of those they victimize. I know that I wasn't your first. Although you didn't have me at all. But I want this feeling to be the last thing you two will feel before I take you from existence. Exposed, scared, and pathetic." She walked over to the men now. She stood shoulder width apart, with her hands on her hips. Both of her hands were dripping with blood still her right hand worse than her left. Only she didn't mind.

They all stood there for another thirty seconds that felt like an eternity, when Charlotte finally said, "Times up." Connor began to stand up, straight as a stick. Nose ring took his hands off of Connors ass and took a step back. Charlotte commanded this of them. Connor turned and faced Charlotte again, with a flood of relief onto his face. Nose Ring had the same expression on his face. Like a great weight was lifted off of them, or that they were awakened from a great nightmare. They breathed heavy as they closed their eyes and thanked God from sparing them their assholes. It was when they opened their eyes—that they felt their terror wash over them again. Washing their relief and prayers away like it was leaf in a river.

The smile that remained on Charlottes face the whole time since they saw her, since she was in the elevator in the parking garage. Since they confronted her and her and Danny. Since they slapped her before and where the mark still remained on her left cheek. Since they lost control of their bodies—was gone. In its place was anger. Fury that brought those green eyes wide and full of the hate that bore into their souls. A hate that felt like it was radiating from her body and reached both of the men. Connor thought he was going to piss himself again at the look of this face, but thought that he had no more to let out of him. But it looked like he didn't have too. Nose Ring aka Mike Walsh was pissing on the ground enough for the both of them. He was seeing the face as well and knew what it meant for the both of them as well. Death.

Charlotte stepped up towards Mike Walsh, aka Nose Ring to her, and put her right hand on his chest with a small bit of force, but it didn't penetrate the skin. All of a sudden there was a glow of orange that was radiating from his body. Unlike Mindy Crass and the others that she took this past week, and the hundreds of thousands she took from her lifetime, she did not go slowly. She knew that if she did it slowly, it would hurt them less. She didn't want that with these two. Soon a little glow went on top of Charlottes hand, like fog on top of earth. Then she made a tight fist like she grabbed ahold of something and pulled. It happened so fast that Connor didn't think he saw it. But he did. What he saw was Charlotte pulling orange mist out of Mike or something that looked like that. When what looked like enough of the mist was out of Mike, Mike collapsed as the mist started to make an outline of a human. Charlotte then took her left hand and put it right next to her right hand, in the center of the mist form. She then pulled the form apart, where it made a large noise like static from an old television set. Then the orange mist disappeared around them. Connor then realized a horrible truth. What she just took from Mike, what she just tore out of him the same way she tore out a piece of lung out of Jess, was his *soul!* His fucking soul! And she just tore it in half. Once again he tried to move—and he tried to scream.

"Too late for that dip shit. I saved the best for last. Tell me, do you like fireworks?"

She did the same to Connor. The last thing he saw was his half naked body collapse away from where he was seeing, which looked like he was standing five inches off the ground. When he turned back to look at Charlotte he felt like he was on fire. He heard the voice of some man yelling "Hey you! Stop what you are doing!" When he felt the fire engulf the rest of him completely. Then Connor Phillips was no more.

Chapter 9

"Oh my God!"

Those were the only words that Tyler could say as he saw the orange light be taken away from the man in the alley. When he saw that the man collapsed to the ground he started walking across the street as if he was a fly taken in by a bright glowing light. If a car, or a bus for that matter had driven down the road at that time, he would have been in big trouble. Tyler walked right through Matt, who had his back turned on the alley when Tyler got off the phone with Tanya. When he turned toward the alley to see what Tyler was seeing, he saw the orange mist dissipate in the alley. He thought he must have saw some trick of the light or a reflection of like from a watch of mirror or something. He followed Tyler while keeping his eyes on the alley, and crossed the street as well, when all of a sudden he saw another figure that was standing in front of another man, pull out an orange mist from him. Then the man fell down to the ground. Tyler thought that this man was dead when he saw this as well. The orange mist gave a glow in the dark alley and they both saw that it was a woman that was dressed in a red dress that had splotches of another red substance. They instantly thought that it was blood. Seeing the strange act that went on their minds went straight to their worst thoughts. Matt's mind began to function once again and the cop in him spoke, "Hey you! Stop right there!"

The woman (to say she had an angry look on her face might have been an understatement) looked at both the men that were approaching the alley. When she saw them, her hand that seemed to be holding the mist in in the middle of the air burst into flames. and scattered all over the alley like the sparks that fly up from a campfire. Both Tyler and Matt looked up to see the sparks go up into the air until they disappeared. The two men looked down and saw the woman start to approach them. Matt reached for his sidearm, when he realized that he forgot it at home. He knew that he was going out with Tyler, knowing full well that alcohol and firearms never mixed well, he left it on his coat hanger at home. So now when he needed it the most, something he couldn't have expected, he was without it. Still he decided he needed to show that he was in control of the situation.

"Ma'am, I need you to stop where you are and show me your hands!" Matt said in an authoritative voice.

The woman smiled as she was making her way slowly toward Tyler and Matt. She was about twenty feet from the opening of the alley. Matt and Tyler both started to back up from where they stood on the sidewalk. As they backed up, the woman started to raise her hands in the *"don't shoot me"* pose. The men saw her do this and then they got a good look at her hands as she approached the opening to let more light into the alley. Their eyes widened and their mouths dropped when they saw her hands. Dipped and dripping with blood. Keeping her smile on the both of them like an insane jester. Getting closer to them. Fifteen feet. Ten feet. Keeping that smile, keeping her hands raised that continued to drip with blood.

"Stop moving!" Matt screamed.

Tyler bent down and picked something up. It looked like a baseball bat at first glance. It looked like a small piece of wood that was about two feet long. A carpenter that was doing remodeling about two weeks ago, inside a snowboarding and skateboarding shop named The Slick Board. On his way to throwing away the excess wood from putting up brand new beams in the shop, he dropped this piece and a smaller square-like chunk on his way to the dumpster in the alley. He saw the pieces and never picked them up to throw them away. Tyler picked up the bigger of the two pieces. His nerves were so shot from being scared, but he reacted on pure instinct. He quickly went to a batting position pulled back on the piece of wood and hit the woman right in her left shoulder, knocking her down onto the ground. While swinging the wood, the woman tried to pull her arm down in what looked like a defense position from the impact. Tyler saw something different. It looked like she was trying to grab to back of his head. Like she was going to rip it clean off his shoulders. With a heavy gust of wind that flew above Tyler's head, she missed. Then hit from the wooden board slammed Charlotte back to the alley wall. Just as quickly as the first time, Tyler pulled the wooden board back into another swing and struck home once again.

"Tyler NO!" Matt yelled.

This time the wood connected to the back of Charlotte's head. She fell down to the asphalt were she laid on the ground. Her eyes closed and the smile gone.

"Holy shit Tyler. Did you have to hit her so damn hard? And on the back of the head?!"

"I-I didn't think I hit her *that* hard. She has blood practically gushing from her hands! You kept giving her commands, and yet she still kept on coming forward! I had to do something to make her stop." Tyler said. His cheeks were going flush with red. He knew that he could have killed her. He didn't want to reach down and touch her neck to see if she had a pulse, because he was afraid that the answer was no. Even *if* this was somehow considered self-defense, he was going to be in a lot of trouble since he didn't see a weapon on her.

Matt looked around and saw that nobody saw anything, or if they did, they were already long gone going to the cops, which was a funny joke on him because he was the cops. He walked up to Tyler whose face looked like it was about to spill tears all over the place. Matt grabbed him to bring Tyler to his feet as he knelt over the woman. He looked down and saw that her stomach was moving up and down, a clear cut sign that she was breathing, but he had to make sure that she had a strong enough pulse. He put two fingers onto her neck, felt, and waited.

"She has a very strong pulse. So you didn't hit her hard enough to kill her." Matt said.

"Are you going to arrest her?" Tyler asked.

"With what? I don't have any cuffs. No, we are going to stay here and and call the police and have them arrest her. If I were on duty I would have reached for my cuf—."

Gunshots and spray of brick building filled the the air that cut off Matt in mid-sentence. Both Tyler and Matt hit the deck and kissed the pavement. Matt looked up to see a man about thirty feet away from them, with his gun drawn, approaching them. He was wearing a suit, that had some blood on the lapel, probably because it was from the head wound that was clearly leaking from the top of his head.

"Police! Don't shoot!" yelled Matt as he started to crawl into the alley to provide himself with protection from the gunfire. The only good this statement did was cause two more shots to be fired at the men's direction.

"Hey we have to go!" Tyler said to Matt.

"We can't just leave a crime scene!" Matt exclaimed.

"If we don't leave, we will be joining these bodies that are laying on the ground." Tyler then extended his arm to show the three bodies. One that was making a really large pool of blood that was slowly being led to a drain in the middle of the alley. The other two were laying on the ground and appeared to not have any injuries, but all three had their pants removed. Matt and Tyler could start to hear footsteps coming closer towards them. Matt nodded. The men stood up and started to run toward the other end of the alley as fast as they could. If the men had shared a mind, it was at this point. Because what they thought was so similar you would have thought it could only come from one mind, and yet the thought was obvious to anyone that was in the same situation: *Please don't shoot down the alley. Please don't shoot down the alley.* They thought this cause any gunshot that would go down the alley would result in one of them getting a brand new hole in them. This thought made them bare down in a dead on sprint, like an athlete in the 100 meter dash. Hoping against hope that they would beat the man that was going to turn down the alley.

Ten yards away from the corner. Tyler turned his head, he saw a foot just turn the corner of the alley. He was so close now, he had to give himself more speed. Only he couldn't, he knew this was all he had for speed.

Five yards. He turned back and saw the figure stand in the alley with his arms to his side. In his right hand, he saw the pistol that was aimed a few seconds ago at him. The man began to raise the gun to his face so he could aim down the sights.

His face. HIS FACE!

There was a click in Tyler's head of recognition that almost made him stop in his tracks. He face forward again and saw that he reached the corner. Since he was closest to the corner he grabbed Matt by the shoulder to bring him into the cover of the gunfire that would start. Once they turned the corner, Matt still kept on running, dodging through cars that were in a parking lot on their way out of the alley. He got past about two when he realized that Tyler wasn't by his side. He turned around and saw that Tyler had stopped just short of the alley's opening.

"What are you doing?!" Matt almost screamed at him. Loud footsteps could be heard from the alley. Coming closer, and closer. Tyler held a hand out to Matt as he was trying to catch a quick breath.

Finally he yelled out something that shocked not only Matt, but the footsteps that were running down the alley. He was sure to scream them so the man giving chase could hear it if he was on the other end of a football stadium.

He screamed in question, "STAUBAUGH?"

Chapter 10

His footsteps stopped cold as if he hit a brick wall. Slowly his handgun lowered to his sides. That voice. That voice sounded so familiar. In the depths of his mind a name began to trickle to the surface that was long buried from a different life. A simpler life. One were your life was at risk, but was manageable because you had brothers who were going through the same thing. Gordon? Gretchen? Gueaser? Green? Green. Green! The name matched the voice in his mind. "*Green*? What the fuck are you doing here?"

Tyler was still in the cover of the building, he didn't know what his old pals intentions were, so he stayed right where he was and yelled back to him. "Hey I got a better question asshole. Why the fuck are you shooting at us? You almost fucking killed one of us!"

Danny realized, even through his splitting headache caused by one of the three dead assholes that were laying back behind him, he was shooting at one of his old battle buddies. How the fuck did he even notice him? Most importantly, what the fuck was he doing here?!

Only he had no time for a reunion. He saw that Charlotte was laying down back there at the other end of the alley, he didn't know if she was taking an involuntary nap, or if she was dead. He hoped for the latter. But he couldn't risk it. Danny started to raise his weapon.

Tyler's eyes widen in panic. "Staubach, stop!"

Danny got his weapon at eye level. Then he spoke so softly that Tyler almost missed what he said. While Matt couldn't hear it at all. "Run Green. Get out of here."

Tyler almost asked what he said. But then it was like the words hit rewind and started to play in his mind for him: *Run Green. Get out of here.* Then just the first part again rang through his head first at a small whisper like the volume his old battle buddy just spoke, then it grew up to a roar. *Run. Run. Run! RUN!*

Tyler turned back and started to run toward Matt's direction in the parking lot, making his way toward the three leveled parking garage. He made it about ten steps when three gunshots rang out in a burst.

Tyler knew that Danny was a crack shot in his days in the army. Judging by the current work Danny was in at the moment, his ability to hit a target probably wasn't rusty in the slightest. Only the three shots that he fired—missed their targets. Tyler felt one of the shots damn near kiss him on his neck, feeling the wind brush by him. The first and last bullets nearly got him, he couldn't feel the second one. It didn't matter anyway, he continued to run like mad toward the garage for cover. Or to try to get a hold of someone for help, like the police.

The two men ran and ran till they ran through the entire parking garage. When Matt turned around to see if they were being pursued, he saw that no one was behind him. Just a lower level parking garage that was full of cars and empty of people. Both men stopped where they were and caught a breath.

"What the fuck was that about? That guy could have fucking killed us!" Matt said with a gasping breath.

"If he wanted to kill us he would have done it. I knew him wh-."

Matt interrupted him. "Yeah and how exactly do you know that asshole?"

Tyler paused for a moment so he could catch his breath. "I knew him from the army, it's a long story. Right now we need to get a hold of your buddies in the Police Department. There are still three bodies and that Scarlet Bitch up there in that alley, that need to be taken care of."

"Yeah your right." Matt said as he pulled out his phone. His hands were shaking something fierce, that they made him drop the phone as he pulled it out, letting it hit the concrete sidewalk. Before he reached down to grab the phone, he tried to rub his hands together to try and stop them from shaking. "What the fuck did we stumble upon, man?"

"I don't know. Personally I'm just glad we were able to get out of there and kept all our blood inside our bodies." Tyler said.

"Yeah, same here." Matt picked up his phone off the ground and started to dial his L.T.'s number on speed dial. The phone started to ring. After three rings, the gruffly voice of Lt. Coyer spoke through the earpiece.

"Hello, this is Lt. Jeffery Coyer."

"Sir, This is Officer Mullen."

"Mullen? What the hell are you doing calling me on your night off?"

"Sir, I need you to listen to me. There are three dead bodies on Jefferson Street. In the alleyway between the parking garage and Mexicano Pub and Grill. It's a blood bath there sir. There is also a gunman and an unconscious woman at the scene. I would have stayed at the scene if I had my firearm. We think we can identify who this guy is if we catch him."

"Hold on, slow down. Your telling me there is an active gunmen on scene?"

Matt thought to himself that the L.T. needed to keep up with him. Yeah it was true that there weren't many gunmen situations that happened in Wausau. But shit, it wasn't like it was completely out of the realm of possibility either. "Yes sir. Use extreme caution when approaching the scene. He has a handgun, most likely a nine mil., I couldn't get a good look at it."

"And you said that you can identify him?"

"Yes sir. When we find him, I know we can identify who he is."

"We? Who's we?" Lt. Coyer asked with a confused tone.

"I'm with my friend, Mr. Tyler Green. Former U.S. Army. He is reliable and seemed to know who the shooter was." Tyler shook his head as soon as he heard his name being spoken about in the phone. The very last thing he wanted to do tonight was talk to a bunch of cops that didn't go by the name of Matt Mullen. Right now his mind was on their encounter with his old battle buddy Daniel Staubach. It was true that Staubach had fired at him and Matt, but he thought that after he identified himself to Danny, they were no longer a threat. So why shoot after them when they started running than just shoot them both at the end of the alleyway?

Matt pulled the phone away from his mouth. "Hey, you will have to talk to another cop other than myself. So you might as well try and love the idea while you have the time."

"Well other than you, I not the biggest fan of cops. I don't know a single person other than cops, that is a fan of cops."

"All you have to do is tell them who the guy was that was shooting at us. Tell them exactly what you saw happen, then thats it. The end."

Tyler sighed a heavy sigh. "I think we both know its never that easy. But I will tell them."

"Great, who was he?" Matt said as he started to raise the phone to his mouth.

"You want me to tell you now?!"

"Well I have my L.T. on the phone right now, so yeah. Right now would be a great time."

Tyler gave another one of those heavy sighs, "Okay. His name is Daniel Staubach."

Matt repeated the name into the phone to his boss. Tyler could hear a small statement that sounded like a question that was going to be directed toward him. "He wants to know where you met this friend?"

Tyler was starting to get annoyed, he held out his hand to indicate that he wanted to talk onto the phone. Matt gave him the phone, cautiously. "Listen. I am not going to be giving my story to fifty different cops to see if I'm lying over something that I witnessed. I am going to wait for you to send some cops over here, and I will talk to them and give my statement. Is that fine with you?"

Tyler looked at Matt, who's eyes were bulging almost completely out of his skull. Talking to his boss like that was only going to get both of them into trouble. Tyler knew this, but he was too busy trying to figure things out for himself. Repeating himself to this guy on the phone and then to the many cops that were on their way was a huge waste of time. There was some rustling on the other end of the phone that was felt almost deafening from the silence that followed. Finally, the man on the other end said, "Son, I am trying to help you. Correction, *we* are trying to help you catch the son-of-a-bitch that killed three people." There was a small squeal of tires that came from the parking garage, like a vehicle that pressed a little too much gas as it hit the pavement, then stopped. It caused both men to look up for a second, then they returned their attention to the phone. "I'm not the bad guy here, so please, try and help us understand what the hell is going on please."

"Like I said, when your man shows up, I will explain all I have seen. I just don't want to repeat the whole story multiple times, cause its just going to be counter-productive." Tyler said.

"I understand. Can you give me back to Mullen please?"

Tyler gave Matt the phone back and was greeted by his friend with a look anger. "Yes sir?"

The lieutenant got back some of his composure back as soon as Matt spoke through the phone. "You are to stay right where you are and wait for a squad car to come pick you up. Once he does, you are going to show him where all this happened at *exactly*. After you show whoever gets there the scene, I'm hearing on the band that it might be Ramsey on his way to you and your friend Green there will give your statements. Is that in anyway unclear?"

"No sir."

"Good. Now tell me where you are so I can tell the squad car where you are." Matt looked around and saw that he and Tyler were just outside the Public Library. He told this to the lieutenant and he heard him relay this message to another person. "Okay they said they will be there in a few minutes just stay there. They will pick you two up and bring you to the scene. I will make my way down there as well so I will see you soon Mullen." The phone beeped, telling Matt that the phone call had ended. He put the phone down by his side.

"Why did you have to talk to him like that? He was trying to help."

"I know he was, but there was no reason for me to repeat myself twenty times so they can try to catch me in a lie. You know I'm not gonna lie and that should be enough." Tyler said. He started to get up off the sidewalk and moved closer to the library, like he wanted to seek it for shelter from everything that just happened. Matt was about twenty feet from him when he decided to yell out, "So what's the game plan?"

Matt looked over to him and said, "Squad car is gonna be here any minute now to pick us up, then we go back to the scene and hopefully catch your buddy there with his gun and arrest him, if he is still there."

"He won't be I can tell you that much." Tyler said almost whispering it to himself.

"Then, while the ambulances and cops are there trying to process the scene, some other cop friends of mine are going to take our statements. It will probably take a while, so might as well prepare for the long haul."

"Fantastic." Tyler groaned

"Well just ease up on the attitude and everything will be fine. You shooting your mouth off because for some reason you don't agree with cops, is a good way to be taken in for a disorderly, or interfering with a police investigation."

"I will try to keep it to a minimum. In the meantime, what is the plan for taking care of Danny Staubach?"

"What do you mean?"

"Well he is a trained soldier, and whatever he has been doing these past two years seems to only improve that fact. His aim was fucking deadly."

"What are you talking about? He missed us three times when he had us practically point blank range. Hardly what I would say as deadly aim." Matt was looking in the direction from where they came, just to see if their pursuer was going to pop up and finish what he missed.

"He's not coming." Tyler said with confidence. "If he was, he would have been on top of our bodies, deciding what to do next. What I meant was he missed us on purpose. I can't speak for you, but the two rounds that missed me when running away damn near gave me a love tap. He could of had us. Fuck, he *should* of had us. You don't miss that close to someone unless you aren't really trying to kill them."

"So why keep us alive? He knows we would go straight to the police."

A squad car tuned the corner on the street and started to make its way to the library. The car had the lights flashing on top, but no siren going. Most likely to keep from spooking off Staubach, Tyler thought. That was alright with him, but if they really wanted to go for stealth, they would turn the lights off as well. The car pulled up and there was a female police officer behind the wheel. Matt came up to greet her. "Hey Ramsey. Turn the lights off will you."

She answered by flicking a button on her dashboard and suddenly the lights on top of the vehicle ceased. "How's that?" Ramsey asked.

"Good." Matt replied. "I'll ride shotgun, Tyler you get into the back. I will show you where to go. Is your shotgun loaded?" He was talking about the shotgun that was placed in the middle of the driver and passenger seat. Usually it was regulations to keep the shotgun loaded when going out on patrol, but Matt remembered that Ramsey forgot to load hers once when she was facing a home invasion in Weston. No shots needed to be fired that day because the two men gave themselves up without a fight. Only afterwards did she realize that the gun was unloaded. If they did need to do some shooting, she wouldn't have lasted long.

"Yeah, I just loaded it before entering the car. It's all yours."

Matt grabbed the shotgun out of the holder, and made sure there was a round in the chamber, there was. It was nothing personal, and Ramsey knew that. "Right along this parking garage, take a right. Right in between the parking garage and the restaurant, is the alleyway that we want. Go slowly so we can try and sneak up on the Staubach."

"What do you want me to do? I'm good with a weapon." Tyler said.

"Sorry buddy. I couldn't give you a weapon if I wanted too. Police policy. You just stay where you are."

"You don't know what you are up against, come on, another gun in his face will help out. Trust me."

"I said no Tyler. If I give you a weapon and they are arrested without a fuss, they could end up walking because of a civilian holding a weapon on them. I don't want to take that chance."

Tyler sat back in his chair, angry that he was just coming along for the ride and not helping out like he should. As much as he wanted to arrest these two, he was really looking for ward to getting the answers from Danny on where the hell he was for the past two years. Two years. He just up and vanished. There were signs at his home that suggested he might have been kidnapped. His living room and his bedroom was found in a mess that was clearly caused by some sort of struggle. There was only one other footprint besides, Danny's that suggested anyone else had been in the house. As far as evidence went, that was it. No blood, no stray hairs, no fingerprints. There wasn't much to go on in hopes of finding Danny, and Tyler went over to his house to help console his wife Amber and daughter Lisa. Eventually the case went cold, and Danny remained missing—until today.

The squad car approached the turn and took the right.

"Okay you see that alleyway?" Matt asked Ramsey.

"Yeah I see it." Ramsey said, sounding a little nervous.

"We need to wait and park right here for the another squad car to block the entrance on the other side." Tyler said as he held onto the shot gun.

"Hold on, I will see where they are at." Ramsey picked up the CB radio and spoke into the mic. "Car 12 this is Car 27, are you coming up to the back end of the alleyway?"

There was a brief pause. Suddenly Car 12 broke through with their transmission. *"Car 27 this is 12. We are in route and will be there in about five mikes, break. Where is your current position?"*

"We are by the street entrance of the alleyway, about half a block away, break. We are keeping eyes on in case we see suspects, break. Let us know as soon as you have arrived on scene. Over."

"Roger that. Stay there we will be there shortly to help block off and keep suspects detained if they are still present. Out"

Ramsey put the mic back onto her dashboard, and began to watch the alleyway just like Tyler and Matt were, and waited. Nobody said anything while they waited. Tyler and Matt were still reeling from their experience that came to all this. Their eyes never moved form the alleyway entrance. Time seemed to slow down for the two men as they waited for Car 12's transmission that they had arrived. Yet time took over the control from here.

There was no movement in the alleyway. When Tyler hit the woman with the piece of wood what seemed like hours ago(which in reality was only ten minutes ago), she was exposed a little bit on the sidewalk with one of her arms on concrete slab. Now he couldn't see an arm or any body part of any sort laying at the entrance of the alleyway. As far as anyone in the car could see, there was no one anywhere. which was very strange considering the time of night. Yes there was a show on at the Grand Theatre, but there weren't that many people interested in going to see it. There were always people walking along this area, wanting to get to the bars or the restaurants, or even the mall. Always someone somewhere around here. Yet tonight on this street there was not a soul that was walking near here. As if the whole street smelled or something that just naturally made people avoid it no matter what. It was very, very erie, Tyler thought.

Still the woman was no longer visible to him right now. Tyler knew that he hit her pretty hard, on account of how much she scared the shit of him. He thought again of her trying to make a reach for his head and missed. The shear weight of the wind that flew past him and almost made his head go bye-bye if it made contact. Seeing the blood again that soaked her hands. That smile—damn that smile. There was a tremor of fear that washed through his body. He tried to push these images out of his mind, and get his head back into the situation that was at hand. There was still no movement for several more minutes that felt like time didn't know how to work.

"*Car 27 this is 12. We are in position waiting for a go. Over*"

Matt picked up the mic this time a spoke in a rushed voice. "Move in! Go!"

Suddenly the Squad car roared to life and drove down the half a block to the alleyway. Ramsey did as she was told and blocked the entrance to the alleyway with a quickness and sudden slam of the brake that would have put most movie stunt drivers to shame. Both her and Matt popped out of the vehicle as if it were on fire, drawing their weapons as they did this. Both of them yelled "Police!" as they pointed down the alleyway and saw Car 12 Block the other entrance of the alleyway. Car 12 as soon as they hit their brakes, shined a light down the alley pavement so they could get a better look at pavement. Ramsey, Matt, Tyler, and the two officer looked around and saw— nothing. There was nothing.

"What the fuck?" Tyler said to himself as he sat in the back of the squad car looking into the alley. "What the fuck?!" He repeated.

There was nothing there. No bodies. No pool of blood. No woman. No Danny. The entire alleyway was completely empty.

Chapter 11

It was 2 a.m. when Tyler finally stumbled into his apartment. He looked around for Max to see if he needed to be taken outside when he remembered that Max was no longer here. He thought he would never get the fuck out of that police station for the love of God. Their endless questions about what happened in the alleyway. The complete play by play, from seeing the blood on the woman's hands, all the way to when they went back to the alley only to find it completely empty, and completely clean of blood, and bodies. Telling the officers the same thing over and over again. While at the same time being asked the same questions over, and over again. Something that Tyler wanted to avoid in the beginning when he talked on the phone with Lt. Coyer. Yeah, he knew that name well now since he was the one that not only took his statement, but joined in with that other hard-ass cop Gentle, like it was him that hid the bodies somewhere.

Only it was worse than that in a way. They flat-out accused him and Matt for making the whole thing up. Sprouting out some bull-shit that the two of them made up that three people were killed by some woman all dressed in red, so they could create some kind of bogeyman figure for the deaths that happened last Saturday, because apparently Matt could not let go that the deaths were simply heart attacks. When they separated him from Matt, Sgt. Gentle got really close and tried to play off being his friend, so Tyler could tell him what the "real" story was.

"Tell me." said Gentle. "What really happened there buddy?" Tyler thought to himself when exactly did we become buddies. Was it when you were screaming in my face, or was it when you were calling me a liar? Must have been when you put me in another room away from Matt that the calls of brotherhood and friendship decided to speak to you. "What really happened in that alleyway?"

"I think you have my story on what happened in that alleyway Sergeant. Just because you separate Matt and I doesn't mean that I am going to change it."

"Yeah, yeah sure." He said this as if to tell Tyler to not worry about that. "You see, let me tell you a story about your friend Matt back there. He has a big head in the office, always wants to be the hero of the precinct. Last week he thought there was something in a case that wasn't. Trying to look for trouble where there isn't any so he can try and get his name in the paper. Maybe even to skip a couple of steps in the chain of command so he can start giving the orders instead of taking them."

Tyler decided to go into *military mode* as he like to call it. Taking his mind back to his days in the military and all the rules and regulations that went with it. He thought about going on with this conversation by giving this prick just his name, rank, and social security number, but that would only piss the asshole off further. Tyler could see that this guys screws were already a little loose if he really thought that about Matt. He knew Matt too long to believe such garbage. No, he decided to give him the old, not to speak unless spoken to. Gentle continued with his rant, although Tyler was barely listening now. Something more on Matt being a glory hound bullshit, until finally he said, "So what do you think of that, buddy?"

"Sergeant?"

"What do you think of your best bud in the next room now?"

"Sergeant, I tuned out of what you said halfway through what you were saying Sergeant."

"Well maybe you need to open up those ears, or get your head out of your ass buddy. Cause you are in serious trouble here."

"Sergeant, how could I be the one in trouble when Officer Mullen and I were the ones that made you and the rest of the Police Department aware of the murders, Sergeant?"

Sgt. Gentle finally sat down in the chair that was right across from Tyler. He had a disgusting grin on his face that said he was going to like what was coming-out of his mouth next. "We have very little evidence that the incident you and Officer Mullen said happened, actually happened. Sure there was blood in that drain in the alleyway like you said, but not the amount that you said there was. Besides That blood looked pretty fake to me anyway. Some kids playing with some fake blood leftover from last Halloween is my guess. Anyway getting back to the point, being that you two cried wolf the way you did, and sent officers and personal to a scene that was pretty much clean of anything, that's a problem to the State of Wisconsin buddy. You and Officer Mullen will be charged for faking a crime which *is* a crime in this state. Officer Mullen will be brought up on charges and fired if I have anything to say about that, and you will be facing jail time." Gentle just stared at Tyler waiting for some sort of reaction or response to this. This whole explanation seemed very thin to Tyler. What kind of charge would that be? Misdemeanor? Felony? When he saw that there no response or even a hint of anger on Tyler's face, it cased him to get a little angry, in which he said, "Are you going to talk to me buddy, or are you just going to sit there all night?"

"Sergeant, are you charging me with a crime, Sergeant?" Tyler said. The time for cooperation was over. If he needed to get a hold of a lawyer, he needed to get ahold of one now, or they needed to release him ASAP.

Sgt. Gentle moved in his chair uneasily. Yet his anger seemed to transform into that small grin on that he had before, like getting Tyler to respond was some sort of victory. "Not at this time." was all that he said.

"Sergeant, then I wish to be released or to be giving my phone call to my lawyer."

After that Sgt. Gentle didn't have much to say. He got up and left Tyler in that room with the table and chair for another three hours. Most likely out of spite for both he and Matt. When he finally was released from the room(not by Sgt. Gentle, it was in fact Officer Ramsey that let him out), he looked at the nearest clock that was hanging on the wall. It was damn near one-thirty in the morning. Tyler was exhausted from all the excitement and waiting that he decided he was going to go home and straight to bed as soon as he found Matt. Only they told him that Matt was still answering questions at this time, and that they were going to keep in touch with him very soon. Only one thought crossed Tyler's mind when he was told this: *Perfect.*

Thinking about all this was giving him a headache. He walked into his kitchen and went to the medicine cabinet, and got himself some aspirin. He needed some sleep, but he also thought that maybe he needed—no—*deserved* a nice nightcap with some Jack Daniels and soda. He made his way from the medicine cabinet, to the liquor cabinet, which wasn't too far away from each other, Tyler was happy to find out. Seeing all that blood off the that women's hands, was enough to make a man drink—*a lot.* Tyler hadn't seen blood in the quantities like that since Afghanistan. Something he didn't feel like bringing up to himself right now.

Yet still there was flashes of a pool of blood in the sand. While gunfire was going off all around him while taking cover behind a small muddy wall. As soon as he saw it, the image just as quickly left him. But as soon as that brief second of sand and blood flashed before him, he suddenly didn't know where he was. He looked around quickly for a second and saw that he was in his apartment. Where was Sammy? Right,— she was gone. Was Max gone too? Yes, he went with her. He looked down in his hands and saw that he had the bottle of Jack Daniels by the neck. He looked around again and saw that he was no longer in the kitchen. He was standing in the middle of his living room. He looked at the bottle once again. Did I drink from the bottle? He place a hand to his mouth and did a breath check. So far, so good. But how close was he to drinking from the bottle like an old stew bum? Something told he that he wasn't far at all.

On second thought, maybe a nightcap wasn't the greatest idea right now. He was already going to have nightmares from what he saw earlier. No need to make them worse with alcohol. He went back to put the bottle back in the liquor cabinet. Once that was done, he all of a sudden heard the sweet, sweet call of his bed. His eyes were droopy when he first entered the apartment, now they were damn near hitting the floor. He walked down the hall and was already imagining hitting the covers. He remembered thinking on the drive from the

Police Department if he was going to get any sleep, after what just happened to him and Matt tonight. He now thought that that was a stupid thought now. He entered his room, and while reaching for the light he was thinking of just collapsing onto his sheets and not even bother taking off—

"Hello, Tyler Green. Did you enjoy your night?"

Tyler stood where he was, in the doorway. He couldn't move. He was staring at his bed transfixed at it.

There was a woman there.

All dressed in red.

The same woman as before with the bloody hands.

She was spread out onto his bed and looking right at him with those stoney green eyes that seemed to gaze almost right through him. Not just him but *any* man that would dare to look into them. Her hands were cleaned off of all the blood. As well as wearing a new dress. The one before was long and moved with the curves of her body. This one had a short skirt that ended at what looked like just above her kneecaps; it was very hard to tell with her lying down and spread out on the bed. It still moved with her body, only it only moved with her upper body instead. While the lower part was fluffed out. To cover the rest of her legs she had on high top red boots that looked like she got them out of an old 70's punk rock store. Her hair was done in two pony tails that were done up on both sides of her head that both shared the streaks of red that went through it along side the black. There was a thought that went through Tyler's head that if Pippy Longstocking had an evil twin, she would most likely look like this. The Scarlet Bitch.

Tyler couldn't say anything. He seemed to have lost his voice upon seeing this woman again. He hoped that he never would see her again. Yet here she was, not more than a few hours from the last time he saw her. How did she know where his apartment was?

"Well are you going to wish me hello? Or are you just going to stand there like an idiot?"

The words were starting to make their way back to him. "Ho— How did you know were I lived?"

"Well you know who my trusted body guard was, so I just got what he knew about you from him. Seems you two have quite the nice long history between you. Afghanistan, Germany, all those nice fun times you two spent together I found very interesting. Anyway, after his story was done, I just used the internet for the rest. And, as they say in *Cinderella:* Bippidy—Boppidy—Boo! Here I am. I have issue with you Tyler Green." She began to get up from the bed, and stood up right before it. "I have great issue with you."

Tyler started to walk backward when he suddenly reached to the opposite wall of the hallway and stopped. "What issue do you have with me?" he said.

"You saw me. And that cannot do. You saw what I am capable of. You saw my ability first hand, and worst of all, you told people about it. All of that simply will not do. You and your friend."

"N-n-no one even believed me when I told them about it. They all thought that my friend and I where just making you up, so we could get attention in the local media." He told her "my friend" so she wouldn't know about Matt, if she didn't know about Matt already. He knew that Danny didn't know who Matt Mullen was through him, so *she* might not be able to know who he was.

"Really?" she sounded genually interested in this piece of advice at the sound of this. "Wow. That still doesn't change the fact, that you know what really happened. Eventually someone is gonna want to listen to you."

"You don't know that." Tyler said, fear rising in his voice.

"I do know that. You think you are the first to see what I can do. I assure you, that you are not."

"I don't even know who you are." he wanted to say more but the words were escaping him, because he didn't know how to follow up this statement. He already knew that it wouldn't matter to her. She was going to kill him or worse, whatever she did to those men that were in that alley.

"You know Danny, and that's enough. I know you can keep a secret, based on what you have seen in Afghanistan."

"Wait, how do you even know about that?" Tyler said with awe, forgetting for a second that Danny was the one that probably told her.

They were both in the hallway now, Tyler still backing up from the woman's approach. On Tyler's right he could see that he was starting to pass the hallway closet.

"Never mind about that, it's not important. What I have to do with you is more important. I was going to offer you a position just like Danny. Have you two work together, once again. But then you told the Police and that's when you kinda tied my hands. Not to mention hitting me in the back of the head. That was really unwise. So…that's that."

That was when she charged at Tyler. Her face went from sad apologetic sincerity, to a viscous smile that said she was going to eat Tyler instead of kill him. That smile could have gone on forever, as if the corners of each side were going to meet at the back of her head and cause it to open her skull up.

Her advance upon him was quick. It took her almost no time at all when she was ready to grab him. Tyler saw this and took only one step back and with even more speed, opened the closet door that was right beside him, and slammed it at her approaching head.

There was a loud CRACK as the door made contact with the woman's head. Tyler could no longer see her, because the door took up the almost the entire width of the hallway. Something he wanted to complain to the landlord about, because in the summer when the wood of the door expanded, the door could get stuck on the wall of the hallway and block you path to get to the bedrooms. Right now, Tyler was glad he made no complaint.

Suddenly the door thrusted back and almost closed Tyler into the closet, but the door was stopped with only a crack between the door and the wall to spare, with the strong and quick placement of Tyler's foot on the edge of the door, still wearing his boots from the night.

"There's no point in trying to fight this." A voice said that came from the other side of the door—only—it wasn't the Scarlet Bitches voice. It was more dark and sinister compared to the light and almost sweet voice that nonetheless, threatened him only seconds ago. Now it was like something took ahold of her voice. As if a demon stole her voice and replaced it with its own.

"I will turn this door to mulch, if you don't let me through." Tyler was almost mesmerized by this change. Then he looked into the closet and snapped out of it. He needed the closet open for more than to hold whatever that was at bay. He looked up above the winter coats that were hanging started to dig in the cluttered upper shelves of the closet.

"You may think by my size that I cannot do it, but I assure you that I can." Tyler was checking on the left trying to keep his foot in place of the door. He pulled a folded up blanket down and put it in front of the door as well, right behind his foot, to help block the door. He tried to see into the top shelf, but the door was blocking the light that was hanging from the hallway ceiling.

"Well you can't say you haven't been warned." He felt around on the left side and felt that it was now bare of anything. He wanted to move to the right side, but he would have to stretch if he wanted to reach the corner of the closet shelf, and keep a foot up against the door. He reached into the dark corner and felt his hand come across a solid object. It was what he was looking for.

Suddenly there was a loud BANG and a thrust of the corner of the door. Like some creature was trying to bash its way from the other side of the door. The strength that it took almost made the upper left corner of the door smack Tyler in the back of the head. The door cracked open from the wall about an inch, Tyler quickly tried to recover the ground he had lost, but his strength was met with what felt like a stonewall leaning against the door. He push with his left hand as hard as he could, only it was no use. He now knew that he had to act quickly if he was going to survive this encounter with this creature, this bitch from hell.

He reached for the object that was a case. A case for his handgun, his Colt .45 that he went shooting at the range every so often. The same handgun he went shooting with Tanya a week ago.

BANG! Followed by a loud crack and another thrust forward from the door. Tyler was leaning more into the closet this time so he wouldn't get hit by the impact of the door. He was scrambling faster now, because that crack that rang true throughout the apartment sounded like the door wasn't going to take much more punishment. Tyler opened the gun case and saw the gun itself sliding around in the case along with the magazine, when Tyler suddenly stopped in his place. He was trying to remember if he filled the magazine with bullets or not. He scrambled and searched in the deepest pit of memory. He lifted the magazine to try and get a feel of the weight of the mag. There was clearly one on top of the magazine, but the weight felt wrong somehow. Like there were bullets in it, but not nearly enough to fill the whole clip. He decided at this point, he didn't have a choice. He needed to send something in this bitches direction, if they would kill her at all. For all he knew the only thing that could hurt this woman was a stake through the heart or a bullet of the silver variety. Still he had to try something.

BANG! CRACK! A piece of the door broke off and was sent flying down the hallway, scrapping Tyler's forehead, causing it to start to bleed. The case fell out of Tyler's hands as well, sending the gun to the floor which he scrabbled to the ground so he could pick it up.

The woman stuck her head through the hole in the door. Strands of maroon red hair dangled from her face. She spoke, but once again it wasn't that sweet voice expected from a woman of her image, but the demon that spoke before, with a smile that was as incident as the devil's.

"Hello again Tyler Green. Whatcha got there for me?" Her smile remained as her eyes locked onto the gun and magazine, then started to make a grab toward Tyler. Tyler just looked at her and felt his fear wash away, and in its place was rage and hate. Without looking, he locked and loaded his handgun in a loud CLICK, followed by a CLICK-CLICK as he pulled back the slider release. The woman's hand was just about to come out of the hole in the door when suddenly the woman's head disappeared, right before the loud BANG, of the gunshot rang in the ears of both the woman and Tyler. Leaving a hole right in the ceiling. There was loud footsteps that were fighting to be heard in Tyler's ears through all the ringing that was vibrant. The footsteps were in quick pace, but we're moving away from Tyler. She was trying to get away! Tyler immediately stayed where he was on the ground and just started shooting down the hallway through the door that was between him and the Scarlet Bitch. BANG! BANG! BANG! He shot in a three round burst like the drill instructors taught him to do so many years ago. After he finished firing he quickly got to his feet to look through the giant hole in the door. The hallway was empty. There were three large holes in the wall at the other end, but that was all.

"You missed me!" Yelled the woman, returning to her regular voice. Then there was the sound of footsteps again, once again moving away from him. There was a loud sound coming from his bedroom. The sound of glass breaking. There were no mirrors in Tyler's room, Samantha took the large one that was over her dresser when she left. The only thing that was made of glass in his room was the window to the outside. Did she just smash it or did she jump through it? Tyler didn't know, but he didn't want to get any closer to his room in case it was some kind of trap—only…

It didn't feel like a trap. Tyler was very silent and tried to listen for any kind of sound. There was still ringing going on in his ears from the gunshots, but it was starting to subside. Instead of going forward, toward his bedroom and the possible trap set for him, he moved backward and moved toward the living room. He looked into the room and noticed the lights were off. He made his way toward the light switch when a thought came to him.

"What the fuck am I still doing here?" He said aloud. He needed to get out of here, but was still squeamish of the idea of going outside with that bitch roaming about in God-knows where—

SMASH!

The window of the living burst into a million pieces of glass and wood, and shot into into the living room. It was the woman that jumped through the window and now stood there behind the couch. Keeping that smile on her face. That predatory smile. Tyler drew the gun on her and froze in place. If she moved at all, he thought to himself, I will put a round in her eye.

"Still with the gun, huh?" The woman said, "Still not seeing that it doesn't make a difference, huh? I can't tell you how many weapons have been aimed at me. I had machine guns, Tommy guns, pistols, throwing knives. Hell, I even had a bazooka pointed in my direction. You think you have more than those men? Cause that is what it's going to take."

Tyler all of a sudden thought back to his clip in the gun. How light it felt *before* he started unloading rounds into the walls and doors of the apartment. Now, it felt like nothing at all was in it. He figured if it was this light, he had either one or none. One or none. Nice.

"Get out of my house!" Tyler said with sudden anger. "I don't give a shit what was aimed at you in the past. All I know is that you will die if you move another inch."

"That sounds all great and fantastic in the movies Tyler. Only this is the real world." Almost in a blur, she went from standing in the middle of the living room, to sticking on the side of the wall. Her speed was so quick that Tyler almost had to do a double take to see that she moved. Then had to get a tight hold onto his sanity to cope with the fact that she was sticking to the side of the wall like a goddamn house fly! What the fuck was she?! How was she doing this? Tyler then had the realization that he was going to die…He was going to die right here with this creature in his living room, sticking to the wall like she was something out of his worst nightmares. Like Dracula climbing the walls of his castle using only his fingertips. He tried to gain his focus again. Tried to concentrate on the situation. Fear was trying to take him. Take him and his mind to a place where he thought all he could do was submit. To surrender and let this creature just kill him here, in his apartment for no reason, or for a reason that he didn't understand.

But there was another part of him that was almost silent when his fear came until now. Tyler never thought of what it must be because he was thinking about all of these things in a matter of seconds. But the silence of this voice was now broken. The voice inside of him spoke a word, a single word. A word that went against the very grain in his being. A word that almost offended him as a soldier. Back in his days when he would repeat his warrior ethos to not only to his drill instructor, but also to himself: *I will always place the mission first. I will never accept defeat. I will never quit. I will never leave a fallen comrade.* Those words, were not just words to him. They flowed within him like the blood in his veins. Made him be a better man than most, he always felt. But now the word that was spoken inside his head, went against all of that. Forsaken the lessons of his time in the military. Worst of all it was being spoken to him in Danny's voice. Danny who was helping bring this beast into his life, he didn't know or why, but he knew Danny was holding some of the blame for this. Yet with Danny's voice it also meant that Danny was helping him somehow. That Danny wanted him to escape. To stop what was going on.

The word that was spoken was: *RUN!*

Tyler was trying to think about what he needed to do. While he was doing this he maintained the weapon to be pointed in the woman's direction. the thing that he needed to to do was to get out of the house, and drive away from here as far as he could. He tried to think about where his keys were. Thinking on where he put them when he walked in, and he remembered that he put the keys on his kitchen table that was only about four steps away. If he shot her, or shot *at* her, it maybe enough to buy some time to grab the keys and head out the door. Then he remembered that he didn't put his cell phone down anywhere. It was still in his pocket! If he could get out of the apartment and drive away, he could try and call the police or to Matt and warn him that he was going to be targeted as well. It wasn't much of a plan. With her speed he was bound to be killed by her no matter what, but it was better than doing nothing. He had his plan set, however long shot he had on success was clear, but again it was better than dying here and now.

All of these thoughts took only a few seconds for Tyler to process. The time was now. He took a step to his right, into the living room, keeping the creature on the wall in the sights of the handgun. He made a quick prayer to God to please give him a final bullet or two in his clip, and that he just misjudged the weight from the adrenaline that was flowing in his veins. The woman maintained her smile, yet still slowly raised her arms across the wall and then digging her drywall covered fingers into the wall, coming closer to Tyler so she could make her kill like a lion hunting on the plains of Africa. Aiming right for her eye, Tyler Green pulled the trigger, and was rewarded with his prayer.

BANG! Then *click*.

Tyler didn't wait to see if his shot hit true. He dropped the gun and turned toward the kitchen table. While running to the table he seen that his left arm was within reach of the doorknob and quickly grabbed it to open the door, and still made a dash to the kitchen table to grab his keys. There they were, sitting at the edge of the table like they were always placed every time he came home. He grabbed the keys and turned to the open door. He was glad he opened the door as soon as he turned around.

He was still moving when he saw her. The woman. The creature. The Scarlet Bitch. She turned the corner of the wall to face the kitchen and Tyler. Her smile—gone. In its place was pain, and hate. In the half second that he saw her face, Tyler all of a sudden felt as if heat rays were coming from her face and beaming down on him with great intensity. Her eyes almost didn't look as if they were green, but they looked as if they had a tinge of red on the inside of her irises. On her left shoulder, there was a wound that was bleeding perfusley from a circle point. It was where his bullet, his last shot from his handgun had entered into her body. His shot rang true after all.

This image did not stop his momentum from getting to the door. If anything it motivated him to move his ass faster. She was now mad as a hornet and was going to go after him with everything she had. He made it to the doorway just as he saw her turn away from him and went into the living room. Only he knew that she wasn't going to the living room, she was going to jump back through the window so she could intercept him as he was making his way into his truck. His truck was about ten feet away from the door, where he always parked it. Right now that ten feet seemed like a mile as he made a mad dash to the driver side. As he was running, he saw a figure moving toward his truck. He knew exactly who and what it was. He opened his truck door and slammed it shut, then hit the locked door button quickly. There was a second when a thought hit him: *if she can bust through a wooden door, what does a glass truck window have?*

Just then, the truck rocked hard and a hand shot through the rear glass window, as if to give him an answer.

"Fuck!" He yelled.

Her hand was trying to grab at the back of his head, but fortunate for Tyler once again, he had a dual cab, so the reach for the back of his head was farther away than she anticipated. She continued to thrash and try to get the back of Tyler, while at the same time he was getting the keys into his truck to try and roar it to life so it could get him out of here. The truck roared to life, Tyler thought about putting the roaring Silvarado in reverse, but then he had another idea.

The woman's hand which had the reminisce of drywall dust on its hand was reaching closer and closer, almost an inch from touching

Tyler. Then she was slammed back to the tailgate of the truck. Instead of putting the truck in reverse, Tyler decided to travel the remaining ten feet of his driveway, and put his truck into drive. Then let his foot drop down onto the gas like a brick falling from the sky and touched the floorboards. The sheer force of the acceleration, caused the woman to fly back. Just as quickly as he hit the gas, Tyler hit the brake and the woman flew forward. Tyler didn't look behind him, but he heard a loud THUMP hit the back of his cab and knew that it was the woman now flying forward, hitting the back of his truck cab. He hoped the she hit her head, the bitch. As he was having this thought, he finally put the truck in reverse, and once again put his foot down on the floorboards, the screeching of the tires was loud enough to wake anyone in the neighborhood, as he made his way down his driveway. He looked in his rearview mirror to see where he was going, and to see if he could see the woman without having to look behind him. He made the end of the driveway in no time, and quickly turned on the street and hit the brakes, once again hear a loud THUMP as something hit the tailgate. Looking through his rearview mirror once again he saw that the woman was leaning up against the back of the tailgate and was staring back at him with the same rage as she was before.

Only now there was another look on her face, it looked like sorrow, but Tyler was also thinking that it was pain as well. He could still see that she was a bloody mess. Her wound on her shoulder was still leaking blood like crazy. From this and his crazy driving that he did in the last ten or twenty seconds, he could see that the blood from her gunshot wound had gotten everywhere. From her dress to the top of her forehead. Yet she still stared at him with those determined eyes. Those eyes. Those eyes. Those I'M GOING TO FUCKING KILL YOU eyes.

Tyler put the truck back in drive again, only this time he waited. He continued to stare at her. Watching her as if to reply to her look. Saying: *Yeah you want to fucking kill me. But do* you *have want it takes?* He continued to wait for her to move. To get up from where she was sitting. Finally after about ten seconds—the woman that was not a woman, started to get up with the same quickness as before. This time Tyler was prepared for this, and for the last time, dropped the brick that was his foot onto the gas. The truck moved forward once again with the same screeching the tires as before, only this time while he was waiting he put the truck into four-wheel drive, giving him more power than before.

Tyler did all of this right as the woman that we know as Charlotte got to her feet. Once again like before the force of the momentum from the truck, sent her backward. This time the back of her knee catching the top of the tailgate, and not even she could stop from falling backward and hitting the pavement of the road.

Tyler only saw her flip backward into the night and kept his eyes on his rearview mirror, only occasionally looking at the road. he needed to make sure that she was gone, or at least staying behind him and not trying to run faster than his truck could go. After he saw her flip over he saw that she was laying on the ground as he continued to drive, but she didn't get up. Did he kill her? Still looking his mirror and looking at her body, he saw that she had landed within the light of a streetlamp. Keeping his eyes on her, he kept driving, not slowing down at all. After he traveled about two blocks, running through two STOP signs without even giving them any notice, he finally saw her start to stand up.

Tyler pushed his foot down on the floorboards some more to see if he could get some more speed out of the beast that was his truck, but he already had his foot down on the gas as far as it could go. He kept his eyes on her as she stood there in the middle of the street behind him, getting further and further away from him. Then he saw that she turned around and started to make her way in the opposite direction.

Tyler took a deep long breathe, as if he didn't breathe through his entire encounter with that Scarlet Bitch. Breathing and thinking about what his next move was going to be. He knew that going back to his apartment from now on was going to be out from now on. He could maybe try Matt's place, because he was the only one who…

A thought burst through his head as he heard Matt's name enter his mind. MATT!!! She said someone was going to be taken care of Matt as well. Shit! I have to tell him. No. To warn him that someone is going to be giving him a bullet sometime tonight. And Tyler knew just who that was.

Matt was making his way out of the Police Department when he heard his phone ring from inside of his pocket. He was about to to take it out when he saw that a figure of a man was approaching him. A man that looked a little familiar. A man in a suit. He was about ten feet from him when he started to pull his phone out, and then he saw the gun.

"Hello, Mr. Mullen. Or should I say Officer Mullen. You and I have to have a talk."

Chapter 12

"What the hell is that?"

There was a noise that was coming from the front of the house. It woke her up from a sleep that felt more along the lines of a coma than an every night rest. Then the noise came out again, only this time the sound came to her with more clarity. It was knocking. Knocking at the front door to be exact. No. Not at the front door, but at the side door where she mainly used to come into the house. Only a few people knew that she used that door. Only a few of them lived in the city, and one of them called her tonight to apologize for a bar fight that happened last week. He said that he was going out drinking with his and her friend tonight, and if he was knocking at his door at this time of night…What time is it anyway? She looked at her clock that was on her nightstand. 3:07 A.M. Said the blue LED lights that shown on her clock radio.

BOOM, BOOM, BOOM, BOOM, BOOM. The knocking rattle some of the walls in the house the person was hitting the door so hard.

"What the fuck is going on? Do they know what fucking time it is?" When Tanya's sleep was disturbed, she resorted to swearing until she knew what it was about. She got out of bed, and went to get her robe. She thought that someone had better be dying or dead for waking her up at this hour. If it was who she thought it was, he was *going* to be either dead or dying.

She moved sluggishly through her house. Before the knocking had occurred she reached that perfect part of sleep that caught a person at their most tired part of the night. The part where dreams were the thickest part of reality at your moment of solitude. Where most of the time, the only thing that could wake you up was the terror from your own nightmares. And even then, depending on the nightmare, sometimes you wouldn't wake up even then. The part where if you were to wake at that particular moment, you would mistaken objects for what you were looking for. Like for instance, when you would get up from this point of exhaustion, and you wished to go to the fridge to get yourself a nice cold glass of milk. While opening the fridge and seeing everything that is in your fridge, you could not make out that stupid carton of milk if it was right in front of your eyes. Because guess what? It usually is right in front of your eyes hiding in plain sight. Instead you grab something that somehow feels right, maybe a little off key in the touching department, but who cares? You are tired and you just want to get that stupid glass of milk in your stomach so you can get your ass back to bed, right? You take what you grab and unscrew the top while you aimlessly grab for a glass from your cupboard. The muscle memory of doing this a thousand times, saves you from grabbing something other than a glass. Like accidentally grabbing a bowl or a plate instead because, well…you're just too damn tired to do this shit anyway, let's face it. But you do grab a glass and pour the contents into it. It is either at this point or right when you are chugging down the glass of whatever down your throat that you realized that instead of pouring milk in your glass, your pour the whole bottle of ketchup or mustard into your glass, and you where just in time to stop yourself from swallowing it, or you are too late and are now trying to find that damn water faucet to wash out the taste in your mouth.

This was the type of tired that encompassed Tanya right now. She was searching for her side door, and was failing miserably at it.

The first door she came to was the one that was right next to her bedroom door and thought that this was it and she arrived pretty damn quick for being asleep. Once she peered through the doorway and could make out the toilet and the shower curtains in the room, her common sense slapped her against the head, and told her she had to keep going. There was another barrage of hard knocking that hit the door. This time Tanya was close enough to hear the voice that carried it, but she could not match the voice to the name of the person.

"TANYA! OPEN UP, IT'S IMPORTANT!"

She was too tired to think. She didn't want to think. She just wanted to go back to bed and go back to the dream that she already forgotten about. Yet she knew that it was a nice dream, because when she was woken up by these hard, angry knocks, she felt satisfied in a way that could only come from a happy thought, or a great dream.

She made her way down her hallway, still looking for her side door to the outside. Instead of turning to her right, she looked into a door that was on her left. and saw it was her extra bedroom. "God Dammit." she muttered under her breath.

After this, she had a brief thought that she was never going to find that fucking door with her mind like this. Another series of hard knocks were closer to her now. they sounded more like hits from a sledgehammer now. BUM, BUM, BUM, BUM, BUM.

"Alright I'm on my way!" Tanya said in an more than aggravated toned. "Just stop that knocking, I already have a headache."

She made her way into the kitchen and saw a figure outside her window that was right next to the door. She peered out to see who it was— and then more anger raised up in her chest. She had a concerned thought that at least in his drunken stupor, Tyler didn't get into a car crash on his way here. Although she was going to make it as uncomfortable for him enough to think that a car accident might be better than to stay at her house right now. And if he was here for some kind of drunken boody call; he had another thing coming. Not that he never thought of Tyler as unattractive by any means, she thought that one: it was still too soon for him to be making any one-night stands with *any* girl for that matter. Two: they were still too good of friends to do any sort of thing like sleeping with each other. Finally, he was most likely drunk from a night out with Matt, and she was dog tired.

She closed her eyes to brace herself from the drunken Tyler that she was about to deal with, and took out a nice long breathe. She dealt with drunken Tyler before and the results were always mixed. There were times when he was sad and borderline pathetic to the sober bystander. Other times he was an absolute delight and was fun to be around. Mixed with the delight, he seemed to have a cool head on his shoulders while being eight drinks into the night. Then, there was the last time he was drunk, or at least she assumed he was drunk. The drunk Tyler that smashed glasses against the faces of guys that were being just a little forceful onto women that he knew. That Tyler was scary to her, but there was another feeling toward that kind of Tyler as well. It was something like admiration. Yes, that was it. She admired him for standing up for her. Yes what he did was crossing a line, but it had a hint of romance that she wasn't use to. Growing up being maybe a little tougher than the boys you hung around with, made for very little romantic gestures, or the ability to recognize such gestures. In a way, it was sweet that he stood up for her when he did, even if the means were violent.

She shook these thoughts away from her mind just then. She wasn't about to deal with the nice romantic side of Tyler. She was about to deal with the unknown side of Tyler. Drunken side of Tyler she thought. Then she opened the door.

It turned out that she was dealing with an unknown side of Tyler. A *complete* unknown side of Tyler that was starting to scare her. She could recognize what side it was but she had never personally dealt with this part of Tyler before. This scared version of the strong willed man that she had known for years. the Tyler that signed up to join the military, and went to some of the toughest schools they had to offer. She saw this and started to fear for herself. Because if something could scare the hell out of Tyler; then what the hell was she going to feel?

"I need to stay here for the night. That's if I can? Maybe even for the week if it's possible?" Tyler said these three sentences with a pause between each so he could take a breath. Tanya thought that by the way he looked he might have ran the whole way here from his house, which was about three miles away. If he was drunk that might be a possibility, but Tyler looked anything other than drunk. He looked like he had just seen all of the ghosts in the world came up to him and tortured him.

"Sure, but what the hell happened to you? You look like you just had just been through hell?"

"In a way, I had just been through hell. Someone or something is after me. And I think someone already has gotten to Matt. I hope not."

Tanya was panicking a little inside, but was trying to remain calm on the outside. "Hang on, slow down. What do you mean someone or *something* is trying to come after you? And what do you mean that someone has taking Matt already? What's going on?"

"It's a long story. Short version there is a woman that was in my house that Matt and I saw earlier doing some really freaky shit, and now she is trying to hunt me down and kill myself and Matt."

"A woman? Like a woman you slept with or saw her sleeping with—."

Tyler cut her off. "NO! Not a woman I slept with, Christ Almighty. Everything is about sex nowadays with everyone isn't it? Sex, sex, sex, sex, sex! No, none that I know of ever slept with this woman as far as I know. Although if I had to put my money on anyone sleeping her it would have to have been Danny."

"Danny? Who's Danny? You aren't making a whole lot of sense?" She saw Tyler start to close the curtains of the living room and was starting to get a little worried. If he was being followed by someone who was out to do him some harm, then she didn't want the person to come here at all. "Were you being followed by anyone here?"

"No, I lost her as soon as she fell out of the back of my truck."

"WAIT! WHAT?!" Tanya yelled out to him. "She fell out of the back of her truck? Did you kill her?"

"No, but trust me if you saw what this woman did, you will wish I did."

Tanya's head was spinning. she was completely exhausted, and was barely keeping her eyes open. Yet she could somehow figure that as long as Tyler was here she wasn't going to be getting anymore sleep for the time being until she knew exactly what was going on. And she very well couldn't get the whole story and start thinking about what to do, until she was somewhat more awake then she currently was. This lead her to say and do something she wasn't at all happy about doing.

"Hang on. Let me put on a pot of coffee. If we are going to figure out what kind of shit you're in and how you plan on dragging me into it, I'm going to need a fresher mind than the one I got on right now. So give me a few minutes, and you just take a seat and relax."

"Trust me," Tyler said. "I don't think there is any relaxing for me tonight?"

"Well now that your here with this shit, that makes two of us."

It took about ten minutes for Tanya to get everything ready to get her pot of coffee set for brewing. Tyler offered to help a couple of times, and each time he was snapped at by Tanya. She was already unhappy about being up at 3:30 in the morning, she was not going to let anybody show her where everything was in her own damn kitchen. The pot was brewing with the coffee. Tanya just stood in front of it watching the coffee be brewed. Jumbled thoughts entered and exited her head as she was trying to make sense of Tyler's words. She turned to look at him, but she saw that he wasn't in the kitchen. She went into the living room and saw that he was still looking outside her window, with the shades drawn closed. He was still looking out the window when she asked, "Are you going to be okay there Tyler?"

He didn't answer. His thoughts were lost to the outside. Lost to the location of whatever woman was trying to kill him for whatever reason. She turned back to the kitchen, she thought she would get there answers when he was ready. Hopefully soon, so she could get back to sleep. But there was a small voice inside her mind that said there would be no more sleep for her tonight. Sleeping was over for now.

The coffee maker made its small beep noise to signal that the full pot was brewed and ready to be consumed. Tanya grabbed her favorite coffee mug that had a picture of The House on the Rock that she received when she went to go visit the Wisconsin Dells. She grabbed one for Tyler as well, it had a picture of the Library of Congress on it, and had a small chip taking off on the handle. She filled up the mugs and put creamer in hers. She thought that if he wanted creamer he could put it in his own damn self, or ask for it. But he made no protest about cream or sugar, or the coffee for that matter, because he was still in the living room looking out the window.

She called out to him, "Tyler! Coffee is ready."

"Can we drink it in here please?" Tyler called back.

Tanya rolled her eyes at this but said, "Yeah that's fine. Just as long as you are going to tell the damn story."

She brought his coffee to the living room like he asked. He turned away from the window long enough to take the mug away from her, then turned back to face the sliver of window through the closed curtain.

"If you are sure that no one has followed you, why are you glued to the window to see if anyone is coming?"

Tyler looked at her with this. He then shifted away from the window as if the act was perverse somehow. That he all of a sudden thought that he was paranoid and was ashamed. Only he wasn't paranoid, he knew that there was trouble out there to kill him and Matt, if they haven't got to him yet. "Sorry, I'm just—I guess that I'm…" he trailed off. He didn't want to say the words that were struggling to get out. But he felt that he had no choice this time. "I'm scared of what is out there. I really am okay. I mean, I have been to Afghanistan and saw shit that made me scared for my life, but I think this beats that by far."

"You are saying that a woman chasing after you, trying to kill you is more frightening than an entire year of not knowing you if you were going to die or not?"

There was silence for a moment, "Yes."

"Well why don't you tell me what happened to you and Matt tonight."

"Shit. Matt!" he picked up his phone and hit a button that speed called Matt's phone again. This was the fifth time since he called from the truck that Tyler was trying to get ahold of him. He thought there can only be three reasons why he wouldn't be picking up: One, he was still talking with his superiors at the Police Department, which was a possibility. Only he wouldn't be in there talking with them for more than five hours. Two, he lost his phone somewhere, which was not likely seeing as he always had it everywhere. Finally, Danny and the woman got him and killed him or captured him. As the phone was still ringing its way to voicemail, he was pleading and praying to God that he wasn't in the last option. Please, please, PLEASE!

As the call went to voicemail: *Hi this is Matthew Mullen, I'm not in right now. If you leave your name, and number I will get back to you as soon as I can. Thanks!*, Tyler pushed the end button already leaving three messages for him.

"Fuck! Still no answer!" Tyler exclaimed.

"What happened to you guys?" Tanya was saying as she was drinking her coffee with small sips.

Tyler took in another deep breathe. Than he began.

Tyler tried his best to recall all of the events that happened. He started right when he got of the phone to apologize to her. Telling her almost instantly after he hung up with her, he saw the woman that was dressed all in red murdering the three men. How his friend Danny started to shoot at him after he thought that he had disappeared a few years ago. Returning to the alley, only to find it empty. The hours of being hassled by the police. Then finally the attack at his house, that led him directly to Tanya's house. He was struggling to recall some parts because he too was battling sleep that wanted to take him, despite all the running around that he did, and the coffee still wasn't enough. Tanya didn't say anything while she was listening to him other than the occasional "What the fuck" that she and Tyler usually said. It took Tyler about twenty minutes to say the whole story and to get as much detail as he could, but once he was finished he felt like he didn't want to say anything more for at least a day. He was exhausted telling this story to the police over, and over, and over again. Telling again and adding the bonus scene that happened at the house was taking him to the point of tapping out for the night and ready to collapse. Only he knew that by the look of Tanya's face, he was going to be answering some more questions again. Turned out he was right too.

"Well. With a bitch like that after you, no wonder you keep looking out of my window." Tanya said. "What are you going to do about all of this? Are you going to go back to the police and tell them what happened?"

"They didn't believe me the first time when Matt and I told them something was going on. They will just think that I trashed my house so I can try to get the attention of the news. Which is really bullshit when you come to think about it. I don't think that they really scrubbed that alley like they should have, if they did they would have found there was a lot more evidence there then they would have seen."

"What do you mean?"

"Well there was a lot of blood in that alley when Matt and myself where running through it. When we returned to the alley after we were shot at by Danny, there was no blood around at all. Not on the ground, not on the walls. But thinking about it now I don't think that they looked hard enough. God, that was a few hours ago, but trying to think about it now with how tired I am it feels like a few weeks ago."

"Well just try the best you can. What are you saying that they didn't look hard enough?"

"I think…" he paused, "I think there was a drain in the alleyway. Yeah I'm pretty sure there was one. I'm not sure if any blood went into there, but I think it would have been worth a look."

"Maybe you can tell them that. It's better than doing nothing about all of this. Someone is after both you and Matt. If the cops won't help you who will?"

"If they wanted to hear from me about it they will get ahold of me and then I can show them when I see it for myself. But right now I just want to get ahold of Matt to make sure he's okay." Tyler started to pull out his phone and set his coffee down on the coffee table in the middle of the room. Tanya started to get up to try and take his phone away. Tyler pulled it away from her reach. "What are you doing?"

"What does it look like I'm doing? I'm trying to take your phone away from you because you have already tried to call him almost half a dozen times already, you told me. Do you really think that he isn't going to call you back if he was able too?"

"You're saying I should just give up on him?" Tyler said this as if what she was suggesting was the most awful and offensive thing anyone could think of or say.

"No." she said in a stone like tone. "I am not suggesting you *give up* on Matt. I would never suggest such a thing, and if you knew me at all Tyler Green, you would know that.

"What I am saying is that if this woman or this man that was your friend—Danny was his name?" Tyler nodded. "Right, Danny. If they have him, there is nothing your phone can do right now to make him answer your calls. It's just not gonna happen. And if they didn't get to him, he will get ahold of you as soon as he can once he has seen that you have called him like a billion times. So what I am suggesting to you right now is to be patient with his phone call—."

"Yeah, but what—."

"I am not finished." Tanya gave him a look that said please don't interrupt me again if you know what is good for you. "As I was saying. While we are waiting for his phone call, we can make some sort of plan on what our next move is going to be."

"Whoa, whoa, whoa. Let's pump the brakes here for a second. What do you mean we? You are not involved here. Getting you involved with this bitch, is only going to be more dangerous, and possibly even deadly for you than you think you know."

Tanya was taken aback and was starting to get very angry with Tyler as he said this. "You think I can't handle this bitch with the big boys, is that it? Think that I might worry about my precious little nails, huh?"

"I think that you don't know what you are asking. People have died tonight, Tanya. If that doesn't at least give you some sort of pause to think about what this could mean for you or for what possibly might have happened to Matt right now, then I need to walk out of this house now. Because the fact is, I have risked both Matt and my own lives tonight just by glancing down that alleyway. I will be dammed if I will risk your life as well."

"That's a nice speech. Did you pick that up from a movie somewhere?" Tanya then looked at Tyler as if nothing he could say was going to sway her from making up her mind. She had that about her. Never tell her what to do or she will put you in your place. Which meant to her sometimes was in the dumpster. Always the strong spirit Tyler thought. Always looking for the trouble that Tyler, Matt or Charlie was in so she could try and prove that she could play ball with the rest of the boys. Only this wasn't about playing some stupid game like they were kids, this was their lives that he was talking about. Whatever this woman in red was, she was one thing for sure. Hell on great looking legs. Ready to kill him and Matt if she didn't get to him already.

"I'm not joking around here Tanya. I don't want you to die. It's as simple as that."

"Then why did you come here?" she shot back.

"What?" The question took Tyler for a loop.

Tanya repeated herself. "Why did you come here? You needed my help. You dragged me out of bed when I was most likely having the greatest dream that I ever had. I don't know for sure, all I know is that I was happy. Got up, let you in to MY house. Made you coffee, and let you tell your story to me about how you and Matt are in danger. And you have the gull to sit there and tell me that this is a far as I go? Because it may be too dangerous?! Well big news buddy! You came into my house, you are now stuck with me. So we can either keep up with this pointless argument, or we can do what I proposed earlier and start coming up with a plan on what to do next."

Tyler put his hands through his hair, frustrated and tired, thinking about what he should do. What he thought he should do most of all was try and get some sleep. Tanya was right. On all counts he figured after a minute. He needed a plan and she wanted to be apart of this. He could try and sneak out and get away from her, but he had no where else to go, other than Charlie's place and that was worse than here. Charlie had a wife to look after with a kid on the way. Tyler thought there was no way in hell he would get him involved.

"Alright." Tyler said, raising his hands up in surrender.

"Alright, what?" Tanya said.

"If you want to help, I sure as hell won't stop you. For the record, I think that you are making a very big mistake."

"Then you let me worry about that. I'have been taking care of myself for a while now, and I don't need anyone to look after me now."

"This time around, it wouldn't be so bad to have someone watch your back."

"Well then, good thing I have you and Matt."

Tyler put his hand on the top of his head as if he was going to say how stupid he was. "Matt! Oh God, I just hope he is okay. They better not have touched him." He was looking down at his phone again. "I'm going to give him another call."

Tanya rolled her eyes upon hearing this. "What did I just get done telling you? If he can call you he will. Just give him some time."

"Yes, but I need to know he is okay." He hit **Matt Mullen** in his phone contacts and raised the phone to his ear. "The best thing he is going to do, is give me a hard time for calling him so many times, and if he doesn't like it, I will tell him to pick up his damn phone than."

The phone was ringing and Tyler was looking at Tanya. She was trying to put on a face that said that she wasn't going to worry about it. Only—Tyler could see that there was doubt on her face. She was just as worried about Matt as Tyler was. It was no secret. He was her friend. Tyler always suspected something more between her and Matt, but he was never really sure about it, and he mostly didn't really care. He was married to Samantha for the longest time and was waiting for either the two of them to do something relationship-wise.

The first tone in the phone rang into Tyler's ear.

If not do a relationship, they should just get together for a night of some no-strings-attached-sex. It would at least release some tension on what the other was like in bed.

Another tone rang in his ear.

Tyler was just trying to get it together and hope that Matt wasn't hurt, or dead by these fuckers. Danny. Danny Staubach. Where the fuck had he been for all these years? He could have at least tried to get ahold of his wife and kid, God knew they were worried about him all the time looking for answers. It made no sense if he was working for the woman in red. Tyler only assumed that he was since he was chasing both him and Matt, then coming back and seeing everything in the alleyway gone. If so, and he was working for her like she said. That didn't make a lot of sense. Not the Danny that he knew.

There was another tone but it was cut off by the sound of Matt's voice. Tyler thought it was Matt's voicemail, but then he realized the voice on the other end was more tired than usual but it was nonetheless, Matt's.

"Hello—Tyler."

"Matt? Oh God, thanks for finally getting ahold of me." Tyler looked at Tanya and seen that the relief washed into her face a little bit, but it was fighting with her classic "I told you so" face to almost not be recognized. "Listen, you don't have much time, wherever you are you need to get moving!"

"Tyler."

"No, man, listen to me! I was just ambushed at my house by that crazy brunette bitch we saw tonight at the alleyway. She said that she was sending someone you're way. She said it would be Danny that we saw..."

"I know." Matt said in a cold stone like tone.

Tyler paused for a second, "You know? Did you shoot him or arrest him, or what?"

There was silence on the phone. A long deep silence that seemed to go on forever.

"Matt what happened?" Tyler saw that the concern on Tanya's face made a comeback, only this time it was clearly visible. She was mouthing the words to him "What's going on?"

More silence.

Tyler waited and was just about to ask Matt again, when a voice that was not Matt's voice broke through on the other end that caused Tyler to go from standing right before the couch, to almost collapsing onto it.

"Hello, Tyler. Didn't think I was that tough did you?"

It was the high pitched, sweet innocent girl voice that was on the other end. The voice that belonged to the women he referred to as the Scarlet Bitch. His hands started to shake as he was holding the phone. It also seemed like he was trying to hold onto his sanity. They got him. *She* got him.

"Hello, Tyler? I think it is rude to not answer someone when they are on the phone with you? Makes me feel bad. Makes me angry a little bit. Makes me want to do bad things to other people's friends. Maybe take out an eye, or a finger. You know what? Maybe an arm will do the trick." She was getting worse with her threats, he knew because he was still not answering back. He wanted to. God did he want to. But it felt like he was punched in the gut and couldn't get a single word out.

Finally with a big gulp of air he forced the words to come out. "I'M HERE! I'm here!"

"Good, glad I finally got your attention." she said, he could hear her smile on the other end of the line. "So here is my question to you. How much is your friend worth to you?"

"W-What?"

"Please don't make me repeat myself. It's counter-productive and really has a tendency to piss me off and make me do nasty things. But since you are new to this I will give you what I call a freebee. Here it goes again: How much is your friend worth to you?"

"He's my friend. Give him back or I will hunt you down you bitch."

There was laughter on the other end of the receiver. "I don't think you are in any position to make threats. No. Not one little bit. But that is not my intention. I have every intention to give you your friend back. But for a price."

"What price is that?"

"A person to take his place."

Tyler wanted to ask her "what" again. Then he remembered what she said before about repeating herself. So he just repeated it for her, "A person to take his place. Place for what?"

"So I can learn what you know. Maybe have some fun with you while I'm trying to get some information out of you. If you haven't guessed by now, it's you I want and nothing but you and whoever you told about me will do. Don't worry about the cops you told, they didn't believe you anyways, but when they do, I will take care of them myself. No, I want you and your little friend you are with right now, the one who is helping you hide from me."

"I'm by myself you bitch! You hurt him at all and I will kill you! You understand! No, forget that, you hurt him at all and the police will be after you to the point where you will never sleep!"

More laughter on the other end. "Let me deal with that. Just don't let them be getting anymore information from you from now on okay? Or else I will find my person in Matt. Maybe even do some more nasty things to him before I need him. You believe that I can carry through on my threats don't you Tyler Green?"

Tyler nodded, then he answered her question over the phone as well.

"Good, Hope to see you soon! And by the way, it's not against the rules to give up yourself. Something more to think about. Chow!"

The line went dead. Tyler let the phone drop between his fingers.

"Tyler what just happened?" Tanya asked, panic in her face. "Tyler? TYLER?!"

Part II:
Run, Run, as Fast as You Can

"*I'm dying, praying.
Bleeding, I'm screaming.
Am I too lost to be saved?
Am I too lost?*

— *Amy Lee*

Chapter 13

Time passed, not enough to where leaves were changing, but enough to where the dog days of summer were starting to howl with the breezy wind, and when the sun was out that it was scorching, but as soon as a cloud would cover up the sun, the smallest cold nip of autumn showed it's ugly head.

Time passed enough to where half-truths and rumors were confused with facts on how both Tyler Green, and Officer Mathew Mullen vanished. Rumors of how Officer Mullen getting murdered and then thrown into the Wisconsin River surfaced and made the newspapers and the local evening news. Adding with new "evidence" that was found by Sgt. Donald Gentle of the Marathon County Police Department, showing the mess that was in Tyler's apartment from his battle with Charlotte, it made Tyler Green look guilty even with the most free thinkers in the area.

No one saw either of them for days…Then weeks…Then months…

After the second week, people started to notice that another person was missing as well. Tanya, who had been so adamant on going with Tyler on whatever it was that they were going to go on, was noticed that she hadn't been at her residence for several days, maybe even as long as a week. Gentle found pictures of her with both Tyler and Matt and get into his mind that she was indeed involved in the disappearance of Officer Matt Mullen. Making both Tyler and Tanya both wanted for the same crime. Sgt. Don Gentle wasn't finished with pining just that crime on Tyler, oh no. He was making sure(but not advertising to the newspapers or the local news shows) that Tyler was going to have faking a crime scene added to the rap sheet. Apparently this was almost more important to Sgt. Gentle than the missing person case for the case in point he didn't really care if Matt Mullen was missing or not.

Meanwhile, the media was having the time of their lives with the story. It was bigger than the Slenderman Stabbings and almost as big as the Steve Avery case that had the documentary of *Making a Murderer*. To Wisconsin, this was the new crime of the year as it was getting more and more buzz. Parents from both sides met with one another on live television during a six thirty news segment. Both mother's were in tears defending one another's boys, while Mathew's father Justin talked for the most part on everything about his son and more. From how well he did on the football team in Wausau East, to his service in Afghanistan, even sharing a memory of a Christmas dinner that Matt tried to cook and burned making the family order pizza from the only pizza shop that happened to be open on Christmas.

Weeks went by as the media kept up with the parents, soon brining in Tanya's parents into the mix as well, being just as friendly, and hoping for the best. When weeks were turning into months, solidarity of all sets of parents was starting to wear thin, as well as hope. Soon, small jabs at separate interviews were taking at one another. Before long, none of the parents would talk to one another. Soon enough, Mathew's parents, Justin and Winnie, believed Tyler killed their son, and the media made sure they caught it all for everyone to see them announce that they wanted justice for their son.

Throughout Wisconsin, what the Blue Lives Matter movement that was started in Dallas, Wisconsin citizen began to solidify. Some calling out "Matt's Life Matters!" around Tyler's parents as they would walk into grocery stores, or into banks. The Greens were becoming the villains that the public couldn't pin on Tyler.

All while this was happening, there was running, and fear, and pain for Matt, Tanya and Tyler. No one could find them. Not even the woman who called herself Charlotte could find Tyler and Tanya. She knew where Matt was, and was happy to have him. Only to make him suffer, but the disappearance of Tyler Green didn't bother her at first, but then as the summer was starting to show signs of the fall, her small and almost dismissible worry turned into an obsessive need to find them.

Chapter 14

There are certain phone calls that physically hurt to make. Where you get a pain in the pit of your stomach that feels like a rat burrowing into your body. Those ones that everyone makes that you know won't end well. Weather its at the doctor's office, or the dentist, lawyer's or accountants where you knew either that the news was going to be bad, or that the person on the other end was going to make life miserable for you no matter what. Friends and family members usually are known to do this, but on the occasional blue moon, your doctor, dentist, lawyer and so on. It happens to everyone. No matter how many years we lived, or how many centuries have passed since before phones existed, there are always the conversations or contacts that you dread to get a hold of. The woman who called herself Charlotte was no exception.

She was flying back from a business trip she just finished with on her private jet. Her hand held her cell phone and was staring in deep concentration on weather or not the situation needed to bring this person in. Surely, there was another person who could fix this problem without using him. Wasn't there?

What she told Tyler Green at the end of June was true, she could wait forever if she wanted to. Time was never an issue. Ever. She waited months for a walled in city over in the Middle-east to be swallowed up by the Black Death, she could go in and feast on the remaining survivor's souls. which lead to about twenty of them. Those memories brought a smile to her face.

Only now there were complications. Her father always taught her to never be noticed in such a high manner. Don't draw so much attention that mobs will be formed to hunt you down and have their way with killing you. That sort of thing happened to her mother so many centuries ago, yet remained burned in her mind as if the stake burning left permanent burn marks in her thoughts. It was a lesson that needed to be taught, and it was learned at great cost to her and to her family.

Newspapers and internet news sites were picking up on the disappearance of Officer Mathew Mullen faster almost each week. Yes it was true that his friend Tyler Green was the one they were looking for on his missing friend, but if they did find him, where ever he was, they would get another listen to the story of the alley of that night and of the encounter at his home. That just simply would not do. She knew that the story was far fetched for most humans to believe it, but what she had learned from her time walking this earth is that if a story is told enough and loud enough, eventually there will be someone who will believe it, even if the story isn't true. That was society, at its most raw form. Although his story is true which all the more works against her. The plain and simple truth was that Tyler Green needed to go away, and the sooner the better.

Only just like the police, Charlotte was having trouble finding Tyler herself. She knew that he must have went to a friend's house after their altercation in the apartment, but where he went after that, she had no clue. After they finished talking to each other on the phone, Charlotte tried and have his phone traced so she could keep tabs on him, and to see if he was going to do what she wanted him to do. She knew that it was a long shot. Humans like him were always stubborn to everyone but themselves. She cursed herself for giving him such an option in the first place. After tracing his cell phone she should have just went to the son-of-a-bitches hiding place and killed him right then and there. But instead, once Danny was finished setting the trace up, he had convinced her that she needed to go right away, and get out of Wausau. Thinking on it for a few minutes, she agreed.

Charlotte herself took care of hauling the cop up from the basement that they just put him in and put him back into the truck they had just pulled him out of on the SUV. They placed him next to both the buckets of water and bleach that they used earlier to quickly wash away the blood that was in that fucking alley where all their trouble began. At first the drain that was in alleyway looked like it was going to clog up from all the years of garbage that built up inside of it. The foliage of the liquid stopped for a brief moment, then something deep down must have given way and soon all the blood and bleach flowed down and was gone forever. Matt's head knocked around on these buckets while she struggled to put him in. Not that he was struggling, Charlotte made sure of that.

Danny did a run-through of the house, and wiped down all of the finger prints they could have left behind on any surface. It took him about a half an hour, but felt like an eternity for him, because the battle of sleep was being waged strong and fiercely within his mind and body. Along with a sense that, maybe it wouldn't be so bad if she was captured or caught. Once he was finished, he made his way back to the vehicle, Charlotte gave him a 5 Hour Energy drink to swallow once they got at the gas station to gas up, and then she told him to take her home. Their time in Wausau was at an end,

The entire time Danny was driving her to her home, Charlotte was staring at the computer screen that showed the exact position of where Tyler Green, thinking if she should just tell Danny to go back so she could finish him. There were a few times she actually did spit out the words to try and get his attention. "Danny."

"Yes ma'am?"

"Tur—turn.... Never mind, keep going."

So Danny kept making his way to take his mistress back home to her King. Continuing to stare at that screen and seeing that he wasn't moving from that spot on the Northwest side of Wausau. She stared at it the whole trip. and continued to watched it as soon as they arrived at the house. Only stopping to drag Matt Mullen into the basement, she could have had him walking down the basement, but she was stressed out and causing a little pain on one of the men that caused some of her misery felt relieving to her. Locking him down in the basement took a few minutes along with some threats, and a few kicks and making him hit himself a few times in the face, helped bring her mind at ease a little. She then dismissed Danny to go to sleep, then returned to the computer—staring and waiting.

Around two hours later she woke up the entire house with a scream. Danny, Matt(who was still tied down in the basement), as well as the King that was residing upstairs. Danny rushed to her in the downstairs Library and saw that the Laptop that she was staring at half the night, was in two pieces on the ground, smashed in screen and destroyed keyboard half. He saw that the bullet wound that Tyler had shot her on her shoulder was opened again after he did his best to bandage it, because he didn't have enough time to stitch it properly before leaving. He forgot to ask her about it before he went to sleep, and by looking at it now, it looked like she had forgotten all about it. Only her rage from whatever caused this outburst started to make it bleed just as hard as it did before.

"What is it ma'am?" Danny asked more than a little frightened

"The signal. It's gone. He must have destroyed his phone."

"Are you sure ma'am? He may have switched it off, or it may have died from a low battery."

"Maybe. And we can use the other laptop to see, but if he is as smart as you said he was, I think he stomped on it for suspecting we were looking for him. So here is what is going to happen, you are going to get dressed and go to where he was last seen on the trace. If he is still there you will finish him off. It was a mistake to keep him alive and wait for him to make a decision. There will be no need to call me cause I will know when it is done, then I will use his friend as the last soul, Understand?"

Danny nodded. He then got dressed into his suit, then left.

Charlotte paced around the library for hours, thinking about Danny to get ahold of his emotions. Concentrating just enough so she wouldn't accidentally start controlling him and send him off the road. Keeping track of a person's emotions was always easy on normal circumstances, but when your nerves were all over the place, your concentration was a little fluttery at times.

It only slightly occurred to her that she did not say hello to the King since she arrived at home. He was always up in the third floor of their luxurious home that over looked the lake. Her mind was completely absorbed by her business that thoughts of him were almost completely absent. She felt Danny leave and still feeling exhausted from the night before. She didn't care. She knew he could handle it, she sent him on errands like this all the time, just not with much urgency as this one was.

What it seemed like to Charlotte, was that Danny was taken his goddamn time to get back to Wausau. He drove under the speed limit dost of the way, and when he made his first leg of the trip into town so he could gas up the SUV. Once he was finished with that, he decided to go into the Kwik Trip gas station to pay, then went over the Family Sit-Down that was connected to the gas station and decided to have some breakfast. She only knew this from the sensation, and happiness he was feeling right now, it was the same feeling he always felt when he was eating breakfast, one of his favorite meals. She picked up her phone and called him. When he picked up he sounded like hell. Under normal circumstances she would let him finish his meal and coffee so he would be fresh for work. Not this time

"Quit eating and move your ass." then she hung up on him before he could respond.

She felt a wave of disappointment flow through him. A few minutes later she felt him feel his irritation with a mixture of happiness that came from the sounds on the radio.

He went on like this for five hours. Charlotte felt his anger as he was coming in contact with some stupid drivers he was passing, she was smiling at these feelings. Soon she felt a relief come to him. She thought that he must have made it to Wausau. She felt her own happiness and relief come at this thought. About a half hour later from his relief, she felt a twinge of fear hit Danny, along with another emotion—a sliver of relief.

Soon she received a phone call. "Hello?" she said.

"It's me ma'am." Danny said in a professional voice.

"What's going on? Why are you scared?"

Danny knew she was reading his emotions, so he was not surprised by this comment. "I went to the address of where his phone was reading last. It appears to be a small rental house where a woman lives. A Tanya Walsh. It appears from the outside that she lives alone. No sign of life, inside."

"What does it look like inside?"

"I don't know, I haven't checked."

"Why not?" When she asked this, she wasn't looking for a response from Danny and he knew this. When she asked this, it meant for him to open the fucking door now, or there was going to be hell to pay. Danny paused for a moment, there was a noise on his end of the line that sounded like a piece of glass breaking, then the sure sound of a lock turning.

"I'm in right now."

"I don't need to remind you to check everywhere in that fucking house. Call me the second you are done." Once again, hitting the END button without another word.

Keeping her senses open, she felt both his curiosity and his caution. There were times in her long, long life where time seemed to drag at its heels and others where the time would run as fast as a cheetah. This was the case of the former. She gripped at her cell phone with a strength that almost crushed it in her palm. She refrained from closing her fist all the way, but when she looked at her phone, there was a nice crack running diagonally down the face of it. She put her phone down, and continued to hone in on Danny's emotions.

Feeling that nothing had changed, her phone suddenly started to ring nearly twenty minutes from when she hung up. "What did you find?"

Danny paused. "Well, he was here. But he is not here anymore. Neither is the woman."

"You knew him Danny, where do you think he could be?" She reached out to him and felt his emotions again. She knew when he lied to her, he thought that he could do it sometimes. Like how he always said he was happy to work for her, or that she sometimes took the souls of babies while they were still in their cradles didn't effect him one way or the other. She knew these were lies, but she knew that even if he spoke the truth on these matters, he couldn't do a damn thing about it.

"If I had to guess, I think he would have gone to one of his Army buddies house."

She didn't pick up a lie on his part, only this answer didn't make sense. "Why didn't he just go to an Army buddies house in the first place if he had to go somewhere?"

"I think he went here because she is either a friend or a girlfriend, or just some broad he is fucking. I don't know, but we will find out. I found the remains of his phone. It's smashed to hell, so he might have thought that it could be tracked."

"Do you think he knew that it was being tracked?"

"No, I don't think so. It looks like a precautionary measure because I looked around and took a closer look at certain objects and saw that they were wiped down from fingerprints. So I think he was just covering his ass and wiping away his footsteps, so to speak. The cell phone was just another precaution."

Again, no sign of a lie. "You are sure?"

"I can only tell you what I'm looking at. A house that is in complete fucking disarray, done by yours truly, with no one inside, wiped down surfaces, and a broken cell phone."

"Alright, no need to repeat yourself." She said. "What about her phone? Do you think we could track hers?"

"We would have to know her number for that. We can look in the local phone books, but I'm not seeing a house phone anywhere. She might be like most people in this area and only have enough money to own a cell phone and a contract. If that's the case, then she might just be unlisted, but its worth a shot."

"Alright do that. See if she has one in that woman's house and then get the hell out of there. The last thing you need is some nosy neighbor looking in your direction and calling the cops on a home invasion."

"Not much a problem with that, cities like these go out on Sundays if there are events in the summer, a nice family breakfast at a restaurant, or to go to church. I doubt if anyone is around."

"Just the same, get out of there." She ended the call, but then had a thought. She wasn't going to keep sending Danny up and down the state everytime they came across a lead of Tyler Green's location or sighting, like a Big Foot hunter. Maybe she needed a man on the ground, or on sight as the military officials like to call it. What harm could that do since she could read his emotions when she wanted. She could get daily updates from him, and give him orders on what to do. To Danny, it would be just like he never left the military.

She thought about what sort of problems this may cause for Danny. She knew that he wasn't really happy here with her. She didn't need to read his emotions for that. But she was mainly concerned that Danny might try and betray her, and maybe help Mr. Green in some way. Maybe help him escape. She thought that was highly unlikely and dismissed the idea. She could read his emotions and if push came to shove, she could control his soul from here and that would control his body. Maybe even make him kill himself if that happened. In the end, she thought that is was a good idea and started to dial **Danny** on her contacts list.

"Yes ma'am?" he knew it was her calling him, from the name on his phone.

"I have an idea. Why don't you stay up there at the house and keep the lookout for your buddy, Mr. Tyler Green."

"I'm sorry ma'am?" Danny sounded slightly confused and put off by this question.

"Look." Charlotte said, sounding angry. "There is no use of you coming back down here, and then you jumping back up there everytime we hear something about that nosy piece of shit. You might as well stay up there until he reappears, or we find some kind of lead."

"For how long, ma'am?"

"For as long as it takes! Is that a problem for you?"

"N-no ma'am, no problem whatsoever. I just must ask you, where will I be staying?"

"Is the house up there too small for you and your lavish needs?" she asked with a sarcastic angry tone.

"No ma'am. It's just…I was thinking…Maybe…."

"Fucking spit it out will you!"

"If we are worried about him knowing who and what you are. Maybe it would be best to stay at a hotel."

"Why?" she asked confused.

"Well, who knows how much he knows now. If he tries to come to the house up here, maybe we could use it as a trap of some sort to take him or kill him."

"Why would he know *anything* about me? Other than what he saw me do to the three shitheads, there shouldn't be anything that he should know about me, other than that he recognized you? Should he?" she reached out and tried to feel for his emotions quickly before he answered.

"No, but I doubt you gotten as far as you have, by being careless in ways such as this." She felt something strange on him, it was reading as the truth like it usually did, but there was a sliver of something that felt like secrecy.

"Alright, fine. We will have it your way. I will make sure to check you in to the Howard Johnson's in Rib Mountain. Don't bother asking for anything nicer because you won't get it. Go get yourself some clothes that aren't too conspicuous, you know so you can blend in."

"Ma'am, I know what conspicuous means."

"Don't get smart with me. Just do as I say. Use the MasterCard. So I can keep track of what you are spending my money on. Don't make me regret having you stay up there, otherwise I will make you regret it. You understand?"

There was no hesitation. "Yes ma'am." saying it like he was talking to an Army officer.

After she hung up with Danny she was trying to think if there was anything else that needed to be done, or could be done about their dear friend Mr. Green. After thinking about it for another half hour, she realized that there was nothing else to be done, at least not at this very moment. She looked at the clock in the Library and saw that it was quarter past three in the afternoon.

Then it occurred to her that she never said hello to her love. She was too obsessed over Mr. Green and trying to get rid of him that the thoughts of her love, her life, *her* soul, were merely an after thought. Her King was the very reason she was doing all of this for. Trying to find this bastard that could threaten what they spent many, many years trying to accomplish. The reason that a man was in their basement this very second, so they could keep him as insurance against Mr. Green. And she had forgotten about him for over eight hours while she was in the house.

She started to climb the stairs to the third floor. The Kings' dominion as she liked to think of it. She still had the tattered remains of her red skirt and shirt on that was now a little redder from the gunshot wound Mr. Green had made on her shoulder. She looked down at the wound and saw that the wound itself was almost completely healed. She would have to cut the stitches out in a little while. Most likely after she saw the King. She reached the top of the stairs on the third floor. *Welcome to the kingdom.* She thought to herself. She did that every time she reached the top of the stairs. She looked around at the paintings that were hung around on the inside walls. There was the *Devouring of Saturn's Son*, along with work from a modern artist that went by the name of Chris Mars, *The Yellow Raven, The Tea Party.*

When she looked on the other side of the hallway, there was no wall at all. Only the one-inch thick glass window that outlooked the lake and the beautiful tree like country side. It was always beautiful to her, she always hoped that her King loved it as much as her. Yes it made the third floor look smaller than other places in the grand house that they lived in, but the view was worth it. The gorgeous vista always made her feel like she was on top the world. Or that she was ruling it.

She made her way to the far end of the hallway to the master bedroom. Opening the door slowly and silently as possible. Like Danny, she could read the King's emotions just by thinking about him, but for the most part, she didn't really want to. She loved him. She loved him so much that to do that felt like a violation to her and to him. She peeked inside the room and saw that he was not asleep. He was merely laying on the bed in his pajamas, looking into space. Blank open space outside the window-wall that was in the room, sitting on the bed, not giving any notice to the woman entering.

"Hello my sweet, sweet King. How are you doing?"

The man did not answer. He grey pale face continued to look out to the west where the sun was making its way through the day. Seeing the journey it still had to make before the day was done. She made her way to the bed.

"I'm sorry that I didn't come up here and greet you when I first came home. I had some—unfortunate problem to deal with. It's not dealt with yet, but soon it will be. Some annoying little fly flew into my business last night. Having to cut our trip a little short. So I stayed up and tried to deal with it before coming up to see you. I know that you need your dose, and I should have come up here to give it to you right away. I'm sorry my love. Do you forgive me?"

The King said nothing. The King didn't move. He gave no indication that he even heard her. Charlotte went on as if his silence was answer enough, that she was forgiven. She picked up his left hand and looked at his gold band that was on the ring finger. After looking at it for a moment, admiring it for what it represented like she always did, she lifted his hand up and kissed it for a long moment. She then set his hand down on his side where he laid down and picked up his right hand. She did this to admire the other ring that was on his ring finger and what it represented. That he was a King. The ring was old. Dragged through time, and the earth and all the trying times that they went through together. In a way this ring meant more to her than the wedding band on the other hand. Once again, after admiring it, she raised the hand to her lips and kissed it. After putting his hand down she looked at his face, noticing that he did not turn to look at her. She took her right hand and turned his head her way so she could meet his gaze.

"Well…Here are my spoils to give you. I hope you like them." After saying this she drew her face closer to his. Like she was going in for a kiss while keeping a hold on bis head. She opened her mouth and by applying pressure on his jaw-hinge, she made him open his.

There was a glow. An orange glow that originated from her throat. Then, an orange mist started to come out of her mouth and making its way into her Kings'. There were small sounds coming from the mist as it made its passage. To Charlotte, she might have heard the sound if she was doing this for the first time. When seeing something for the first time, and experiencing something new, you notice the small things, in the event like the sights, smell and sound. As time goes on some of those senses eventually go away from you as the repetitiveness goes on. For Charlotte, it was the sound. During this act of giving as she thought of it as, she could always hear everything else other than the sound of her gift going into her beloved.

The King always heard the sound, and knew what it was. It was always the same, yet always different. Like a snowflake, you knew it was snow, but every flake was unique and different. He heard it overtime, he received his gift. His dose, as she liked to call it. It was the sound of screaming. Screaming men, screaming woman, screaming children, screaming babies. All taken, and given to him. All apart of him now.

He heard everyone that was entering him.

Charlotte finished the passing, and ended the act with a intimate kiss. "One more sweetie. One more. Then we can begin." She said this as she rose from the bed, and walked away from him. The King just turned his head and looked back outside. Wrinkles that almost completely covered his face, were beginning to disappear, Hair that was thinning, and almost a snow white, began to thicken and start turning grey. Soon, his hands that were covered with age freckles and were rough to the touch, would be wrinkle and spot free, and smooth as they were in the days where there were horses instead of cars.

Right as Charlotte made her way to the doorway and exited into the hallway, she heard the only three words from him with this visit. After hearing them, she paid no attention to them and made her way down to the basement, to pay visit to a guest in the house. "Perfect. Just Perfect."

That was the beginning of the long months of waiting. While getting updates from Danny everyday, sometimes twice a day on what ever he heard. Mostly what he found was nothing, but he found out that the woman who resided in the house that Mr. Green was last seen in, had almost completely vanished as well. Danny found out that this was never mentioned in any of the news, because he found out that a friend of the woman's family came to take care of the house as a favor to her. Danny tried to get information from him in a friendly manner, and learned that the man thought that the woman named Tanya Walsh, was on a vacation, or at least that was what he was told. Danny told the man that he thought it was odd that she would just pack up and go on a vacation out of the blue like this, but the man didn't seemed too concerned about the matter. Saying that as long as he earned some money for taking care of the plants and the pets, she could go away for as long as she wanted.

Life had been long for her, but these months seemed to never want to end. She was talking to Mr. Matt Mullen almost everyday when she is at home. Trying to milk as much information from him as she could. But he was a hard one to crack, clearly military trained or had some sort of advanced police training that would stop him from spilling his guts. Whatever it was it was working so far, and she wasn't exactly keeping the gloves on with him. Some of the things she did to him where downright sadistic even for her taste. But that didn't stop her from doing them. Smashing the toes on each of his feet with a hammer made her cringe. His screams when she did it were so loud she thought she was going to hear something from the King himself to keep the noise down. Still he managed to not talk to her. There were a few ways to make him talk. There was a truth serum out there that could make him tell the truth no matter what. Only there was no guarantee that it would work, there were a lot of hit and misses with the serum she heard about. One where an Al Quada operative used it on American soldiers and thought he was getting an exact location to set up an ambush, only to discover that the soldier they were interrogating set the ambush up in the case in where he was captured. He thought of the question on where they set up the ambush, in place of the actual question that the Al Quada operative was asking. It produced an answer that seemed to work for the capture and they ended up walking into an ambush. This loophole in the serum was exposed in the internet, and went viral for survivalist and survivalist classes all over the world. So even if she was able to get her hands on the serum, there wasn't a hundred percent guarantee that it would work. Besides, she had a better way to get the truth out. Better, but would cause her personal dissatisfaction.

Most phones didn't work on planes, even if you put them on airplane mode. But when you pay damn near a thousand dollars worth of upgrades so that you can get service anywhere, you can call from where ever you damn well please. She stared at the name on the phone again: **Dr. Walter Falkes**. Looking at it as if willing it to go away, as if to make him go away from all of existence. She had power, but not that kind of power. Her thoughts broke out again about if she really needed to do this. Calling *him* of all people to help try to find out about her little pest. Her pest and whoever was with him. That Tanya Walsh woman. Pests that needed to be dealt with yesterday.

These brought on fresh memories of her mother. He mother so beautiful as she wore here white dresses and tended to the sick. Healing everything that nature could throw at her. If she lived long enough to treat the plague, Charlotte knew that she could do it and save thousands of human lives. But they shot themselves in the foot instead. Killing her and burning her on the stake while chanting "Witch" at her. Humans. Always scare of what is different. Even if it helps them. Dr. Walter Falkes was there to see it as well. She wasn't, but she knew when her mother was dead, through his and her emotions. Feeling the absolute pain that shot through him and then shot through her at the same time. The overwhelming sadness, grieve, and shock of someone watching their mother's flesh burning and turning to black ash right before their eyes. Her father was there as well, and he could not do anything about it. Not before, or after.

She didn't think that if these people found out about her that they would get the torches, pitchforks, and stakes out to burn her. Only she knew that if her story was believed, they wouldn't hesitate to try and find a way to kill her. Finally, she was finished with staring at the contact on her phone. She made her decision hours ago when she took off from Los Angeles. She press the contact information and press the icon that showed a phone.

There were two rings when a male voice in a sarcastic and devilish tone answered. "Well, well. It's about goddam time you call me. You getting too good for the likes of me now that it's coming to the time with you and the King? Old King Cole is still around isn't he? Or is this a call to report his tragic demise?"

Charlotte didn't say one word to him and already she was regretting ever putting his contact info in her phone, nevertheless calling it. She took a deep breath. "Glad to see you still think that you are funny. I guess I should call more often to try and brake that hope you have in the back of your mind."

"Not even a stone cold bitch like yourself could break that thought process in my head. So tell me. What the fuck do you want?"

"How can you talk like that? Aren't you in some sort of hospital? That's where you like to hang out isn't it?"

"I'm at home right now. You caught me at a time when I wasn't working. Shocking I know, that never really happens. Then again, since the fucking telephone has been invented, you only managed to fucking call me a grand total of three fucking times. And this is the third time!"

"Are you expecting an apology?"

"You think I'm that fucking stupid? To think that out of all that souls you steal from these people, that you would think to keep one for yourself. Hell no, you're not that smart."

Charlotte was biting at her bottom lip. She knew that this was what he wanted. To go back and forth, back and forth with the arguments, and cheap shots. Only she didn't have time for this.

"As much as I would like to hear every criticism about me from the likes of you, I did get ahold of you for a reason."

"That's way I just asked you what the fuck it is you want. Jeez, almost sixty years since we talked last, and I see you feel behind on cleaning the wax out of your ears."

Charlotte ignored this. "What I want is to borrow your special talent. Your green talent."

"Shocker! Only calling me so you can use something of mine. Typical Everlyn, just fucking typical."

"My name is not Everlyn anymore. It's Charlotte. Charlotte Brisbane. You might want to know that when you get here and talk to me around people."

There was a sudden burst of laughter on the other end of the line. The laugh was loud, and dragged on for almost thirty seconds. Charlotte waited patiently for the laugh to simmer. When it finally did, she spoke, "Are you laughing at my name?"

With the laughing dying down, the man said, "Yes, but only half of that laugh was for your name. The other half is the fact that you think that I'm coming by you. That's pure comedy right there that Dante couldn't touch."

There was silence on Charlotte's end of the phone line. "What do you mean? You're saying you are not coming."

"Wow, you finally got that. Congratulations."

"Why not?"

"I don't make long trips. Especially to…" There was a pause. "To—where are you now?"

"Lake Geneva, Wisconsin."

"Yeah, that place. I don't go to Lake Geneva, Wisconsin. Sorry, bad experience. Are we done?"

Charlotte pulled the phone away from her ear, and pressed it against her forehead. She was getting a headache and was on the verge to crushing her phone in her palm. Thinking for a while, she put the phone against her ear, and spoke. "How much do you want?"

"What?"

"How much money do you want? That's why your doing this right? To squeeze me for money? You always tried to dry me out just to try and shove it to me one way or another."

A small chuckle from the other end, "Believe it or not. I don't care about money these days. The last time I took money from you, I did the smart thing and put it in a savings when the interest rates were remarkable. Over a period of sixty years, That money grows into some impressive numbers to where I can live off of the interests, and the many I make from working at hospitals, for decades and decades. Especially the hospitals I've been working as of late. So no it's not about money."

"Then what is it that you do want?"

"Well we will talk about that as soon as you come over here."

"Wait! What? I'm not going over there."

Again there was small chuckling on the other end of the line, "You know, you are the one who needs me. So if you want me, you will have to come get me. Thats one of my prices, and I only have two. So come over here and find out what the other one is. Or not, and you can try to fix your problem by yourself."

There was silence for a long time. So long that Charlotte thought the man on the other end of the phone hung up on him, so she pulled the phone away from her ear to check that the line was still active. Only the silence was on her end, she was thinking about how unpleasant he was going to make this unless he got his way, but the truth of it was that she needed him. She needed what he had. So once again she took a deep breath, and asked him, "Where do you work and live now?"

"Ah ha! I knew you couldn't keep away."

"Tell me before I hang up and throw up."

"Just come to the Massachusetts General Hospital. I will make you an appointment for ten A.M. tomorrow morning."

"I am halfway across the country right now!" she screamed in the phone.

"Don't give me that, I can hear the engines of a jet in the background. My guess is that you make enough money, that you have a private jet on standby, all the time. So just tell your pilot that you have a new destination, and then I will see you tomorrow. Or Are you having second thoughts?"

"With you, I always have second thoughts. But I will be there in the morning."

"Great! See you tomorrow, big sister."

Charlotte hung up the phone and touched the intercom that connected to the pilot. She then told the pilot her unexpected new destination. Almost gritting her teeth the whole time she told him the new destination.

Chapter 15

There are few crimes in our world that are more terrible and inhuman as rape. Most victims of rape can attest to this, for the effects it has on a person, weather male or female, can leave wounds and scars both physically, and mentally for years, if they ever get over such an experience at all. Some of the most evil and violent people, use rape as a scare tactic to keep their victims corporation floating away from them. Others have done rape, to assert dominance of a certain area, such as a prison.

Then there are others that are considered the lowest of the low, and perform rape for the pure enjoyment of it. Men or woman that have to dominate over a person, and abuse that dominance. Sometimes this is the only way the rapist can feel any kind of pleasure. Webster's dictionary has many definitions for the word rape. One is for the name of an Old World herb. Another is to force someone to have sex with you by using violence or the threat of violence. But the definition this narrative is trying to make point goes as such: an act or instance of robbing or despoiling or carrying away a person by force. If by definition this is rape, then Dr. Walter Falkes is by far the most sinister, and dangerous rapist that ever walked the earth.

What makes him a rapist in this context has nothing to do with forcing his penis into another person, or his sexual drive. Quite the contrary, the last time he ever truly had sexual intercourse, was before there was a secession from the union.

No. His needs for dominance far exceed those of mortal men.

Dr. Walter Falkes works at the Massachusetts General Hospital as a psychiatrist. Some of the top brass executives often like to brag to their inner most circles of doctors, rich friends, and basically anyone who will listen, that they were lucky to grab such a excellent doctor such as Falkes. The patients he treats get diagnosed by such mental disorders as: Post traumatic stress, severe schizophrenia, psychosis, and manic depression. This alone would be nothing special to any other administrator of any hospital, just another doctor doing what they are paid for. No big deal, no problem at all, thank you and good-night. What made him stand out was the quickness he found such mental disorders. Usually, unless it is such clear cut circumstances, it can take months or even years to properly diagnose an individual of the before said mental disorders. Dr. Water S. Falkes M.D., had a record of diagnosing psychosis in a matter of hours. Doing this once, would have been chalked up to good research and a keen ear and sight on one patient, and giving a handshake as well as a helluva good note in his personal record and at the bar. Only in the beginning of his career, this was a common thing. Almost weekly. If there was ever an award for diagnosing the most severe mental disorders in a year by a single doctor, Dr. Walter Falkes would have been giving Rookie of the Year on his first year as a doctor. Well, first year under his current name that is, but that was neither here or there.

Patients that had no personal history or family history of any sort of mental disorder, showed various symptoms of psychosis, schizophrenia, and of course, post-traumatic stress. The strange part of patients was, that they showed no sign of these symptoms when they would first go to Dr. Walter Falkes' private practice for something else that was required of them or by attending on their own free will. Only after seeing Dr. Walter Falkes himself, did such symptoms occur. From a person on the outside looking in, this was very suspicious of the doctor himself. When it was becoming a common day occurrence at the practice, an investigation was soon called in to look at the records of Dr. Falkes. Unbeknown to him, a team developed by the Florida State

Board of Mental Health, and the state police, with the cooperation of seven patients, sessions of Dr. Falkes with the patients, were video taped using lapel cameras, and microphones. When he wasn't around his office at night, investigators searched and tested his personal office, his personal bathroom, public bathroom, waiting area for patients, even the secretaries office for potential drugs that could cause these types of mental breakdowns and episodes.

Ultimately what investigators found was this: *nothing*.

There was nothing strange that was going on in the scene going on in his private practice. The search for drugs in the entire office areas came up clean. Not even suspiciously clean like something was being washed away daily to hide evidence. No. There was nothing there, no trace of any such drugs, not even an aspirin. The walls, ventilation systems, drinking water, hell, even the air humidifier was all searched, tested, and all produced a negative result for any kind of drug.

The patients that helped with the investigation however found something out for themselves. Of the seven people, (three woman and four men) six were treated for mild cases depression, stress, and one woman for post pardon depression after just having a baby. One of the seven patients, a man named Justin McCarthy, went into Dr. Falkes office with a clean bill of mental health. He was looked at at by two psychiatrists to help treat him for a mild case of depression after his girlfriend Kelly had left him after he tried to propose to her, and she told him no. When he went into the office of Dr. Walter Falkes, he received a different diagnosis altogether. A very, very, different diagnosis.

During the video recording of the session, there was nothing visibly wrong with the session that Dr. Falkes gave to Mr. Justin McCarthy. When the incident occurred, Dr. Falkes asked Justin, "Have you had any other girlfriends, since you broke up with Kelly?". There was no harm in this question. There were no signs that Dr. Falkes was being disrespectful, rude, even leading in anyway. Just a shrink trying to get the full story, so he can help treat his patients.

Justin McCarthy paused for a long moment. Dr. Falkes appeared to not notice at first as he was writing on his notepad in front of him about five feet away in a chair. After about thirty to forty seconds later, he looked up and saw that Justin did not answer him. He looked at

Justin confused and asked again, "Justin did you hear? I asked if you dated any other woman after you and Kelly broke up?". There was still silence for a little while, with a look of puzzlement on Dr. Falkes' face. Suddenly, there was a loud scream coming from Justin that was not visible on his lapel camera. He shot up out of his seat and would lunge toward the doctor and try to get his hands around his throat. He was trying to kill him. Dr. Falkes resisted by holding his hands out and grabbing Justin's wrists. The secretary outside of the office heard what was happening and called security to help retrain the man. When security guards came in, Justin was trying to get ahold of Dr. Falkes' green tie and tried to tighten it around his neck.

After he was taking away and formally arrested, doctors that saw him and treated him before going to see Dr. Falkes, had to do a double take when looking at the man, and looking at the file of their previous notes. It was like night and day. Running series after series of toxic screens to see if he was drugged by any drug all came up negative. What the doctors concluded after study Mr. Justin McCarthy was that he had suffered a psychotic break from reality. He remained in Central Florida Behavioral Hospital for about four months, until one day his doctors and nurses were coming in to give him his medication when they saw him laying dead in the middle of the room. Choked to death on his own tongue.

Other than the incident with Mr. Justin McCarthy, the investigation lead nowhere. Dr. Walter Falkes was, in the eyes of the law and the state medical bar, cleared of any wrongdoing. His cases were chalked up to a keen eye, and ear, as well for a great knowledge of the symptoms of mental illness. If only that was all true.

The real truth that laid behind the sunny green colored wearing, sunny face with the blonde hair, six foot built figure was a monster of the most perverse kind. To him, his patients were mere toys. Toys that not only could be broken, but *needed* to be broken. And everywhere he went, every corner, every building, anywhere, his toys would be walking around waiting for him to play with them.

He told his sister that he was going by the name Walter Falkes these days. He went by many names as the centuries have passed: Allen Miller, Jonathon Grenwald, Elmer Wallace, William Tye, Henry

Botten, Connor Armstrong, after he walked this world under his true name of Kolat, and under all names he did the same thing. The game that never loses it excitement or mystique: reading and destroying peoples minds.

To say that Kolat merely reads minds is an understatement. To him the mind is like play dough, he can mold it into whatever he wants, add to the dough, take from the dough. He can control what a person sees, what they hear, what they taste, and what they feel, all by a simple look. Like a radio tower that tries to get a direct signal to a certain radio, only then taking over the radio completely if it really wants to. His favorite hobby when he did this, was to rape a person.

The victim didn't matter, men, woman, children. It mattered not to him, they were all his toys. If walking down the street of Boston where he now resides, and a person happened to walk in from of him on the street, it was the perfect opportunity for his game. What he would do is put an image of a man or a demon, or an animal if he was really feeling creative, and have the creature overpower the person and have their way with them. Only the challenging part was to place the image in a memory from the persons past. He like to do this to happy events in the person's life, like a birthday, job promotion, hell even the birth of a child. He then would place it in the person's mind by merely willing it there like a silent thief in the night. Once placed in the mind, and if the unfortunate person still happened to be traveling in the same direction as he was, he would bring the memory to the forefront of the person's mind as if they were hit by a semi-truck. Then he would watched what happened next. If there was a big response to this from the individual, he would focus again on them and make it seem as if they were experiencing it right then and there. Telling the person's brain to move the muscles around certain areas, to spasm in terror, if the the creature or person that was raping them had claws to open them up, the brain would intentionally open itself up and begin bleeding.

By this time the person would begin screaming in real life, or crying or vomit, or fall to the ground and weep like a child. The response was almost always the same. He looked and walk by at these outburst like a child looks and walks by snow falling from the sky, seeing every individual flake like a piece of art in a museum. Walking away with a smile on his face.

Even though he did that on the street, his work was far more interesting. These days he no longer just sat by in a chair and watched people on couches, peeling away the layers of their mind like an apple. Now he administered medicines and treatment plans—while simitaniously making the patients worse. Getting into their heads and bringing to light their darkest fears as well as fears they never knew they could be afraid of, as well as making them fear pointless objects. One patient he made them afraid of a ballpoint pen, no reason, he just made a trigger in the person's mind to scream and become terrified every time the person looked at a pen. This was his fun, his satisfaction. The satisfaction grew sometimes, when the people he would torture out on the streets, went to him to help treat what he did to them without ever recognizing him. To him that was splendid, like a gift he sent himself from the past. He would treat them, while making them worse. Just like everyone else.

Only he had to put a little bit of a rush on treatment for today. It was 9:30 and he was meeting a patient right before he would meet his sister. This was one of his favorite patients: Toby Thompson. Toby is a twenty-six year old recovering drug addict, that had a mental break(not Walter's doing) as he was was high on crystal methanphynamines, when he snapped and tried to kill a homeless man that was outside of the abandoned apartment complex on the east side of Boston, by beating him with a piece of chainlink fence post that was laying on the ground. He was doing heavy detox treatments before he came to Dr. Falkes, and when they finished the treatments, they found out that the mental break may have been caused by the drugs, but was there to stay for the foreseeable future. After the psychiatrist diagnosed the patient of psychosis result of mental break, Dr. Walter Falkes decided to pick up the patient and treat him himself.

That was seven months ago.

He saw Toby everyday at least once. In Dr. Falkes' mind, Toby was like a ball you would toss against a wall if you got bored and had nothing to do except throw it. Only disguising it as real medical treatment.

He walked down the hall toward Toby's room, meeting several doctors and nurses along the hallway as he did.

"Hello Dr. Falkes." said Miss Connie Tames, a nurse that helps him with patients every once in a while. Every once in a while he takes a peek into her mind and sees that she imagines sneaking him into a closet and doing—extra curricular activities with him. Almost every time he sees her this image usually flashes before his eyes for only a small moment. It gives him a small smile.

"Good morning Miss Tames!" As he passes, he sends a small message to her brain. She all of a sudden misses a step in her walk as she felt a small delightful spasm on her inner thigh. She too starts to smile. She notices that happens a lot around Dr. Falkes, and thinks her body is trying to tell her something.

He says good morning to about five other doctors and nurses when he finally arrives at Toby Thompson's room. Like always, he knocks three times and announces himself before entering. He always tries to identify where Toby is in the room, so he can keep a lock on his mind, and so he isn't taking by surprise and tackled to the ground by him, unexpectedly. He knows he shouldn't be here alone, rules in the hospital state that when seeing a mental patient, one should always be occupied. Only he knew he would be safe, because he could read the man's every move. It was best if no one saw what they were going to do anyways. He entered the room and saw that Toby was sitting on his bed, staring to the empty wall. Most patients had pictures hung around their room, of family, friends, or the drawings that they made in the activity area. Toby had none of these. He wasn't allowed near other patients due to his prone and repudiative behavior of attacking them in the past. Nor were any drawing utensils giving to him in the precaution that he might sharpen them into weapons of some kind. As for pictures of family, he never had any visitors from friends or family to give him any pictures of them. According to statements giving to the hospital, there was no room in the family for and abusive drug addict.

Whenever Dr. Falkes thinks about that statement he couldn't help imaging a ballroom full of people with a man in front of them behind a podium saying: "And the Parent of the a Year Award goes to..."

"Hello Toby. How are we this morning? Did you sleep well."

Tears instantly started to fall down the side of his face as he heard Walters' voice. He said, "Please—please just go away." he started to cry, on the verge of uncontrollably. "I just want to go home. Why can't I just go home?"

The nice facade of Walter's face was gone now. Only the predatory smile from his evil deeds (that became his resting face it seems) took its place. "Because you are unwanted Toby. Unwanted by your family and friends. If we release you—if *I* release you—there is no telling what you might do out there in the world.

"But here, you are wanted by me. I want to be your friend. I want to help you get better. I want to help you get rid of all of your demons" He sent Toby an image of a huge beast entering the room through the door. With two large horns on top of its head, with a red liquid covered all over its body. Toby saw and thought that it was blood. The thing was covered in blood. Muscles blew out of its body as if the thing worked out since its conception. Looking down he saw that it was naked and that the things penis was well a foot long at least, dripping with blood as well. On his feet, each toe nail had claws on it that were inches long, and sharp as razor blades. Toby's crying was turning to screams.

"Shhh. Shh-shh-shh. There is no need for that" said Walter, but the the screams kept coming from Toby. In an instant Walter made the demon disappear. Toby saw this and stopped screaming but continued in hysterical crying. "You…ah, ah, ah. You monster! Why are you doing this?"

"I'm not doing this to you at all." Walter lied. "You are the one that sees these things. Like I said I am just trying to help you." Walter saw in Toby's mind that he was going to charge at him. Reach out his hands and try to choke the life from him. Walter quickly threw into his mind a peaceful feeling of a meadow covered by flowers, and Toby was right in the middle of it. This didn't take away from Toby's anger. No Walter didn't want that. Instead it just confused Toby on where he currently was. Toby was looking around hysterically. getting up from the bed and trying to find where Walter was.

"I will check on you in a few hours. I have another appointment I have to make. You take care Toby." Then he got up from the bed and started to head out of the room. When he turned around to shut the door, he looked through the window of the door and saw that Toby was still looking frantically around the room, tears streaming down his face. He was crying as he was getting more and more lost within his own mind. Walter locked the door and walked away. Making sure he would make him lost in that field for a good three hours. That should be good enough.

He entered his office only to find that it was not empty. What greeted his eyes made him think about one of the biggest modern cliques in the world. Sitting behind his desk was Charlotte, or whatever her name was nowadays. She was dressed in a red shirt and somehow she found a pair of red jeans that looked like Ralph Lauren's worse nightmare as they were red and had cuts all up and down the legs. His desk was covered in the front so you couldn't see his legs if you were entering the room. No. She had her feet and legs on top of his desk, that was how he knew about the god-awful jeans that she was wearing.

He knew what this was too. This was her little petty way to get back at him for making her fly all the way over here from wherever she was now., instead of just going straight over to her place. Only Walter, a.k.a. Kolat wanted her to know that she did not own him like a slave from the old days, no. If she wanted to use him, she was going to have to get down on the disgusting jeans and start begging and kissing his feet. The days of using his abilities for free are long gone.

"Well, I see that patience is still eluding you these days as they have all your life Anoaka. Get those fucking legs off of my desk now if you want any hope of me doing you any favors." said Kolat.

Charlotte, a.k.a Anoaka dropped her legs to the ground and got up from the chair. "You think using my true name will scare me Kolat? A tactic equivalent to you pounding on your chest. You're pathetic as always."

"Oh, sorry *Charlotte!*" He said the name in a dragged out sarcastic tone as he made his way to the chair behind his desk. "I forget that you feel as angry and pouty as a child that just got spanked if I don't use the fake name you give yourself for this stretch of years. How many names has it been since we saw each other last?"

She sat down in the chair that faced his on the other side of the desk. "Like seventy years or something like that. I haven't really kept track. When you told me that it was sixty years since we last had our conversation on the phone, I'm thinking: and yet it seems like yesterday. Guess that's how much you bug the shit out of me."

"Once again Anoaka, you are tugging at my heart strings and make me want to help you more and more with every insult you throw at me. Or have you forgotten that you came here ask me to help you with your whole missing witness bullshit?"

"Get the fuck out of my head! Why can't you just try and have a conversation with a person like everyone else for once in your life?"

"Because, with you it will be a lot of bullshit that you have more power than me, that you hold the key to survival, and that soon all of this will be…BLAH. BLAH. BLAH. BLAH. That kind of bullshit. So I might as well just skip that part and get to the part of what you want." There was a brief pause. "What I got was that you want me to read the mind of the friend of the shit stain that got away from you, so you can call up Danny, your new house pet, to go and kill him. Only that he was friends with this witness at one point in his history. Hell, more than that, they served together in Afghanistan according to him. Which in my estimation, makes them way more than friends, they are practically brothers. Yet it doesn't matter, you are still gonna want him to kill him. Then when that is complete, you are gonna get the last soul you need for the King so you can after all these years, no, centuries, finally start trying to conceive children of your own to continue what we do. Did I get most of that right?"

"Yes. You did. So will you help me?"

The woman who's true name was Anoaka stared at the man named Kolat for a moment, when all of a sudden her head was starting to sting and weigh what felt like a ton. The light that was shining through the window was starting to blind her as she started to feel on the verge of vomiting all over Kolat's desk.

She started to yell but then lowered her voice as her own yell was starting to pierce her ears. "STOP it…Kolat of the Green I demand that you stop this at once and get out of my head!"

"The years I always knew made you stupid Anoaka of the Red, but I had no idea how stupid they made you until now."

Pain still radiated into her head that made its way all through her body, she was trying to focus her ability on him as much as she could, but it felt like her abilities and her mind were about a million miles away from one another. With all of her thought she searched for the Kolat's emotions and his touch that she did to him all those years ago. After a few moments that seemed like years to her, she finally found it and started to think of the only word that could come to her now: *up*.

Kolat's arms suddenly spread out like he was about to replace Jesus Christ on the crucifix, and started to make his way up toward the ceiling. Caught off guard, he had a surprised look on his face as he was flying straight up in the air, until it was replaced by pain as he made contact with the ceiling. As soon as he hit the ceiling with a hard thud that left a nice bump on his head he would find out later, he immediately started to fall down to the ground. As soon as he started to rise, he lost his hold on Anoaka and her pain that was in her head from the severe migraine that he was causing was starting to go away, only it was going very, very slowly. They both started to get up to their feet.

"Do you want to know why you are an idiot Anoaka, or are we going to go at it like the old days?"

"How dare you call me that! I could kill you and have your soul faster than you could think of a proper way to try and kill me. You have no right to talk to me like that!"

"I have the right for our survival you dumb red stain! You expect a man to kill another man after they shared a bond of serving with each other in combat?! He would rather die then do something like that even if you try and control his body. Last I checked, I didn't think you could even do that from half a state away! If anything he will try and warn his friend Tyler of what he is dealing with and how to kill you or us! From what I picked up, you have not touched this Tyler Green at all have you?"

Anoaka said nothing. Just glared at Kolat as the pain was going away in her head, and the sickness started to subside.

"Then you really are risking everything. What you need to do is go after the fucker yourself. And don't give me the whole 'I tried that already and he got the best of me', no, he got lucky. I can see the whole thing now, and tell you you could have easily killed him if you didn't want to show off and try to scare him, instead of just killing him.

"The second reason you are an idiot is you still didn't get the last soul you need until you find this Tyler Green. That is what truly takes the cake on stupidity. Once again you are trying to show off with the dramatics. And its going to cost you everything if you keep it up."

"If I wanted a lecture on how to run my life, I would have ran to father. The only thing I need to know is will you help me read the mind of Matt Mullen so I can kill Tyler Green?"

"Only when you have paid my prices."

"*Prices*? As in plural?"

"Yes, one of them is to be paid at this very instant without question. The other can be paid when you return."

"Return?" Anoaka looked at him skeptical. "Where am I going?"

"You are going to a patients room right now. His name is Toby Thompson. You need one last soul and it is going to be his."

"What? Who is he?"

"He is quit essentially a nobody. He has no friends or family that visit him and have disowned him after he suffered a mental break. I am going to send you in your mind on what to do to him after you take from him what you need. So you can cover your tracks."

"Why won't you be there?"

"Because I saw him right before this meeting. That would be suspicious looking to say the least if I went to go see him only minutes after saw him before. Here, take my lab coat, it has all the keys in the front pocket to get into the room. Take what you need, I will send you what you need to do after through thought in about two minutes." He sent her the room information to her through his mind. She gave him a very pissed off look.

"I had my own plans for how to do this."

"Yeah, I saw. Very poetic and childish. And a complete waste of time and chivalry toward your King. This way it is done and over with. Now do it if you want my services, or leave my lab coat, and leave my hospital." He got up and gave her his lab coat. He checked his pockets to make sure that the keys were inside one of the front pockets.

"Doesn't everyone know each other in places like these?"

Kolat gave her an inquisitive stare. "Do you not want to get the last soul? Or better question: do you not want my services anymore?"

"Of course I need your abilities. Otherwise I wouldn't have come all this way. I am merely asking if I will be spotted and recognized as someone who doesn't work here. This is pretty last minute."

"No, you are trying to get out of this because, like I read in your mind, you have plans for this sort of thing. Don't try and hide shit from me. I can read you like a pop-up book. Besides, this isn't your first time and you know better than anyone that most people won't even notice you even with your hair and your outrageously red outfit." He looked her up and down quickly at her all red clothes as he said this. "You know what? Scratch that. I have some clothes in my personal bathroom that you can wear quickly. Go in there and change, then come back out here and get a move on with what you have to do. Then come back here and you will have just one more thing to do before you have my abilities. So go on and change. Go!"

She went inside his private bathroom and change into some mens clothes that looked slightly too big for her. She was decided to put on the tie because she knew that some women could pull off the tie look and she thought that she was one of them. After she put it on she put her hair up in a bun so it would make her look more like a doctor, that gave a shit about her job. All the while being pissed off that she was already at the whim of her asshole brother. Always wanted to have the upper hand in any situation was how he always was and always had to call all the shots when it came to the two of them. She was loathing every word that shot out of his mouth as he was here. She had her own way of doing this. Her own way and act of devotion she wanted to do to get that last soul for her King. And now this piece of mind reading shit was ruining it for her. She hoped that he heard that in her mind. He always liked to sneak into her mind while she was undressing as a child. Trying to get a look at her breasts and her vagina and seeing what he could never have. Only in his fantasies. She knew this because he told her in the heat of augments he was on the verge of losing. Always when he failed to try and make a fair point, he would throw some hidden truth at her hard to try and catch her off guard. The day that he told her that he sneaked into her mind while she was undressing in front of a mirror, indeed did the trick. Once she was finished getting dressed she looked at herself in the mirror and studied herself to see that everything was in place. Then, in an act of defiance, she lifted up her hand in front of her, and shot the bird at the mirror. Thinking of just in case Kolat was watching her.

She appeared out of the bathroom, grabbed a piece of paper that was sticking straight up in Kolat's hand and walked straight toward the office door to go out into the hallway. She didn't give Kolat a glance, or even a thought, which she hoped had made him disappointed. She opened the piece of paper and knew that it had the information of her next victim on it, her reluctant victim for both prey and predator. She closed the door behind her hard, but not slamming it, and made her way toward the room that was shown to her in the piece of paper. Several people walked past her on her way to whatever room she was going, and none of them gave her a second look. She thought that the clothes she was given by her brother seemed to work out just right enough for her.

It took her about ten minutes, but she finally arrived at the room she was supposed to be at. She saw that there was a window on the door that had wires placed in the glass. She looks through it. She saw a man that appeared to be lost. He was looking all around as if he was blind and trying to search for something or someone. She opened the door and heard that there was a small creak in the door hinge that let out a tiny squeak. The man didn't react to the noise, she didn't know if he was deaf, didn't care about anyone enough to look at whoever was coming into the room, or the he had indeed not heard anything because he was trapped in his own horrors. Courtesy of Kolat a.k.a Dr. Walter Falkes.

Watching him like this made Anoaka feel something that she hadn't felt in a long time for another human: *pity*. Pity that this person fell victim to Kolat's mind games that he got sick pleasure of. Pity to know that his suffering was merely because of Kolat's boredom, and his need to mess with minds. Pity knowing that he wasn't the first, nor was he the last.

Only this sense of pity—didn't stop her. Less then a minute later there was a flash of orange that shone through the window of the closed door. Only one person saw the flash of orange, but didn't see or hear the body of Toby Thompson drop to the ground. It was Jane Otteson, a woman in her mid-twenties and brown hair, wearing a patients' robe wandering the halls with her head leaning against the wall of the hallway. She suffered from severe depressive schizophrenia and had common hallucinations of random objects or events, such as while she would eat the chair that was standing next to her would catch on fire, or that certain people would have worms or insects crawling out of ears, and noses and eyes. When she saw the flash of orange that came from the room she was approaching slowly from about twenty feet away, she closed her eyes. Thought to herself that it was all in her head, there was no orange flash. If not for the doubt in sanity, she would have known that she was not merely seeing things. Well—at least not this time. As she came to the room on the opposite side of the hallway, she made it a point to not look at the door, or inside the window. The flash may not have been real she thought, but she didn't want to see what was inside the room in case her mind wasn't finished playing tricks on her. So as she passed the room, she kept her head against the wall with her eyes shut, having the wall continue to guide her down the hallway.

Ten minutes after Jane Otteson passed the room, Anoaka appeared from the room and closed the door behind her as quietly as possible. She then walked down the hall and made her way back to Kolat's office. What she left in Toby Thompson's room was his body hanging from short bedsheets that hung from the bars on the window. Some of the doctors will say that he showed no signs of suicide, but it was not uncommon for patients to think up strong and effective Sudden Suicides, what they like to call them. They would think oh well, and then pick up the pieces.

When Anoaka got back to the office, she saw that Kolat had his briefcase in his hand sitting onto of his desk with his feet on the ground. Like he was waiting patiently for Anoaka to come back from her little trip.

"Ready when you are big sister." he said.

"Ready for what?" she thought that he was talking about the *other* price that had to be paid. *He* was the one that was a mind reader, not her.

"I'm ready to go. Well I just need to get to my place and grab some clothes, but then we can make our way to the plane afterwards. Why, what did you think I was talking about?"

Anaoka gave him a look. "You can read my mind. You know what I was thinking about asking you."

"Just because I can read minds, doesn't mean I turn it on all the time. Takes the mystery out of life, sometimes, when you know everything."

"What about the other price that needs to be paid?"

"Oh, yeah, we will get to that. Just not right now."

Anoaka looked at him with distain. Every minute of his presence was starting to become more and more irritating.

With that, they made their way back to Wisconsin. Back to home. Back to have a little chat with Matt Mullen.

Chapter 16

The biggest understatement of the decade right now would be that Matt Mullens existence was a bleak one. If you were standing next to him when you said this to him, he would try with all the strength that he could muster to try and beat the living shit out of you for pointing this out, and not helping him. The problem was that he would only be able to manage to maybe spit on you with some inaccuracy, being that all of his limbs were tied down to the floor. Tied enough to where he could maybe get to his knees and elbows, but not loose enough for any of his limbs to touch one another. His body was also covered in bruises and dried up blood that the woman named Charlotte did herself. He was completely naked, which left him freezing most of the time. When he first got to wherever this place was, he thought it was a house, it was nice and toasty down here in the dark basement, or dungeon as what it felt like. To where when he was naked it was somewhat of a relief to be giving somewhat of an escape from the scorching summer air that sometimes plagued Wisconsin in the July and August months. Then the nights in a dark underground basement, touched his skin for the first time all those months ago. He all of a sudden didn't mind the scorching summer air all that much.

Now, he didn't sleep most nights because those summer nights were making their way into crisp, cold autumn air that froze him. Sometimes when the woman would make her way down for her regular torture sessions, she would see that he was almost dead from near hypothermia. Then, she would get a thermal blanket for a few minutes so he could get warmed up—only to take it away and make the cold air wash over him, only feeling worse after having the touch of heat on him. That blanket, that fucking blanket. He grew to hate it after it was used on him over a dozen times. It was just another torture method that the woman was use to using. And she had used a lot of torture methods, some he was surprised he lived through. Most that made him feel dirty—like the crowbar. Never again with the crowbar. But right now, his hatred was aimed toward that stupid fucking thermal blanket. Special Thermal for victims of hypothermia. The kind they sell at Gander Mountain, so in case you fall through the ice while you are ice fishing and need to get warm fast. She had it just laying around down here in the basement. He thought about that most days when she wasn't around. Staring at the blanket that was always just a few feet out of reach each day. Just so he couldn't reach it. Most days he wouldn't try to reach for it because he knew that he would get a few minutes of warmth each morning when the woman came down to continue her torture. Only there was a problem now. She told him that she was leaving for a few days—maybe even a week. That was along time when you were stuck down in the basement. It felt like months. What was worse is that she only left him enough meals for about a day. A bowl of rice, that didn't look like it could feed a starving baby in his eyes, and two peanut butter sandwiches. In her exact words she said, "That is all I have for the mongrels today, try again another day."

He wished he could have beaten the shit out her right then and there. His mother always taught him never to strike a woman, but she was no woman. She was a monster. Sadistic to the core, and there would have been no remorse for beaten the shit out of her if he could. Not for what she did to him, and what she was continuing to do to him. Things that the government couldn't think up that were completely medieval. Things that weren't even possible for a human being to comprehend, let alone do. He gave a cold glance at the crowbar that was leaning against the wall. Like a strange predator that leaned against a lamppost waiting for its next victim.

Like it was watching him.

Matt looked away and couldn't bear to look at the thing. What she made him do with it. What she made him do to himself with it those weeks ago—or maybe it was months. Time was strange down here in the so called basement. Other than the food, there was the blanket, the *crowbar*, a chair, the ropes and Matt of course. For a basement, not a lot was kept down here. Not golf clubs, Christmas decorations(if she celebrated it), or any decorations for that matter, any thing that could be used for storage, certainly wasn't stored down here.

People were stored down here. People who crossed this woman, whatever that might be. People who may have seen what she is. Whatever she is. Locked away to be punished for sticking noses in her business. Tied to a floor with no clothes on. Barely any food to survive, while shitting and pissing yourself where you lay or kneel. Then, torturing you by using your body against you. How can she do that?

How can she make my arms and legs move the way she wants them? Don't I have any control over my body at all? How can she make me do those things to myself?

He asked these questions constantly to himself, and overtime he did again and again—he looks over toward the crowbar like he was now. Shuddering again at the mere look of the object, then turned away, bringing on him the shame and pushing the tears out of his eyes.

It always directed his thoughts back to the two dead bodies that where found next to the Glass Hat in the middle of June. When he saw the small piece of red fabric and thought that it was nothing worth looking at. When in truth it was probably one of the biggest clues to who could have killed those two men, even though to anyone else now, it will never go down as a murder. Not if he was going to die down here.

Small red fabric…

Was it silk? Maybe it was.

Biggest clue of them all. Biggest clue.

Red. Red…

"REEEEEEEEEEEEEEEEEEDDDDD!" he screamed as loud as he could. He hoped that one of his screams would help catch the attention of the man that helped the woman, the one that Tyler knew back in his Army days. He tried to do this even though he knew that the basement was probably sound proofed. But maybe if the man who helped the woman was anywhere in the house, there was a little hope he might give him more food. He never saw him since he was taken down here. She could have just as well possibly have killed him, which with her was never out of the question. He didn't know how long her sort of "assistance's" stayed within her employment and lived to tell about it. He doubted that they lived to tell anybody, anything. He knew if he had her powers, he wouldn't let anyone know and let them live.

Still he continued to yell every once in a while. The alternative was to give up.

Sleep was starting to take over his thoughts, and he was trying to resist going to sleep as much as he could these days. Sleep brought back dreams that were more along the lines of memory. And the memories that showed in his dreams, turned them into nightmares. He tried to fight it as much as he could, he really did. Being in the position that he was in, he tried to do push ups the best that he could so his blood could keep moving. It was hard because of his left foot, he knew that it was broken at least in two spots and it was hard to place his toes onto the ground when that sort of pain reached him. For a while he used the pain that was in his foot to try and keep himself awake, but after a while, his body got so used to the pain that it no longer worked. So he tried push-ups instead.

Lifting his left foot off the ground he started to push onto the ground.

One…Two…Three…Four…Five.

Moving up and down now, he tried to go a little bit faster. But he was so weak that he could already start feeling fatigue creeping in.

Ten…Eleven…Twelve…Thirteen…Fourteen…Fifteen.

He was starting to get winded. He started to take heavy breaths now to try and compensate for the loss of energy. No, NO! He had to concentrate now. He knew that he could do more. He had to keep his blood pumping. He had to stay awake.

Twenty…Twenty-one…Twenty-two…Twenty-three…Twenty-four…Twenty-five.

Pain was starting to make its presence known to Matt now, in his arms. Sweat was starting to show on his forehead, despite the cool air that surrounded him. Exhaustion, was starting to take him. Even though push-ups will keep your blood pumping and keep you awake for a little while, it is a poor substitute for caffeine. Eventually you will have to stop and rest, and when you do, exhaustion makes its move to make way for sleep. Weakness from the months of staying in the same spot started to curl its slender fingers around Matt's arms and very slowly started to tighten into a fist. In Matt's military days, he could have pushed up to around seventy push-ups in two minutes, now he was struggling to make it to thirty. He started to slow down more and more as he kept pumping his arms.

Thirty.........Thirty-one.........Thirty-two.........Thirty-three... He collapsed to the floor, and closed his eyes and focused on his breath. Only while having his eyes closed—the nightmare started seeping into his mind.

The door opened for the first time since he was taken from the parking lot of the police station, and taken to the basement of this place. The light that came from the ajar door, almost completely engulfed the dark basement and felt like searchlights going off inside of his brain. Nevertheless, he looked toward the doorway on top of the stairs. He saw the woman start making her way down the stairs, then hit the lights on in the basement. The pain that the lights gave him from the top of the stairs felt bad, but not as nearly as the pain he felt when the fluorescent lights came on all around him in the basement. Matt shut his eyes quickly to try and adjust them, not noticing the woman standing in front of him until he could see straight. When he could see shapes, colors, and make out objects, he saw that the woman and looked straight up at her. She looked at him like she would look at an insect. Distain, and hatred, mixed in with a desire to kill. He knew that she could too. He was there in that alley, he saw what she did to those three men that were in the alley with her. Thinking back on it, brought him a feeling of fear as he gazed upon her.

"So." the woman said. "Where is your friend? The one that was in the alley with you?"

He looked at her and tried to give her a face that revealed nothing. "What friend?"

"Don't fuck around with me Mathew, you know who I am talking about. He is the reason I took you instead of just killing you. You may think that you want to thank him for that, but you won't. Not after I am done with you you won't."

"No matter what you do to me, I'm not giving you anything." Matt said with a defiant look on his face.

"You say that now." she said with a smile on hers. "You will think twice in the not too distant future." Then she bent down and touched him on his nose as if he were a pet dog waiting for a treat. "You have no idea what is in store for you. Fuck! I don't know what is in store for you! I guess that makes it exciting on my part. I think I'm just going to hit you with whatever just comes to mind." She then bent down and reached for his right wrist that was restrained, and released it. Matt looked at this with confusion, only she didn't meet his look and merely continued toward the left wrist and started to release the restrains on that as well. Matt looked dumbfounded at her. After all the threats she was going to let me go? He looked back and saw that she was starting to make her way toward his feet and ankles. After she released them, she made her way back to stand before him. She looked at him for a moment. Then he was looking at himself and started to make his way onto his feet.

Alright? If this bitch wants me to leave, or have me loose, she can have me. But I am going to beat the shit out of her for kidnapping me! Matt thought to himself. He started to make his way toward her—only—he stood right where he was. He tried again to move his legs—but there was nothing. He stood right before her. Right before her as she smiled that God-awful smile that told you that she knew a secret.

"Trying to go somewhere, Mr. Mullen?" she said, making that smile that already seemed impossibly large get even bigger. "Trying to do something to *me*, maybe?" putting a hand on her chest as she was referring to herself. "I have a dangerous touch Mr. Mullen, a *very* dangerous touch. You should try to know what you and your friends get yourselves into before you put your noses in other people's business. Didn't your mother ever tell you that?"

Matt tried to speak but felt enormous pain as he tried to open his mouth, that he threw back his head in pain.

"I can control your speech as well. Just so you know what I am capable of. Now let's get to it. I am going to ask you some questions, I want you to be completely honest with me. As soon as I know you are not lying to me, I will let you go. And what I mean by not lying is that you lead me to the capture or death of your friend. Do you understand?"

Matt tried to speak again. This time finding that he was able too. "You don't like to beat around the bush I see."

"Believe me, Mathew. The bush isn't the thing I'm going to beat if you don't answer me truthfully."

"What happens if I don't answer at all?" He said this knowing that it sounded extremely juvenile, but it was creating the anger that he wanted in her face. It may not be much of a victory, but it did make her lose a little bit of her concentration on what she was doing. That was what he was taught, if ever in situations like this.

"I will treat all non-answers as lies. Simple as that, now do you want to talk or should I just show how much control you truly have lost in this place?"

Matt paused a moment, and looked away from her to make it look like he was considering his options. Even though he already made up his decision on what he was going to do. He was not giving in to this monster. No matter what she did to him. What exactly could she do to him, make him move around like a puppet? Better than giving her anything that could help her find Tyler. That was when he made his decision indefinitely—he wasn't going to tell her a damn thing.

"You know what cunt? I don't give a shit what the fuck you do to me. Go ahead. Make me walk around like Pinocchio tangled in strings. Hell, make me dance to the Village People for all I care. I just hope you keep me alive long enough for Tyler to come and kill the shit out of you and his good ol' boy he knew from way back in the day. 'Cause once he does, you are totally fucked."

The woman looked at him with no hint of emotion on her face. She just stared at him for what seems like hours to Matt. Then, a large smile, that horrible, evil smile that she gave him a few minutes ago, that she gave both him and Tyler back at the alleyway. All in that moment, the terror that was absent in his time here, made its roaring appearance with that smile. She wanted him to say just exactly that. Give her a big "Fuck you" right in her face, because now—she can really start to have some fun.

"Well…if that is how you truly feel…" The pain started bloom in his toes. Like a tiny little tick just starting to borrow into the skin on the tip of his toes. Then it shot like a bullet as fast as his nerve endings would allow, all the way up into his chest. Matt screamed and screamed as loud as his voice would allow, on the edge of his vocals bursting in his throat. He tried to move, but the woman was using her powers to make sure he stayed standing right in front of her like a disciplined soldier. He wanted to move more than anything. He wanted to tell her everything she wanted to know right then and there, and he was just about to—then she closed his mouth. She closed it to stop the screaming. She was so close right there to getting all the information that she wanted, he thought to himself later. Only now she was having too much fun. Nearly five seconds after she shut his mouth, she stopped the pain flowing all through his body. The pain still vibrated all around him, but it was starting to fade.

"Oh what next should I do? Oh…I think I know just the thing. Let's go get that crow bar over there." She gestured her left hand to point toward the crow bar that was laying just under the stairs. Matt's body started to move toward the stairs, walking sluggishly at first but then the woman made him straighten up and walk toward the underside of the stairs that was kept and used a a makeshift storage. When he looked underneath, all he saw was the crow bar, and a rolled-up blanket of some kind that was on top of a mat that was used in gyms. His hands were used by her to pick up the crow bar and then he made his way back to the woman, where he stood in front of her.

"Do you know what I am going to do to you Mathew?"

Matt gave no reply.

"I am going to beat you with this crow bar, only I am not going to lay a hand on it. I am going to make you beat yourself up, until I think of something better to do to you. And you are going to start doing this, right about.............now."

The crowbar that was in his right hand about halfway from the curve of the bar to the flathead pointed end, was risen above his head, at the same time his hand placement on the bar went from halfway, to being slid down to the flat pointed end right before the bar started to go flat. His right hand then came down and came down hard onto his left foot. Without stopping, it came up again and then came down onto his right leg, right below the kneecap. Then again onto his left thigh muscle, again onto his right kneecap, again on his groin. Again, and again, and again, and again—and again. The pain was unbearable. Screams of complete agony filled the basement, and wouldn't be surprised if they were heard all throughout the house. He noticed earlier that the door remained open when she came down here. His screams must have reach someone's ears other than theirs.

If someone did hear, they didn't care.

She continued to use the crow bar to beat him using the commands from his body. Even though he felt every blow and was in complete pain to the point where he knew that there were definite broken bones; his body never slowed, never faltered, never strayed away from standing in the one spot where she command him to stay. Yet he continued to raise his right arm up; then bring it down hard onto himself on some random part of his body. A few times he hit himself in the head along his jaw, where he could feel the rising of blood and some solid object move around in his mouth. Having control of his mouth again, he spat out the blood—and the tooth that he knocked out of his jaw. She even got clever about where to hit him and through some clever move that he was barely conscious for, managed to hit himself in the right arm. The same arm that was holding the crow bar that was now soaked with blood.

His screams were starting to die down now, all he felt now on his body was pain. His right eye had been hit and was starting to swell over, but with his left he could see that the crow bar was soaked with blood. He could start to feel his grip on the object loosening his hand. "Good." he thought to himself, "Maybe when its coming down on one of these swings it will fly out and strike her right in the temple. Then maybe I have a chance to—to." Only now he thought that he was kidding himself. Pain was everywhere and with each strike, causing more in fresh spots. There was no way he would escape even if that happened. No way.

As his grip was fading fast on the crow bar, his right hand took another raise above his head and then—stopped. It stood up above his head as if he were a inaccurate representation of the Statue of Liberty. He thought more like the Statue of Pain and Suffering.

"So…You ready for the first question?" asked the woman that Matt could now barely see in front of him.

Being horse from the screaming that he did as well as the immense pain he was feeling, his words were coming out in little sniffle like sounds through his sobs of pain. "Mmm….mmmmmmm…..mmaaa…..aaaaaaaaa. Kkkkkk…Iiiiiiittttttt. Sssssssssssssssss…."

"Alright I get what you are trying to say. Shit, you only did this to yourself but not wanting to cooperate. And holy shit! Did I really do a number on you. You look worse than any of Muhammad Ali's opponents, after fifteen rounds. I think I might have to take a picture of you after this because this might be my greatest work. You just determine if I should continue it further or if I stop for the day. Mind you it's still pretty early in the day. So here is the first question. Where is your friend Tyler Green?"

"Hhhhheeeeeee sh-sh-sh-sh-shoooouuuullld ba-a-ee at h-h-h-his ho-ho-ho."

The woman cut him off, "Ho-ho-ho, what are you fucking Santa Clause? No, I know what you are saying. 'He should be at his house' am I right?"

Matt just nodded.

"Well he is not at his house. There is no trace of him after I made my special appearance there the other night. So you need to tell me where he would go in an emergency. A house of a friend that he would really trust. A house that is not yours."

Matt froze and stared at her with intense eyes. What she was asking, he simply could not give her. Not because he didn't know where he could be, but in fact quite the opposite. Other than Matt himself, he thought that Tyler would only trust two or three other people to help him out of any type of jam. Of those three, one was Samantha his soon-to-be ex-wife, so he knew that was now one of the last places Tyler would go. The second he was thinking of would be Chucks' places, he probably wouldn't go there with a problem of this magnitude for the fact that Chuck had a wife and kids to look after and think about. Besides, Matt didn't think they were all that close; for the reason that Tyler knew that Matt had his own distain for Chuck, likewise for him. So he felt that he might feel inclined to pass on any help toward himself.

That left only one other person in their circle of friends that he would trust enough to help him out was Tanya. Sweet Tanya, that you would have to think twice before you cross her. Still, when he looked at this woman that was making him torture himself with a crow bar, and then thought back to Tanya; there was no question that she would be out of her depth.

"I-I-I-I d-d-d-d-on't kn-ow wh-wh-where he is."

The woman looked at him, again displaying that smile. "That's not really an answer to my question. You dodging the question with an answer that is close to the answer tells me that you are lying to me. You *do* know where he is. Or at least know who he is with. Tell me. Tell me now or I will begin again."

Matt could suddenly feel one of his legs moving on its own. The pain from his injuries was starting to rise up within him again. But he just looked at her; silent and stone faced in the wake of the rising pain and the certain threats of more pain to come. Then he said the words that were going to haunt him until the day he died. Words that sentenced him for what was to follow. Pain, humiliation, violation, and brushes with certain death that drove him to the very limits of sanity. But also became a promise to himself. A promise that told the woman in red that he was not going to talk anymore to her about him, or Tyler, or anyone else that would cause her to hurt or kill. Words we all heard spoken from defiant lips that were only three syllables long, but told you all that you needed to know about a person. He spoke them without any hesitation. He summoned whatever strength that was left in him, to say it clear and without stutter.

"Fuck you."

He expected the smile to fade from her face; for the woman to get upset and start commanding his body to begin again with the self-beatings on his body almost at once. Yet, she just stayed right where she was. Not moving from her position at all, as if she were a statue that hadn't noticed him at all. Still keeping that same sadistic smile. After the words had left his lips and saw that she kept the same face, he realized something horrible; this was exactly what she wanted him to say.

"Okay. That is how you want to play it? Fine. We will continue." she paused for a moment. "Only this time I don't think I am going to beat you. No. I have something else in mind. Something quite uncomfortable—well, for you I imagine."

Matt then, involuntary, got up onto his knees. Pain from the both of them was unbelievable. "Ah, ah." he said as he was letting out sounds of the pain. When on his knees, the rest of his body, stood ramrod straight once again. Still looking at the woman as she was watching him with enjoyment. He then was forced to bend down and grab the crow bar that he let go of and still felt that it was wet with blood. Grabbing still, with his right hand. He shot back up into a straight position, feeling every ache and pain through his body. Then to his horror— she made his upper body bend down, so that his face was kissing the ground, with dust going into his nostrils. His arms were laid out on his side; while his buttocks was up in the air as if he were a duck dipping its head underwater. Then it hit him what she was planning to do next, and started to resist as much as he could. "No. No. NO. NO. NO. PLEASE! PLEASE! NO! DON'T DO THIS! PLEASE! PLEASE!" But his cries, might as well have fallen on the ears of a statue. For she did nothing to stop what she was going to do. As he lifted to crow bar up and placed his hand on the flat end of the crow bar, her smile grew wider as if it were the smile of the devil.

The crow bar and the hand made its way toward his buttocks slowly. He screams were louder now. "PLEASE STOP IT! STOP. STOP. STOP. PLEASE I BEG OF YOU!" but a small part of his mind that was buried in pain knew that she wanted him to beg. Wanted him to realize that she was in control. Always in control. His hands still kept their course, as he spread one cheek of his buttocks.

She said one last thing before she made him do this. "I hope you enjoy it as much as I will." He then inserted the flat end of the crow bar, into his anus. There was nothing, nothing else but tears, blood and screams. Screams that seemed to have no end in sight.

And the smile of the woman.

Matt woke up from this nightmare that was a reality for him. That first time was without a doubt the worst for him. He remembered as it was going on that he was going to tell her. Tell her so she would make it stop. The pain, the horrible, violating pain. Then as it continued he realized that even if he did tell her—she would continue to do it to him after, maybe even until he died doing it to himself. That was the worst thought. So even though he screamed then and many times since that horrible day, and night, he kept his mouth shut toward her. Yes, he did tell her lies, which led him to feel even more pain in many other different ways, but it was necessary he always told himself. So he wouldn't tell the woman the truth about what he knew.

Now his concern for himself was almost completely gone. He knew that he was going to die in this basement. Starvation was probably going to be the cause. He was out of food now. He ate the rest of it right before he went to sleep this time around. If his sleep patterns were going only at night time(which he highly doubted), and each wake-up was the beginning of a new day, then he would be on day sixty-eight. He didn't bother lifting up the water bottle, he knew that it was now empty. He was just stuck here with no food now, and no water. Waiting to starve, waiting to die, waiting for the beatings to continue.

Hours passed him like cars passing a statue in a cemetery, slow and malevolent. The urine that was around his legs from when he last pissed the last couple of sleep cycles ago, was still around him. There was no where for it to go or to be evaporated. So it just stayed right by his knee just like the shit that was now caked on part of his legs. He tried his best to move his body away from where it normally rested on the floor to where he went to release himself, but there is only so much space he was allowed, and he had been there a long time. Eventually, his pile of urine and shit slowly made its way into contact with his body. Making him feel even more dirty than he already felt about himself alre—

A noise that would seem like a small squeak and completely ordinary to anyone else on the outside, rang like a shotgun blast in the constant silence that filled the basement nonstop. The doorknob from the door on the top of the stairs leading into the basement began to open. The door flew open and before Matt could turn and get a good look at the woman, she quickly hit the lights that cause instant blindness throughout his eyes.

"What the fuck An…Charlotte? It smells like shit down here. Don't you take care of his leavings at all?"

That sounded like it came from a man? Matt was thinking to himself. His eyes were still trying to adjust to the light, because all he was seeing as he was looking toward the voice was white light.

"I thought he was the type of person that could pick up after himself. Beside he looks so comfortable in it don't you agree?" said a voice Matt knew all too familiar. Only now after how long, he finally had a name to this bitch. Charlotte. Only he caught that the man was going to call her something else at first, but then repressed it and called her Charlotte. Probably a fake name. Still it was better than not calling her anything.

"Yes well I don't agree with it at all. If you are going to keep a prisoner, you must clean up after it at all times. Now, I have to work with the smell of shit and piss fighting over the attention of my brain. Thank you very much for that."

Matt caught another thing right there. He called him "it". Meaning this man, whoever he was, had no intention of helping him at all. No. He was going to help *her*.

"Somehow. I know you can manage it. Now please get to work on him."

Matt lifted his head as the shapes were starting to appear before him. He saw the woman who's name is Charlotte. All dressed in a red shirt and jeans that looks horrible. Complete with a pair of red tennis shoes. Matt had a small thought that no one would ever really go out in public and wear that sort of thing. But his attention was toward the man that was with her. He was almost just like Charlotte, dressed from head to toe in a certain color, only it was a suit like he was going to go to the office right after he was done with whatever business he had to do here; only the color was not red; it was green.

Green leather shoes that were a dark green that looked like he had rotten eggs all over them. Pant suit, jacket and tie that were all matched to the same shade of green, Matt thought that the only completion of this image was if he sat down on the Blarney Stone and kissed a shamrock that was in his hand, he would be mistaken as a leprechaun.

What the fuck were these two? Staying with the same color of their clothes. Since Matt saw the woman in the alley, it has been nothing but red. Red, red, red, red, red. Now Mr. Luck-of-the-Irish here with all the green that a man could legally pull off in public right before him. Something was with these two that just wasn't adding up. Tyler and himself stepped into something bizarre to say the least.

"I can't." said the man in green. Charlotte gave him a look of anger.

"What do you mean you can't? That was why I brought you here!"

"I see you have starved him as well as kept water from him for a long time."

The look was continuing to be thrown at the man by Charlotte as if she was trying to burrow a hole into his skull with it. "What about it?"

"It needs to be fed and watered for me to be most effective. I was hoping to have this talk in private, because now he is going to fight his way from receiving any food or water, but you force my hand once again with you and your stupid rules. So now you need to feed him or I am going to have a lot of trouble to helping you out."

Charlotte, looked down onto Matt, as Matt stared back at her. He wanted to fight having any food or water to stop, whatever this man was going to do to him. Only, Matt knew that this play just wasn't in the cards. He was starving and needed food badly. Water would be just as great touching his dry and cracked lips. He saw in her eyes that she saw there was no fighting the need for food or water with him. He just wanted a taste of either. "I will be right back." she told the man in green, but looked directly at Matt. A minute later she was up at the top of the stairs and closed the door behind her.

"Forgive her. She can be quite the idiot sometimes. Especially around me. Just because I am always the smarter of us. So she really can't help it too much. I understand that your name is Matt. My name is Walter. I would ask you 'How do you do?', but I can see that you are pretty much on the other side of well these days. Tell me, has she washed you down since you have been down here?"

"Not really." Matt's horse voice said.

"I figured as much. She really is a stone cold bitch, isn't she? Leaving you down here, chained to the floor to rot apart like a laid to waste pumpkin. Tragic, I think. Just downright tragic. I will have to have a talk with little Miss Charlotte as soon as she makes her way down here with your food."

The man in green just stood where he was and looked at Matt without another word. Nor did Matt give him anymore words. He said he would talk to her about the condition in which he was kept, he didn't say that he was going to try and convince her to let him go. He would rather have him tell her that.

A few minutes went by as the two men stayed silent where they were. Matt chained to the ground while the man in green stood right before him, when the door to the basement opened once again. Matt looked to the top of the stairs and saw that it was Charlotte with a tray with a bowl and a glass with a substance in it he could only assume that it was water. There was a disgusted and hurtful look on her face as she was stepping closer to the two men down the stairs. When she reached the bottom, she dropped the tray down onto the ground with a loud BANG! that echoed throughout the basement. The bowl that was on the tray tipped over, spilling the rice that was inside, and the glass of water tipped over as well, but mainly spilled inside of the tray. Leaving very little inside the glass. Matt didn't care. He would have eaten it if she had spat in the rice and water. He was that hungry. He started to devour both the rice and the water that was in the glass and tray as soon as it hit the floor.

"That was unnecessary Charlotte. You must not want my help if you insist on pulling such childish pranks on this poor man."

"Spare me and him with your false sympathies, Walter. Just get on with it." Matt looked up at the both of them as he was continuing to eat.

"I need to wait until he is finished, but isn't there something that you could do in the meantime?" asked the man in green.

"What do you mean?" asked Charlotte.

"There was another price to be paid while you required my services, and I believe that it is upstairs right now. Or more accurately, someone. Go to him and finish your stupid poetic romance right now. Do it. And by the time you are finished, I will give you what you want."

Matt felt the fear in him now. *Give her what she wanted! Who was helping Tyler out! What the fuck was this guy? Some expert torturer more skilled than controlling how his body moved? And who was upstairs now that needed her attention?* Matt stopped eating as he had these thoughts, and just stared at Charlotte. She looked at him with her wide green eyes with her angry look. Either he said something in front of Matt that wasn't suppose to be said in his presence. Or she was not looking forward to what he was talking about. Whatever it was it caused her to stare at the man in green for what seemed like an eternity. Then without another word she turned and looked down at Matt, taking a good look at her handy work that she made in the last few months, and smiled at him. She then started to walk away and make her way up the stairs, and then closed the door behind her.

The man in green then looked down at Matt, and produced a small malevolent smile of his own. "Finish up eating, then we can begin."

Matt spoke through a horse voice, "You didn't tell her to wash me off like you said you would."

"No—I didn't. But I will once we are finished." the man in green started to walk toward Matt. Matt's fear rose within in him.

There was screaming of both kinds in that house as that day went on. In the basement, Kolat was both getting the information that Anoaka desired and had his fun as Matt screamed and wept from digging and discarding information from Matt's mind. As well as putting new and fresh nightmares in his mind that tore Matt's sanity apart. Kola found that what his sister had done to Mr. Mullen already pushed him to the brink of insanity already. In Kolat's mind, what he did to Matt was very little compared to what he was used too with other people. Nonetheless, he got some information that his sister required, but he was going to wait in the shit and piss smelling basement until she returned from paying the price that he required her to do.

The price that was required of Anoaka was to stop putting off what was required of her. She was to go to her King. Her King that was by her side for so many, many centuries and finally enable the act that she was waiting for, instead of waiting for some stupid act of love in which they were going to act upon. It was time. The King had reached the proper amount of age and now it was time. And now she had the final soul that was required for him. No time but now.

She made her way to the third floor of the house and enter the King's room. There she saw him standing before their closet getting dressed. She went over by him and stopped him from going any further. She spoke low, soft, and loving words to him as she turned him around and put an arm in him shirt that made its way down toward the belt of his pants. Her lips met his and after a small and brief flash of orange that made its way into her King's mouth, it was followed by her tongue.

They made their way toward the bed, and completed their work that she yearned for for so long. Her screams were loud and filled with pleasure.

Chapter 17

Danny heard his phone start to ring as he was walking down the streets of Wausau. He reached into his suit pocket and looked at the name, then felt his heart sank a little bit. He answered it, "Hello?"

"What are you up too?" asked Charlotte.

"I am walking down the street getting ready to eat lunch over at the Mint. Why? What's up?"

"Yeah, well lunch is canceled. You need to check out these locations. One of them is pretty far away. But the other is in the Wausau area, in the township of Kroenewetter. Its all apart of the Rothschild up there here is the address."

She gave him both the address that was close by and the one that was far away. Finally after the summer had past on, Danny thought it was going to take forever to get a lead on his old friend. Not that he was really complaining about being away from Charlotte and her sadistic ways. In a way having him up here somewhat looking for every little clue was sort of like having a working vacation. Yes it was true that he was going from place to place at whatever little whim that Charlotte was giving him, but he never really thought that his old friend was going to stick around in the area after what he saw Charlotte doing in that alleyway a few months ago. Tyler was always trying to do the right thing when it came to doing the right thing, which sounds like gibberish but it usually just meant that it caused more problems for him then there should be. He knew that Tyler would always try and do the right thing, even if it cost him his life.

"Are you still there Danny boy?" Charlotte asked in a tone that told him she was smiling.

"Yes ma'am. I am still here I will go and check these out right now. I will keep you informed on what I find."

"Thank you Danny, you do just that." then there was a click on the other end of the line. Then his phone went back to the menu screen, and he put it back in his suit jacket. Then, his phone rang with a text message, he pulled it out again and saw that both the addresses were on there so he wouldn't forget. He thought that she must really have faith that one of these places houses Tyler and whoever is helping him. Danny was probably thinking that it was the woman who's house he went to where he found Tyler's broken phone. Only, he checked that woman's place, her family, any other places that she might have own. There was nothing. She may be with him, but she was hiding him really well. Danny knew that a lot of the locals had cabins that were up in the northern part of the state, and that Tyler was more than likely up there somewhere. But going up there from lake to lake, and cabin to cabin, would be like trying to find a needle in a haystack. Maybe even a little worse, up in those places you couldn't even ask any of the neighbors if they knew of anything, because they mostly kept to themselves when they would be in their cabins unless they were inviting other people to come and join them. If you were not part of their group—you might as well forget talking to them unless it was to wave and spread your cheer and happiness that you were having on those lakes. Those many, many lakes.

Danny knew that Minnesota got its popularity by saying that it was the state with ten-thousand lakes, but he knew that Wisconsin had more lakes than Minnesota. Wisconsin was out-laking Minnesota by over five-thousand more lakes than its neighbor. The reason this isn't more known is two reasons: one, nobody cares, and two, most of the lakes that are in Wisconsin had no names to them at all. Some of these lakes had cabins on them, that only the locals would give them their own makeshift name. Not known to the state of Wisconsin, so they would(in the states eyes) have no name. If you were a local this was no problem, if you were an interloper, you had a problem finding your way. As well as finding anybody you were looking for.

Danny went deep into talks with Charlotte on why he shouldn't go up there on her request and just start looking at cabins. Stressing that the work would take forever without any real knowledge that Danny was getting any closer to his old friend's hiding spot. In fact, he might just be moving away from him and in the meantime, start causing waves that might be heard from Tyler or his friends that were hiding him. Making Tyler disappear altogether. "Or cause him to make mistakes." she said as her only argument. Explaining to her that it was highly unlikely because he reminded her that Tyler was a skilled soldier that knew how to evade an enemy if he wanted to, she finally relented and told Danny that he was to stay in Wausau until they found out further information from the man that was being tied up in the basement of the house. Danny agreed to this and stayed in Wausau at the old house on the far side of Rib Mountain since then.

While being here he was sincerely looking for any type of clue that Tyler was in the area, even though it was highly unlikely, he still maintained that he was still doing his job. Though most of the days were filled with looking through newspapers that brought up the story of the missing place officer now residing in his lady's basement, he found no new information on Tyler. Some days he would be sent to check out a certain location and another, always finding nothing on Tyler. Danny started to think(and would have guessed right) that Charlotte was just guessing in certain probable spots on Tyler's location. At one point she thought that he was in Sturgeon Bay and he should try and check out one of the islands that were off the shore. He had no idea what made her think of such a location, but he checked it out nonetheless, because that was what he was ordered to do. Still finding nothing.

As it went on he started to enjoy himself and visited these places, like he was a tourist. He knew that he was hoping that Tyler wouldn't be at any of these random spots. Mostly because he wanted Tyler to win at this game. He wanted him to kill Charlotte and this King that was walking about on the third floor of the house. Visible for all to see but Danny. He never knew exactly what they were up too, but he knew if it involved a person that stole the souls of people, it was nothing good. He thought that if anyone could at this point beat Charlotte, it was Tyler. As much as he hoped never to find Tyler, he had hoped to at least help him beat Charlotte. He knew that to get past Charlotte's ability was close to impossible, no matter how far away you ran. So… he continued his search—and continued to find nothing.

Of all the locations that were always sent to him, none of them had been addresses. Set in stone addresses. This told Danny that Mr. Matt Mullen—must have spilled the beans on his and Danny's friend. Danny knew that Matt was more than likely going to end up a corpse by the end of the day if they led to Tyler. Which made Danny's heart sink, just a little lower. Vacation for the time being…was over.

First things first. He was being sent to the Kroenwetter address and started to approach it twenty minutes after receiving the text. Looking around the neighborhood he could start to see houses that were lined up in a row of their lots. The beginnings of Halloween decorations and leaf changing in the trees and in the yards were making their way into the season as well as the neighborhood. Kids were running around playing in the leaves as parents were racking them into piles, while the kids were hopping into them. Sometimes making a bigger mess than before, sometimes just keeping the leaves on top of the pile and merely broke them into smaller pieces upon themselves. Danny watched these kids and adults in their lives, not noticing him as he drove by. They were laughing and yelling at one another, all in all having a good time in each others company.

Danny envied them. He wanted that more than anything right now. To have little ones and play with them in their sandboxes, their leaf piles, in a pool. Try an tickle them until they couldn't take it anymore, play with their action figures or their dolls. He wanted that. He wanted that more than anything right now. Kids to protect from the world and monsters that he had come to know in the past two years. To have a home on a street just like this with a small house to have. Not the mansion that he resided in now with the female equivalent to the bogeyman. He yearned for that peace, that salvation of a simple life. He thought that he would never enjoy such simple and unattainable dreams such as what he was passing now. Sometimes when you have been helping evil for so long, you never learn where you pass the point of damning your soul. He didn't know where, only that is was in fact, damned.

His GPS told him that he needed to take a left on the upcoming intersection, then the destination would be on his right. He approached the intersection and signaled that he would be turning. He approached the house; a nice one story house with white siding on the top half of the sides, while finished with brick siding on the lower half of the house. There was a nice maple tree in the front yard that was complete with a rope swing in one of the branches. There was an attached garage, with a big dark green garage door on it. Danny thought this garage door was a little oddly mismatched because the major colors that seemed to go with the rest of the house were white and brick red.

He didn't pay anymore attention to the features of the house. Danny was mentally preparing himself for what he was going to have to do once he approached the house. He knew what Charlotte would want him to do: *ask questions first, then kill who was there.* Danny always thought this approach was counter productive, so most of the time he would waited it out until someone was there alone and then corner them and get answers out of them by whatever means he had to do. He couldn't do it that way this time, because he got a feeling from Charlotte that time was all of a sudden of the essence.

So what was he to do?

He thought it over in his head and thought that the only way to go through with what he had to do was to do it Charlotte's way. He was going to have to cover his tracks the best he could if it came down to that. Maybe wait until night had fallen to remove the bodies if there was more than one. Who was he kidding? He would have to wait until night had fallen anyway if he was going to kill anyone. He looked at the house again, seeing if he could see any walks of life. So far he couldn't see any movement…but that didn't meant the place was empty. He hoped it was empty. God, oh God did he hope it was empty.

He started to get out of his black SUV, and started to make his way up the driveway.

Charles was having a hard time getting things to work on his offset press. The ink that he was using must have had its lid open just a hair, which caused a lot of the ink that was in the can of cyan, to be dry. If he had another can, there wouldn't be much of a problem, but that was the last can of cyan he had until he got paid at his other work. He had enough money now to order a fresh can of cyan ink, but that wouldn't help him right now, because you couldn't just go and pick up this kind of ink for an offset press over at the local Walmart. You had to special order it; which costs a lot of money in the first place; and he and Cindy had to still get groceries so they could survive until next paycheck.

If he could just get enough ink out of the can to finish this job of business cards and stationaries, they would be able to pay for more than a months worth of groceries, a fresh can of ink, and get his boy's Halloween costume before the prices gone up enough. Jordy would love that! Only he was thinking he was at one of those famous crossroad points when you are on the verge of just finishing a job to get you that nice paycheck before the paycheck, and was just one thing shy of completing the job. In this case, a few more ounces of cyan ink. Sometimes life just sucks when it can't give you just a small break that way. He tried to dig deep in the can with his Puddie knife, bring to scrap some working ink together to put in the offset press' ink well. He was making it work well too. It thought that maybe there was hope left for him after all. Cindy would think that there are some small blessing if he could get this job finished. Things were tough these days, and he knew why. When you tried to help your friends out, there was always a little suffering that went your way, a little sacrifice of happiness. Only in time, you knew that it would be paid back. He knew that helping Tyler was the right thing. It just was causing a bit of a strain on himself more than he would like. He pitched in with Tanya to help get food to him up at the cabin, but without Cindy knowing about it, it had to consist of some financial magic on his part. Sure they were bringing in two incomes, but these days it was harder when you were providing food to someone that was wanted for questioning and possible kidnapping by the cops.

As soon as the reports came in that Tyler might have kidnapped Matt, he knew it wasn't true. Charlie had his own reasons for disliking Matt, but he knew that Tyler and Matt were way too good of friends to do that to each other. Besides, if he was laying all his cards on the table, he thought that Matt would be able to take Tyler if it came down to a fight between the two.

Charlie was remembering back to when Tyler came to him early in the morning at the beginning of July, Tanya right beside him, asking for his help. Waking up before his wife got up, and seeing them cross his yard, he met them at the front door before they rang the doorbell. So not to wake up Cindy and Jordy. Opening they door he looked at them with dumbfounded confusion. "What are you two doing here?"

"We need your help Charlie, and we need it without involving your family." said Tyler.

"What do you mean? Is it dangerous?"

"Yes." Tyler said to him. "It is very dangerous, but you are the only person that I know she can't find. Otherwise I wouldn't put your family in danger."

"Put my family in danger? What is this?" Charlie was starting to get upset at the mention of his family potentionally being put in harm's way. "You better start giving me answers before I start helping you out in any way. Not even money for gas."

Tanya stepped forward. "Listen Charlie, we will tell you everything that you need to know in due time, but right now, we need to hide somewhere that is out of town. Do you know where there would be such a place?"

"Doesn't your family have a cabin up north somewhere Tanya? Why don't you go up there and hide out?"

"Charlie, we already thought about that and we know that that wouldn't work. The person that is after Tyler, now knows most likely that I am helping him out. If they know that, they will have someone waiting for the both of us. Please Charlie. Do you have somewhere for us to hide out for awhile?"

"I have a cabin up in Eagle River. It barely gets touched in the summer months because it's not like its near a lake or anything. But I don't want to give it to you until you do some explaining."

Tyler started to step forward and looked deep into Charlie's eyes. Charlie saw a lot of exhaustion as well as anger that didn't look pretty on the surface, and knew that it was even uglier only skin deep.

"Charlie. We need to do this now, okay? I promise you, we wouldn't be here if it was important and if we could avoid the risk toward you. But we need to move now! All we need is the address, we will make our way up there and get in our way if you don't want to surrender the keys to avoid suspicion from your wife. I will understand that. Please don't make me get your family involved by coming in and asking them for the address. I don't want to do that."

Charlie looked at him and knew that he meant it. "They are asleep. I will tell you just please don't wake them." He gave both Tyler and Tanya the address to the cabin. "There is no need to break in. There is a key under the first step on the far left side, you can get in that way."

"Thank you Charlie. I will explain everything when I get a chance."

"You better. I will see you next weekend to get that story. I don't need to tell you that you owe me, do I?"

Tyler didn't say anything, he just looked back at Charlie as he was making his way back toward Tanya's car and gave him a nod. Then, they both climb into the vehicle and drove off. He didn't see the two of them until he drove up to his cabin like he said he was the next weekend. By that time, he was mad as a hornet that just found out he had been swatted at. He drove up to the cabin alone, except for a couple of newspapers that were in the passenger seat next to him. Each of the papers contain two big pictures of both Matt, and Tyler. Headlines of missing Police officer. Both men missing. Tyler Green suspected to be culprit. *What the fuck did he get involved in?*

When he got to the cabin he got the answers he was looking for. Sympathized with him for what had happened. As soon as the story was told, he had plenty of questions; all of them answered, but for the life of him now, he couldn't remember a lot of them that were so important. He knew a lot of the questions were about the woman that was after the two of them. Those questions seemed like they would never go away.

He snapped back into reality when he looked at the ink can and finally figured that he wouldn't get that last scrap of cyan out of the can. He gave up and decide he would have to get a new can, when he felt the sudden urge to go to the bathroom. He notice that he was going to the bathroom more and more this days. He hoped that he wasn't starting to get that cancer that made you pee a lot. That would be the day. Hiding a potential fugitive and his friend, while slowly going broke trying to help out feeding them when suddenly…BAM! The big C. Coming up to bite you right in the ass. Or was it the groin? He didn't really know, but he did make a mental note to himself to make a doctor's appointment abou—

There was a knock on the door, followed by a DING-DONG of the doorbell. He always thought that people need to look around on doorframe so they could find the doorbell. Knocking on the door seemed so stupid over just looking for the bell. Whatever. Someone was at the door.

"Coming!" he yelled out from the bathroom. He was in mid-piss when the knock/doorbell came to his ears. He pushed a little harder so that he could finish faster. Once he finished he zipped up, washed his hands quick and and made his way to the front door.

As he turned from the hallway to the front door, he saw that the image through the foggy glass on the door that it must have been a man in a suit. His mind immediately went thought about where Cindy and Jordy were, then he remembered that they were out to go to the Cedar Creek Indoor Waterpark, for the last weekend special that they were throwing for the end of summer. Thinking to himself that he would just have to scare off a local Jehovah Witness, he made his way toward the front door, prepared to let the gentleman down lightly that he had already been saved by Our Lord, Jesus Christ.

He opened the door, "Hello can I help you?"

The man in the suit grinned, "Yes. Hi. I'm Special Agent Moore with the Federal Bureau of Investigation. I was wondering if you could answer a few questions for me?"

"If you are FBI, can I please see your badge?"

"Oh yes, sorry. I forgot to get it out." The man in the suit said and then pulled out his wallet and flashed his badge very briefly that Charlie couldn't read the words that were on that badge. Something started to smell fishy. Yet he kept his eyes on the man and gave him a smile.

"Thank you, Special Agent Moore. What do you have to ask me?"

The man flashed a smile at Charlie. "Well, for starters, I was wondering if I could come in?"

Charlie hesitated for a small moment, but then opened the door and said, "Of course, sorry. Seems like you are not the only one that is forgetting stuff. You; your badge, me; my manners. Please come on in!"

"Thank you so much." said Special Agent Moore. "Lets talk in the kitchen. Is your family home at all?"

Charlie stopped stunned for a moment. "How did you know that I had a family?"

Moore pointed to the wall. "There are picture on the wall. Unless those are someone else's wife and child you are posing for?" he gave that smile again. Only this time it looked a little pushed upon his face.

Charlie chuckled, "Oh right. No, they are not here. They are out for the afternoon. Tell me what is this about?"

The smile on Moore's face disappeared, and turned into a grimace. "Do you know the whereabouts of Tyler Green or Tanya Walsh?"

Charlie looked at him for a second, then answered, "I don't know who that is?"

"Which one?"

"Excuse me?"

"Which one don't you know? Tyler Green or Tanya Walsh?"

"Neither of them. Who are they?"

There was a moment of silence as the man in the suit that called himself Moore stared at Charlie.

"You know I see that you get the Daily Herald."

"What?"

"The Wausau Daily Herald. The local newspaper. I see that you have a subscription."

"Yeah?" Charlie was a little confused by this turn in the conversation. "What about it?"

"I also see that you have a radio, a television, and on the outside I swear I remember seeing a dish on your roof. Am I correct?"

What does that have to do with Tyler Green or Tanya Walsh?"

"It just confuses me to think that you have no idea who they are, when they have been the subject of news for quite some time in this area." The man that called himself Moore continued giving him a face of complete loathing toward Charlie. "Seems like everyone in this city or the surrounding area's would know who they are. Wanted for the known whereabouts and safety of Officer Mathew Mullen. You are telling me you don't know who they are?"

"My wife is the one that reads the news in our household. That is her subscription." *Oh shit* he thought to himself. *I don't want to get Cindy involved with Tyler's crap. Now this guy is going to want to talk to her about Tyler and she won't hold back because she knows that I am friends with him. Fuck!*

"You are saying that you have no idea about Tyler Green?"

"That is right, and unless you have a warrant I am going to have to ask you to leave please."

The man in the suit just stood where he was. "I'm not going anywhere, Charles." The way he said "Charles" made Charlie shiver a little with fear. "You are going to tell me where they are and what you know about them. *If* you know something that I don't already know. And you are going to tell me…now" Moore started to walk towards Charlie. Charlie was against the counter. He saw that the knife rack was behind Moore, that was a major problem.

"Who are you? Really?"

"Didn't Tyler already tell you who I am? I know you two must have been talking. Where is he Charlie, or I swear there will be no pieces left of you for your family to bury."

At that moment, for some crazy reason, Charlie's fear dissipated. He looked at the man square in the face and saw that the man winced as he did. "Danny. Oh Danny. Yes he did tell me about you. About how you helped him get away. Why do that if you were going to hunt him down and kill him? Why not kill him then, on that night in the alley? Why?"

Danny stopped and froze where he stood. Words escaped him as silence filled the room with the look of Charlie looking at him curiously. What could he say? The only thing that came to him was the truth. "I want him to kill her."

"What?" asked Charlie. Confused

He regretted the words as soon as they were spoken. Almost everyday since she freed him from that bunker two years ago, he wanted her dead. He was afraid of her. Afraid that she would decide to kill a whole family one night of decide that she needed to go out and pick up a stranger and just kill him for his soul. For two years, all he knew was fear. He was afraid now that she was sensing this conversation. He needed to stop.

"Tell me where he is?"

"You want him to kill her?"

"Shut your fucking mouth! Just tell me where he is."

"I'm protecting my friend, I can't tell you where he is."

"Ha…Then you leave me no choice." Danny pulled out his gun in one quick movement and shot Charlie right in the kneecap.

Blood splattered up onto the walls and the cupboards in the kitchen, as well as on Danny's suit. The screams that came from Charlie were almost deafening, but Danny thought that he didn't have time for that.

"Tell me now where they are. Tell me, and I will let you keep the other leg, and still might have a chance to walk again. TELL ME NOW!"

Charlie tried to keep his screaming under control by biting his lip, but it was no good, the pain was too great. He held his leg for a long time it felt like when suddenly it roared back with more pain as he felt pressure on his leg. He opened his eyes and saw that Danny was putting a foot on what was left of his kneecap. The smell of blood filled his nostrils, and found that the pain made him loose control of his saliva as he began to drool onto the floor. Danny screamed at him, "WHERE IS HE MOTHER FUCKER?"

"A…At m-my cabin……..he he's th-there. With-with Tanya." he spoke through tears and sobs.

"What's the address?"

Charlie gave it to Danny, it took a long time as Charlie was fighting his way through the pain to tell him. When he was finished, Danny's face went blank and started to pull something out of his suit jacket. Charlie was relieved to see it was a phone. he pushed a couple of buttons and then should it to Charlie. "Is this the address?"

Charlie looked at the phone and saw that it was. He also saw that it was sent from another person, and was confused by this. "Y-yes. H-How d-d-did y-you….get th-that ad-address?"

"Never mind about that. Right now you need to worry about yourself more than anything." Danny said as he started to adjust his suit.

"Ar-are you l-l-leaving n-now? I-I n-need a d-d-d-doctor. P-pl-please call m-me an am-bulan-ce" Charlie sobbed.

Danny started to walk away from him. He got halfway to the door down the small hallway from the kitchen when he said. "Sorry, no hospital, under orders." He then pulled out the gun again from his jacket and aimed it at Charlie's head.

All that Charlie thought about before his time was up, was the faces of both his wife and son playing at the waterpark. How they were having a wonderful time and how they were going to be so horrified when they would see him laying here on the ground. Then there was a big white flash that went before his vision, and then darkness.

Danny moved a little ways down the hall so he wouldn't get anymore blood splatter on him anymore than there already was. He knew that he had to move fast if he was going to get this body moved before the wife and child would make their way home. He was so over taken by the man's question about what happened in the alleyway, that he forgot to ask him when the rest of his family was going to come home. "Fuck." he said aloud.

He moved over the man and made his way to the cupboard under the sink. He looked down and saw what he was looking for; garbage bags, and to his luck, there were black. If they were white, or if they simple didn't have an garbage bags, he had some plastic is car that would work just as well. Unfortunately it was clear plastic, but that wouldn't matter now that he found some black garbage bags in the house.

It took him almost thirty minutes to get the body in the plastic garbage bags(all in one piece) as well as cleaning the kitchen of blood spatter before he was ready to go. He went outside and looked around the neighborhood. He saw no nosey neighbors by his judgment anywhere, as he looked at all the windows and doorways of each house. He then backed his car up the driveway, so that the trunk was facing the front door. He quickly popped the trunk and then made his way back into the house.

Once again he looked around the neighborhood for any lingering eyes. Judging again, and seeing none, he lifted the heavy, heavy dead weigh that was covered in plastic garbage bags and made his way to the trunk. Lifting dead weight was never easy, and Danny hated it more and more each time he was forced to do it. Yet he was prepared for how heavy the man was going to be and got him in the truck quickly. Once in, he slammed the trunk down and looked around, he saw someone walk past a porch window briefly, but didn't think that the person saw him. Still he thought that there was always the possibility that someone snooped in his direction and thought it best to get the hell out of here. He got in the car, started it up, and drove away.

Ten minutes later, as Danny made his way on Highway 51 North to his next destination where Tyler was going to be, Charlie's wife Cindy and his son Jordy pulled into the house just as they finished swimming at the Cedar Creek Lodge. Not knowing that as soon as they got in the house, a man they both loved very much, wasn't going to be there.

Chapter 18

Walter White.

Walter White. Walter White. Walter fucking White! That was all that could run through his mind right now. Tyler was a fan of the show *Breaking Bad* like most of his Army buddies when it first came out. It was done really well for a television series and was one of his favorite shows all the way up until its end in 2013. The whole concept of making meth was a little unpleasant for his taste, but he like what it would take for someone who has been good for so long, to turn into a drug lord that had no problem with killing people.

What made him think about Walter White right now was the last episodes in the series. In the series, he is stuck in a cabin that is surrounded by snow in the middle of the woods. All alone and without his family and friends. Cops looking for him everywhere. No one wanting to help him without needing a lot of money for the time. He remembered that he had to give the man that was helping him get food and supplies for his cancer another ten-thousand dollars so he could stay for another hour for the company. It was incredibly sad to see him have a wonderful—if not flawed—life with his family, to being reduced to becoming the most wanted man in the United States.

Right now, Tyler could sympathize with Walter White. Right now, in a way, he was Walter White.

He looked out the window of the cabin and wished that he could make his way to the road and just go for a walk down the thin gravel lane. To take a car and drive into town and go through a store, without anyone noticing him and grab for the phone to get the police. To go to the nearest lake and go for a swim without anyone riding in their boat and noticing him. Mostly, get Matt out of whatever hell he was going through, and kill that bitch that took him.

He wanted to.

He wanted so many times to go and take the car from Tanya and just drive down to wherever he was with his gun and come up to the woman and shoot her square in the head. He saw that she could bleed. That she could be wounded. He had done that to her; right on her left shoulder, he saw the blood. There was something else there as well; her anger. That bullet didn't slow her down at all. If anything it motivated her to come after him faster so she could kill him as fast as she could. She failed this time, but would she if he came to her, on her home territory? Most likely. He thought that he could try and get some help from either one of his old Army buddies, or hell maybe even his dad might be able to. He scratched those plans as soon as he took a look at Tanya. At the time she was watching T.V. and and was watching *The Wizard of Oz* on a DVD that was left up here by Charlie and his family. That also got him thinking about Charlie.

These people. His friends, that he cared about so much. Tanya, Charlie…Matt. All of them were now in danger because he put them in danger. Matt was taken, Tanya on the run with him. If someone found out that they were here, they would drag Charlie into the nearest police station along with his family. Tyler could have that. No way. Not one more person, it was too dangerous.

So he had to find a way to arm himself. That was what he told himself next. Tanya had her handgun on her which was good. When they left her house, Tyler convicted her that they had to swing by his house and he could pick his gun up off the floor after his altercation with the Scarlet Bitch. Only when he arrived at the apartment, it was flooded with cops. They turned onto the street and saw almost a half a mile away, where his apartment was, squad cars and lights that filled the area. Getting his gun at his house was no longer a sane option. After they arrived at the cabin, with the stern talk with Charlie. Tyler found that there were two hunting rifles in the see through attic. He got them down and cleaned them and found that they could be very useful; once they had ammunition. Now the problem with that was to get the ammunition…in town. That was going to be a problem.

As much as the community of Eagle River was friendly toward strangers, they were not in particularly in good spirits, he was sure, of potential kidnappers. Tanya was able to get some ammunition, but it had to take repeated visits to the local gun shop, so they could stock pile some of it, until she was told she reached her limit for the next six months. That wasn't easy considering they didn't have a lot of money in the first place. In total, they had six boxes of rifle ammunition, and two boxes for Tanya's handgun.

Tyler wished he had his iPhone with him right now. Wishing he could do anything other than watch one of the five movies that were laying around in the cabin. Even playing a game on a smartphone sounded thrilling to him at this point. Only—he smashed his right before he left to come up here to this cabin in the middle of nowhere. Probably wouldn't work up here in these trees anyways.

Through the fog of realizing that Matt had been taken, and the exhaustion that he felt through that night, he tried to tell Tanya at the time everything that happened in the phone call. Hearing Matt's voice, hearing the threat, it was the final nail in the coffin on his sanity for that night. He was frantic, more about Matt being taken and what the woman was going to do to him. His mind was starting to go all over the place, and rightfully so. He experienced what she could do. It was terrifying, and now Matt was going to experience something way worse than he did.

Tanya did her best to try and calm him down. At one point, Tyler tried to climb to his feet and try to find Matt as soon as they could, but he only got to his feet when he started to waver and land back onto the couch.

"You are in no position to do anything. You are dead on your feet Tyler." said Tanya

"We need to get Matt!"

"We will, but you also need to rest. You are no good to Matt if you are beyond the point of exhaustion. We will go and get him when we wake up from some rest."

Tanya retrieved some blankets and a pillow for Tyler to sleep on the couch. He almost went to sleep instantly as his head hit the pillow.

When he woke up he saw that the sun was shining and almost didn't know where he was. When he looked around for a few seconds, everything that happened earlier in the night came back to him. He picked up his phone that was on the coffee table and saw that it was close to quarter after nine. He had only six hours of sleep. He looked at his phone while thinking that that was probably all the sleep he was going to get. He had to do something about getting Matt back and away from that woman. He thought about getting a his gun back at his house. Didn't he know someone that had an AR-15 he could use or buy from? Yeah. He thought he did. That would help with trying to kill the woman. She said last night that she lived all those many years and that she had been shot at and still hadn't been stopped, but she bled just the same after he shot her. Even at the unlikely chance that she wouldn't be killed by gunfire, she still bled and that had to help. Didn't it? It mattered, but he had to figure that out later. Right now he had some calls to make. He swiped his finger crossed his iPhone. When his screen knocked he saw that his phone call app was till on. He was about to go to the contact option so he could get ahold of Rusty at the indoor shooting range he and Tanya went to over a week ago, when he stopped. He looked at the most recent phone call option on the phone and saw Matt's contact info on the screen. He stared at it. Thinking to himself: *She knew how to get ahold of me through Matt. She could be tracking me through my phone. Couldn't she?*

He saw it in movies all the time. Although he knew that movies didn't get everything in real life right, he knew that it wasn't too crazy to think that she couldn't be tracking him right now through his phone, was it? The technology is out there. He knew that. And…she did have a lot of money. With a lot of money—you could get almost anything you wanted with very little questions if any questions at all. He thought that he didn't know for sure that she had a lot of money. That was just a wild guess. But the doubt started to creep into his mind again: *how much money did you actually need to get what you were hunting for? Buying something like that wouldn't take much at all, would it?*

The questions were starting to mount up in his mind. One of his Sergeants told him when he was young and dumb in the big wide world of the Army was: *If the questions start to mount up. Assume the worst and don't take any chances.* Tyler always thought that was good advice. Only it would mean that he would have to smash his phone. He thought about just taking the battery out of it. But he knew that with iPhones, there was a special way to take out the battery that he didn't have time for.

"Hey." said Tanya as she started to shuffle into the kitchen. "Do you want any of the coffee from last night that I can warm up? Or I can make a fresh pot along with some breakfast? Your call?"

"There might be a possibility that she is tracking my phone."

Caught off guard, Tanya said, "Huh?"

"There might be a strong chance that the woman is tracking my phone."

"The woman that is after you is tracking you through your phone? Do I have that right?"

"Yes, I think she is."

"How do you know this?"

"I don't really know for sure. But she called me from Matt's phone, instead of her own. Why is that?"

"To make sure that you picked up." Tanya said.

"Right. Cause being scared and possibly alone, I wasn't going to pick up the phone if a strange number called me after such a traumatic night. I get that. Especially since Matt was the one with me. But maybe she was using it to get a lock on my phone as well. Like she might have a device or an app on her phone to track this phone that is in my hand."

Tanya looked skeptical. "But like you said, you don't know for sure. Maybe your exhaustion is getting the best of your mind?"

"No, because I feel refreshed right now. Sure, I could use coffee, but that's normal. Besides, I don't think this is a 'completely out of the ballpark' kinda theory. Cops have done it before to catch criminals."

"Do you know that from anywhere other than the television?"

"No of course not. I don't know of anybody that could use that other than maybe Matt. But I know that the technology exists. They tried to use that kind of tech to try and hunt down Osama bin Ladin's courier that eventually led to him."

"Again, you saw that in *Zero Dark Thirty*. A movie. Other than saying that it's *based* on a true story, there is no guarantee that they used that kind of device to locate him. It is just a movie."

Tyler's anger was starting to show a little bit now. "You're kinda missing the point. Either way if it is based on a movie or real life, the technology exists! That is what I'm trying to tell you! It may cost a pretty penny, but the technology exists nonetheless! Judging by what she was wearing last night, it looked like she could afford such items."

Tanya raised her hands as if she was attempting to surrender. "Okay, okay. Lets say she has this device. What do we have to do in order for her to stop tracking your phone?"

"The only way I can think of is to smash it."

Tanya looked at the phone that was in Tyler's hand. Saw that it was a brand new iPhone that she knew Tyler could barely afford at the time. Actually, she knew that it was a birthday gift for him from Samantha. She didn't know if he just wanted to smash the phone because it reminded him of her, or if what he was saying that he was being tracked by this woman made sense. She guessed either way, he was going to smash it eventually.

"Alright. When are you going to do it?"

"Do you have a pen and paper?" said Tyler

"Uuhh, yeah. But what do you need that fo—."

"I need to write down Matt's number. I don't have it memorized, and I think that scarlet bitch is going to have it for the foreseeable future."

Tanya looked around on her counter top and landed her gazed on a notebook that was under some envelopes that contained this month's round of bills. She picked it up and tossed it as well as a pen, towards Tyler. He looked at his phone and started writing a ten digit phone number on a piece of notebook paper. He then ripped the paper out of the pad and stuffed it in his pocket. At the same time, he put his phone on the ground and went to get his boot at the front door. He put the boot on his foot quickly, then walked over to where he played down the phone, and smashed it with his heel.

"So…You're not wasting any time on that are you?" Tanya said sarcastically.

Tyler gave her a look. "At what point do you think that any of this is funny?"

Tanya then looked down on the ground, a little ashamed of cracking jokes at a time like this. "Sorry." she said. "Just trying to lighten the mood a little bit. I know that this is serious, and I'm sorry."

Tyler looked down at his feet now. "It's okay. It's just…I'm just really stressed by all of this. We have to get moving now. If what I think is true, then we are going to have some company here real soon. I don't really want to take that chance. So grab what clothes that you can, toiletries, towels, anything. Any essentials. We leave in about five minutes."

After that they made their way to Tyler's house to find the cops; then made their way over to Charlie's to get his help in hiding them at the cabin; waiting a few months to maybe conceive some sort of plan, weapons, ammunition; until ultimately bringing them here to this point. Waiting…and waiting.

Looking out of this window, he no longer could take it anymore. "We need to get the fuck out of here."

Tanya still watching *The Wizard of Oz*, rolled her eyes at hearing this and replied in a dreary tone, "Yes. I know we do Tyler. But we need to wait until the cops stop looking for you." She then put her attention back to the screen, as the cowardly lion enters the story. Right now, that was exactly how he felt. Cowardly.

"No. No more." He walked toward her and shut the T.V. off. Catching her full attention. "We need to leave and get out of here now."

"Why? Whats wrong? Do you see something out there?" she looked out the window and saw that it was raining. How long had it been raining?

"No there is nothing out there. I just want to get out of here and start doing something instead of just waiting here to be caught."

Tyler started to look out at the nice autumn day and then started to reminece as a memory came to him just then, which carried him off. "I remember looking out of windows when I was a kid and being amazed at looking at the woods that played just beyond our lawn. Thinking that there was always a beautiful world out there in those woods. Of course my mother told me and my brothers that we weren't allowed in those woods, but when she would go to work, we would make the woods our playground. Building forts out of sticks and small fallen trees after storms would knock them down and start creating paths in the woods. Those were always fun times. They grew when we started growing up and got int hunting and trapping. Making duck blinds, turkey blinds, and tree stands for hunting season. Jeez, hunting season is gonna be here soon enough. Guess I'm going to miss it this year."

Tanya didn't say anything. She just stared at him.

"Only I guess now I'm the one that's being hunted huh?" The question was rhetorical, but he saw that Tanya was nodding her head solemnly. "What are we going to do? We can't stay here forever."

"No we can't. But we have no idea how to find Matt or the woman, and even if we did, how do we know that she can be stopped?" Tanya and Tyler have been having this discussion for months. Every time it would be the same and every time it would end the same. Only this time Tyler wasn't going to stand for it any longer. He moved toward the bedroom where the two beds were and went toward the closet. He started to pull out a bag that they brought with them, and then went to the dresser and started throwing clothes in it. Tanya followed Tyler into the bedroom. "What are you doing?"

"You can stay here for another day, but I can't stay here anymore. If I keep moving around, it will be more difficult for them to find me. You should go back home to Wausau."

"Yeah, sure, okay!" Tanya said in a sarcastic tone. "If you really think that the police aren't going to think that I'm not involved in any of this, you are kidding yourself."

"The cops can't prove anything that says you were involved."

"Are you stupid?!" Tanya was starting to get angry now. "We left my house with pieces of your broken cell phone laying on the ground. All the cops need to do is look up the serial number on the back of the phone know the the phone belongs to you. Secondly, you are forgetting that the reason we fled my house and smashed your phone was because you thought that the woman was tracing your cell phone. If she was then, then she knows *my* house was where your were last known location was, and if no one has been there the past three months, it might tell *everyone* in the world that I am now involved."

Tyler stopped packing long enough to watch Tanya and her declaration. After she was finished he continued to toss clothes into his pack. "Just tell them hat you were on an extended vacation somewhere, or that I took you against your will. According to the news, that's not that far of a stretch."

Tanya couldn't believe what she was hearing. "You are an idiot. If you think for a minute that would throw you to the wolves just to save my own skin, you are indeed an idiot, and no one is going to believe that I was in Mexico for three months without telling anyone including my own parents. They just won't Not only that, that sort of travel would leave a paper trail of some sort I'm sure, because you can't leave the country without a passport." she paused for a moment and looked at him closely. "Why are you trying to get rid of me? Seriously?"

That stopped Tyler's packing, dead in it's tracks. How could he answer such a question her? Should he tell her that he was starting to develop feelings for her that were blooming into more that just friendship? That seeing her getting hurt would be worse than suffering the worst death he could think of? Or tell a lie and say that she was wearing out her welcome or some shit along those lines? Even though that he really didn't want her to go at all. He felt deep down in his heart that they would never be a couple. Not in a million years. Tyler thought that they had stepped into that friendship zone for far too long to become anything other than just friends. maybe friends with benefits someday, if they were ever so daring to cross that line, but he knew that was a sure way to end a friendship rather than make it stronger. If he couldn't have her, than life without her would be a most unbearable place to be apart of.

"I-I know that this hasn't been easy for you. I can see it everyday on your face. You are regretting ever opening the door of your house to me. I know you will deny it, but I can see it on your face. You don't want to be here. i don't blame you, because I sure as shit don't want to be here either. So I'm not going to give you an order to get out of here. No. I'm going to leave and try and finish this on my own."

Tanya stared deep into Tyler's eyes and didn't like what she saw along with what she was hearing.

Bullshit.

Everything that he was spouting out of his mouth was pure bullshit. For once she knew that she didn't want to be anywhere else on the planet than here with Tyler. She knew that he wasn't lying about what was going on. Why would he? There was a moment in the beginning of all of this that she thought that maybe he was crazy. That he might have kidnapped Matt for some weird twisted purpose, but that was all before the phone call from Matt himself, and then from that that woman. The sound of her voice that was barely audible from side of the room through the phone, it made her shiver with fear hearing how sinister and cruel she could be. After that, there was no question that Tyler had been telling the truth. She was here for him, no matter what.

Now he wanted to spring this bullshit on her like he was trying to do for months, so he could try and find Matt and the woman by himself?

"You are so full of shit! Don't give me the whole 'I know you aren't happy' bullshit. I get it, you don't want me to get hurt, you want to go in on alone. Fine, whatever. I don't care what you need to tell yourself. Because for the last time, this shit isn't going to work. I told you back at my house, that I am with you until the end of this. That means until we get either Matt back, or that insane woman is taken care of. So if you are going somewhere, be sure to keep room in my truck for my bag because I'm going too."

"No you're not."

"Yes I am."

"No, you're not!"

"I have brothers so I can do this forever. Yes I am."

Tyler screamed out in frustration. "Goddammit!"

"Why don't you want me to come with y—."

"I CAN'T RISK LOSING YOU ANYMORE!" he yelled in her face while holding onto her shoulders. "I can't risk your safety anymore. Everyday I feel that things are getting worse and worse. The longer I stay here, the worse things are getting out in the real world. It scares the hell out of me. it scares me even worse that I am dragging you along with me in this mess. I can't do it anymore. It's becoming too hard for me to bare. I know you can look after yourself, you have told me so more than once, but i feel that I reached my limit on letting you come with me this far. That is why I need to leave. I need to settle this on my own, knowing that you are safe."

Tanya again stared at Tyler with a face filled with awe. "You clearly don't understand then. We are both beyond the point of no return here. There is no 'Oh sorry we went this far for nothing, might as well turn back'. No, there is none of that. I knew what this meant to go along with you. I am not stopping now. i can't stop now. So if you want to go somewhere, that's fine. Let's grab our shit and let's get outta here. But don't think for an instant that you are leaving without me. You are going to need my help. Besides, you need someone with more brains than you along for this ride." She looked down at his bag that had a few objects of clothes in it. "You are going to need to bring more clothes than that, you maybe have enough clothes for like a day at the most."

Tyler looked down and saw that the only things he put in his bag were a pair of pants, a shirt, and some toothpaste. "Yeah, I was just rushing out the door as fast as I could, I guess I need a little more than this." With that, they both made their way to the bathroom to pack. Tyler didn't like it. Not at all. He cared too much for Tanya now, and he was risking her life for his at this point on and it made him feel like garbage.

While the fight was going on, a black SUV pulled off of the road that connected to the driveway of the cabin that once belonged to the Tyler's late friend. Danny looked at the cabin and saw that smoke was rising from the chimney. People were in the cabin just like the man had said. Danny just had to check it out now to see who was in there. If it was Tyler, things were about to get interesting.

Chapter 19

Anoaka felt a tremor of emotion enter her. Normally she didn't feel those, not unless something was happening with someone that is under her control. She reached out and tried to feel for Danny. Once having a lock on his emotions, she felt a mixture of both excitement, and worry. Most of the worry came from the worry of Danny losing one of his friends. This lead to a mixture of weather or not he was going to go through with what had to be done. Something Anoaka was worried was going to happen.

She grabbed her cellphone. She had a slight hesitation on whether to call Danny up or to just go ahead and use him. After thinking about it for a second she decided to give him a call, hoping that his cellphone would work in whatever backwoods he was in.

Danny felt his phone vibrate in his jacket pocket. He made a grab for it, and looked to see that Charlotte was calling him. Now what? His nerves were a little shot from where he was and how sure he was that his old friend was in that cabin. What did she need to add to make his day even more complete?

"Hello ma'am."

"What are you doing right now?"

"I am right outside of the cabin that our dear friend Tyler Green and Miss Tanya Walsh are currently hiding out in."

"Good. So what are you going to do about it?"

Danny took a long deep breath before answering her. "I'm going to go in there and take care of them both. Just like you requested ma'am." Danny waited for a reply. There was silence on the other end that seemed to drag out into eternity. "Ma'am? Are you still there?" He knew she was, otherwise he would have heard a beep on the other end of the line signaling that the call had ended. "Ma'am?"

When she spoke, her voice was not that of an innocent young woman that made her seem to spread her beauty through her voice, but the low demon voice that she reserved for her prey. Filling Danny with fear and realization with every word that was being transpired. "Good. Now I am going to make sure you doing it right this time."

Danny started to feel the pain spread throughout his body. His thumb slide over by itself to hit the END button on his phone, then slide back into his pocket.

She started to bring out the souls that were kept within her, out into the library as she put down her phone. Screams of mothers, fathers, and children tried to roar and reach her ears that grew deaf to the sound. She stood up from her chair and outstretched her arms as if she were imitating Jesus on the cross. As her arms reached out from her sides, a glow of orange smoke, raised from her arms as if she were on fire. As this was happening, screams that were coming from the souls she kept for herself, raised to a higher octave as they were their pain started to rise within them. Soon, one by one screams were slowly dying out, as they were being burned and split apart from themselves and bringing the energy and the focus that Anoaka needed to control everything that was Danny over a great distance. It was very difficult, and she had to be careful that she didn't burn her own soul in the process; but if she was successful, Tyler Green and his little girlfriend would be dead and rotting in the woods of northern Wisconsin.

She dug deeper, and burned those souls harder with her concentration. The screams rose within her, as the orange smoke rose higher off of her body.

Kolat was just entering the library to she what his sister was up too, when he saw what she was doing in the middle of the room. About to give her shit for her lacking taste in style and color(once again wearing a nice red skirt with her stupid pigtails), he stopped short as soon as he noticed to orange smoke rising off of her. He knew that he would catch hell if he disturbed her now. She might even be mad enough to send her Red powers onto him…not that he wouldn't be ready for it. Still, best not to meddle, besides if she was successful, his time here might be over. That was good news for him. He hated his sisters place.

Curiosity started to nibble at the edge of his mind. Maybe, just maybe, he could sneak a peek at what was going on. It was risky, he never tried anything like that before and it might throw off Anoaka's concentration. Bringing out a nice and scornful wrath. Only, he didn't think so. He was thinking about trying to be careful and very lightly touched her mind. He was sure that would be enough for him to look into her thoughts.

He was right.

What he was seeing was woods that were surrounding a cabin. He was moving closer to the cabin at a very slow pace, like he was fighting himself from trying to either get closer or to resist the force moment. Trying to look in a little harder into her mind to try and see who's body she was in, so he could look into their thoughts was pushing it. He was merely doing this to observe, not to constantly dig for answers. Besides, with what she was going nuts over that past few months, it could only be one person; Danny. He man that served as her helper. He never met the man, but judging by him helping out his sister, he concluded that the man was probably nothing special to anyone; most of all, by Anoaka.

He stopped his thoughts, and took in hers. He stood there, not more than ten feet away from his sister, watching her thoughts unfold as she was taking control of another human being, so she could kill another. Kolat hoped it would succeed too. So he could get the hell outta here.

Both Tyler and Tanya were in the middle of throwing in some socks and toiletries into their bags, when Tyler raised his hand up for Tanya to stop what she was doing and to be quiet. He thought he heard something. Something like twigs snapping outside and feet being dragged along the ground. As he tried to stop all movement around him and Tanya, he heard the sound was getting louder. He made he way toward one of the windows that was covered by curtains and peeked out to get a look at whoever was outside. At first he couldn't see anyone because he angle was off and he thought that the movement was starting to make its way around the back. He quickly made his way to the opposite side of the house toward the back, looking through another window and saw who it was. Seeing Danny trying to make his way up to the only door of the cabin filled him with terror. Mostly because he saw what was in his hand.

A handgun.

Probably the same handgun he used to shoot at him and Matt back in that alley. Tyler looked over toward Tanya and pointed toward the closet in the hallway, then made hand gesture into a gun. She understood and made her way quietly toward the hallway closet to retrieve their guns. She knew that only the deer rifles were in the closet. Their handguns were in the kitchen cupboard that was closest toward the door. The deer rifles were enough, but if they missed him in a shootout, reloading was going to be a little slow compared to the Colt that he saw that Danny had on him.

Tyler was looking as Danny was making his way up the stairs. Was he hurt or something? Why was he dragging his feet along the ground and now up the stairs? Something was wrong with him, only he kinda knew that after the last time they met and he was shooting at him. Tanya came back from the hallway closet and handed Tyler a deer rifle with a scope. He didn't think that he would need the scope if they were going to do a firefight in here—

Suddenly there was two loud gunshots that made both Tyler and Tanya jump as they were loading their guns, then a loud BANG as if the door was getting kicked in. Tyler slammed the small magazine into his rifle that held the five rounds, then locked and loaded. He held his rifle aimed down to the ground but was ready to raise it up if he needed to. His right ring finger was pressed lightly against the safety, so when he raised up the rifle, muscle memory would kick in and turn the safety off. He quickly positioned himself in front of Tanya, ready to make his way out into the hallway. Tanya held his arm as if to stop him, and Tyler quickly looked back at her to see what it was that she was doing. She looked at him and started to shake her head, he saw that she too was scared. He lifted his elbow that was being held back in a quick movement that said, "Get off of me" and lined up against the wall next to the door as if he was going to breach the room. He quickly glanced down the hallway, then just as fast, brought his head back behind the wall. From what he saw, no one entered near the hallway. Hell he wasn't sure that Danny entered the house yet.

He waited.

And waited.

There was a long creek coming from the door in the main room that was attached to the living room and kitchen, and lead to the outside. The only door that did so.

There was hard footsteps making their way through the cabin. Tyler decided to peek down the hallway again. Only this time, he mounted and stuck close to the door frame, aiming the rifle down the hallway for the first sign of Danny. He listened for anymore footsteps from other people, but he didn't hear anyone else. He thought that this was foolish because he heard the limp, or stagger that was in Danny's walk that was not right. He must be hurt or something. He still sounded like he was moving fast enough as he was making his way throughout the house, but still there was something in the steps that was off from any other person walking. Tyler just couldn't put his finger on it.

"Mmmmmm-Tttttyler!" said the all too familiar voice of his former battle buddy, "Tttyler, ge—get oooooout of hhh—here!"

What the fuck was that? Did he just try and *warn* me? If he was here to kill me, why would he do that?

"G-go! N-n-now!" Danny's voice was trying to scream this, but it sounded to both Tyler and Tanya that the man had something trying to block his mouth. They still heard his footsteps in the cabin, moving along throughout the place. Tanya was looking at both Tyler and the doorway leading to the hall, looking and feeling confused about what was going on. Tyler stayed right where he was, waiting with his rifle aimed down the hallway. Ready to kill the first thing that moved when more words came from Danny.

"Y-y-y-y-you neeeeed t-t-t-o g-ggget ouuuut! N-N-NOW!!" screaming the last word out as loud as he could, "S-s-s-sh-sh-she is ya-ya-ya-using ma-ma-ma-me! K-K-KILL YA-YA-YA-YOU!!"

Tyler wanted to respond. To tell him that he knew that. Why the fuck else was he here shooting down a door and marching through the place that they were staying. But he didn't want to give away his position. Still…why was he warning them? That didn't make any sense. He kept his hands steady around the rifle, thinking that he was going to show himself any minute now. Only…what if he took his old friends' advice? Both he and Tanya could get out through the window with next to no trouble and sneak out the back side of the cabin. It could be be done in less than thirty seconds. If they both jumped through the glass.

Only what if this was a trap? He would be risking both of their lives on whatever Danny, the man that was after them with a gun, was saying to them. Not exactly a smart move that way either. Maybe, he could send Tanya out through the window to see if there was any danger that was expected for the both of them. Thinking about it some more he went against it. He would be putting Tanya in unnecessary risk that could lead to her being killed if there was something out there waiting for the both of them. It lead to taking a risk, something when you life was on the line, you didn't really feel like doing.

While thinking about this, Something showed up in his periferlle vision. Without thinking, his body reacted to this new development like he set his mind to respond; to shoot at anything that moved. Without thinking or aiming, he pointed in the general direction and pulled the trigger.

The rapore from the shot was deafening in the small enclosed hallway, that it caused Tyler to have loud ringing in his ears. When he looked at the area where he took his shot at he noticed a small hole in the floor near where the foot had been. Only there was nothing else that was in his sight. No foot, no blood to indicate that he hit anything. Just a hole and the knowledge that he missed. "Fuck." he mumbled to himself.

When the ringing started to subside, he heard more talking from Danny, "T-T-T-Tyler! G-gggget ow-owww-out! Sssssssshe i-is g-g-g-go-go-going to k-k-k-k-ki-ki-ki-kill you!"

No point in playing that he wasn't here anymore, now that he ruined his own element of surprise. "Hey, buddy! Nice to see you too. You show yourself to me, I will make sure *I* will kill you! Got it? And what the fuck is wrong with your voice?"

Tyler was looking down on the floor down the hallway when he said this. In that time, Danny's body got into a position to use the wall of the hallway as a shield, then raised the weapon to eye level.

Suddenly Tyler saw quick movement down the hallway and raised his eyes up. He saw Danny, pointing his gun at him trying to get a fix. Tyler quickly reacted and went for cover in the room, when three shots ripped past him merely inches away, and damaged the door and the wall opposite of the doorway.

"Looks like your the one trying to kill me. Buddy!"

"I-i-i-it's h-hher!"

"What do you mean? *What* is her?"

There was footsteps that were starting to move in the cabin.

"M-m-move-m-ments" that was all that Danny said.

"That little bastard!" Anaoka said out loud to herself. "You're going to pay for your words."

Tyler had to stop Danny's advance. He took his rifle in his left hand and looked at Tanya with dread. Tanya looked back at him, then looked at the window. "We need to move now." she said.

Tyler took the rifle then pointed it down the hallway and started to fire blindly. After he finished firing three shots, he turned to her. "We don't know what's out there. He might have that woman out there, or whoever else is helping him out there."

Speaking in a hushed voice with a sense of urgency, "We don't have a choice. He is making his way down toward us." Then she lifted the window open and cautiously looked outside. First looking toward her left, then slowly towards her right, all while Tyler shot twice more down the hallway. He pulled his rifle back and started to reload with the barrel pointed toward the door. Once he looked back at Tanya, she was already halfway out the window.

"Get your ass back in here!" he scowled at her.

"How about you get your ass out here so you can have a chance to live?" As she told him this she was looking around the area, looking to see if anybody else was here. "I think he came alone."

"He said that *movements* was her? I don't know what that means, but she might be here. So keep a lookout."

"Alright."

Tyler finished reloading his rifle and stopped moving. He listened hard, past the ringing that was going on in his ears, and waited to see if he could hear Danny's movements. Danny might have been sneaky, but in a cabin where everyone heard every footstep, it was damn difficult to be sneaky. Still next to the doorframe, Tyler raised his rifle at the doorway. Inching himself closer, he started to peer around the doorframe itself. Inching closer….closer….closer….

He peered around and saw that the hallway was empty. Trying once again to listen he didn't hear anything. The ringing in his ears had abated a few seconds ago, and even then, he could still hear things.

Now he heard nothing.

Silence in the cabin.

Tyler was thinking about staying right where he was, he turned his head slightly to his left so he could keep Tanya in his sights, and he knew that they should stay together.

Only, he had to know where Danny was. He was dangerous and sly. A combination that was never any good when you were on the opposite side. He looked again at Tanya and saw that she stood right where she had been. Still looking out for anyone. Maybe if he just went to the end of the hall…

No. No! Stay together. That was important. Thinking back to the military, he knew that let the enemy separate you was one of the worse things you could let happen. If he knew that, Danny knew that. Probably what he was going for.

Tyler started to back up with his eyes down the hallway, moving around the doorframe so he would have some cover. Once he had his cover he turned and looked toward Tanya, ready to join her outside, when he saw that she was gone.

"Tanya? Tanya?!"

Looking out side the window, he saw that she was nowhere to be seen. He thought that maybe she went around the corner of the cabin. If that was the case, his idea of not being separated already took a shit.

Suddenly, Tyler heard a loud SMACK of the door. He turned to his right and saw that Danny was jumping from the door to the cabin, down over the stairs and making a run for it. Tyler tried to raise his rifle but it got stuck in the window, by the time he lifted it to aim. Danny already turned to corner of the cabin.

"TANYA! LOOKOUT HE IS COMING RIGHT FOR YOU!"

Tanya was on the far right side of the cabin, ready to turn toward the front toward the road, when she heard Tyler scream out to her. Right then and there she was thinking that she had made a mistake by leaving the window. She started to backup, but she lifted her rifle up toward the corner of the cabin as she was making her way back to the window. She glanced back because she knew that there were a few sticks that made their way up from the ground and she didn't want to land on her ass after being tripped up by them.

Trying to make her way back, she heard something that sounded like sticks rustling to the front of the cabin; and they were moving around fast.

"It's him." she said to herself.

She stopped in her tracks. Hearing the leaves and sticks move closer to her…closer…closer…

The movement sounded like it was right on top of the corner of the cabin now. She took aim with her rifle.

Something popped up from the corner of the cabin, and just like Tyler reacted in the cabin, she pulled the trigger. Only unlike Tyler, she hit what came from the corner of the cabin…after she got a look at it, she wished she didn't.

It was a log. A small log that they stored outside for the fireplace.

"Shit." she tried to pull the bolt back on the rifle so she could load another round into the chamber, only it stayed where it was without budging. How could it not budge? She cleaned this rifle just the other day—

She heard movement from the leaves again and looked up. There stood a man holding a holding a Colt .45 right at her head. The man that Tyler had been talking about ever since that night in the alleyway. Danny Staubach. He had a suit on that didn't seem to match all the stories that Tyler told about him when they were bored and just wanted to pass the time by telling stories. Tall and broad in the shoulders, but he stood like he was going to keel over. Walking closer he looked like he was struggling to move his legs at all.

These only gave Tanya minor mental notice. What she thought of most of all, was that she was about to die. And she was scared of dying.

"Don't move a goddamn inch Staubach!"

Danny's head turned to see Tyler on the opposite corner of the cabin. His rifle pointed at his body. Remembering to aim small miss small to himself, Tyler was focusing on the knot of Danny's tie. If he missed the knot, he would still hit a big portion of his body.

"Drop your gun Danny! Don't make me kill you!"

"Pl-pl-please…" Danny started to say, but then his head jerked around to his left which seemed like it was cutting off what he was going to say. Then when he looked back, his eyes were pleading and scared, while his mouth became a dark, hollow voice that reminded Tyler of the change in the woman's voice. Right then, he knew. He knew what it was that Danny was talking about in the cabin. *She* was controlling him. This whole encounter, *she* was the one that was attacking him. "*I don't care Mr. Green, if I have to kill this bitch first before I turn the gun to you. I'll do it. Even if shot, you won't stop me. Just like that night in your apartment.*"

"It's you. The woman." Tyler said in disbelief. "That's…that's impossible."

"*Very good Mr. Green. I would give you more credit for figuring it out if Danny boy here didn't try and tell you himself….uh! He has been fighting me this whole time which has been making things difficult. He will be punished after I use him to take care of the both of you.*" Danny's head started to turn to take aim back at Tanya, who stood still with shock and terror on the conversation that was taken place.

Tyler snapped out of it. Still aiming at Danny's tie knot, he decided to take the shot, he was out of time. He pulled the trigger.

He missed his target, the tie knot that was right in the center of his broad shoulders. But he did hit the left shoulder. The arm that held the gun pointing at Tanya. Once hit, the shoulder pulled more to the left, throwing off the barrel pointed at Tanya's skull, and went off. Sending the bullet into a nearby tree.

"Nice shot. But you think that will stop me?"

"Don't do this! Don't make me shoot my friend!"

"Oh! Since you asked so nicely, I think I will just go home." Danny's right arm moved to his left to take the gun from that hand. *"But not until I'm done with all of you!"*

Quickly once again the gun was raised up and took aim. This time, it was aimed right at Tyler's head. It was so quick that Tyler almost didn't have time to react. When he spoke to Danny/the woman, he had his gun pointed to the ground. The speed in which the gun was pointed at him was incredible, that the only reaction that Tyler could do was to get down. He bent his knees down to to where his ass slated on the leaves that were touching the ground. At the same time he lifted his rifle and took aim. Danny's gun fired to where Tyler's head had been less than a second ago. Sending the bullet to fly right over his head and into the woods. Tyler's muscle memory took over, making sure his fingers hit the safety as soon as the gun was raised and then took aim and fired three rounds.

Tyler's mind was thinking to only wound Danny. Wound him to the point where he was incapacitated. While firing he made quick little adjustments to his line of fire that he sent one bullet into the right shoulder, then two in his right leg. One he was sure, was sent into the kneecap. Sending him to the ground in an instant.

There were no screams of pain. In fact something worse was on his face; a smile. The same type of smile that was on the woman's face; all knowing, full of malice, deceit, and evil.

Danny, or Danny's body, started an attempt to get itself up with his left leg, the only limb that was till good enough to work on its own.

Still maintaining that smile. His arms were trying to move to help him up, but from what Tyler observed was that they seemed to not want to move or refused to.

"Still coming. Still…..coming to get YOU!"

Tyler approached Danny and raised to rifle once again. Pointed and pulled the trigger. *CLICK.*

He was out of rounds. The thing that was controlling Danny tried to move a little faster now. Looking at the right hand he saw that the gun it held was laying on the ground and tried to make a move to grasp it once again, but Tyler came down and hit Danny in the head with the buttstock of the rifle. Causing Danny to fall to the ground and appear to knocked out.

Tyler wasn't taken any chances. He kept his eyes on Danny, making sure that the woman controlling him wasn't going to come back and surprise them. He reached into his pocket of his pants, swearing that there were a couple of rounds left to load into his rifle. Sure enough there were two left. He loaded them in the rifle then kept it pointed at his former friend. "That bitch was controlling him the whole time. The whole fucking time!" He was talking to Tanya without looking at her. After a minute of not hearing a response, he quickly glanced at her and saw that she was on the ground. Her eyes were red and full of tears. "Are you alright?" he said, moving back toward her and falling to the ground next to her, all the while as he kept his eyes on Danny.

"He was going to kill me. *She.* She was going to use him to kill me. And I just stood by and almost let it happen.", she said through sobs.

Tyler put an arm around her. "But she didn't. I wasn't going to let that happen to you. Danny's down now. He can't hurt you anymore. Once he wakes we are going to get some answers out of him.", he then related to her, "He's not going to hurt you anymore"

"He didn't hurt me. He almost *killed* me! And it wasn't him in the first place. You said it yourself. *She.* That woman. She is the one that was controlling him to kill us. It sounded like she wasn't even trying that hard. In the end it was like she was toying with us. How can we stop her if she can control anyone? How?"

Tyler took his eyes off of Danny and looked at Tanya's. "I don't know. I just don't know."

Right as the blackness set in on Danny's vision, Anoaka, put her arms down and almost collapsed to the ground that she needed the end table that was closest to her to keep her at least on her knees. The amount of souls and energy she burned through, was extremely taxing. Though she was very weak, it was almost an afterthought compared to the fury that was taking over. She grabbed the lamp that was on the end table, and threw it across the room, even though it went only a few feet away, it smashed on the ground.

"That could have gone better."

She turned and saw Kolat standing by the doorway of the room. "How long have you been there?"

"Through the whole thing. Was it just me, or did you seem to be a little sluggish through that whole out-of-body experience. I mean, jeez, you couldn't even walk straight."

"Shut your fucking face Kolat. That fact that you went inside of my head through the whole thing might be a reason, don't you think?! And now, I have a dead servant, and two living troublemakers on my end. Probably because of you!"

"Oh, spare me your blame. I didn't touch anything inside of your head that would have effected your hold on dear ol' Dannyboy. I was merely at an observation point. Besides, from when I looked back, it seems that you were waving trouble controlling him from the start. So if you want to blame anyone, blame yourself." There was a long pause in the room. "So what could have caused your lack of control?"

"He was fighting me. I said that load of bullshit to you because I'm furious. He was fighting me the whole time I took him over. He was able to talk to them as I was trying to use him."

"I know. Has that ever happened before?"

"No." she answered him even though she knew he could just look inside her mind. "But I'm not going to let them win. I need that phone over there, can you please hand it to me. I can't walk at the moment, and this needs to be done right now."

Kolat did as she asked. He went over to the end table where the phone last rested from Danny's earlier call and handed it over to Anoaka without any hesitation. Anorak was glad for that. She started dialing the phone with shaky fingers. Kolat shifted in his stance, "And I don't think Danny boy is as dead as you think."

There was a small movement of fallen leaves that was coming over in the direction of where Danny lay. Tyler looked up and saw that Danny's head was moving from side to side. Slow at first, then it began to pick up speed to the point of jerking around violently. Moans of pain made their way to screams as Danny now became fully concise.

Tyler got up from where he and Tanya sat on the ground. Tanya maintained holding his hand, still scared of what could happen to both her and Tyler.

Tyler had his rifle at the ready, in case the woman took control of him again, or if this was some sort of trap that was being laid down like a medic going to a wounded soldier, only to be shot by the sniper. Danny started to cry for Tyler in his pain.

"Tyler! Help me! Please! Help me! I'm bleeding pretty bad and the pain: oh God the pain!"

"How am I suppose to trust that this isn't some sort of trap."

The pain for Danny was so great that he couldn't really think. All he knew was that he wasn't going to try anything to prevent the help that he needed. So he said the only thing that might help him. "I don't know, but she isn't here now! I need help now so I won't die!"

Tyler looked uneasy at Danny. He turned to Tanya, "Can you hold a rifle?"

Tanya looked confused, "What?"

"Can you hold a rifle? And if at all possible, shoot one if you need to?"

Tanya looked around and saw that her rifle was laying on the ground from when Danny/the woman, got the jump on her. She went over and picked it up. "Y-yeah, I think so."

"Good. 'Cause I am going to go and help him out to stop his bleeding. If he tries anything, I will do my best to get out of the way, then you will shoot him. Understand?"

"You think it will come to that?"

"I don't know, but I won't leave anything to chance now. Do you think you can do that?"

"Yeah."

"You sure?"

"Just get over there and help him. Get some fucking answers out of him as well. I what to know what all of this weird shit is about and what the fuck we are facing."

"Yeah. Same here." With that, Tyler made his way over and knelt down next to Danny. He saw that his old battle buddy was indeed bleeding really bad. Especially in his right leg where the two shots tore through him like he was made of paper instead of flesh and bone. Tyler started to undo Danny's tie so he could have a makeshift bandage for the leg. For the two wounds that were on his shoulders, he was thinking about ripping some of his suit off to try and pug the house that were gushing the blood out of him. "What the fuck is going on Danny?"

It was obvious to anyone with eyes that Danny was in an extreme amount of pain. Tyler didn't think that it might be great enough to where he might not even remember his own name. "Your being hunted. I thought you would have figured that out by now Green?"

Looks like he's well enough to be a smart-ass.

"Listen old buddy. I feel for you, I really do. Last thing I wanted to do was shoot you. But if you don't answer my questions, or if you give me attitude or resistance in anyway, I will leave you here to bleed to death, alone in the woods. You understand?"

Danny started to look at Tanya, standing about ten feet away, with a rifle pointed right at him. Tyler followed his gaze and said, "Don't look at her. She's not going to help you either, not unless I ask her to."

Danny looked back at Tyler in a pleading, sad face. "Please. She will kill me if I tell you."

"Maybe. But then again you will die if you don't. So…. choice is yours buddy. At least if you tell me, you get to live a little longer."

"Okay. Ask your questions." he said this through winced teeth.

"Who is the woman that is after me?"

"Us!" Tanya interjected.

"Right. Who is the woman that is after *us*?"

Danny was gasping for a deep breath, "The name that she gave me is Charlotte Brisbane." he exhaled quickly, then took another breath.

"I know she has other names and alases, but I only know her by that name." Another exhale.

"What is she? How can she do the things that she does?" As he asked this. He started to wrap the neck tie around the wounded leg.

Danny winced and screamed as Tyler did this. Once Tyler was finished with tying it off, he gave a small bust of chuckles, "When you figure that out, let me know." Another breath. "I've been with her for two years, and I still don't know" Breath. "I know for one thing, she isn't the only one."

"What do you mean?" asked Tyler. He started to rip the inner shirt of Danny's suit.

"I mean that there are others that she knows with abilities." Breath. "I don't know how many, but one for sure. I don't know his name." Tyler looked at him to see if he was lying. If he was, he was doing a damn good job of it. He was most likely telling the truth because he didn't think that this Charlotte would tell a mere minion that had the possibility of betraying her, that kind of information. He was sure that after a while, Danny would wear out his usefulness, and become another one of her victims that he saw in the alley.

"What is her ability, or abilities?"

Danny took in a deep breath, Tyler was thinking it was to try and fight the pain. "I don't know exactly what it is." Another deep breath. "But I know that it has something to do with manipulating souls."

"Oh my God." Tanya said aloud. Her mouth remained open in shock. Tyler was just as equally shocked, but that can't be right.

"Souls? As in, *souls!?*" he said.

"Yes. She takes souls and uses them for her needs. Her and the King?" He coughed and wince at the pain that it caused from his movement. He took a second to recover from the pain. While that was happening, Tyler started putting fabric from the shirt, in the wound on the right shoulder and started to press down hard.

"Tanya. I need you to come over here and press this piece of cloth onto his left shoulder."

"Wait, what? What if he tries to over take us?"

"Put your left knee on his inner elbow, it will stop him from making any kind of move. Hurry. He might not have a lot of time!"

Tanya put her rifle on the ground and did what Tyler said. Pushing down hard onto the wound with the cloth, causing Danny to scream out in pain. When his screams subsided, they could hear a faint sound in the distance. It sounded a lot like sirens. Police sirens.

"Who is the King?"

"I don't know." A short heavy breath. "I'm not…allowed to see him." Heavy breath. "Swear to God."

"But you know where he is?" Sirens in the distance started to get louder.

"Yes." Another breath. Tyler noticed that the pressure he was applying wasn't enough to stop the bleeding, and he was holding down the best he could. "They are in Lake Geneva, Wisconsin. 554 Bayview Dr., The big ass house." Another deep breath. "Matt is there too." Breath "If he is still alive." Sirens were ever so close now. Maybe a mile or two away.

"If she can control souls. Why can't she control us and have us kill ourselves or something?" Tanya asked this. Looking up to see where the sirens were.

"She has to touch you." Breathing heavily. "She needs to make a physical connection first before she can control you." Tyler thought about this. He realized that the Scarlet Bitch was close a few times to touching him. The closest was in the alley when he hit her over the head with the piece of wood. Another close call was in his apartment. Close, but no cigar. Both he and Tanya's souls were safe as of now. "Once she does that, you are under her control, or her victim."

There was a vibration that was coming from Danny's chest. Tanya realized that it was coming from her side of Danny, and used one of her hands to get the phone out his pocket and looked at the number. It said CHARLOTTE.

"Oh God! It's her!" she said.

"Give it to me." Tyler said. He took the phone and slid it to answer.

"Danny's phone." he answered.

"Is he dead or alive?" said the perky little voice that Tyler knew to be the camouflage of Charlotte's true voice.

"He's still alive. Not unlike you if you come up here and try to do what you used him for."

"I see that Mr. Staubach, my Dannyboy, has been blabbing his mouth off. How…unfortunate for him. I hope you enjoy your wait."

Tyler was confused by this. At the same time he heard the skid mark sound of a car slamming on its brakes on the gravel road. Along with the opening and slamming of doors. "What do you mean?"

"As you sit in jail. I'm coming for you." Then her dark voice made it vocal appearance, *"And there is nothing you can do to stop me!"* The line went dead.

Suddenly, both Tyler and Tanya were thrown back away from Danny as Danny's arms lifted the both of the up and into the air with sudden force. As they landed back on the ground, Tyler saw that Danny was making his way for the handgun that was laying on the ground. Tyler had enough time to think of Charlotte, and that it was her that was doing this. Danny was screaming in a combination of terror and agony.

Tyler raised a hand to try and reach Danny, but it was too late.

Danny took the hand gun and through his screams, put the barrel of the gun in his mouth. Then, pulled the trigger.

Blood sprayed out the back of his head, along with a white matter that Tyler later realized as he was being put into the squad car, was either brain matter, or pieces of skull. Most likely it was a combination of both. What was most important, was that he knew that his friend from another life was now dead. Tanya had a look of shock on her face as it was happening, then full on screamed her head off as the trigger was being pulled. Tyler could only sit in shock, until the police arrived and pointed their handguns right at their heads. Tyler didn't even remember the cuffs that were slapped on him, or the entry into the police squad car

Eventually, as the both of them were being driven to the police station in Eagle River, Charlotte's phone call rang through to him, and he became scared to death. She was coming for them.

Part III:
The King

"Hope you got your things together.
Hope you are quite prepared to die.
Looks like we're in for nasty weather.
One eye is taken for an eye.

Well, don't go round tonight,
Well, it's bound to take your life,
There's a bad moon on the rise."

—Tom Foggerty

Chapter 20

"Welcome back, Mr. Green."

Tyler sat there. Once again in that chair that was being overlooked by a a giant piece of glass that looked like a mirror, but wasn't. Sitting across a table to Sgt. Gentle, once again. Tyler didn't even hear him. He was still trying to process what was going to happen to him. *How* it was going to happen. For Charlotte, it would be all too simple. Merely touching one of the cops that would be hanging around the lobby. Control him or her, then have them come into one of the cells, and shoot both him and Tanya dead. If she had the power to do that, that would be the way that he would do it. No one would ever trace it back to her. Just another cop that had access and chose that opportunity to kill a potential cop-killer. Hell, if it was played that way in the media, people would probably rally around and cheer for the guy.

No matter how he pinned it in his mind, Tanya and himself were in deep shit.

"Hello? Earth to Tyler Green." Sgt. Gentle waved a hand in front of Tyler. "Am I getting through to you?"

Tyler snapped himself out of his thoughts and looked at Sgt. Gentle. He looked angry. More angry than the last time he saw him. Tyler already knew that by looking at him, that he would interpret every word that came out of Tyler's mouth as either a lie, or a means of insult.

"There you go. You have a lot of questions to answer, *buddy!*" He dragged out the word "buddy", probably because he remembered that Tyler didn't like being called that, all those months ago. So now he was going to bring on the autumn resurgence of stick poking. "Questions like where Officer Matt Mullen is located? What did you do to kill him? Why did you kill him? Did it have to do with the fake crime that you said you saw in that alley all those months ago? Huh? Was it going to back fire, so you needed a real crime to prove that you witnessed one? Or did you just want to join the glorious ranks of 'Cop-killer'? What did Mr. Daniel Staubach do that made you think that he deserved to die? I'm not going anywhere, so I can just stay here all day if you like. Sitting here staring at the walls."

Why even bother with this guy? Tyler thought to himself. *Anything I say is wrong. Talking to him was a complete waste of time. Besides, I'm going to die here anyways, right? Even if I could convince them that this was all the work of some soul taking bitch, I would still need to post bail in order to get out of here.*

He thought that he was in deep, deep shit. None of which had anything to do with the cops.

"Well, you sit there and daydream a little while longer. Like I said, I got time."

Tyler looked at him square into the eyes. A revaluation came to him. "What is your problem?"

The cop that sat straight in his chair with his arms crossed against his chest, gave a chuckle and a cocky smile. "What's MY problem?!" He said, yelling the word "my". "Said the criminal that either kidnapped or killed one of my fellow police officers. I knew that you were trouble just by looking at—"

Tyler interrupted this clique by repeating himself. "No, What is your problem? You had a stink about Matt and myself the very first time I entered this room. Saying that 'being a friend of Matt Mullen was enough for me to be trouble' or some shit like that. What was your problem with Matt?"

Sgt. Gentle sat there making the smile vanish before Tyler's very eyes. What replaced it was anger and embarrassment. As Tyler said this he noticed that Sgt. Gentle's eyes shifted from side to side like he was trying to give a glance at the mirror behind him so he could try and see its reaction, or the reaction of the people behind the mirror. "I think I'm the one that's asking the questions Mr. Green." He brought his gaze right back at him, but Tyler saw that the man's face was starting to turn vermillion from anger.

Tyler didn't stop. "No. I think it's very interesting that now as my best friend is captured, and has been captured for several months, that they look at his best friend, than the cop that disliked him more and more everyday. Matt told me that very night when we went out to eat that you always rode him on every little thing when you worked together."

Tyler didn't like himself very much for attacking Sgt. Gentle like this. He didn't like the guy that much, but he knew that he really didn't need or deserve any blame on what was happening to Matt. But he couldn't tell any of them what was really going on. Tyler knew that the woman now known to him as Charlotte would not hesitate to kill everyone in here if that was what it took. Which meant that he needed to get the hell out of here.

"We are not talking about me. We are going to talk about the guy that just died right in front of you where we found you, and what you had to do about that. As well as Matts whereabouts."

"I would love to tell all about that, and wish I knew about Matts whereabouts," Even though he had some idea about where he was, "but this is where I'm going to tell you I need my lawyer."

"You tell me something on what happened, I will get your lawyer for you." Tyler was sure that he had to get him his lawyer post haste as soon as he ask for it. This last part that was said, he was sure, was some last attempt for him to give the man on the other side of the table anything to work with. He would get none. Tyler sat where he was and stared at the man. They looked at each other for a minute before, Sgt. Gentle got up from his chair with a disconcerting look on his face. Like he wanted to choke the life out of Tyler.

After he left, Tyler waited about another twenty minutes in that same room until another person opened the door and showed his face in from the crack.

"Are you Mr. Tyler Green?"

Tyler had his head facing down on the table when he heard the voice coming from the door. "Yeah that's me."

The man brought the rest of himself through the doorway. He was wearing a suit and tie and held a briefcase. Making an easy deduction, Tyler figured this was his lawyer. The man went and sat in the chair that held Sgt. Gentle not so long ago, and put his briefcase on the table and opened it. "I'm glad I found you. My name is Richard McCoy. I will be representing you in court."

"You got here pretty fast compared to what they made out how long it was going to be."

"What exactly did you tell them Mr. Green?"

"Nothing. They asked their questions, but I don't have any time to answer any questions right now. Miss Walsh and myself need to get out of here as fast as we can. Where is she?"

"From my understanding, a Miss Tanya Walsh is being held in the woman's section of the jailhouse on the other side of the courthouse. It's good that you didn't answer any of their questions," he pulled out a file from his briefcase and started to skim through it, "because you and I need to have a conversation on where you and your friend need to go from here. I had the guards go and retrieve Miss Walsh for me, because I will be representing the both of you. Seems you two are in one hell of a situation.

"From what the paper and news outlets are making out, you had something to do with the disappearance of Officer Mathew Mullen over three months ago."

"I didn't—"

"You just stay quiet until I'm finished, and maybe until Miss Walsh can come and join us, okay hard nose? Disappeared for three months living in a cabin owned by a Mr...." He flipped a page on his file, "Charles Grenwalt. A man with a wife and a little boy that lives right here in the Wausau area."

Tyler almost forgot that he was now in Wausau. The past day had been a blur since they arrested him. Word spread that he and Tanya were arrested in Eagle River, and as soon as that happened, a transfer order appeared from a judge saying that he was going to be sent along with Miss Walsh in his original county upon their request. Tyler was sure that pressure from the Wausau Police Department as well as certain citizens form the local area had something to do with that. Maybe to try and get information on their missing comrade. On HIS missing comrade. He did have some, but to give it to them was just going to get them killed.

"Mr. Green did you hear me?"

"Huh?" He snapped back into the moment.

"I was talking about—"

There was a knock on the door. When it opened, there was a guard coming into the room arm and arm with a handcuffed Tanya.

"Tanya!" Tyler exclaimed.

"Hey Tyler. When they said I was going to meet my lawyer, I was thinking that I would be seeing you."

Richard stood up from his chair. "Hello Miss Walsh. My name is Richard McCoy, I will be representing both you and Mr. Green here."

The guard interjected, "Please wait one moment while I get another chair, so you can be seated and cuffed at the same time."

Tyler was a little angry at this. "Is that really necessary? She can just sit in a chair she doesn't need to be cuffed to the table."

"It's standard procedure, you don't like it you can have this conversation back in the cells, separately."

Tyler remained quiet after that. He stared at his own cuffed hands on the table. "Do what you need to do." Tyler grumbled.

"Well thank you for your permission sir. What would I do without your approval?" the guard gave him a sneer.

"That will be quite enough of that. Please retrieve the chair an then leave us please." Richard ordered. The guard did as he was told without another word. Only plenty of evil looks that Tyler paid no attention to. Once the chair was in, Tanya was cuffed to the table, the guard left them in peace. "I was just explaining to Mr. Green, what kind of situation you two are in right before you entered."

"I know what kind of situation we are in. Deep shit." Tanya said.

"From a legal standpoint, I would say that you are spot on. But we will have to wait to see what the evidence shows up."

"Evidence? Legal standpoint? No. That's not what I'm talking about at all. Im saying that if we stay here, in this jailhouse, we are going to die. She won't let us live long now that she knows where we are, and knows that we aren't going anywhere."

Tyler looked at her. "Yeah, I agree. What are the chances of us getting bail?"

"You need to be arranged before the judge first. Once you enter your guilty or not guilty. Which in your case I would enter in guilty and pray for the best. They will set a bail amount for the both of you."

"When is that going to be?"

"It will be in a few hours. You two are quite the celebrities. They want to hear from the two of you right and quick. After we get finished talking, the cops are going to want to talk to you as well. With me present, of course."

Tanya looked befuddled. "Hang on, why do you want us to plead guilty. We are not the guilty party here."

"It doesn't matter." Richard said. "The way you two have been missing for three months and now are showing up with two dead bodies on your hands makes you look pretty damn guilty. They were taking polls throughout the state weather or not to bring back the death penalty for you two. For the record, the polls say no."

"Two dead bodies? What are you talking about? There was only Danny Staubach that killed himself in front of us?" Tyler said confused.

"If you were paying attention right before Miss Walsh walked in. I told you that the body of one Charlie Grenwalt was found at the cabin. In the trunk of a car that was at the scene."

"Wait? What!" Tyler exclaimed.

"Charlie is dead?" Tanya said as she started to burst into tears.

"Appears he was shot about four times."

Tyler was stunned and devastated. Charlie had been his friend for over a decade. Now he was gone. Dead because he dragged him into all of this shit. Shit that all started from that night in that stupid fucking alley. Now…Charlie's wife and son were without their husband and father.

Tyler felt about the size of a grain of sand. He just wanted to die himself. If he stayed right where he was he figured, that just might happen.

Anoaka started to get dressed and get ready for the drive ahead. She always had a driver to take her everywhere ever since the automobile has been invented. She knew how to drive, but she never really enjoyed driving. She could try and hire someone on short notice, but she didn't want to waste time or to get anyone involved and witness what she was going to be doing at her destination. It was how she got into this situation in the first place.

She dressed in blue jeans that were red and a red shirt that had a big black butterfly over that front. With the streaks of red in her hair, she just looked like any other depressed looking goth girl after she applied all the make-up on her face; making her look white as a sheet, with dark blue eye shadow. She looked at her artwork on her face and deemed it acceptable. Not how she normally dressed, but it was necessary to have some form of disguise.

She made her way out of her bathroom(in their nice house, The King and her each had separate bathrooms on the third floor bedroom), she spotted her love standing right out in front of the window, as always, right next to the bed. His face was looking younger as the days were passing since they made love a couple of days ago. Since she poured the souls into him that he needed. The grey hair had all but completely disappeared from the side of his head, His cheekbones on his face were starting to fill out once again, and his arms were starting to retain the muscle that time took away from him. "How are you doing my love?"

"Fine." said The King.

"You keep looking out that window, I'm gonna start thinking that you want to fly right out of it." she said with a chuckle.

The King didn't say anything. He continued to look out onto the lake all the way to the shore on the other side where he noticed two people, one small and one big, fishing off the end of the dock. From his window they looked like ants to him, but still he could see that they were enjoying their fishing time. Getting use to the vision that he had lost just a few days ago, to now be back right as rain was always a bit jarring for him.

"Liking the view I see. Well, I will be leaving soon to go take care of some business. Are you going to see me off, or should we just say our good-byes here?"

"What kind of business is it?"

"Oh I just have to swat some annoying flies. Hopefully I will be back sometime tonight. Otherwise I will be home first thing tomorrow morning. I don't want to get too tired and start dosing off the road you know so I might get a hotel."

"Are those flies, the young man that has been in our business?"

Anoaka smiled at him. "Well, one of them is that man, Mr. Green. Once I get done with him, I don't think he will be in anyones business anymore. Are you coming down to see me off?"

The King didn't move. "I think that I'm going to stay up here for a while longer. Have a nice trip darling."

Anoaka's smile turned into a small frown. "Okay. See you either tonight or tomorrow morning. Be a good royal highness okay?" Then turned his head with her hand to look at hers and gave him a nice long kiss.

She made her way down to the driveway only pausing once, to look at the door that lead down to the basement where Matt resided. Well…what was left of him that was. As she continued, Kolat made his way toward her, dressed in a green suit and holding a cane like he was an aristocrat, as she was stepping out the door. She didn't have time for his antics and tried to brush him off.

"Oh, dear sister!" he called out to her in that "I'm a pure fucking delight" tone of his. She slammed the door behind her, hoping that would be some sort of hint to leave her alone. Unfortunately she was never that lucky when it came to her brother. He opened the door that also lead him to the outside, following his sister. "Sis-ter…. I have a question for you."

This made Anoaka stop in her tracks and roll her eyes up to the sky. "What is it, brother?"

"What the hell am I doing here right now?"

"Excuse me?"

"I have fulfilled my purpose, have I not?" He said as he was swinging his cane from side to side. With the tone that he was giving her, she was thinking that she could take that cane and smash it against his head. "You could try to take my cane, but I assure you that you would not be fast enough and than I would have to punish you with it instead."

"Stay out of my fucking head Kolat."

"I will as soon as you answer me."

"Yes you have fulfilled your favor to me. Is that what you wanted to hear?"

"No, I want to hear that I am no longer needed and that I may go home to my hospital."

"Your mental hospital, don't forget that. Why are you asking me to be dismissed Kolat? You are a big boy. You have been for the best part of a millennium, if your don't count the dark ages. Could you be afraid of…"

Kolat interrupted her. "Don't fool yourself with such pipe dreams in your head to think that for a moment I am afraid of you, Anoaka of the Red. I merely was asking if you needed my services anymore and what you would give me to stay. That is all.

"Seeing that you must not have anything more for me to do and that you are on your way as you speak to kill the shit-heads in that jailhouse, I suppose I can take my leave. No?"

Anoaka barely thought about it. "Yes fine. Go back to your warped sense of a home and be sure to get yourself examined while you are there. And by the way, don't you ever use my full title in the open again. Do you understand me?"

"Then never use my real name in the open like you just did, twice." Matching her look of distain in her eyes. "Good luck Charlotte. Don't fuck this errand up."

She turned away from him without another word and got into the nearest car that was in her enormous garage. Ironically, it was the red Ferrari. the same one that she used to pick Danny a little over two years ago. She reflected on that for only a second. Followed by a mutter of just two words: "Fucking asshole." Then she was off.

Near the same time that Anoaka or Charlotte whisked herself away in her nice Ferrari out of the driveway, Tyler and Tanya were just on their way back to their cells after spending some of their valuable time in a courtroom for their hearing. The judge was less than pleased with their pleas of not guilty, along with their lawyer Richard McCoy, thinking that with guilty plea that they could get a reduced sentence without having to go to a jury trial. Only now that they pleaded not guilty, his options on defending them were now very limited. He heard their story about the woman that took souls and killed people, along with having Tyler's old Army buddy control his movements and sent him to kill the both of them after he witnessed a crime in an alleyway that had no victim. He was going to be crucified by the partners of the firm he let them go on the stand with a story like that.

The judge wasn't impressed either. Thinking that Mr. McCoy would have persuaded his clients a little better to take the punishment and move on, was the best course of action. Only now the county is going to have pay for a high profile case with a police officer still missing.

As for setting a bail; one-million dollars each, the judge seeing that they were a risk to the safety of the state, as well as a flight risk. As they heard the judge's explanation, both Tyler and Tanya sunk in their seats. Tyler thinking he was going to melt inside his orange jumpsuit. Maybe he was just hoping for that. All his hope for survival was now gone.

When finally getting back to their cells, Tanya stood in the cell until the door slammed shut behind her. Almost immediately she fell to her knees and broke down crying. Tyler went and sat down on the only thing that resembled a chair in his cell which was his bunk and put his face in his hands. He too almost broke down crying, knowing now that there was no way for him to get out of here before that woman showed up to kill him somehow.

Even in the face of waiting for his death, he couldn't help but think about Matt. Hoping he was still alive, somehow. Hoping that since finding him that Charlotte, the Scarlet Bitch, hadn't killed him or made his life a living hell, even though, logic and doubt creeped in and slapped him with a hard truth and said that Matt *was* dead or in terrible enough condition to make him want to be dead. These past months, thinking about Matt was hard, but it kept him going to try and find a way to rescue him.

This time, Tyler felt that he had failed him. Sitting here in this cell waiting to be killed by that bitch. He failed him for sure.

Chapter 21

An hour passed by. Tyler calmed himself more or less as he sat there on his bunk. He had no idea when Charlotte the Scarlet Bitch was going to make her way to the jailhouse, if she hadn't made her way here already, but he still had his body prepared for what ever was coming his way. If a guard was under her control like Danny was, and tried to open the door to shoot him, he was going to be prepared. What chance he had with his bare hands and facing a man with a gun—he didn't really want to think about *those* odds. He just knew that he wasn't gonna roll over and die, like so many he was sure did before that faced this woman.

He kept his eyes on the cell door, waiting for whoever it was that was coming for him. He half hoped that it was that Sgt. Gentle that was always giving him such a hard time. That would feel pretty good as he took him down to the ground. Well…*if* he could take him down to the ground was what he should be thinking. Even if it wasn't Sgt. Gentle, the guard would still have a gun, and probably wouldn't hesitate to use it on him if he had a chance and think that his own life was in danger.

"Oh, who the fuck am I kidding." he mumbled to himself. "I can try and fight my way out of this as much as I want." he than thought about the outcome of everything: *Let's say I do get out of here through fighting with a guard for his gun, escaping my cell, making my way through the jailhouse that is full of guards, finding Tanya's cell, somehow free her from her locked cell, then get out of the jailhouse, and avoided every cop that surrounded not only the city, but basically the whole state. How the fuck am I going to stop that thing? The thing that walks around as a woman. Charlotte. Her name is Charlotte.*

He thought long and hard about what he had to do. Only there was no clear way for him to beat Charlotte. He remembered shooting her. He saw the blood coming out of her shoulder. Then, the clear horrible angry face, and the march toward him afterward. He knew that if he could he could shoot her again. Despite what she said to him that he couldn't shoot her, clearly proven her wrong. But what good did it do? She was still alive after the shots, worse, she was pissed off and still kept on trucking along to kill him.

He shook these doubts away. He told himself that it didn't matter. He still needed to get Matt out of whatever hell she put him through. If he was still alive, he had to get to him and to do something about Charlotte. He would try to get a gun. If he could get out of here, by God, he would go and get a gun and pump her full of leaky holes if that was what it took. Because he knew that she needed to be stopped.

After he had these thoughts, reality sunk back in as he came back to looking around the cell. He was still trapped in here. And she was still making her way here as well. Like a trapped rat in a cage, waiting for the cat to come and swallow him. Yet he sat there on his bunk and he waited.

Charlotte, also known as Anoaka of the Red, just passed the exit on Highway 51 north that lead to Plainfield. If she was driving a sedan, her estimated time of arrival would be around an hour and a half at best. That was if you had a full tank of gas, had no bathroom breaks, and followed the seventy miles per hour speed limit that the state just recently added five miles per hour higher than the previous year.

Charlotte/Anoaka was in a Ferrari. Gas tank was indeed full after she filled it up in Lake Geneva, that followed a few waves from the locals that always admired her taste of cars. She did not grab anything to drink or to eat, so she had no need for a bathroom break in the foreseeable future. She did travel the speed limit, only if there was an area that had reported speed traps and areas she was a little uncertain of, but mostly she hit the pedal to the floor where the needle on her odometer would sometimes just grace that one-hundred mark that glowed nice and blue. Then she would let go of the pedal just in case there were any hiding police cruisers that were parked along the highway. Granted if they did pull her over there wasn't much they could do, she could outrun even the most well maintained police cruiser, but she didn't want any attention drawn to her then necessary. Yes a red Ferrari was means to get attention, but she wanted to get to where she was going as fast as possible.

At her current rate, she would be at the Marathon County Courthouse in just shy of forty-five minutes. She could hardly wait.

Tyler almost fell asleep as he sat there on his bunk, watching and waiting to jump the next guard that might come into his cell. His eyes weighed as much as lead weights on a diver. Lack of food for the past couple of days since his encounter with Danny, Danny's death, being arrested, then transported to Wausau from Eagle River, until finally going to court and meeting in front of a judge that pretty much told him that he wasn't going anywhere for the foreseeable future, was taking a toll on his mental state as well as his physical state.

His eyes were just about to close for good, when there was a sudden CLANK that came from his cell door that it woke him up from the daze that he was in. He forgot what he was supposed to do for and instant, until he saw the guard that was coming through the doorway with a cart. A food cart by the look of it. It had plastic trays with plastic covers on top of them. Lunchtime, it appears, has arrived at Marathon County Courthouse.

"Stay where you are, and don't get any ideas." said the chubby guard that pushed the cart and pulled out a tray of food. "I hope you like sandwiches. 'Cause if you don't—I guess it's a case of tough tittie said the kitty." He placed the tray on the far opposite side of the bunk to where Tyler was sitting.

Tyler was just staring at the man. Observing him, looking for a gun if he had one. He looked at his belt and saw that there wasn't one. That—was a problem. His only hope was to knock him down somehow.

"What are you looking at?" The guard said following Tyler's gaze. "Looking for a way out, that doesn't include a legal way? Good luck with that! You would have a long way to go and be taxed and sent to the Big Big House if that happened. Judge doesn't put up with that shit here. Word of advice; shut up and don't do anything *more* stupid than you have already done." Then he was on his way out of the cell, backing himself out in front of the cart.

Tyler barely heard him, he was thinking that since he was backing out he could push the cart far enough to hit the man against the wall. Maybe getting lucky and hitting his head against the wall and knocking him out. He saw things like that happen on television, when watching those attempted prison escapes, didn't he?

Then sense started to come to him, just in time like it almost always did before he was about to do something stupid. Thinking to himself, he thought, "I can't do this. I can't make things worse by trying to escape from jail. That's a sure way to make things way worse. If the guard was right, then I would be detained in a more secure place, making it harder to fight of any attack that Charlotte would make on Tanya and I. What shit I'm in. Fuck. I don't want to die here. No way. Not like a rat in a cage."

He turned to look at the food that the guard left and thought that he should eat it, so he could keep his strength up for what was coming. But then depression was starting to sink in again. What was the point? He was going to die right? Why make time last longer? Why?

There was a sudden flash again of Matt. It was the of the last time he saw him, on that night they went out just the two of them for a time on the town. A much needed time out for Tyler, coping from the news that Samantha dropped on him. Remembering how much fun the both of them had just to hang out.

Then an image popped up that showed Tanya. Tanya who decided to help him with whatever came there way in this nightmare. Who went into hiding with him to go and help find Matt. Whatever it took to make sure their friend was back with them. He twinged at his heart to think that she had sacrificed so much for him. Then sank again after he realized how close his was to giving up on her, right here and now. It started to make Tyler loath himself. He…no, they. They did not come all this way for him to give up. If not for himself, at least for Tanya.

Then a smaller flash of a face appeared before him, one that he had not expected, but was there nonetheless. Samantha. Sammy, his Sammy. The way she looked like before she was unhappy. With her hair out loose in the wind that looked like golden leaves in a tree, rustling to and frow against her head, with a big smile that always melted his heart whenever he looked at it. And those eyes…those green beautiful eyes that sparkled. He missed her. He missed her for months now. What she must have gone through thinking that he was this monster that the news was making him out to be. When instead he was fighting a monster, a real one. With teeth that were sharp and its touch was lethal. Coming in the form of a woman.

"I'm not going to die in here. The fuck if I'm going to die in here."

He picked up his tray of food and began eating. He knew that he was going to need all of his strength. He didn't stop eating until the tray was picked clean. A half hour later, when the guard came back to pick up the tray, he watched him only to defend himself in case that Scarlet Bitch was using him to kill him. The guard gave him a look like he didn't give a shit one way or the other, collected the tray and left.

Forty-three minutes from passing Plainfield she arrived at Marathon County Courthouse and was completely annoyed with what she saw. Anoaka looked at the building that housed both the menaces that caused her so much stress, and thought that the building was always deemed ugly in her eyes. It was not the first time she ever saw this building. Oh no. Every time when Danny drove her pass the building whenever she made her way onto Grand Avenue, she would see the monstrosity of a long grey looking building that was covered with local patriotic, official decor. Such as the statues of the first human world war, as well as the statue of the police officer that stood for the service to the community. Oh how it made her want to vomit all over the street right here and now.

Which didn't make her feel bad about having to kill any of the pigs that were inside.

She had no love for law enforcement, true. Though the same could be said that she had very little love of any human being, unless they were loyal to her. Police officers of all sort weather, local, State, or FBI, she always felt that they could get particularly nosy about business they had no particular need to be apart of. Cops and federal agents crossed her path a few times; the latest was in the fifties when the country was going under a giant witch hunt for commies that they deemed were a threat to the American way of life. She killed them and made it look like they fled the country with a bunch of federal money. That wasn't easy to do, but she got it done.

That was the last time she encountered any police officer, other than the standard speeding ticket, or parking violation her aliases would take care of. That was until today, from what she was about to do to get in. If she really wanted to, she could just march right in and go get Tyler herself. Taking nothing but touching a few police officers that could be her distraction from the rest of the police force, while going to find the cells where the two little shits were and killing them both. Like taking souls from a couple of babies.

But she didn't want to be notice, like always. Even to her, the precautions that she made to keep anyone from noticing her, made life boring and complicated at times. Only it had to be done.

So what needed to do was to gain access to the inside—she waited in the parking lot that housed the police cruisers. She waited and waited.

Looking at the door that was the closest to the parking lot. The one she was sure was accessed only by officers of the law. She would walk back and forth in the lot, giving glimpses to the cop cars and the busy traffic that would pass the courthouse. At one point, she leaned against one of the cruisers and just started playing with the driver side rear view mirror that was attached to the door. Facing it up toward herself to give herself a once over. Looking at the curves of her body and the darkness that contrasted her pale skin.

She felt an urge, almost a need, to rip the mirror off the vehicle, toss it on the ground and smash it with her heel. She was sick of this and wanted it to end right now. Wanted those two dead, at this very instant. The past couple of months have felt like this. For the past few months she felt this way, and was downright sick of it.

"Hello. Can we help you miss?"

She had to get herself under control once again. She discovered that her face was twisted in anger, but she was not facing the direction of the voices. She adjusted back into a smile, then turned around to see two cops heading her way. The one on the right of her, and the closest to her, was white, skinny, short man, that had his sunglasses, even on such a dreary day, saw on his name tag that his name was Dodson. The other was a stocky woman that went by the name of Adams, had a build to her in not only her arms, but her ass and chest as well from Anoaka's point of view. She did not have her sunglasses on like her partner, but she seemed to have her hand move slowly to her side arm; a taser judging by the bright yellow handle. Anoaka wasn't going to use violence, she didn't need to. She stretched out her hand to greet them both.

The woman moved her right hand from her belt and slowly picked it up the shake the hand that was offered, right after her partner finished shaking it as well. With a firm grip, she shook the hands of both the officers as she said, "My name is Mrs. Brisbane." she finished shaking the hands at the same time she finished her sentence. She didn't say anymore. She didn't have to. Both the cops turned right around, pain in their eyes with a drag in their walk.

She took them over immediately.

She felt their anguish, but she didn't care. If anything it gave her more pleasure to feel their pain and suffering just for being what they were; human and cops. She followed right behind them as they made their way back to the door they just exited from the courthouse. She noticed that the door could only be opened with a keycard that only cops of police officials had on them. Anoaka made the woman cop grab for her card that she saw was right on the side of her belt on one of those retractable belt accessories. As the woman was swiping the card on the pad that was attached to the wall, she saw and felt the pain that was on her face from the reflection of the door window.

She opened the door and made both the officers walk into the building. The door was about to close on her, until she quietly held the door open a little bit so it wouldn't lock on her, making her fresh new recruits do a little scout ahead of her. She listened carefully through the door, listening to anyone else that might be near the doorway and give the two officers a "Hey, did you forget something?" sort of chat. She had them stop in their place and heard no ones voice. The only emotions she felt were the fear and pain that were in both officers, there was no hope of seeing someone. That was good for Anoaka. "Just going to make my way in." she said quietly to herself, letting herself in the building. "No need to make a ruckus." She made the two officers move forward into the small space that was in the courthouse.

The interior, in her opinion, was incredibly worse than the exterior was. Why did they decorate with the color brown? Did they want people to be depressed all the time when walking into this building, or just the sense of no hope? She guessed she could she the latter point of view for the local judicial system. Best not to get hopes up, and just let the criminals face the reality that was before them: ugliness. It wasn't so much that the carpet and walls were brown, but the furniture that was just in the opening was also brown, pictures on the walls were mostly brown in primary, with wooden rails that seemed to surround everywhere the hallways lead to, as well as the the room that lead to the outside. Once again she had that sense that she might need to vomit from this people's attempt at decoration. She moved up to both the police offers and whispered in their ears. She didn't need to do it, she could tell them what to do do with her mind. She learned to work her ability that way a long time ago. But she had a feeling she had to say it out loud, if only to tell their conscious minds what she wanted them to do. "Find Tyler Green and Tanya Walsh. Kill them, and anyone in your way. Go." She hesitated on the second part of the last sentence as she gave a thought if any cops would try to stop them. She gave them the answer right there then.

The two cops started to walk through the room to make their way toward the hallway. Their walks once again staggered, took each an dreadful step toward their goal, while Anoaka waited until they both reached a distance away from her, then followed slowly down the hallway. This was the day, it had to be.

Tanya steadied her thoughts. Well…to the best of her ability. It never escaped her that she and Tyler were in great danger, even in the jailhouse. She thought back to Danny, there was little else to think about while she was in her cell, unless it was to contemplate how extremely fucked she was from the oncoming storm the bitch was bringing with her—but even then—that too brought her thoughts into a loop back to Danny. Danny laying in the woods, shooting his own brains back into the woods. Just after he had the jump on her and almost killed her.

No. That wasn't Danny. She never knew the guy, but there was something strange that was going on with him that changed him… at least she thought. The voice that changed into the dark thing that spoke, from the cries of someone that was trying to help a dear friend of his.

The getting shot and not being able to register it as pain was another. At least not registering it at first. It came back to the screams of pain after he came back to his supposed "normal" self. After Tyler was holding her for comfort—for almost getting killed.

That was nice. It was comfort from man that she hadn't had in a long time. Not for about five years since she was in love with Sean Crew, until he died from a stupid motorcycle accident where he was showing off on Highway 29, standing on his seat at sixty-five miles per hour and then colliding with a pulled over pick up truck and was killed instantly.

Killed instantly. Killed instantly.

Killed. Killed. KILLE.

Dead. Killed meaning dead. Dead, like Danny.

Fuck. Going into that loop again. Fuck.

She looked around her cell, almost the exact same way that Tyler did a few hours ago. Like Tyler, she was alone in this cell. Thinking it was probably for reason of being so high profile of a case. Or that they were willing to make an example of the both of them.

Right as this thought came to her, her cell door opened. The loud crank of the lock being unlocked was thunderous in the small cell, followed by the squeak of the hinges that sounded like they needed a whole bottle of WD-40 sprayed on them. The squeaking was so loud and seemed like an eternity it was so annoying. Tanya hoped that whoever it was, was here to get her out of here for the noise alone of that fucking door. When she looked up after straining her eyes and her ears to the sound of the door, her heart sank deep into her chest.

"Hello Miss Walsh." Said Sgt. Don Gentle.

Well no way in hell this guy was going to let him out of here. "Hello, Sgt. Gentle. Anyway, you are here to get me out of this cell?"

Gentle gave Tanya a smile that looked like it was on the burst of laughter. "You better keep dreaming Miss Walsh."

"I'm thinking more along the lines of just a different cell. That door is fucking annoying as hell. At least do something about the squeaking, please! WD-40 will clean that shit right up."

Sgt. Don Gentle pretended like he didn't even hear this. He brought with him a file and was looking into it as Tanya was giving her pleas to him about the squeaky door. "Says here that this is the first time in your adult life that you have been arrested."

Tanya didn't say anything.

"I say adult life because when you were a minor you were caught with shoplifting at the age of thirteen. It says: Stealing a bottle of alcohol. At age thirteen. That is pretty young to get caught with alcohol, don't you agree?"

"In this state, it's not all that surprising. We have the most alcohol related crimes in this state than any other state in the country. That includes California."

"Yes that's true. But rarely are they at the age of thirteen. Nor does that make it okay." There was silence for a few moments as Sgt. Gentle looked up from the file and started to stare at Tanya. She just stared back at him, not saying anything. She knew where this was going. That she was nothing but a troublemaker in his eyes, and always would be. How most cops looked at her after she got arrested for such a stupid thing that her and her friends did along time ago.

Before she was arrested, she would wave at every cop, and they would wave back. Look at her like she was the nicest little girl that they came crossed, and to herself, she was. She was always helping people out with whatever needed to be done. Her friend Kacy, had a dad who was a farmer. They always hung out together. Their favorite thing that they always did was to go swimming. Sometimes in the river, or in a lake, but mostly at the city pool over in Medford. Sometimes they would bike together, and other times they would have either one of their parents take them to the city pool. On times they were stuck with busy parents they would make due and use their bikes to go to Lake Esadore. In the summer Tanya would try to bike over to Kacy's parents farm everyday. When Kacy was old enough, around ten years old, Kacy would have to do chores, preventing her from going swimming. She said that her dad said that "We all had to do our part, so the farm can grow, and we can do the things that we want to do". That made sense to Tanya. When this problem occurred to Tanya, she went over to Kacy's father, Anthony, and asked what she could do around the farm to help so Kacy could get her chores done faster, so they could go swimming.

She didn't just do that with Kacy, she did that with all her friends. Most of the time it seemed like she was helping them out more than going out to play. But in her mind, if helping them got them to come play with her, than that was what had to be done.

She got a reputation of being helpful around Medford. Teachers at school looked toward her to help a student if they needed help with something they didn't understand. Police officers would always give her a nice wide smile of approval that said, "That there is a nice young lady".

But once Tanya and her friends did that stupid crime, everything changed. Her middle school friends and her were told by their parents to never drink until you were at least eighteen years of age. Tanya, Kacy, and their other friend Kala were wondering what the big deal was one night. It was just like drinking water wasn't it? The three of them went into Kacy's parents liquor cabinet, and took out a bottle that read Absolute Vodka. They knew that they couldn't have much so they each just took a swig so Kacy's parents wouldn't notice. The taste felt like it would make their mouth as well as their throats catch on fire. They immediately put the bottle back and then left the rest of the liquor alone. At least for a whole week they did.

They would sneak drinks here and there from each others parent's houses. Eventually getting wise to the fact that their parents would catch on that booze was missing from the bottles, and that there were only a few other people other than themselves that could have been taken it. A few *young* people. That was when they got the idea to steal a bottle from the grocery store.

Only they got caught.

The judge that provided over the case gave each of the girls probation, and one hundred hours of community service. Standard sentence that rang home for the girls. All three of them. Having never stolen another thing for the rest of their teen years, and never had a drink of alcohol, until their graduation night from high school. Only the damage, in the communities eyes, was already done.

No more the happy smiles that came Tanya's way when she would walk down the street of Medford. People saw her, and addressed her as a troublemaker, always and forever. Never giving her or her friends a smile over a stupid mistake. Just like what Sgt. Gentle was given him now. Like a bug that needed to be squashed, but you didn't want to be the one to do it because you didn't want to get your shoes dirty.

"What do you want me to say Sgt. Gentle? That I'm sorry for that stupid crime? I think you know that I am. And I don't see how this story has to do with the situation at hand, do you?"

"Anyone's arrest record, always has to do with the situation of the time, in my opinion." he said. "This is proof that bad things aren't so uncommon for you is it Miss Walsh?"

"I hardly think that an arrest for shoplifting over twelve years ago, hardly means that I killed anyone or kidnapped them. You might actually have to do some real police work, Sgt. Gentle. Otherwise you might have another Avery Case to deal with."

Their was a flare of anger in Sgt. Gentle's eyes. The Avery Case, which was now a national attention grabber, always made him and every cop he knew flinch as soon as they heard of it. A case with very little proof, and the look of police covering something up, just so they could put a man that got compensation from the state two years before, for being put in prison for a crime he did not commit.

"You better watch your tone Mi—."

He was cut off by the sound of gunfire outside of the cell. He turned to look at the door with his hand on his sidearm. Tanya's face grew with terror.

Tyler shot to his feet, as the shot rang clear and close to his cell. "What the fuck?!" he said in panic. Then it dawned on him that he somehow forgot: she was no longer coming.........She was here.

Dodson was the one that first came across Officer Paul Craig in the corridor. After a look of confusion on Craig's part that lead to a question of "Did you forget something, the both of you?", which lead to the pull out of his weapon, and a pulled trigger. Officer Craig fell to the floor, dead before he was even aware of what happened. You couldn't blame him. Who expects to get shot by someone they worked and got along with? Weather you blamed him or not doesn't matter. He was the first to die in that courthouse.

The shot rang out everywhere in the building. Judge Faber, who was speaking to a young man named Morris Metz about his traffic record on the other side of the building. After the young man that he was ticketed for going twenty-five miles over the speed limit, he stopped in mid-sentence where he was going to cut the boys fine to a hundred and fifty dollars, instead of the two-hundred and fifty. Instead raised his head in panic, looking toward the door of the courtroom, then to his bailiff for security where he had his hand on his sidearm that was a taser. Officers that were at their desks, suddenly raised their heads. Along with clerks, civilians, the police Chief, the Sheriff, and one K-9 unit dog. Not to mention the twenty-three inmates that are being kept in the jailhouse.

Officers Dodson and Adams walked over Officer's Craig's body, each catching a foot on his chest as they did this. Dodson's gun was still smoking from the discharged shot. Tears were going down his face as this was happening. For his fellow officer that he unwillingly shot, and for the pain he was feeling from not having control over his body.

Adams was also in tremendous pain, but was also incredibly scared. No way the academy could train for a situation like this. No, sir. She felt that her right hand grasped around her gun as well and was pulled out of her holster, holding it in her hand. She knew that the woman that was making this happen, was going to make her shoot the next person that appeared. Just as she thought it, two more officers appeared from around the corner of the narrow hallway, guns drawn.

"What happened? What happened to Craig? Is he ali—."

The officer named Hanson, was cut off. What he saw next reminded him of the movie *Pulp Fiction*, seeing both John Travolta and Samuel L. Jackson's characters raising their guns at the exact same time.

That was exactly what Dodson and Adams were doing now, raising their guns and pointing directly at himself and Phillips right behind him. Hanson didn't raise his gun in response, shocked at what he was seeing. Phillips behind him didn't see the action until it was too late. He was staring at the body of the dead officer on the ground as soon as he saw that there were two cops already at the scene, he never thought that they could be the shooters. Hanson looked at them and had enough time to think of one thing: "It was them, they're crazy." He then saw the flashes of light coming from the barrels, the feeling of pain from the impact of the bullets, until finally seeing the sad distorted faces of both Adams and Dodson. Like they were incredibly sorry for what was happening to them.

Tears were flowing freely now from Officer Adam's eyes now. She was trying to scream now, to try and warn people not to come near them, but there was nothing but the sound of air coming out of her mouth. There was incredible pain in her throat now. Dodson was mentally counting the bullets that he discharged at the other officers, hoping that he was almost out of ammunition. Yes, that would mean that he would wound up getting shot, but he didn't think that he would survive this encounter anyways. With the pain that was going through him, with no way to express it, he didn't want to.

They both continued down the hallway. Staggering into the jailhouse area where they noticed a controlled entrance into the jail itself. There was a armored door that was attached to a booth with a wide window. Inside there were control panels and monitors right before a guard. The guard was looking at the monitors, frantically. Both Adam's and Dodson knew that there weren't any cameras in the hallway where they shot Hanson and Phillips, so the guard possibly seeing him as a threat might be out of the question. The guard that was named Brian Tessmere, grazed his eyes on the monitor that showed directly out side the booth and saw both Adams and Dodson. He turned around with wide eyed fear and approached the microphone. "I can't let you two in. We are on lockdown until we catch whoever is doing the shooting. Keep your guns drawn to see who comes down the hallway."

Dodson stared at the guard, his own eyes filled with fear. He suddenly felt his right arm that was weighted by the gun in his hands, to lift up. He thought that it was going to lift to try and shoot the glass of the control booth. Good. Then that bitch that was controlling him could use up all the bullets from his gun and be pointed out as the shooter, then be taken out and maybe even be lead to the woman that was waiting in the waiting room in the lobby.

Something was wrong though. He could feel the weight of his arm raising, but he noticed that it didn't raise right in front of him. Instead it lifted and stretched outward from his right side, like he was exercising with a heavy weight. As soon as arm was out stretched straight out, it stopped. Then adjusted to move maybe an inch, maybe two forward, then once again stopped. Dodson couldn't move his head to see what he was pointing at, but looking at the guard that was in the booth, and the horror that was growing there along with the disbelief of what he was seeing, he figured that he was probably aiming at his partner of four years—right straight in the head.

"What the fuck are you doing?!" Yelled Brian in the microphone. "You're going to kill her!"

Both of them could not speak, but they both simultaneously mouthed "Please. Please. Please."

Fresh tears pouring from not just Adam's face, but Dodson's as well. Brian the guard looked dumbfounded and horrified at the same time. He shook his head very slowly, thinking that he wanted to help them, even though he didn't understand what was going on that Dodson was pointing his gun at Adam's head.

Was he taking her hostage? Was he the one that was doing the shooting? And if so, why was he doing it? He wanted the questions answered, but he couldn't let him in. No way.

Dodson's thumb pulled the hammer back, and maintained its position aimed at Adams. Brain thought that it was an eternity since the strange standoff that was before him started.

Then, in a quick motion, Adam's left hand move in lightning speed and pushed the gun in the air while her right hand came up and hit Dodson straight in the throat. Dodson went down, while the gun was stripped from his right hand by Adams, then holding his throat with both hands on his throat, struggling to breath. Adams had the weapon pointed at Dodson, keeping her face on him.

As soon as he saw that Dodson was down, Brian Tessmere pulled out his taser, hit the gate door button, and moved out of the booth to give Adams support. "You got 'em? Jesus, what the fuck?! He was the shooter huh? He was the fucking shooter! Adams, give me your cuffs, quick." Brain looked up from looking at Dodson, and saw the big black eye of the gun barrel that was just pointed at Adam's head. Then a sudden flash, and Brian fell into darkness.

The spray of blood and brains seemed to get everywhere. The wall that was directly behind Brain, was instantly soaked with red, with white chunks that seemed to be mixed in. Adams looked down and saw that Dodson was just as soaked with Brian's blood as the wall. Brian himself landed right onto Dodson's chest and poured the grey and red remains of his brains onto him as well. Dodson got up, looking like he took a red shower and followed Adams as the two walked through the open gate door that Brain forgot to close behind him. Adams, who also had blood on her face, noticed that Brian didn't just forget to lock the gate behind him, but also forgot to hit the alarm button that rang out for a lockdown and a serious situation was going on in the facility.

Adams was trying with all her might to try and push the button, it was inches away from her since she entered the small control booth. She saw her hand raise up and felt a glimmer of hope. It hurt more to try, but she thought that the pain was worth it. And by-God it was working, wasn't it?! She was going to push the button! No more people were going to die! She was closer, a mere two inches from the button, moving her hand closer as she tried to outstretch her index finger to push it. Behold her finger did indeed outstretch. This time the pain receded some, she was an inch away....

Then her heart dropped as the pain came back and her hand moved past the button to press another button. A button that was close to the alarm button. Only this button wasn't going to help her, or Dodson, or anybody else in the jailhouse.

It was the automatic inmate cell door release button. A few seconds later, she could hear all the cell doors that were closed in the jailhouse, slam open.

Chapter 22

Tyler was pacing around in his cell. There were more and more gunshots being heard from the courthouse, and he wasn't the only one that was hearing them. Cries from other cells could be heard. Mostly filled with "Get me out" and "I hear gunfire, what's going on?".

Tyler was about to join these cries, even though that they probably wouldn't do much good. He thought that even if the building was on fire, the guards would be little inclined to help them out. There were certain rules about that sort of thing, not that they would tell any of the inmates what those were. In times like those, or like these, they don't tell you those things until its too late.

There was a silence from the gun fire. So far there had been five shots that had been heard through the jailhouse, but since the silence of the gunshots, the panic had started to set in. Not just for the inmates that were around Tyler in the other cells, but in Tyler as well. She was here. She was here and she was going to get in just as he had predicted before. Using some guard as a way to distract all the other guards and cops that were in the jailhouse. Then in the confusion, Charlotte, the Scarlet Bitch, or some other guard or inmate or person that was under her control, will come in here and kill both him and Tanya. All too perfect a plan. Didn't even need to be that thought out all that long. Just using the mask of confusion, that was all it really takes. That's all it takes, and now he and Tanya were just sitting here, waiting to die. Waiting to die, like cows waiting to be slaughtered.

One more gunshot rang out and then there was silence.

The yelling and cries of wanting to be saved had suddenly stopped. There was no noise now. Not even a graze along the cell doors, not a yell to see if anyone was alright, nor another gunshot that was followed after that one. That last gunshot seemed to speak it all: People were dead in that direction.

The silence was deafening that Tyler wanted anyone to speak up, anyone at all. To scream for their lives, to beg to be let out, anything. ANYTHING!

There was only one sound that followed that last, horrifying gunshot, it ranged loud to every cell in the jailhouse, and made Tyler scared out of his mind.

With the sound came the visual; his cell door was opening. After his, every door in the place seemed to open on cue.

There was the sound of mummers. Soft whimpering ones that were attached to voices not two minutes ago were going nuts with pleas to let them out. Now they figured that maybe the safest place for them was to be locked up. There were mummers, along with small scraps on the ground from the sandals that they gave to the inmates instead of their shoes, that could be heard from his own cell. Unlike many of the other inmates, who were cowering away from the cell doors, Tyler stepped forward, wanting to see what was going on; accessing the situation that had been drawn for him. He poked his head out when someone yelled at him, "Hey you, get back in your cell. I'll get out my taser if you don't. The doors will close in a little bit, so get back in there!"

"I don't think so." Tyler mumbled to himself.

"What did you say?" said the guard that was now marching toward him, pulling his taser out of his holster. "You talking back to me son?"

Tyler paid no attention, he looked down the hallway from where he came from when he arrived at his cell. The main opening and the only way out of the jailhouse was that way. He had to find Tanya, she was in a lot of trouble now, just like him.

"GET YOUR ASS BACK IN YOUR CELL!" screamed the guard, now standing maybe three feet behind him. His taser drawn. Tyler turned around to look at the guard. As he was turning, he was thinking of a plan to wait until the guard got past him after he entered his cell, then try and slip past him as the guard would try and make sure that every other inmate was staying in their cell. After all, he couldn't really stop them all could he?

Once Tyler turned around, he saw the guard; big with a puffed out chest with the taser drawn out onto him. He had the laser sight on, telling Tyler he was serious about using it. That was good, he just wished he would stop pointing it at him. He thought his, when something else caught his eye. The look on the guards face, which Tyler didn't see, frown at the lack of attention that he was receiving, he then turned around and saw that there was another inmate that was behind him. He barely had time to register that the man was bald and almost a pasty pale white while being slightly on the heavy side, but his shoulders didn't appear to him that he was merely fat, before the man lifted up his fist and punched him square in the knock out button. Tyler judged that it probably wasn't the man's first time ever doing that. He looked on the ground and saw that the taser was just out of the guards reach. He bent over it and picked it up, giving the inmate a glance, and saw that the inmate had other ideas about the now ownerless taser. Tyler had his hand on it when Baldy lifted a boot that was making its way toward his wrist. Tyler was quicker than the oncoming boot and swiped it away while quickly standing up to meet the inmates gaze, stumbling back a little from the speed in which he reacted on. "This isn't for you," he said to the inmate, "but I need it for protection, so please don't make me waste any juice on you." He lifted the taser to show that he was serious.

The inmate looked like he was about to make a charge at him, but then Tyler looked at Baldy's face and saw that he was thinking better of his odds. Tyler thought that was good enough, he couldn't linger here knowing that death was on its way toward Tanya and himself. He made a dash toward the opening corridor.

Anoaka decided to get up as soon as she heard the last gunshot. She knew what it was, feeling the pain and the loss of all hope from the woman, followed by the shot; she knew that the woman cop Adams shot the guard to gain access to the jailhouse.

So Anoaka was on the move down the hallway, walking ever so slightly just in case some other pig made their way out into the the hallway to the jailhouse. Though she was quiet, border line to the point of stalking prey, she carried herself with a very malicious smile. There was no way for them to escape this, no way. This was what she was waiting for. She was not going to be denied what she wanted.

"No way." she said to herself. "No way. Not this time. Not if I have to burn this whole city to get them." She meant it.

"What the fuck is going on?" Sgt. Gentle said to himself, but Tanya took it as if he was talking to her.

"It's her. Fuck! She here and she is going to kill us!"

Gentle turned away from the opened cell door and looked at her, "Kill you? What do you mean? Who?"

Tanya went from scared to a little pissed off, "Well what could I mean?" She said sarcastically, "Someone is coming and is on their way to kill us. Well, Tyler and myself, but I'm sure other people don't really matter to her."

"Her? Her who? Who is doing this?" Sgt. Gentle was starting to sound a little scared himself, she started noticing that as soon as the gunfire was ringing throughout the building. That was good. He was right to be scared.

Tanya decided to give him some but not all the information on who was coming their way. She would have to fill in the rest later,(if there was a later) but right now there was just no time. "Her name is Charlotte, Tyler tried to tell you about her back when everything happened to him back in the alley, three months ago. She has been chasing Tyler and myself ever since. The woman you didn't believe him about is here, and she is coming to kill us."

There was a yell from a familiar voice outside of the cell door that was above the confused and scared voices of the other inmates. "Tanya? Tanya! TANYA WHERE ARE YOU!"

"OVER HERE TYLER!" she yelled this right at the same time Sgt. Gentle pulled out his sidearm. This was not a mere taser. He lifted up his gun, and took aim at the opened cell door. Tanya looked at him in disbelief, "What are you doing? You can't shoot him!"

Without looking back at her Sgt. Gentle said, "I'm prepared to defend you and myself from anyone that comes through that door."

About ten seconds later, Tyler was slowly looking into Tanya's cell, and saw that she was there, he smiled. Then his eyes glanced at the weapons-drawn Sgt. Gentle, then he frowned again. "Tanya, are you alright?" he asked.

"I'm fine"

"She is doing alright, but you better not step in here unless you want your brain to spray all the way to the cell behind you. I don't know what is going on here, but I will be damned if I will let you take advantage of the situation and try to escape. You are going to prison, boy. I am going to make sure of that."

Tyler looked at him, disbelievingly. "Right now, I'm just trying to survive what is coming. You heard the gunshots I take it? There is gunfire coming this way and all I know is, that we need to take refuge somewhere, or we are going to die." he turned to Tanya. "She's coming, you know that right?"

"Don't you talk to her!" Sgt. Gentle scowled at him. "You have until the count of three to get the fuck out of my line of sight, or there is going to be a discharge coming from my gun. Do you understand?!"

Tyler stood where he was, saying no more. He knew that talking to a scared man set in his ways was ludicrous. Anything that popped into Sgt. Gentle's mind now would seem like a good idea. Only what popped into his mind now was to stay here and potentially shoot anyone that steps foot into this cell. Tyler understood, he was scared as well. But he was not leaving without Tanya. So…..he stayed right where he was. Right in front of the cell door, with anger smeared all over his face.

Sgt. Gentle stood in the cell, not believing that Tyler wasn't moving. He wasn't going to take any of this shit. "One….Two…."

That was as far as he got. Tanya came up behind him and gave him a backhanded fist to the back of the neck. Knocked down, but luckily without his finger on the trigger so not to send a rogue bullet, he turned to Tanya, only to be greeted with her fist to between his eyes. He went out cold.

"Remind me not to piss you off ever."

"Yeah well, he had been pissing me off since you had been telling me about him at the cabin. For the record you were right. He's a fucking moron."

"We can talk about it later, right now we have to move. Pick up his gun, and don't forget his clips; something tells me will are going to need them."

"Ya think?!" Tanya did as he said and took the gun from Gentle's hand as well as the clips. She looked down at the unconscious asshole that wouldn't believe either of them if his life had depended on it—which it did—and decided to grab the handcuffs that were on his belt as well.

"You really think we are going to need those?"

"I don't know. All I know is that we have nothing right now and we are pretty much going into a blind fight. I would take a whoopee cushion if it would help us survive." she said this while shoving the cuffs and the gun clips of ammunition into the sports bra that the jailhouse gave her to use. She had no belt, and she figured that she was going too have to use her hands, so she figured her ladies were going to have some company…painful bra-filled company.

"Well…in that case…" he leaned down over the KO'd officer, and took his night stick. He had a thought that cops weren't allowed to bring their weapons into the jailhouse section of the courthouse. Wasn't that a rule? Maybe. If it was, Tyler had no time to think about it. He and Tanya needed to get moving. He looked at his new night stick and the taser he took from the other guard. Then, he looked at Tanya and the Barreda Police Issue. She pulled back the chamber to see if it was loaded, she saw that it wasn't, nor did she expect it to be. She pulled out one of the magazines from her breasts and locked and loaded, lifting it up to look down the sight. Tyler observed this until it was finished. Thinking that even though she was in jailhouse orange and that they were about to fight for their lives, she looked really good to him right about now. He shook this out of his head. Need to focus. Get into that military mode. He looked her square in the eye, "You ready?"

"No. Who can be really ready for this? But fuck it. Here we go anyway." They both made their way into the main cell hallway.

As soon as getting outside of Tanya's cell, they took a right; heading in the direction toward where the gun fire was heard last. Some inmates were walking around near their cells, mostly just wondering about the gunfire that was echoing throughout the courthouse. Their curiosity made them look, but most weren't that stupid enough to leave the safety of their own cell without some sort of weapon. Tyler lead the way, holding the taser out in front of him. He took a look at it, then called behind him. "Hey Tanya, I need the gun."

"What? What's wrong with the taser?"

"The taser would work with what we are about to face. It makes sense that you use the taser behind us, in case someone tries to take our weapons, okay?"

"Well then why don't I just take point?"

"Because I know what this bitch looks like, okay? So just give me the damn gun."

"Okay, okay." Tanya mumbled. "This doesn't change the fact that I'm the better shot."

Just so she would stop talking and so he could get back to the situation at hand, Tyler agreed with her.

They were quiet now. Tyler with the gun leading in the front, and Tanya with the taser glancing occasionally to their rear, they slowly started to make their way forward. The silence was everywhere. No longer were there the screams and yells of the other inmates that were slowly making their way behind them with overstep they took, staying in the cells. Some came to their doors and gave a confused glance, followed by a "You're not supposed to be out here" whisper toward them. Some saw the gun and quickly made their way to the farthest point they could reach in their cell, short of going through the wall itself to reach the cover they would be satisfied with. One or two that saw the two fellow inmates armed with police weapons, gave their support with their own little whisper, "Yeah! Fuck the Police. Do what you have to do." Tyler had no intention on killing any cop. Even if they were under Charlotte's control, no doubt about it that she was probably doing this attack that way. But he thought that if he could just disarm them and maybe knock them out, that might be enough. It worked with Danny at the cabin. Well....at least for a while. It was the waking up part that killed Danny in the end.

He heard footsteps, and stopped quickly. He looked around to see if he could use one of the cells as cover, but he was out of the holding cell area. Up ahead, he saw a hallway that went about ten yards before it took a sharp left turn. Before the hallway was a barred door that was wide open for anyone to come in, or come out. Tyler looked behind him and saw that there was a cell about ten feet from where they passed and signaled to Tanya by pointing that they had to make their way into there. Tanya didn't hesitate, she heard the footsteps too, and make a quick and silent dash toward the cell. Once in they saw that it was occupied. An old man that had a major problem with body odor. "What the fuck are you two doing?" he said loudly. "Get the fuck out of here, this is my cell!"

"Will you be fucking quiet!" Tyler quietly scowled. "You heard those shots before? Well those responsible are on their way. So shut up!"

"You can't tell me what to do." mumbled the stinky old man. The fact that he was whispering told Tyler that the man wasn't totally without some form of obedience. "Just like those fucking cops, telling you what to do and how to do it. Well fuck them and fuck you too. You try any of that prison target ass practice on me, I swear to God I will make sure that you have the worst fuck of your whole life."

"Good to know, now shut the fuck up." The man did, with a look of disgust on his face toward Tyler, but looked at Tanya like she was the last piece of pumpkin pie on the Thanksgiving table, and began to stare at her.

Tyler leaned against the wall that was right next to the cell doorway. Holding the handgun in his hands as if he were praying with it. As he heard the footsteps getting louder. He noticed that it sounded like there were two of them that had limps. Shit. She got to them. But two? How the fuck could she control two at the same time? Fuck. Fuck, fuck, fuck, fuck, fuck me!!

He waited. He gave a look toward Tanya and saw that she was frightened. He didn't blame her, he was frightened too. She was over by the far wall, opposite side of the old man, who was also quiet but seemed to take no notice of the situations he continued to look at

Tanya. She lifted up her sandals one, by one, making her way to Tyler, trying not to make a sound. Tyler thought to wave her off, but he also thought that she needed to hide, so instead he offered a hand to her to help her reach him as quietly as possible. She took ahold and was pulled next to Tyler, watching out for the night stick that he put down his pants, on his side.

More footsteps came closer, it was the only other sound they heard other than each others breathing. There was a clank noise of metal on metal, Tyler thought that it was maybe the sound of handcuffs, or a gun, that hit the barred doorway that lead to the cells.

Then there was silence.

No more footsteps. Along with the footsteps there was the sound of rustling keys before, but that also had stopped. There was nothing. Just the empty hollow scream of silence. Tyler was hoping that someone would speak, so that it would be broken, but it only continued. In that silence he found only uncertainty, he always had. Uncertainty of what had to be done, of weather or not they had gone deaf or not, or weather they were going to survive whatever uncertain act would follow. He was starting to silently panic now. Closing his eyes trying whatever he had to do so he could hear something in this silence that seemed to stretch on forever. *Calm down, calm down,* he thought to himself, and that already was starting to help. His thoughts were deflating the crazy panic that was filling inside his head like a balloon. He continued to stand there, and listen.

Now that the panic was leaving him, and his ears were ready to pick up any sort of sound that the jailhouse would give to him, he did hear something and it shocked him. It sounded like shallow breaths that were followed by three little sniffles at the end of each.

It was crying. Like the crying of a small child. Yes, he was certain of it. He turned to Tanya and saw that she heard it too. Mouthing to him the question, "Is that crying?"

He nodded back to her slowly. He fought the urge to look out of the cell. He wanted to see who he was dealing with or who Charlotte played her claws into to cause such pain, but then he reminded himself that he would probably get shot.

Just then he heard another sound. There were more of the knocking sound of footsteps that were making contact on the linoleum floor. Tyler thought it was a cop marching on the way to stop whoever the cops were that were shooting, but there was something different about these footsteps. If they were the steps of a cop rushing in to save the day, how come the steps seemed so relaxed, as if the person was going for a stroll? Not just a stroll, but like the person was having a good time, borderline ready to skip, as the sound of the steps was starting to get further apart from each other, yet the volume of them increased

KNOCK….KNOCK………KNOCK……………KNOCK…….

There was playfulness in those steps, and that was when he looked at Tanya and saw that she knew who it was as well. As soon as her footsteps stopped the two cops started to move forward. Tyler turned his head to look at the cell doorway. Waiting to grab an arm or hit a head with the night stick that he grasped as Charlotte made her way down the hallway. The footsteps made their way right before the cell door, and Tyler saw the barrel of the gun slightly enter the cell then stop. If it made its way in here further, he would grab for it and take the guard in he…..

"IF YOUR GOING TO FUCKING SHOOT ME, SHOOT ME. YOU CHICKEN SHIT MOTHER FUCKER. I FACED DOWN THE FUCKING GOOKS IN 'NAM, YOU THINK I'M AFRAID OF A PANSY ASS LIKE YOU?!"

Tyler was startled by the old smelly man's scream that he lost his concentration. Just as he regained it, the gun barrel was gone and Tyler heard the shuffling of limping legs move on to the next cell. Tyler breathed very slightly, knowing that Charlotte was really close and he didn't want to give himself away. Only he heard her laughter from about a few feet away, in response to the old man's backtalk. Tyler gave him a look, at the same time he heard cries and pleas of not being killed. He lifted a finger to his lips to tell the old man to shut the fuck up, when he heard footsteps approach from the other side of the wall. Only—they were moving away from them. Moving away until they finally stopped.

Tanya was looking at Tyler, and gave him a nudge to the shoulder that caught his attention. Mouthing, "What are we going to do now?"

Tyler shrugged, all he could think of was to stay right here. If they moved they were dead. If they made a sound they were dead. The only good thing was that Charlotte wasn't making the two cops she had against their will, shoot up the jailhouse. He didn't know if that was an act of mercy, or to preserve bullets so they could use them on them. If Tyler could guess, it was probably the latter.

Tyler looked in front of him and saw that the old smelly man got up onto his feet. He gave Tanya a look that told Tyler all he needed to know about the pervert. He turned his gaze away from her and started to make his way toward the doorway. Tyler attempted to make a grab at him, but could only do it in the lightest way possible so he wouldn't make a sound. The old man swatted air in front of him that told Tyler that he needed to get away from him. He made his way to the doorway and stopped. He looked both to his left, seeing the cops continue to look into the cells, then turned to his right. When he turned right, Tyler saw that he was looking slightly up in the air. "Hey missy!" the old man said to both Tyler and Tanya's horror. "Yeah you! You look pretty hot all up there in a police uniform. Say, you want to know what a real man feels like? I will make you feel things your high school sweetheart couldn't imagine! I will give you one hell of a ride."

Tyler and Tanya's eyes bulged from their sockets. This wasn't happening, no way. This old fuck was crazy. Here they were trying to get away from the psychotic bitch that had been hunting them for the past three months, and here was this old smelly con trying to fuck her! There was only one thought that came through his mind now, and if he could read minds like Kolat, he would know that Tanya was having the exact same thought as he: *we are going to fucking die in here.*

Anoaka ignored the old man as much as she could. She was trying to keep her attention on Adams and Dodson searching the cells. But the cat calls were starting to get on her nerves. She was perched up on the corner of the wall, with her left leg bend so she could sit on it while her foot kept her in place. Her right leg, stretched out in front of her placing her right foot on her left side wall to keep pressure up against the wall. She looked like an owl perched on the corner trunk of a tree.

"Come on sweet thing, don't let my age get in the way of a good time. Haven't you ever heard the old sayin' 'The older the berry, the sweeter the juice'?" She did, in fact heard that one before, back in the nineties when a few old men tried to pick her up when she was out on the hunt for the King. They picked her up alright, for about a minute while they were alone and then never seen again. "I know I'm not much of a ride to look at, but I assure you that the motor runs just fine once you get this diesel engine started!"

That was a good one. So good that she was trying to stifle a laugh, only she couldn't help but crack a small smile on the left side of her face. The old man saw it a cracked a smile of his own. "Yeah come on baby! I promise I won't take long. I can see you got things to do, how about *I* be one of those things!"

She was losing her concentration on the two cops, as she gave an eye roll on this last comment. She heard that one before, and it was starting to get on her nerves. She thought about going down there and shutting the old man up. It wouldn't take a whole lot of effort. She could hop on down there, give him a smile, push him over to a corner of the cell, and then poof! No more headache. Yeah that would be a good idea. After all the man was old, they would think that he just died of a heart-attack from all the excitement or what not. She was already going to make it look like Mr. Green and Miss Walsh went on a killing spree to escape. Well…what's one more body?

She hopped down onto the ground and saw that the old man had big smile on his face that looked a little hollow in the dental department. She might be doing him a favor after taking a closer look at him. Life was not kind to this man, then again he was in here so chances are, all that roughness was probably his own doing. Live hard and *try* to die young.

Fool.

As she approached him, she started to give him, her best "I want you" smile that she could give. Looking at the man, you would think that it would be hard, but she had decades of practice. Getting closer to the man, nearly ten feet away, the old man started to enter his cell.

That was good, she could kill him without that much more of a fuss and with a little privacy. Then she could get on with finding those two troublesome bastards.

She entered the cell doorway, when there was a sudden appearance of a long black object that was thin, but then started to grow in width. It hit her square in the temple and had her fall backward, but not out. All the same she felt her hold over the two cops fall away from her, as she struggled to figure out just what the fuck had hit her. Then she figured it out. She was hit in the face with one of those night sticks that the pigs always carried around with them. And she was hit in the head by the same amount of force only a few months back. Mr. Green was in the cell. When she looked up her suspicions were confirmed as she lifted her head in time to see him running down after her, lifting the night stick once again and then bringing it down home free. She didn't have time to respond, all she could do is wait for the impact. When it made contact, her head slammed down onto the linoleum, just as she heard voices of protest saying "Stop right there!"

Tyler finished the swing and saw that he knocked her out cold. The very next thing he did was drop the night stick, and raised his hands over his head. At first he thought that the voice came from the hallway that lead to their way out, looking to his right, he saw that no one was there. Looking toward his left, he saw Mr. Not-so-Sgt. Gentle himself pointing right at them, making his way slowly toward them. Tyler thought that the hit to the back of the head must have really done a number on him, but he couldn't worry about that now, they had to get the hell out of here while the Scarlet Bitch was out for the count.

"Come on!" he yelled back at Tanya who was in the cell doorway.

"Damn, boy! You really knocked her the fuck out! Didn't your mother ever tell you not to hit ladies?"

"Yes she did, but that thing is not a lady. Tanya let's move!"

"Just a sec!" she yelled back and picked something up quickly off the ground. Tyler didn't have time to see it, he just made a grab for her hand quick as she leaped off the ground and started to make a run for it. They didn't know how much time they had until Charlotte came to, but they didn't want to stick around to find out. Besides, it was a miracle in itself that there were no more guards and cops that made there way down the hallway. Judging by the way Charlotte was dressed in a cops uniform, he had a sneaky suspicion of that.

As they made their way through the corridors that took them a few minutes to navigate, he understood why. Wausau was a big city in the sense that is was bigger than the surrounding towns that populated most of central Wisconsin, but its police force was not the biggest as in the terms of Milwaukee or Chicago. Judging by the amount of bodies that they passed in the hallways, Tyler would be surprised if half of Wausau had its cops either available to them or alive. Neither took count as they were running to make it out of the building, but Tyler judged that there were at least eight that they passed by. One was right in front of the gate booth that people needed to go through to enter the jailhouse. They both stopped to a pair of bodies that seemed to have nothing wrong with them. "Looks like Charlotte has been having fun on the way here."

"Please don't say that. It's been horrible looking at the bodies of all those…those…well let's face it. Kids. Kids with badges, pretty much." She started to sob.

Tyler held her by the face so he could get her attention, "I know honey, I know. But listen to me. Right now we have to get out of here, but we can't do that wearing these orange jumpsuits. People will come over and try to stop us, if they see us leaving like this. Especially cops. So we need to put on the tops and the pants of these two cops to get out of here. Do you understand?"

"Yes." she could only give a one word answer, anymore and she risked breaking out in sobs just for having the mere thought of what they had to do.

They reached down and started to undress the two bodies of the cops that couldn't have been older than twenty-three. Tyler finished getting the top off of the body he was working on, when he saw that Tanya was having trouble getting the top off of hers. Her hands were shaky something so fierce, that Tyler thought that she must be freezing to death. He put his right hand on top of both of hers. "It's okay, I will get your while you watch out for her or anyone else. Here, take the taser, just in case." he handed it to her and noticed she was relieved to get up and move away from the bodies. She looked at him for a second.

"Thank you."

"No problem, just keep your eyes open, I'm counting on you."

It took him about two minutes to undress the bodies, then they each took turns watching out for other people, while the other quickly put on the uniform. Neither of them thought to take their jumpsuits off, knowing that it would just take too much time. Nor did they fuss over the shoes, putting their jail sandals back on because they just needed to look alright from a distance.

"Dammit. No keys. We are going to need some kind of car or we're fucked."

"Don't worry about it. Let's get a move on."

Tyler was confused by this. He knew they sure as shit weren't going to take the bus. They needed wheels to get as far away from here as possible. He was going to tell Tanya this, but then he noticed that she was already down the hallway that was opening up to a lobby. When she got in the lobby she saw that there was a door that led to the outside. Once she checked that there wasn't some sort of SWAT team ready to bust through, she opened the door and made her way to the parking lot.

"Tanya, we are going to need to get ahold of some wheels, it's the only way to get out of here fast enough."

She had a small smile on her face, "I know, and I don't think we can get away faster, than if we drove that." she pointed to a vehicle, and he turned to see where she was pointing, and then—he smiled too.

He saw a fire red Ferrari in the parking lot. He turned to her ready to say that they would most defiantly need the keys for a car like that, seeing as he couldn't hot-wire any type of car, let alone a Ferrari, when he saw that she had the keys dangling right in front of her, bearing the unmistakable Ferrari logo on the side of not only the key, but a keychain that was attached to it.

"Where the fuck did you get those?"

"As soon as you knocked that bitch to the ground, I saw that they fell on the floor. They must have been loose on her pocket or something. So right as we were leaving I picked them up as fast as I could."

"Good God woman I love you!"

"Love me later. We need to get the fuck out of here!" She tossed him the keys, knowing that this was too much car for her to handle right. He loved her a little more for that.

They hopped into the car and roared the engine to life. He noticed that even though they both passed through hallways of death, the roar of this car gave him an erection. He backed out of the parking space, made his way out of the parking lot, and was driving away from Marathon County Courthouse, where there was a monster being kept for the time being.

"Where are we going to go?"

"We need to stop and get some decent clothes or something. We can't drive around looking like this." Tyler said.

"Stop by my house quick so I can pick up clothes, shoes and some money that I have stashed. I can change in the car, and then we can stop in a store and run in to get you something to wear. Then we can figure out where to go from there."

"I already know where to go from there." Tyler said in a serious tone.

"Where?"

"The address that Danny gave us. 554 Bayview Drive, Lake Geneva. Matt is there and I am going to get him back."

"Tyler. We aren't ready for that. We have no idea what's waiting for us there."

"I know what's *not* waiting for us there. That Scarlet Bitch that just tried to kill us for the third fucking time. She will be stuck up here while we have her ride. Plus, when we had to take the clothes of the two cops, I took one of their guns as well as their ammunition. We are not going to be anymore ready than we are right now."

"Tyler. It's just. It could be dangerous."

"Have we experienced anything else lately?" it sounded like a joke, but his face said that he was dead serious. "If you don't want to go, I understand, and I don't blame you. Just tell me where you want to get off and I will do that. I just need a little money so I can get by for a few days. I don't see it going further than a few days."

"Is that how long you think you are going to survive for? Just a few days?"

"I don't really know. I just know that I am going to get Matt back, weather he is dead or alive."

Tanya took along sigh, "Just take me to my house." Tyler understood, he started to make his way through the town streets. He couldn't blame her for wanting to get out while she could. Fuck, he wanted to get out right now as well, but he knew that he needed to get Matt back first. "Wait for me when we get there. Hopefully the cops didn't find my hidden gun stash. Something tells me with this trip, the more guns the merrier."

Tyler smiled.

Anoaka was pissed.

Thermal nuclear pissed.

Right around the time Tyler and Tanya made their way to her car, she woke up to a big blurry orange blob that seemed to surround her. Once her eyes focused, she saw that she was indeed surrounded, but by the inmates that looked at her with curiosity, mixed in with fear.

"Stay right where you are! Don't you move a muscle."

Anorak looked up and saw that Adams the female pig, was standing directly on her right with her gun drawn on her. Charlotte didn't listen, her head hurt too much for her to give a shit on what the pigs wanted right now. She touched her tongue to her lips and could taste the copper that was her blood. She started to get up, looking around angrily for either the cocksucker that sucker punched her, or the cunt that was going to be nailed onto his corpse when she got ahold of them.

"I said don't move! Move again and I will shoot you!" at this the small crowd of inmates that surrounded her started to back up. They were curious about the cop that got beaten up, then had guns drawn on her by her own people, but not enough to get blood all over them or worse, get shot along with her.

"You better do as she says," said the other pig that was named Dolton, or maybe it was Dodson, she couldn't figure out which one at this point, and didn't really give a fuck. She started to get to her feet, when she noticed that Little Boy Pig Dolton, started to come forward and started to raise his gun above his head like he was going to give her the hand stock of his pistol to her face.

No. No fucking way was that going to happen to her again. Not one more fucking time, ever.

Seeing this added fuel to her rage, making her concentrate with all her strength.

The gun was about to make its' way down right on top of her head—when suddenly it stopped. The look of authority that was on the little pig's face, fell through its thin layer that was held up by fear this whole time. Anoaka stood up, and stood up fast. She went and grabbed the nearest inmate that was a thirty-year old man that had a red beard with glasses, and tore off his head from his shoulders. Blood sprayed everywhere, as well as the screams and the yells from the other inmates. Only, Anoaka didn't stop long enough to admire her handy work. She ran over to a small woman that might have been in her twenties, that had black hair in a ponytail who was there doing some time, because she preferred buying crystal meth, rather than buying baby formula for her three month old. Anoaka ripped her arm off, holding the socket in place and then ripped the piece of bone that remained in the arm and stabbed her about five times with it, before moving on with her stab work on a young boy that couldn't have been more than eighteen. The school called the cops on him, for threatening a teacher after he said that "He was going to beat the shit out of him." for giving him an "F" on a paper about the Civil War, his favorite topic.

She wasn't done yet. Blocking the exit so no one would escape, she continued her onslaught. Driving her arms into chests, ripping off breast of woman, and penises of man, while breaking their legs so they be in complete agony, while filling the jailhouse with their screams of pain and horror. It was a massacre of the cruelest kind—done by bare hands. She gorged herself in their blood. Filling up her shoes that she stole from a cop along with soaking the uniform, until it couldn't absorb anymore and began to drip onto the floor. Along with the smell of blood, that had that coppery smell, there was the smell of shit from the ones that were already dead releasing all bodily functions. The smell in the air was that of a slaughterhouse, and a portable outhouse.

"Please, no!" was what was heard the most on her ears and her deaf soul. Along with their screams of pain and death.

Officers Adams and Dodson were the only ones that were not being killed. As she continued to move around them as some tried to hide in nearby cells, or tried their luck to make a run for it, the two officers saw everything. Splashes of blood went crossed their faces as if they fought a battle in medieval times. As their faces grew red from the blood, they also twisted in anguish and horror. Eventually, they both vomited where they stood, because they had no choice. What they saw was too much for the sanities to bear let alone their stomachs.

After about five minutes of killing and mutilating(not necessarily in that order), Anoaka stopped her blood soaked rampage, until she saw that there were only three people left; Officer Adams, Officer Dodson, and the smelly old man that was in his cell.

The old man didn't do anything while the killing was going on. He knew that there was no point. That mean, blood soaked bitch was going to get him no matter what he did. Weather he ran, or tried to fight her off, she was going to kill him, for leading her into his cell only to get bashed in the head. So…there was no point in doing anything really.

She made her way over to his cell, dripping with blood and holding her gaze at him with horrible anger that was made worse with all the blood covering her body. "You have been a bad….BAD old man. Haven't you?" she yelled the second "bad" as high as she could. "Tricking me into thinking that I was going to have myself a sweet time, getting fucked. And then you sprang that piece of shit Green, and his cunt on me." She was approaching him slowly into his cell. "Causing me to bleed from the head and having just the most… ACHING headache. What do you have to say for yourself, you dirty old fuck?"

The old man named Trevor, gave out a long sigh. Knowing this was his end and not wanting to show this bitch that he was afraid. Even though he was scared to death. "Well, I don't see any mark on your pretty little head now. So I think you are going to live."

"Flattery will get you no where."

"Oh. Well in that case—judging by the mess you made out there, I'd say that that piece of shit named Green did the right thing and knocking you the fuck out. Shit, now I wished I would have joined in, instead of wanting to fuck you. Do what your going to do and then get the fuck out of my cell." With that, Trevor turned away from her and looked straight ahead toward the wall.

She tore out his soul, and ripped it into little pieces, before burning them. The remnants scattered out of the cell and spread out throughout the jailhouse, like butterflies being released from a jar.

She walked out of the cell and looked at the two blood splattered cops that kept their exact positions as before. She saw tear trails that led down there cheeks, cutting through the blood, along with a stream of vomit that covered part of their uniforms where there was no blood. She didn't say anything. She thought to herself, that she wasted enough time here already, and soon the rest of the cops were going to show up. She would kill them too if she had too. No point in trying to play it quiet. She reached out a hand to the both of them. A giant flash of orange later and their souls, their undying souls unless she deemed them to die, were hers.

She walked out of the jailhouse gate that led to the hallway, before their bodies hit the ground. She reached her hand down into her pocket to grab the keys to her Ferrari, when she realized they were not there. Her eyes grew with horror, thinking that she might have dropped them while she was killing all the inmates. But then a sharp memory hit her. She remembered after getting hit in the head the first time today, she heard a faint sound of metal hitting the floor. She turned and looked at the spot where she fell down, looking all around and seeing nothing. The blood was making it hard to see anything, but then a thought occurred to her. "No. NO. NO. NO. NO!"

She started running toward the door where she had come in. Dreading to see what she would find.

The only survivor of the Marathon County Jailhouse Massacre, was Sgt. Donald Gentle. After yelling at Tyler and Tanya to stop right where they were. Sgt. Gentle, feeling wobbly from the hit that Miss Walsh gave him(giving everything she could at him, and she wasn't a weak woman), fell down again and hit his head on the linoleum floor, without putting a hand out to stop his fall, causing him to be knocked out again. He woke up on the floor, staring at a body that seemed to be staring at his legs, while starting to create a pool of blood around him. No wait, that was his own blood, looking at it he saw that it wasn't that much, but still he lifted his head and gave out a murmur of "What the fuck?" before the screams started to ring into his ears, along with the sounds of body parts doing something they weren't supposed to.

In her throws of killing, Anoaka saw the knocked out cop on the ground, along with the small pool of blood that gathered around his head, and assumed that either Tyler or Tanya killed this cop so they could escape from whatever cell they were in. Thinking nothing of him like she did all cops, she continued painting the floors red.

All the while, Sgt. Don Gentle continued to lay there and played dead, while the dead gathered around him, as each second passed.

Now he got up, his face crusty with his dried blood, and wept as he saw the dead that surrounded him. Shortly followed by vomiting up whatever food he had in his stomach.

Chapter 23

They stopped at Tanya's house, with very little trouble. She was in and out in less than five minutes, which as far as they knew no one had seen them. She went in and grabbed new clothes, being sure to hide the cop uniform that she had taken, deep into the back of her bedroom closet. Hoping that once this was all resolved, or if, that she would get rid of it in the burn barrel she had out in the back. She had some cash that she hid away for times when she knew, life might come a little hard, and in her opinion this qualified. It was only about two hundred dollars, but she figured that they could live off of that for a few days.

When they got back onto the road, they stopped over at the nearest Goodwill, Tyler gave her his sizes, then went in and got him nice button up flannel shirt, along with two pairs of jeans, and a nice jacket just so he wouldn't freeze to death with the cold days that were ahead. Tyler knew that it was only temporary, but with the clothes that he was wearing followed by driving a nice hot red Ferrari, he knew he clashed more than he ever thought possible. They then grabbed something to eat at the nearest Hardee's drive thru. Then it was off to their destination.

The Ferrari had a GPS on it, and once they typed in the address that they needed to get to, it was under the saved destinations menu under the heading **HOME**. With a smile on Tyler's face and a grimace on Tanya's, Tyler hit enter and their course was set.

"Do you think this will be over?" Tanya asked.

"I hope so. I don't know about you, but I would be happy if this fucking nightmare would end any moment now."

"Yeah no kidding."

"Right now my focus is to get Matt. We will deal with that bitch Charlotte as soon as we have him."

There was silence in the car for a few minutes, the only sounds were the constant revving of the car, and their own thoughts, until Tanya finally spoke up. "That's not enough."

Tyler turned to her as soon as she spoke this, while turning to keep watch on the road, periodically. "What was that?"

"It won't be enough to just get Matt. You know it, too. She will keep coming after us, no matter what.

"But in case you haven't noticed, we now have an opportunity to come out on front. Hell, we *are* out in front on this ball game now!"

Tanya was confused. "What are you talking about? What ballgame?"

"The ballgame that has been this chase! For the past three months she had been pursuing us, now we are on our way, in *her* car, to *her* house! That's big! And chances are, she knows where we are heading. If not, she is going to be in for a huge surprise!"

Tanya thought about it for a few minutes, and thought about the opportunity that they had. They talked in the car for a few minutes more as they were driving down on Highway 51 South. passing small gas stations and waysides as they spoke in depth on what they needed to do, and to convince themselves of the courage that they desperately needed in order to pul this off. Knowing that what they were doing was facing the beast itself, and possibly not living through the experience this time.

As they were speaking, Tyler noticed that the gasoline light on the Ferrari lit up and that they needed to stop to fill up the tank. "Go up a few more miles and there is a truck stop over on the exit to Neenah. It's directly after the truck weigh in stop."

"Alright." said Tyler.

Once gaming up was finished, with Tanya paying for the gas of course, they continued back on the road.

"Keep an eye out for the nearest Target, or Walmart that you can find that has an outdoor center attached to it. We need to make another stop."

"Okay?" Tanya said confused and skeptical, "Mind you the money we have is very limited. We can't just spend as much as we want."

"Relax. What I'm getting would cost us forty dollars at the max. Besides, it has to do with what we are going to be doing." Tyler explained for a few minutes, which Tanya then understood and kept her eyes peeled for the next available exit that would have a convenient store near the highway. They didn't reach one until they entered Madison, where they saw a Walmart in all its blue and brown glory. Getting off the highway, and going into the store, took them about fifteen minutes before they made their way back on the highway. It helped that Tyler knew that most Walmarts are virtually the same, and that the sections were almost always near or close to the same spots as the other store locations.

Once they were on the road again, the GPS told them that they were about eighty-three miles away, with an estimated time of arrival of an hour and twenty minutes. With the Ferrari at their disposal, they knew they could easily cut that down—they just didn't know if they wanted to.

At the time that Tyler and Tanya entered Madison, Anoaka was just making her way into a vehicle that wasn't rundown into the road, and making her way out of Wausau.

Her massacre inside the jailhouse costed her more than she intended. At the time she thought she still had her Ferrari at her disposal, so she thought that no matter what she would be able to catch both of those cretans with hardly any trouble. Little did she know that right after Tyler and Tanya took her Ferrari, the police departments from Mosinee, Rothschild, Merrill, and the SWAT Team from the Wisconsin State Police Department, made their way to the building of the Marathon County Courthouse. In the midst of her onslaught, the separate police departments began to surround the building and place it under lockdown until they could get all the remaining people that locked themselves in different rooms throughout the building to safety.

Right as Anoaka was making her way to the door that she used to enter the building, she turned the corner of the hallway only to see the alternate colors of red and blue light up the wall from the door window, stopping her in her tracks.

After several seconds that filled the silence of the lobby with curse words of a unique nature, she decided that she needed two things: a new set of clothes, and someplace to hide. Near the lobby there was a bathroom for men that she went into and went directly toward the sink. She knew that she threw on a men's police uniform, and hoped that would throw whoever off of what she was as far as the sex, just like going into the men's room. As far as she knew, she killed everyone that ever saw her in this building, Hoping it was going to stay that way. Having no scared little sons of a bitches come in here and and see a woman covered in blood, taking off a police uniform, also covered in blood. Talk about awkward. She ripped off the shirt and the pants right down the middle, until they were both in halves, threw both pieces of each in the sink and turned on the faucet. The water was turning red as it started to fill up and battle to drain itself past the shredded clothes. Meanwhile, Anaoka went to the other sink and started to wipe off the blood, that was slowly drying on her face, as well as her arms and her legs. Not the first time she had to clean off blood in such a short amount of time, but it was never easy.

Nearly ten minutes later, she poked her head out of the men's room and saw that the coast was clear, so she left the restroom, leaving the faucet run with the bloody clothes left in the sink. She made her way back down the way she came and went to go find her clothes that she had on before. The red shirt with the skinny jeans, saw that they were still in the locker of the cop's locker room, and put them on. As she was doing this, she started to hear the sound of yelling in one of the rooms for people to "Move out with your hands above your head" tone of voices. Garbled from the layer of stone wall, but she was able to understand what the man said. She quickly went and hid in one of the lockers, tears welling up in her eyes.

She was in there for about ten minutes, waiting for either the voices to pass or for them to find her. She heard the small sound of boots creeping along on the floor, trying to move stealthily through the locker room. Several other footsteps followed into the locker room. There were either four or five by Anoaka's guesswork. Little stomps here and there threw her off on their exact positions in the locker room, but she could tell that some of them were closer to her now. Then in an instant, there were no sounds. No more footsteps moving around in the locker room. They couldn't have left, because she knew that one of them was over on her far right side, when the exit to the locker room is over on her left side. Something was about to happen, and she better be prepared.

Suddenly, in perfect unison, the lockers were all forced open at the same time. They had no locks on the doors because everyone trusts everyone in small police departments to small cities. With a whirlwind the doors opened and weapons were drawn on whoever or whatever was inside. Anoaka let out a huge scream, and covered her eyes and her head with her arms. "DON'T KILL ME, PLEEEEASE! DON'T KILL ME! OH MY GAAAWD!"

The cop that was covered from head to toe in tactical SWAT gear stepped back and yelled out, "PUT YOUR HANDS BEHIND YOU HEAD, AND GET DOWN ON THE FLOOR!"

"THEY KILLED, EVERYONE! THEY KILLED THEM ALL!"

The cop stopped yelling as he pushed her down to the ground, touching only the back of her shirt, and started to zip-tie cuff her with his tactical gloves. "Who did? Tell us who?"

"THE MAN AND THE WOMAN!" she said through tears and hysterics. "THEY WERE WEARING ORANGE JUMPSUITS AND STARTED KILLING EVERYONE!"

They pulled her off the floor, again from the back of her shirt, and looked straight into her eyes. "Which way did they go?"

Calmer and making sure another stream of tears tipped from her eyes, down to her cheeks. "They....they went into the jailhouse. That was the last I saw of them, but I heard lots and lots of screaming! Please, get me outta here, PLEASE!" she screamed the last please into the officers face.

The SWAT officer turned to one of his men, "Take her outside with the remaining survivors. The rest of you on me. We are going into the jailhouse to check it out."

The officer went and grabbed Anoaka at the cuffs of her hands. She got onto her feet and started walking at a quick pace throughout the locker door, while the SWAT officer that had her aimed his automatic rifle down the hallway where the other officers were going to be heading. The rest of the team appeared a few seconds later at the door opening, giving both the officer and Anoaka cover. Once they appeared, the officer turned away and concentrated on the hallway that was ahead of him, while Anoaka followed, still crying and not fighting the movements of the SWAT team member.

The officer escorted Anoaka outside, where they was an area that was reserved for people that were taken out of the building. When she entered the outside she saw that the muggy day that started was starting to become dark with more, thicker clouds coming along over Rib Mountain. She also looked over to where she had parked her Ferrari, and saw that it was gone. Though she hid it on her face, she was absolutely livid internally. Curses were flying through her head while at the same time she was imagining what she was going to do once she was going to get her hands on them. She thought about taking the woman's soul and slowly feeding it to Mr. Green as he was bleeding from his crouch, after she removed his testicles.

Even though she thought this, she filled with despair and worry. This was the fourth time Tyler Fucking Green escaped her. The third time while she was face to face with the bastard.

She was chasing him all over the damn place like Ahab with his fucking white wale. Only this time it was worse, Moby Dick didn't sink her ship this time, he fucking took it away from her. Now she was stranded up in central Wisconsin, while two people that should be dead in her eyes were walking around and making her look like a fool.

She didn't have time for this. Throwing herself a pity party and waiting for God knew what. She had to get out of here and get out of here, fast. While she waited with all the other people that were evacuated, she made her way to the back of the crowd. When she was there, she merely pulled her wrists apart, making the zip-tie cuffs simple fall apart to the ground. Using her quickness and the opportunity of everyone looking at the courthouse and jailhouse, she snuck away from the crowd of people as if she were smoke. Once she left the area of the courthouse she made her way toward the mall that was right next to the courthouse. She did this, because she knew that she had to get to her house that was locked up on the far side of Rib Mountain, there would be a spare car for her to use instead of just having to steal one from some random person she was going to have to kill. Going to the mall meant that there could be some pay phones, or a land line for her to use to get a taxi to the house. She may not have her phone, but she did have her credit and debit card.

It took her no time to get to the mall, and lord and behold, there were some operating pay phones that were still hanging around to mall administration hallway in the southeastern side. She was putting change into the phone after the administrator broke it from the twenty she got out of the ATM, when someone passed her and placed their arm on her exposed shoulder. This caused her to snap her head to her left in such a fashion that you would have thought it was going to spin off if it didn't stop so suddenly. It caused the woman that touched her shoulder to step back little, and in a timid voice asked Anoaka, "Are you alright?"

The question confused Anoaka, "Excuse me?"

"I think you might be bleeding behind your ear."

Anoaka took a finger and wiped behind her ear and felt that it was wet with some inmate's blood. "Oh, it must be from when I just banged the top of my head in the car door. I will be alright. Thank you for noticing, I will go clean it up."

"Your welcome." A smile replaced the woman's concern and she continued to walk down the hallway, she turned her head back to look at Anoaka with a fleeing glance, then she turned to enter into the mall.

After the phone call to the cab company, she went into the woman's bathroom that was right next to her, and she checked her hair and any other body part that might have any exposed blood visible. Cleaning the back of her ear, as well as the bottom part of the back of her neck, she got all the visible blood off of her. She found herself getting carless. Having blood from a victim exposed on her skin was beneath her. She has had centuries of practice. *Centuries!* This was not like her to have her mind reduced like this from the stress of these two bastards. She cursed herself for seeing how far she had fallen from this whole affair. Looking into the mirror she took deep breaths to calm herself down and to clear her mind. Then she left the woman's room and waited for the cab to arrive.

The cab ride was short and without conversation, Anoaka made sure of that. A few times the pungent woman with the green lens sunglasses tried to strike up conversation about the weather with her, and Anoaka ignored her on all attempts. After the last attempt the cab lady mulled to herself, "Stubborn little tart aren't we." Anoaka heard of course, but far from cared. Her mind was on the situation at hand. She thought about her next move, which was to check out both addresses of Mr. Green and then Miss Walsh. She was sure that they would be at one of those places. There was no where else to go. She would check there and hopefully end this there. As she thought this, she had a brief glimpse of Danny that flashed for an instant. She shook it away, wondering why he showed up now of all times. Even wondered why the traitor showed up at all. Dead and good riddance to the bastard.

The house was locked, and Anoaka had every intention on keeping it that way for the foreseeable future, but she needed to get the keys to the blue Camaro that was the remaining vehicle that was in the garage. All other cars were in her house garage in Lake Geneva, minus the black SUV that was up north in Eagle River due to Danny's failure. Again showing up in her mind.

She had no key. So she broke a window and quickly made her way to the alarm and shut it off. She did like this house, so before she left with the keys to the Camaro, she took clear plastic that was used to cover the attic windows from being too drafty in the winter, and used it to cover the broken window. Then she was gone.

She went to both houses, and found nothing. Well—she didn't find either Tyler or Tanya like she had hoped. She thought about where they could have gone. Back to the cabin? That would be stupid, considering that she knew where it was now. Maybe another cabin? Highly unlikely, that pig Mullen said that Mr. Green and Miss Walsh only had a few friends, and Kolat would have picked up on that if he was lying or who any other known friends were. Maybe there were friends that he didn't know about. After all, you didn't know that Danny was his friend once upon a time. Danny? Danny? *Danny!*

There was a flash of seeing the last images that Danny saw. And hearing the last words that he said. She didn't hear all of them, but a cutoff of when she was going to re-enter his body to control him. Part of a bigger statement but cutoff. In her memory she heard: *eva, Wisconsin.*

Lake Geneva, Wisconsin.

That traitorous fucker gave them her address! Not just her address, but the King's as well.

She thought about it even more, Even if he didn't tell them, they had the Ferrari. It had GPS and had her address saved in the GPS. Holy Shit!

She looked at her clock and guessed how long it was before they left. She was horrified to find out that they took off from the jailhouse about three hours ago. Rain started to fall as she ran from Tanya's house to the Camaro. The next instant she was on the road, cursing the whole way down the street.

There wasn't rain as Tyler and Tanya passed Janesville, but could see that it wasn't far off. Dark clouds were coming in and looked like it was about to dump right on top of them. Tyler stopped at a gas station to fill up the red Ferrari, while Tanya was still napping since they left Madison. She said she only wanted to get a little sleep before they arrived at Lake Geneva, so she was sleeping for about an hour. Tyler thought about waking her to see if she wanted anything to eat quickly, but he couldn't bring himself to wake her up just yet. He topped off the gas tank and went inside to pay.

"That's a hot ride you got there buddy!" the clerk behind the counter said as he took the two twenties that Tyler gave him.

"Yeah, she drives nice."

"Someone who drives something like that, usually travels with plastic." the clerk said as he gave him a suspicious look.

Tyler didn't hesitate, he didn't have time to be under some watchful eye of a gas station attendant. "Yeah well my wife had enough fun with the plastic this whole week. So, I figured I would give it a break. You have yourself a good day." He looked up as he said this and saw that the clerk was looking inside the car from his window. They were probably about ten yards away to the car from the building, but he was acting like he was right next to it, seeing if Tyler really owned it, or really had a wife. Tyler saw that he saw that there was indeed a woman asleep in the from seat, because Tanya started to stir and woke up with a big yawn. She looked around and saw that they were at a gas station, right as Tyler started to make his way back to the car.

"Do you want anything?" he asked her.

"No thanks. I just want to get this over with."

"Yeah me too." Tyler started the engine and they were back on the road.

"Any ideas on what to do after?" Tanya asked.

"Nope. The only one I can think of is turn ourselves in, hopefully with Matt still alive."

They drove on for another forty-five minutes. Indeed it did start to rain right as they entered Lake Geneva. They bypassed most of the city as they entered toward the lake roads. From there, both Tyler and Tanya saw the neighborhood that they entered.

If there was any suspicion that Charlotte and this King were full fledged soul stealing murderers, they were probably quashed with the mere appearance of the neighborhood they entered in. Tyler once heard from one of the guys at work that Lake Geneva was the rich man's city in Wisconsin. By the look of the houses he saw why. Each entrance to a driveway had a gate to it that lead up to a concrete driveway that had heaters embedded in them so they was no need for shoveling or plowing snow in the winter. Each driveway was connected to a two or three story house that usually was made entirely of brick, logs, stone, with the option of marble columns that graced the front porch before you would knock on the front red door that had a crystal window.

"Yikes." said Tanya, "Ya think they have enough money in this neighborhood?"

"Nope." Tyler said sharply. "You need seven figures just to keep the lights on around here." he was joking, but he wasn't really sure he was too far off on that figure.

"TURN LEFT AND THEN THE DESTINATION IS ON YOUR RIGHT." the GPS navigation lady said. Tyler drove past the street while pressing end for the GPS.

"What are you doing you missed the turn?"

"Yeah, I'm not going to park in the driveway for element of surprise reasons. Besides, we have some setup to do. Once we are done, we are going in to get Matt."

Chapter 24

It was raining hard now since they parked the Ferrari. Tyler had to rush outside to the trunk to get the supplies that they needed. Once he looked in the trunk, he realized that the objects looked peculiar as they sat in the small trunk of the Ferrari. He grabbed to the two bags and the small red backpack that he bought and brought it inside the cab of the car.

"Where are we gonna put everything together?" Tanya asked.

Tyler looked around outside and saw that the rain was only gonna get worse before it got better. They couldn't put it together outside, the rain would ruin it. If they wanted the explosion that they wanted, the only moisture that could be allowed would have to be from the chemicals themselves. Tyler thought that they didn't have time to go and travel someplace dry to put it together. Nor did they want to risk being seen by other people on what they were putting together. "We're gonna have to put it together right here, in the car."

"Okay?…Only it's a little cramped in here."

"I know, I don't like it either, but the way I see it, we are just gonna have to make it work."

"Seems to be the motto with us." Tanya said, despite being scared, she cracked a smile.

"Yeah, no kidding."

They worked for almost an hour. By the time they finished it was full dark that they had to turn the car back on to see what they were doing. Halfway through, Tyler looked up at the clock that was on the dashboard and saw that it was eight-ten and night, when he finished it was closer to eight-thirty.

The end product was two thermos's that were filled with homemade explosives with two short cloth wicks that were at the top of both of them that they used from a torn handkerchief. The hardest part was to make the hole that was on top of both of them. It took Tyler a while to try and make them with the small two dollar pocket knife that they got, but after holding the knife on top and then smashing it against the Ferrari door a few times, it made a nice enough hole for the wicks. Mixing the chemicals was all done by memory from Tyler's military training of advanced explosives. They Army never directly trained Tyler how to do this, the most that they did was showed him the mixture of most homemade explosives. He remembered after the class that he and a few of his other buddies, Staubach included, were curious on what the exact recipe was to make bombs. So they all went to the nearest internet cafe and looked up the recipe. After some long convincing to the C.O., on an afternoon of nothing to do, they put together a class on how to make homemade explosives in a pitch. Just in case someone from the company found themselves needing to blow up an enemy with some fertilizer in a field. The class was a success, he thought, seeing as how everyone that participated seemed to have a good time blowing up shit—literally.

The process stunk up the car, but it wasn't like it was *their* car anyways. The only things that worried Tyler about the bomb was: where they were going to place it in the house, how much time they had to get away from the bomb, and how big the blast was going to be? Judging by the weight of the thermos's, he and Tanya had about ten pounds of explosives. Not enough to blow everything toward the sky, but enough that if it was placed in the right spot, like a gas main, to start a nice uncontrollable house fire. That was only thing he could hope for at this point. Waiting, of course to get Mathew out of the house first if he was still in there, from when Danny had told them only days ago.

"Are you ready?" Tyler asked.

"Fuck no, are you nuts? No one could ever be ready for this shit, yet here we go anyway." Tyler placed the bomb in the small red backpack that was only big enough for a small kid to carry on it's back, and they both exited the Ferrari; guns drawn as they both made their way into the dark, cold, rainy night. Tyler lead the way as they made there way toward the wall only a few feet away from the driveway gate. Tanya put a hand on Tyler's shoulder. "Wait!"

Tyler turned to see what was wrong, when he was greeted by a pair of lips onto his. The kiss wasn't long, maybe only a peck in the sense of length, but long enough to get Tyler's blood running. "Good luck Tyler, let's get out of here alive."

"Absolutely."

He put his gun down the front of his pants, making sure the safety was still on, then interlocked his fingers so they would form a sep for Tanya to place her foot. Tanya looked at it for a second. "You want me to go first?!" she asked with disbelief.

"Yes. You are the smallest, so you need to go over first. When you get on the other side, I want you to be ready for anything that comes your way, I will be over there as soon as I can. Got it?"

Tanya nodded, the rain making her look like a worried puppy that thinks its going to be in trouble for something that it might have done. She put her foot in the hands as soon as she put her gun her her right hand, then lifted herself up onto the wall. She stayed on top for a while as she turned herself around so she could land on her feet. Pushing herself off the wall and then frantically looked around to see if there was anyone or anything that was around. She looked at the house and was amazed.

She saw that the entire house was made of stone on the outside, with big marble columns that graced the front. The first two floors had individual windows that were spread out every ten feet or so for a grand total of sixteen for the front side alone. Where she landed in the yard, she could see part of the house's left side and see that the side had another two windows for each floor. She couldn't see much of the right side, only that it was connected to a three door garage.

The grandest feature of this house was the third floor alone. All the lights were on inside the house and she could see through the windows what was partly inside. With the third floor, she could see almost everything. The outside walls of the third floor were made entirely of glass. Either glass, or some sort of strong glass that could put up a nice resistance to the weather outside, but still everything was visible for everyone to see inside, as well as whoever was inside to look out to a most glorious view of the lake.

Looking in on the top floor, Tanya saw the stairs that lead to the third floor along with the entrance to another room that was dark. She never saw a house like this ever. She heard a noise behind her and saw that it was Tyler landing from the wall right behind her.

"Are there any dogs, or guards around here?" Tyler asked.

Tanya forgot all about looking for dogs, guards, or even fucking lawn gnomes, she was so distracted by the house. "Uh.. none so far."

"Well keep your eyes peeled, and quit looking at the house. Once you've seen one you've seen them all, and we got a job to do."

"Yeah, you're right. I'm sorry."

"Don't be sorry. Let's find a side entrance. Maybe there's one in the garage over there." They started to move across the yard slowly in the rain, trying their best to stick to the dark parts of the yard in case someone would spot them.

After about five minutes, they found a door on the far side of the garage and found that it was locked. Moving to the back of the house, they both saw a combination of woods and garden that seemed to take over the backyard with paths and stone mounds that had what appeared to be waterfalls, at least that's what Tanya thought they were now as the storm continued. What lighted most of the back yard was a glass porch door that leaked out light onto the garden and the trees, as well as a stone back patio complete with some of the most beautiful outdoor furniture Tanya had ever seen.

Tyler saw all these things as well, but his mind was more viewing them as obstacles then of objects to be adored. His mind was at the job in hand, and the job at hand was to gain entry into the house. He approached the door at quietly as he could, but with the rain beating down he could have showed up in the backyard in a semi-truck and still not be heard. Still he wasn't taking any chances. He reached the side of the glass patio door and peered in to see inside. He was peering into a kitchen of enormous size and beauty. Black marble counters, that surrounded an island in the middle of the kitchen, with pots and pans hanging above the island. On the island itself, was a second sink that he could see as he quickly glanced and saw another one over on the counter connected to the wall over by the stove on the far end. On the other side of the room was an opening to what he could see was possibly a dining room, his angle of view only gave him the look of the back end of a chair.

He turned back and looked at Tanya with her soaking wet hair and shivering body. He then turned back to the door and reached for the door handle, hoping and praying that it was unlocked. He knew that the was probably his only realistic way into the house, no matter what he was going to use this door even if he had to break his way in. As he put his hand on it, he said another little prayer to God, begging him to that he won't have to break the glass of the door, until he thought to himself that God probably didn't make such stupid requests. He turned the handle and found that it was indeed open. He breathed out a silent "Thank you" to the sky and began to enter the house.

Though the both of them entered the house quickly they still remained quiet as a church mouse. Their clothes were sopping wet and dripped all over the floor. Normally Tyler wouldn't give a shit about something like that, but he was worried that either he or Tanya would slip and cause a noise. "Watch your footing." he whispered to Tanya, "We don't want to slip and let someone know that we are here."

Tanya just gave a nod that Tyler didn't see. Tyler was looking around to see if they were indeed alone. The fear that was building in him made his head move around at every crevice of the kitchen. His breathing was becoming frantic, and thoughts of how they both just stepped into the last place the would ever go into made its way through his head like a deadly virus. His breathing was getting worse with deep breaths that were inhaled and then exhaled, then quickly inhaled and exhaled. He repeated this many times before he felt a hand on his shoulder. He grabbed it and turned around with the gun out, pointing at whoever had him.

"Calm down Tyler." Tanya said, with a look of fear on her face as Tyler slowly let go of her hand and lowered his gun. "Calm down and try to relax." She then said something that told Tyler that she knew he was scared, but wanted to keep moving just the same. "Just take it one room at a time. I'm here with you."

This time, it was Tyler that nodded at the advice. He stopped and slowed his breathing until he got himself under control and got his mind back at the situation in front of him. As where he stood right now; he could not see anyone in the house. But the house was big and full of rooms, and he was going to search every single on of them until he could find Mathew.

Once again, he started to move vey slowly through the kitchen and turned toward the room that looked like a dining room. They entered and saw that it was connected to the living room on his immediate right. Tyler saw that the room was lit up with the table set up, it looked like the house was expecting a dinner party of some kind. Tyler looked at the table and saw that there was a place at the end of the table that wasn't set up. He looked at it curiously and wondered why? He counted and saw that the table could seat sixteen very comfortably. So why would there be and empty spot for the dinnerware?

Unless—a person here already eaten. Eaten and cleared their place at the table.

Wouldn't they set the place back up, or a servant do it? Were there any servants at all? A place this big had to have them, right?

Maybe.

Tyler kept moving hoping these questions would answer themselves as they made their way through the house. Tyler made a hand signal to show that they were going to enter the living room. Tanya knew she couldn't answer that she understood with her mouth, so she tapped his shoulder to tell him that she received the message. As they moved into the living room, they could hear the soft sound of the tapping rain onto the windows while looking around. They saw that there were several sofas in the room that seemed to surround a huge television set. The grey sofas were completed at the ends with end tables that each held a lamp that help the chandelier on the ceiling with the lighting of the room. Tyler thought that the room was big enough to go dancing in, and found it strange that it would be used as a living room. Tanya thought that the room was huge and saw that without anyone in it, it seemed very empty. On the opposite side of the sofas and chairs, they saw that the red front door that was in front was just as red on the inside as on the outside; or so they assumed, having only seen the door at night. At the entrance to the door played a big staircase that lead to the other two floors.

They both made their way to the foot of the stairs, and Tyler was just about to go up them when Tanya tapped him on the shoulder to get his attention. Tyler turned around, and started to hear the low rumblings of thunder. Tanya pointed toward the direction of the other side of the staircase and saw another door that was almost hidden away by the staircase. Tyler gave her a nod and they started to make their way toward the door, Tanya being sure to point her gun up the stairway in case she saw anyone. She kept her eyes and gun on the staircase, until she entered the room that she spotted.

When she turned around, all she saw were books. Books on large shelves that seemed to be thick enough to hold as many as you could think of. They both stood in wonder at the mere size of this library and wondered how could anyone have the time to read all of these. Maybe they were just a sort of insurance so you would never have enough to read in a person's life. I guess if you had all this money, what else would you spend it on?

They made their way through the library selves and saw no one. Tanya tapped on Tyler's shoulder and brought her mouth to his ear. "Would this be a good place to set up the bomb? With all these books, it would make this place go up like nothing."

"It would be a good spot, but I'm looking for some kind of gas main. Maybe if we find some gasoline in the garage, it would be able to catch fire onto the books. Otherwise it's just a big bang in a close to soundproof room."

"Well, let's check out the garage after this and see if there is any."

After clearing the library, the exited from another door on the far right side and entered a hallway that lead to a door at the far end. There was another door on the right side of the hallway, and saw that it was an empty home theater. They spend very little time inside and saw that it was obviously empty before they both made their way to the door at the end. Sure enough it was the entrance to the garage. Just like all the rooms the entered, it too was empty. After they cleared it of people, Tyler told Tanya to keep both her eyes on the door, while he looked for some gas. He found some in a corner of the garage that was right next to a car that looked like something fancy James Bond might drive in a high speed chase. Right there next to the rear driver tire against the wall, was a red container that was about half full of Unleaded gasoline.

They both made there way back to the library and went to the corner that was immediately to their left as they entered the room. Tyler looked up to the ceiling and saw that it was about nine feet from the ground to the ceiling.

"Grab some books." he said to Tanya. He put down the bomb right in the corner and started to grab books by the arm length and toss them onto the floor. Some of the books were old and ripped pages form their bindings. Tyler took those pages and the books and started throwing them on top of the bomb, being sure to leave the top of the backpack open and clear of books so they could get a proper light on the fuse. Tanya was helping out by taking every book she could lay her hands on and started to remove the paper from the bindings making a small pile of paper all around the corner. Tyler looked pleased and took the can of gasoline, and started to throw big globs of the liquid onto the pile. As well as on the shelves that surrounded the bomb and and the books that on them.

The smell of the library reeked of gas. It was so bad that Tyler was glad that they were still soaking wet, otherwise he would worry all their moving around would cause a static charge that would already kill them and anyone that was in this house; if there was anyone. "Let's get the hell out of here. When we get Mathew. I want you to take your box of matches and light them on fire. Every single match that is in that box! Then, throw it over to this corner, making sure to hit the pile of books. The fire that it creates, should be enough to light the fuse of the bomb and then, BOOM, BOOM, BOOM. The house started it's trip up into the sky."

"What if I can't make it?" Tanya asked.

"Then I will take my box of matches. That's why I bought two. I will probably be carrying Matt, but somehow I will get to it, if it comes to that."

Tanya didn't say anything. She thought that if Tyler had to do it, it would mean that she would have to be dead.

They made their way up the stairs to the second floor and cleared every room that was there. It was once they got to the second floor, that they realized they could still smell the gasoline from the red can that they used. It didn't matter. They still had to continue on and clear the floor.

The second floor was filled with eight big bedrooms. All of them were clear of anybody even touching the rooms. Tyler figured they would be used in case Charlotte would ever be expecting guests. Judging by the state the rooms were in; nobody must have set foot in those rooms in at least a year.

The only one that seemed to be touched was the room on the far north side. It was Danny's room. Tyler entered and saw that there were clothes that were hanging in the closet. Most of them were suits, but Tyler recognized a few plaid shirts that were from American Eagle; the same types of shirts he would wear when he would go out for a guys night out when they served together. Not only that, but he found a picture of his wife and kids that was in a frame on the end table next to his bed. The fear that flooded Tyler earlier when he entered the house stayed with him up to this point, but now it was being replaced with anger.

"One more soldier lost." he said as he looked at the picture.

Tanya whispered. "What did you say?"

"Nothing. We aren't going to find anyone in here. Let's move on."

It was here when they made their way to the third floor.

The stairs turned in a swirl as they entered the third floor, from there they started to get a glance at the outside from the window walls that made up the whole third floor exterior walls. Tyler was looking ahead of him and Tanya to see if there was anyone ahead of him, but even he couldn't resist the view that was before him.

The storm broke out in lightning streaks throughout the sky. Making the pitch black night light up to see the view of the lake that the floor gave to anyone that was on the other side of the glass. It looked amazing. Along the shores of the lake, both Tyler and Tanya could see the lights of houses that were scattered, making orange tinted lights look like fireflies stuck on leaves, waiting for the storm to pass. Bolts of lightning, followed by the thundering rumbles that shook the earth were seen striking various spots among the trees as well as on the lake. Tyler was thinking of how this view would look if the lights were off in the house, but he wasn't that curious enough to find out.

He brought his head back into the his purpose for being here for the third time. Even though the outer walls were made of glass, the interior ones were made of wood. White carpet laid on the bottom of their wet shoes, as they moved more slowly throughout the the hallway that seemed to drop off with the placement of wall-window. There were two doors on the wooden side of the hallway, and Tyler decided to go to the first one that was closest to them, causing him to go right. Tanya continued to provide the two of them rear security, only this time it seemed more simple, with there being only two places to scan her eyes. Still, she found it difficult with the light-show of the storm going on outside. Tyler opened the door and found that it was a bathroom, The third one they found since entering the house, although this one had some toothbrushes and toothpaste on the topmost part of the sink, with a shaving kit as well as other toiletries such as deodorant, aftershave, tweezers, and assorted combs. The bathroom wasn't just connected by one door, the door in which Tyler entered, but two. On the other side was another door connected to another room. The two doors seemed to separate the bathroom into a mini-like hallway that separated the sink and toilet, from the shower and linen closet. What also caught Tyler's attention about this door—was that it was ajar.

Tyler motioned his hand to Tanya for her to come over to him. He did it for a few seconds, because Tanya had her head turned away from him as she kept her gaze on the other door, the stairway, and the raging storm that was taking place. Once she glanced toward Tyler, she made her way to his side as quietly as she could. Tyler whispered into her ear. "I think this is where the King stays."

She went into his ear and spoke as lightly as she could. "Are you sure?"

"This is the only bathroom we have seen where there is any sort of toiletries laying about. The rest of the house seems to be untouched."

A voice boomed from the other side of the door, opposite side of the bathroom. The voice had a worn out British accent, from an older type man. Tyler knew from Danny that there was a man here named the King, or that was what Charlotte called him, and knew that after searching most of the house for Danny or this King, that this had to be one of the last places they could be. Still, the sound of a voice he never heard before, sent fear throughout him, knowing that either he was going to have to kill this man, or this man just might kill him. "I can hear the two of you whispering, now are you going to come in or am I going to die in here waiting for you? Mind you, we will be waiting a long time, and time is short as it is."

Tanya put a hand on Tyler's shoulder, holding him back and shaking her head. Tyler looked at her. "We need to find Matt, and he might be the only one here who knows where he is."

"I do know where he is." The voice shouted back. "But I need your help for me to show you where he is."

Tyler was confused by this last statement. He decided to go through the door at the man's request, but he was dead set on taking as many precautions as he needed to. Tanya still had her hand on Tyler's shoulder, but Tyler pushed along through the bathroom anyway. He opened the door and saw that the room was almost completely pitch back. The only light that was showing through was the flashes of light from the lightning that was scattering from another window-wall. Judging the distance from the other window-wall on the other side of the bathroom, Tyler thought that width of the third floor couldn't be more than fifteen yards. Tyler used the light from the bathroom to look for a light switch. There were two switches right next to the door and Tyler flipped both of them. Light filled the room and stayed, unlike the flashes of lightning.

Tyler saw that this must be the master bedroom. Along the interior wall and right next to the bathroom, was a doorway that lead into a walk-in closet that was filled with clothes. Past that, were dressers that couldn't have stood taller than three feet, but stretched out several yards with columns of three drawers each about two feet wide. In the center of the room was a coffee table that supported a fifty inch flatscreen, that was plugged into an outlet on the floor. A few feet from the coffee table and the flatscreen, was a king-sized bed with red sheets that had black borders on it. Sitting on the bed, dressed in a suit and tie and staring out into the storm and listening to the constant relaxing tapping of raindrops on the window, was a man that had pure black hair and pale grey eyes that Tyler almost mistakenly thought that the man was blind; that was until the man turned and stared at him, where Tyler saw the man's cornea's and that it was his iris's that were grey.

Tyler raised his gun at the man, keeping him in his sights as the man laid his eyes on the two of them. He turned the safety off, preparing himself for whatever came next. His finger lightly touched the trigger ready to give it a nice squeeze.

"Are you here to kill me Mr. Green? If so, wait just a little longer so I can help you retrieve your friend?"

"You said you know where he is?"

"Yes I do, but I need your help in order to get him."

"Who are you?"

"That…. is a long story in itself." the man let out a large sigh, "You probably heard your friend Daniel Staubach as well as my wife call me the King. But since you are here to end my life, you may call me Edward. That was the name giving to me me so long ago, before I disappeared."

"Why are you called the King?" asked Tanya.

"Oh…I see. You want the questions first and the location of your friend second. I will be happy to answer all your questions, but first we need to get Mathew, I don't know how much longer he is going to last without someones help."

"He is still alive?"

"I don't know. I need help leaving the third floor, and I haven't left since early this morning. Last I heard he still was, but that was well over twelve hours ago. We need to hurry fast." The man named Edward, who was also given the title King got up from the bed and started moving at a fast pace toward the bathroom door. Tyler raised his gun up at the man's face.

"How do I know you are going to take me to Matt?"

The man looked at him for a moment, a look of impatience, and frustration combined, bored into Tyler's eyes. Tyler kept his eyes locked onto Edward's. Not trusting the man at all and wasn't about to fall for some sort of trap. Then, Edward, the King, walked up and placed his body right against the barrel of the gun. "Trust me or don't, it makes no difference to me. You can shoot me now or later, only if you shoot me now, you will guarantee your friends death if he isn't already. Shoot me later, and you might still be able to save him, what is it going to be?"

Tyler was thinking on what he should do. He decided to himself that he was going to let this man help them if that is what he said he was going to do. Tyler pulled the gun away from the man's body, but kept the gun on him, in case this was some sort of trap.

The King moved past both him and Tanya and went through the bathroom. They followed behind him, until he stopped short of the stairwell. "This is where I'm going to need your help."

"What?" Tyler asked.

"The third floor is as far as I am allowed to travel. I need you both to grab me and take me down the stairs."

"Why?"

"I assume you are familiar with my wife, and what she is capable of, am I correct?"

"Yeah?"

"Well she has made sure that I can not leave the third floor with out the assistance of a willing person. I need one of you to help me down the stairs by grabbing my arm and fighting my resistance."

"She is controlling you as well? Why would she do that to her own husband?" asked Tanya.

"I will tell you after we get your friend. So, which one of you is going to help me?"

"I will." said Tanya. Tyler was about to protest, but saw no need to. He was going to stay next to the both of them in case Tanya was shoved down the stairs or thrown down them by this man. He would keep his gun on him, and if he needed more help going down the stairs, he would be more than happy to give it to him. "Where are we going?"

"We are going down to the library. He is kept in there, or a place that is near there. Now please, take my arm, and don't let go." Tanya did as she was told. She interlocked her arm with the King and held onto it with her left hand onto his forearm. "You are going to have to start walking down the stairs."

Tanya did so. She took the first step, and was met with immediate resistance. She started to pull and pull to try and get the man to move and yet he wouldn't budge an inch; or he *couldn't* budge an inch. She continued to pull as hard as she could, even feeling Tyler start to push on the man's back, when she looked up at the man's face. The King's face was completely red, like he was also trying his absolute best to try and move his legs, or that he was in a great amount of pain trying to achieve this feat. Finally it Tyler that was able to move the legs as he gave the left one a nice hard kick from the side of his foot to the back of the heel of the King's foot. The foot then pushed onto the lower step, almost causing the King to fall down the stairs. That didn't bother Tyler too much. He did the same to the right foot, he was about to kick him in the shins so he could make his way down the rest of the stairs, until both he and Tanya saw that he started to move his legs down the stairs by himself.

"Still a little hard to move, but it is starting to come a lot easier now. Thank you Mr. Green." Tyler didn't respond to then man's gratefulness. He kinda wanted to have his chance of pushing the man down the stairs.

They moved slowly down the stairs but started to pick up the pace. "Where in the library is he? We checked the whole room and didn't see him anywhere."

"Well then I guess you haven't checked the whole room then, have you?" Tyler was getting red in the face as he heard this. He never liked being treated like a fool. Not from his sergeants back in basic training, and certainly not from the husband of some soul sucking bitch. "The entrance had always been a secret, even from me for the longest time. Until one day I stumbled upon it. She knew that I found out about it, hence the reason I wasn't allowed to leave the third floor."

"Like Rapunzel, locked away in her tower, huh?" Tyler shot at him.

"Almost exactly that." said Edward. "She must have more secrets she didn't want me to stumble upon, as well as preventing me from doing a few other things."

"What kind of things?" asked Tanya.

"If there is time, I will let you know. But I do know that time is short. She already knows that we are talking to one another."

"She is keeping tabs on you?"

"No more than a husband and wife usually keep tabs on one another these days. Only with her, it comes with the standard built in equipment. Right, now here we are." They entered the library and all three took a step back from the fumes of gasoline that filled the room. "So that is why you both reek of gas. Planning on starting a fire?"

"Of sorts. You got a problem with that?"

"Not even a little bit. Come, follow me."

Tanya and Tyler looked at one another for a second, taking in the King's answer to the rhetorical question. Of course they didn't care on what he felt about them about to destroy his and Charlotte's house, after all, they were the ones that had the guns. Not that the fact that he said it didn't bother him? What? Even the statements earlier about if Tyler wanted to shoot him now or later, were a little off setting once he heard them. Tyler assumed the King was just trying to make a play to try and save his own life, but now—he wasn't so sure.

Edward, a.k.a, the King started to make his way to the far left corner in the back of the library, and stopped in front of s shelf full of books. "You are not going to tell me that there is a secret door right there are you?" Tyler said. Just then, Edward pulled on the wooden side of the shelf and it started open on hinges just like a door. There on the other side of the self, was a door. "You got to be fist fucking me."

"Say what you want Mr. Green, but it fooled you once you made your way in here. Think about that." They gathered in from of the door as Edward pushed the door open.

What greeted them was a smell like no other. It was as if they opened a manhole cover to a sewer. The smell was a combination of shit, piss, and possibly other organic material that was rotting in the darkness.

"Oh my God, that is horrible." Tanya said right before she started to dry heave on her knees. Tyler had to step away from the door entirely for a few seconds, hoping the gasoline filled air would help dull the smell of whatever was down there. Only….he knew what was down there. *Who* was down there.

Edward pulled out a handkerchief and put it over his nose and mouth. "There are lights over here somewhere." He searched for a few seconds until his hand had reached them on the opposite side of the doorframe. Bright lights filled the dark, death smelling hole. There was a sound of moving chains coming from below.

"Matt? Mathew?! You're alive!" Tyler moved to the opening of the basement. "Thank God buddy you don't know how much…"

Tyler stopped in his tracks on the first step, as he saw what he was talking to.

Tanya glanced up from her knees, happy that she managed to hold onto the food that was in her belly, only to subject her eyes to what she was smelling. She turned form the doorway entirely and found that her eyes gave her stomach too much for it to hold on any longer. She vomited a few feet away from the doorway. She went on for what seemed like an hour, but in reality was only for a few minutes. Afterward she broke into long sobs while repeating the same phrase over and over again. "Oh my God. Oh my God. Oh my God."

"Tyler…..Tanya…..you came for me." The thing said as tears broke from it's skeletal face. Just as a smile broke from it's lips. "It's me…Mathew."

Chapter 25

It was Tyler's turn to vomit now. Instead of going back toward the library, he leaned to his right and let it go off the edge of the stairway. Once he was finished, he looked up at what remained of his best friend.

Matt was completely naked and chained onto the floor by both arms and legs. There were sores on his palms, elbows, and knees from being on all fours for so long. There was pile and puddles of both urine and feces that was around his legs and thighs, his legs were filthy from being caked by the shit for a long period of time. The worst part of this, was the crookedness and odd formation of Matt's legs. They were obviously broken in several places, one of the bones was close to pultruding through the skin. It was clear that the pain was so incredible, that Matt decided that it was best not to move his lower extremities at all; even to go to the bathroom. He just let himself go where he laid, and let it pile up. Gashes and bruises were all over his frail, skinny body, that was once muscular and well toned. Small piles of hair gummed onto the floor with the help of the puddles of dried blood that gathered around him. Charlotte never bothered to clean him up. Dry blood was stuck onto his upper body and arms just like his own feces was stuck onto his legs and buttocks.

His face…was unrecognizable from the face that was in Tyler's memory. His nose was broken—several times since he stayed here, and was never put back into place. Cuts and big black bruises that were black covered his forehead and his eyes, making him look like he had the eyes of a raccoon. Teeth were missing from what Tyler saw as Matt tried to smile at him. His smile was strained and Tyler couldn't blame him for that. He thought that Matt's very existence knew nothing but pain.

Connected to Matt's left arm was a long clear tube that was connected to an IV. Next to that were several pouches of blood that were also connected to his arm. Tyler figured that this was the most medical treatment that Mathew had received since he was captured. An I.V. to help keep him hydrated and possible not die from whatever infection he would no doubly receive from his wounds, and blood so he wouldn't die of blood loss. Tyler wondered how many times he tried to grasp those tubes with his right hand that was chained up away from the left, trying to kill himself by just bleeding out.

Tyler saw images of survivors of the Nazi concentration camps he saw in books and videos in high school. Frail, walking skeletons that would beg for food and were an inch away from death from those that still had the ability to draw breath. That was now Mathew Mullen. His body eating away at itself for three months, till it got to the point of where he is now. A shadow of his former self.

Tyler turned to Edward and grabbed his by the collar of the suit. "You fucking bastard!" He punched him and threw him down the stairs. Edward went down and landed hard onto the floor. While Tyler started to go down the stairs, he threw his gun up in front of himself and then snatched it out of the air, so he could hold it at the end of the barrel. Leaving the handle to be exposed.

Edward started to get up onto his feet, when Tyler reached the bottom of the stairs. Just as Edward looked up at him, Tyler threw back his hand that held the gun and quickly brought it back as if he were hitting in the major leagues. The end of the pistol made contact with Edward's cheekbone, sending him back to the ground, about a foot away from the pile of human shit.

Tyler grabbed Edward by the suit jacket. "YOU COULD HAVE STOPPED THIS! YOU COULD HAVE SET HIM FREE! WHAT THE FUCK IS WRONG WITH YOU PEOPLE?! AREN'T YOU A FUCKING HUMAN BEING?!"

Edward had on a blank face. "I haven't been a human in a long time." The pistol whip made a big cut onto Edward's cheek, but he made no sign that he was in any type of pain. "He wasn't the first one I tried to save. There were many more. So many more that I couldn't count them all. So many years, filled with so many dead. I tried to leave that third floor so many times on my own, but once she touches you, there is no hope."

Tyler let go of Edward, understanding. "She touched you, and made sure you never left the third floor."

"She only did that once we had prisoners here in the basement. Once I found that this place existed, I tried to free many that came in. But like I said, once she touches you, there is no winning. She knows what you are feeling, because she can feel it too. Not just me, but the ones she keeps as well." He turned and looked at Mathew as he said this. "She knows what we are doing right now because of that. Believe me when I say that you are a rarity to get this far."

"LET HIM GO NOW!" screamed Tyler. Tanya was able to get a hold of her stomach and started to make her way down the stairs, crying as she did this.

"You.....you came for me." Mathew croaked out from a silent dry voice.

"I will do as you wish." said Edward as he started to get up off the ground. "Miss Walsh, I know you just made it down here, but could you get a bolt cutters that is over there under the stairs? Thank you very much."

Tyler lifted the gun and aimed it at Edward's eye. "Get it yourself."

"Very well." said Edward, sounded as if they were putting him in a bind. He retrieved the bolt cutters and saw that Tyler drew the gun on him once again. He walked over toward Mathew and wrinkled his nose at the smell of piss, shit, sweat, blood, and dirt all combined. It was awful, no matter how many times your nose was greeted with it, your soul would never get use to it. He bent down onto the concrete and and put the clip onto the chain. He pulled the two handles of the bolt cutters together until they met each other. As soon as they made it to an inch from one another, there was an audible click from the penetration of metal and just like that, Matt's right arm was free.

Edward repeated this act, three more times. Once he was finished, he put the bolt cutters down on the ground and started to move forward to help Matt up.

"Don't you fucking move an inch!" Tyler said in a "don't fuck with me" tone of voice. "Stay where you are."

"He needs help." Edward said to him. "I was merely trying to help."

"Look at him. Does't look like he can feel anything other than pain."

"You came f-f-for me Tyler….you came." repeated Mathew.

"Yeah, buddy." Tyler said as he started to move down the stairs. His nose also wrinkled as he got a more potent whiff of the smell that took up the whole basement area. "I came for you and I'm going to get you out."

"Let me help you." Edward said, with his hands and arms spread out as if to say that Tyler needed to put these to good use.

"I think you and your cunt of a wife have done enough!" Tanya said this in a sharp hiss that made aTyler turn to make sure that it was coming from her and not someone else. Edward looked like that had giving him a blow emotionally, on a face that until then had been like a statue with emotion. Still his resolved was undeterred.

"You may not like my wife for what she had done to him, but it wasn't me. Let me help at least get some food into him and clean off his legs. Time is not on your side because Anoaka will be here soon I'm sure of it."

"Anoaka?" Tyler said in confusion.

"Yes Anoaka. Anoaka of the Red. My wife that has been the misery you have been experiencing for months, and the woman that has been my misery for centuries." He now looked pleading at both Tyler and Tanya. "The woman that I want you to kill."

If Tyler and Tanya went beyond the strength of human emotion and were able to keep stone faces at the sight of what remained of Mathew Mullen, they still would have shown at least a raised eyebrow of interest at the mere mention that the King that was so precious to the woman or creature that had been pursuing them for so long, really wanted her dead as much as she wanted them dead. The looks that Edward the King was receiving now, were of shocked confusion. It stood in the air for a long time, seconds in reality but felt as if they were hours. The silence was broken from an unlikely source, that spoke unlikely words.

"Trust…. him. He's telling……. the truth."

Tyler looked down at Matt, keeping the handgun raised. He looked at what remained of Matt's face that was caked with blood, and saw that his eyes were staring right at him. The eyes seemed to look at him with all the pain and misery that he had experienced, washed away from his face and he saw the look that he knew from his friend so well and missed so much. The look of "trust me, I'm not fucking with you". Tyler understood then that Edward was there to help, and so he lowered his gun and made his way to the basement floor. "Come on and lets get him upstairs. See if there is anything that he can eat slowly in that kitchen of yours."

Edward bent down and helped Matt get up without letting his his legs or feet make connection with the ground, knowing that his legs were in shambles anyways, letting them touch the ground was only gonna cause more pain to the point of sending Matt into shock, and possibly killing him. Tyler went under his right arm to help. He looked at Edward with anger, but was a little impressed to see that he didn't care if he got his hands dirty, as he put one of his hands on Matt's buttocks that was covered in shit, an lifted him up. Tyler would never like him, but shit did that cause him to respect him just a little bit.

Matt was giving out small cries as he was moved around. His legs dangled as he was lifted into the air by the men, causing them to hurt even worse than when they did just laying on the ground as worthless sticks. He was forced to move them every now and again, and when he did they caused him such pain that it made him reach tears overtime he had to do it. It was painful, but necessary. Now as they dangled in the air, not touching the cold concrete floor, his eyes once again filled with painful tears. He couldn't see anything from them filling up his vision with aqua uncertainty. Once he blinked them away so they would fall down his face, his eyes fell onto something that caused him to cry out, and struggle in the men's arms. The pain was great, but in that instant, he didn't care. He just had to get away from what he saw. Even if it killed him.

His eyes landed on the crowbar.

"NO! NOT THAT! NEVER AGAIN! Please! Pleeeeease! PLEASE..........!"

His last "please" was the most painful for all of them to listen to.

It took them ten minutes to get Matt upstairs after he struggled with them. His eyes never left the crowbar as if he were afraid it was going to jump out at him. Once they were clear and made their way back into the library, Matt's pain cries were hard to listen to and made Tyler want to drop him because he was causing him too much pain. They stopped for a few seconds and discussed where they were going to put him.

"We could put him in a car that is in the garage?" Tanya said. "We came here for Matt and now we have him, so let's get out of here and take him to a hospital."

Tyler thought for a moment, thinking hard about their options. But a fact came screaming at him when he thought about Tanya's idea: *She will never stop.* Of course she would never stop, we offended her, hurt her, witnessed her and escaped from her. Even if it cost her her life, she wouldn't stop. How could you escape something like that? But he knew the answer to that too: *You don't, you just fight back.*

He shook his head to get back to Matt. "We will get him to a hospital, but we need to help him first. Besides, I think we need to do something while we are here, don't you think so Edward?"

Edward looked at him with a shine of delight. "Yes I think *you* do."

"Let's take him into the bathroom by the kitchen. We can wash him up while he sits in the bathroom and gets washed off as gently as we can. Then, we can give him some sort of smoothie or something. Anything that is liquid. Sound good?"

Tanya wanted to ask what they needed to do while they were still here and had Matt, but she was afraid of the answer and just nodded her head in agreement.

"Besides, the King here has some explaining to do. A nice talk while there is still time."

"Don't—face her—Tyler." Matt said taking deep breaths in between his words. "She—will kill—you."

"Hold on, buddy. Let's take care of you first."

They made it to the bathroom and laid Matt down while running the shower onto his chest. Tanya took the shower head and moved it all around Matt's body, from his chest, down to the legs that didn't look so great.

"Oh my God Mathew." Tanya whispered as the water was washing away the shit and revealed only purple, red, and black skin where only white caucasian skin use to be. "She destroyed you didn't she?"

Matt said nothing. He was fighting a battle between the nice warmth of the water that he hadn't felt in months, as well as the pain of his legs and body from getting anytime of pressure on his wounds.

"I'm going to get you something to eat." said Tanya as she walked away from the bathroom and left Edward and Tyler in the bathroom with Matt. Tyler turned to the King and asked the question that had been on his mind for months.

"What is she?"

Edward took a long deep breath. "She couldn't really answer that question. Although she is not the only one, I can tell you that. And her story is quite remarkable. Too remarkable for any human to live. Her people called themselves by a name in a language that was lost in time. They were called 'Muliak'. People of Life."

"There is a whole tribe of her out there in the world?"

Edward shook his head. "No, the tribe is long gone now. I'm not sure how many are left, but I know that she told me that she had a father and a brother, and that they are the only ones that are left. Whether that is true or not I couldn't tell you. The tribe was killed by some internal conflict that eventually spread to involve humans. It happened over a thousand years ago."

"Her line has been around for over a thousand years?"

The King looked at Tyler as if he was missing the obvious. "No. She remembers it."

"Remembers it?" Tyler paused for a moment. "Like—she was fucking there?"

There were sounds of a blender in the kitchen that were making a loud noise, but either they didn't hear it or they ignored it. "She told me she was a little girl at the time, but yes. She does remember it."

Tyler was taken aback, "She's over a thousand years old? How old exactly?"

"She told me she was born in 706 A.D., so that makes her One-thousand, three hundred and ten years old. She never really celebrates her birthday."

"Yeah I bet after the first couple hundred, they start to loose their charm." Tyler said disbelief. "How old are her brother and father?"

"I have no idea. I have never seen her father, or hear her mention him ever in the five hundred years we have been together. Her brother, I have only met a few times since we've been married."

Tyler's eyes grew wider than he ever thought was possible. "Wait! You are over five-hundred years old? I thought you said you were human?"

"If you recall Mr. Green, I told you and Miss Walsh that I haven't been human in a very long time. At least, I don't know for sure."

Tanya came in and gave Matt a liquid shake of some sort, that had green chunks mixed with a grey substance. "Here Matt, drink this. The only thing I could find to make was a Kiwi-Strawberry-Banana smoothie. It's not much but it will get something in your stomach. What did I miss?"

"Alot. In one word: alot." Tyler said, and got her up to speed.

"Holy shit. If you are human, how are you still alive?"

Edward looked at all of them and answered in two words. Two words that in a way explained a lot about her and a lot about himself, but only made sense to him. "The Red."

There was silence for awhile. They two men and one woman looked at Edward, waiting for a further explanation, while Edward was waiting to see if they got it. Finally he asked, "Haven't you ever wondered why she always wears red?"

"Not really. I have only seen her twice, once when she was in a nice night gown that was studded in red sparkles and the other when she was wearing red jeans and a red shirt. I mean sure, it touched my mind once or twice, but I was trying to get the fuck away from her as well."

Edward looked at them. "It's a mark of her tribe." He took a long sigh and then spoke. "When she was born, they had a way of testing her ability as soon as she came out of the womb. What they did was take a sharp knife and take it to her small hand. The pain in the baby, triggers something inside of them and reveals their powers. When she was stabbed in her small hand, it caused a vibration in the man or woman's soul, as well as her mother's. Those were the first people to have ever touched her, and when she felt that pain, she caused them to be manipulated in some way. So…from that day on, she was sworn to wear something that was red on her at all times. A symbol of her tribe, of her title, and of her power."

"Manipulating souls. Why hasn't she just manipulated mine, or Tanya's yet?" Tyler asked.

"She hasn't touched you yet. That is why you still have yours."

"Wait." Tanya said. "If she manipulates souls, what does she do with them?"

"That depends. If she is really mad at the person who's soul she is taking, she can burn them in her hands, or rip them apart, but what she really uses them for is life.

"The people in her tribe are not humans. They already live for a couple millennia, so they don't need human souls for that reason, but what she uses them for is for two reasons: the first is to give her strength. The souls give her amazing strength, speed and power to use a soul that she controls in a human body."

"Like he controlled Danny at the cabin." Tyler said.

"And h-how she con-con-controlled me, for s-s-so long." Matt said looking ashamed.

"Yes, to both. She can control people in close range from herself with no trouble at all, but what she did with Danny hundreds of miles away from here, took a lot of souls she had to make happen."

Tyler didn't understand what he meant at first. Then he did. "You are telling me that she burned souls to control Danny so he could try to kill us?"

"I'm afraid so."

"That cunt." Tyler said. "How many have died from her?"

"The number is incalculable." he said in dismay. "She has committed genocide with numbers that have to be in the hundreds of thousands over the centuries. She doesn't care who, and with the wealth she has collected over the centuries, she could buy her way out of situations if that was what it took. If that wouldn't work, she would just kill whoever got in her way. However way she would have to."

Silence once again crept into the bathroom. But then a question arose in Tanya's head that she had to ask. "What does her power have to do with you being over five-hundred years old?"

"Right." Edward said as if he just remembered the original question again. "There is a second reason to use her power, is to give the souls to another human being to prolong their life. Ever since she saw me, I guess she thought that she had to have me. That's not boasting, that is just what she told me she had to do. To be by her side and continue her and her families line."

Tyler felt like he was going to throw up after hearing this. Was he going to have to run from a whole family of soul suckers? "Oh boy."

"Are you alright?" Edward asked.

Tyler looked up and saw that he looked as if he was about to vomit in the toilet. "Yeah, you just freaked me out that's all. She got you, so she could fuck you!?"

"Wait," Tanya said, raising a hand. "I thought you said that her and her brother and father were the only ones left of the tribe? Do human babies not count in the Muliek?"

"Me being human is the only reason it has taken this long. For a human to spread the line, they need to have been alive for so long before they can get a member of the Muliek pregnant. It's not a tribal law, that's just the biology of how it works. Right around the time you two came into the picture, I needed only a few souls before I reached the right age to get Anoaka pregnant. I had been dreading it since the beginning of the twentieth century. But when you two *did* come into the picture, it delayed it for only a few months. Right when you met her brother, Mathew, she gave me the last souls that she needed to get pregnant by me."

Tanya spoke up. "You are the man. Can't you just *not* have sex with her?"

"Using my soul." He said it like a statement. "How else do you think she could get herself a baby with my sperm? She kept me on a third floor for years, making me have sex with her, caused her no mental endurance problems, believe me."

"Right. Sorry." Tanya faced the floor.

Tyler looked at him, his eyes locked onto his. "Why you? Of all the people, in all of history, why did she pick you? You talk about her not like you are soul mates or with any real affection. Why did she pick you?"

Edward took another deep breath and lowered his eyes to the floor now. "Because I'm a King."

A moment of silence passed between everyone until Tyler spoke up. "Is that supposed to mean something to us? Other than a pet name I've been hearing?"

Edward looked on the ground as if he didn't hear him. "I am five hundred and forty-six years old. I know this is America and everyone here is obsessed with themselves in this day and age, but do any of you know any kings that were alive at that time?" He was greeted only with silence. "That's how you know you are old, when no one knows who you are to the point of not knowing history. There isn't time to give you the full story, but I will leave you with my name: Edward V. If you guys survive what is to come, you can look me up yourselves and put the pieces together. But I am looking at you and see that we need to get you into a car and get you to a hospital that is close by," Looking directly at Matt he said this. "but not too close if you understand what I'm saying."

"One last question." Tyler said, getting his feet from sitting on the toilet. "Is your wife pregnant now?"

Edward stopped and looked at Tyler as if this was a stupid question and he should be slapped across the face for asking it. "I don't know, but tell me this: Is that gonna stop you from doing what needs to be done?"

Tyler said nothing to this. He just stared at the man's eyes for a while before he started to help Matt turn off the shower. Tanya stayed right where she was. "You are not serious in thinking that we are going to stick around and try and kill her? Right?"

Tyler looked up at her, "You aren't staying here Tanya, but I am."

"Like fuck you are!" she exclaimed. He eyes bulging from her skull.

Matt looked up at him and was about to say the same thing, instead he chimed in. "Y-you think you have a ch-chance against her?

T-t-trust me you don't! I did-did-didn't live this l-l-long to see my best fr-friend die for me by t-t-t-taking on my kid-napper! There w-w-will be another way, there al-al-al-ways is!" He started to run out of breath hallway through saying this, that in the end all that came out was a hiss of a voice.

"This is the only way right now. Trust me, I thought of every other way I can. But I need to at least draw her fire so you two can get away. Then once you are clear, I can use that bomb on her to see if that will stop her. Do I have a chance at least with the bomb, Edward?"

"If she has more souls in her than she usually does, I would say no. But as far as I know, she hadn't gone hunting for other souls since she took over Danny and started to make her way up to you. So.... it might work, you never know."

Tyler looked at them, "See! There is hope after all!"

Tanya wasn't buying it, "Yeah, but that bomb is covered with gas, if you haven't smelled it since we last past it, that you would be killed too before you ever made it out of the front door! Don't you see?! Either way you die here!"

"Then At least I die stopping her from killing two people I love. That alone is a victory in itself." tears were welling up in his eyes, "Please don't fight me on this Tanya, I have to get my head in the game."

Tears were streaming down Tanya's face now. Matt looked at Tyler with pleaded eyes that were screaming at him to not do this, but he didn't say anything.

There were no sounds except the long breaths taking by Matt for the pain he was feeling. They all just stared at each other, taking in that this might be the last time they all saw each other again. Tears were streaming, but the cries wee internal. Finally, it was Edward that broke the silence.

"Well if you are going to do this, this is what I think you should do to get away. You do it this way, you two will have a great chance of leaving undetected."

Chapter 26

The storm winds were starting to get worse as Anoaka drove into Lake Geneva. Pushing the car the best that it could and succeeding in pushing it only a few inches to the right side at the most. She only noticed it indifferently, as her mind was on other things. Her mind wasn't even on the storm that was around her, violent as it was becoming. Her eyes were seeing everything that she needed to in order to drive. Stopping at red lights, and making the turns that she needed to, even down to turning on the windshield wipers so she could see through the ongoing rain.

Her mind, was a different story altogether. Since she left Wausau and made her way down to Lake Geneva, she outstretched her mind to see if she could reach out and touch the King's or Matt, the fucker she was now regretting of not killing before making her way up here in the first place, or at the very least let Kolat deal with him before he left. If he left. At this point, Anoaka hoped he didn't, but she thought that her luck wasn't about to let him ignore her request that he get the fuck out of her house, this time. Either way, she didn't count on it. She reached out and continued to try and reach out like a toddler reaching on his tippy-toes for a cookie that was on top of the fridge, while he was on the ground so far from the jar; and just like the child, failed to grasp what she sought for.

Her temper was almost a thing of beauty, if you thought long verbal burst of words like "mother fuckers" and "fucking dead rats" and other obscenities were something of beauty to be heard, but nonetheless it would have been enough to make the nearest sailor fresh on leave turn red. Her anger seethed all the way until she reached Janesville, which only took her two hours to reach by not giving a shit of the speed limit that was posted on the main highway. The posted speed was seventy miles-per-hour; she was going nearly one-hundred and ten. Even in her anger riddled mind that sought only revenge, she would have had the sense to slow down in the areas she knew had speed traps in, but the truth was—she wanted to be pulled over.

She didn't want to be pulled over in the sense of getting caught by the police for committing a crime. Oh no. Something like getting pulled over for her excessive driving speeds and anger could give the chasing pig a reason to look at what had happened today in Wausau at the courthouse. Maybe making a connection to the blue shirted pig and calling the rest of the drive to surround her that could give her a nice chase for a while, before she would eventually have to do something that she was going to regret and kill them all and find an escape somehow. Despite such unlikely odds, Anoaka never for an instant thought that she could die from something like that. Just like she always knew that she was going to kill Tyler Green. This wasn't from some advanced look into the future, no, that was just the way her confidence worked. It worked to the point to where it wasn't even confidence, it was mere certainty in her mind that that was just the way that was going to happen, even when those events that she forecasted, turned out to be wrong.

And she was wrong a lot these days.

No she didn't really want that to happen, but with her trying her best to try and reach out to her love, and that little shitstain that was down in the basement, she could have used the souls from whatever pig that pulled her over, to maybe get a better feeling on weather or not Tyler had gotten there yet, or not. As much as she wanted souls for that reason, she knew it was a bad idea to get pulled over at this point in time, even though her confidence was high, she knew that her and the King had to get out of Dodge as soon as possible. The mess that she left back there might have a possibility to lead back to her, even though she was pretty sure that she got rid of anyone that could have seen her face. Still, she ended to be elsewhere for a while that was for sure. Just as soon as this was all finished.

She continued to reach out and touch her husband, but to no success. Her weakness from burning up all those souls a few days ago to control Danny, took its toll on her. If she had all the souls that she had before the burn, she would be able to pinpoint how the King was feeling while eating a sandwich, but now while driving closer and closer to them, hundreds of miles away, she couldn't feel anything on her King, nothing at all.

It wasn't until she got to Janesville, only a little more than an hour away, by traffic laws that was, that she started to feel a twinge of emotion from someone. But from who? Her King? She didn't know right away, she was still a long distance off. If it was her King, why would he feel—relief? Maybe they didn't get there yet and he just got out of the shower or something; that was what she told herself. She drove a few more miles and then casted out another grasp of emotion, like a fisherman casting for fish. This time she felt something stronger and from who it was coming from: Mathew, the shitstain from the basement.

She felt like she was going to throw up, not only had that son of a bitch lived for all these months, even through the times she was starving him, Tyler and his whore showed up and found him in the basement. But wait….hold on. If they found him, and he was in the basement, that meant that…that—

Her foot dropped onto her pedal until she could feel the floor on the bottom of the car. How dare her King show them where he was. How fucking dare he! Quickly as she accelerated toward Lake Geneva, she casted out another grasp for emotion to try and reach her King. She grabbed him until she felt like she got ahold of him and felt that she gotten ahold of two people for sure: one feeling relief with pain, the other feeling caution and…and…relief?

What the fuck was going on?

There was a constant change in emotions as she made her way to Lake Geneva, merely minutes away. They changed here and there, but for the most part they remained ones of relief, and eventually made their way to sadness, but then back to relief for both the men. It threw her for a whirl, but it confirmed that the bastard and the bitch were in fact at the house, there was no question now. It didn't matter. She was just about to enter Lake Geneva, and from there, it was only minutes away from her house. She would take care of them soon enough. If she had the souls, she would try and take care of them now, maybe make Matt look like he was convulsing with a seizure. Then when they came close to check on him, make him reach up and tear out the bastards throat with his teeth. Bet he would love that the mother fucker. After that make him choke the life out of the bitch. The sweet part about that was that no matter how much that she would hit him with her failing strength, it wouldn't help her. She would just make sure that he would have a tighter grip, because no matter how much she would try, nothing could stop her once she controlled another's soul.

Only, she didn't have any souls to use on Matt right now, so she tried and put that way of thinking out of her mind. Still, wishful thinking.

She entered Lake Geneva with satisfaction, and a healthy bit faster than the speed limits allowed, when she first felt that something was wrong. Very wrong. Suddenly she couldn't feel that shit stain Matt anymore. There was nothing. She stretched out further, further than she thought was ever necessary fro someone that was so close now. In fat with this close, she shouldn't have a problem at all trying to feel for anyone that she touched, let alone a nothing like Matt Mullen. She kept feeling around—still, she only felt her King, who felt himself now filled with unease. What was going on there? Still the unease, still the unease.

She continued to drive to make her way down to Bayview Drive. Panic started to fill her up as she was heading into an unknown situation. She pushed it aside as she was trying to get her head into what was going on, and what she had to do to those fucks that were inside her house, with her King.

She turned onto Snake Road. Her turn onto Geneva Bay Drive was coming up and she only let up on the speed of the Camaro for the turns that needed to be made, but once she made them, her foot touched the floor once again.

She felt something new in The King's mind—preparation. That Son-of-a-Bitch! There was nothing that could convince her now that he wasn't helping Tyler and his bitch anymore. After she was going to finish with her annoying flies that were hanging around the house, The King and her were going to have a little chat. The kind that usually never end well for him. She wasn't going to kill him. Oh no. But he was going to feel some pain, and she was defiantly going to feel some pleasure; one way or the other. Even after all these years, he still tries to resist her. After all the love that she gave him, even after saving his life all those centuries ago. If not for her, his uncle would have killed him for sure; like everyone thinks he did anyways. If not for her, he would have lost his head as a boy, along with his brother.

Brief images of her, seeing him as a boy for the first time. A young king he was then. Not knowing what to do with his kingdom, and confused of why he was in the situation he was in in the first place. Along with missing his father, the former king. Seeing him as this cute blonde boy in the days when those kind excited her the most. Young, handsome, and having a country to run, were all the best features a girl like her could ask for. She was a girl back then; a girl in her people's years she was. Yet, she knew that she wanted to spend eternity with him as soon as she saw him sleeping all alone in that castle. As much sleep as he could for a boy that was afraid for his life.

When he awoke, he was even more afraid of this child woman, that look like she was maybe seventeen, but really not even close to that. Several lifetimes from that in fact. He asked her who she was, and all she replied to him was, "The woman you are going to marry. And the woman that will save your life, your Majesty." That was the last time she called him that.

She was brought back to the present as soon as she turned on Bayview and saw something that she dreaded: the Ferrari.

She expected it, but still it made her anger fly right back into her head and spread through her body like the worlds fastest plague. She almost stopped her car to take a look inside, but she knew there was no point, she knew that they were already inside, from Matt's emotions. Instead, she turned the Camaro down the Bayview and saw her house. Full of light from the stone sided bottom, to the transparent third floor; all covered with lights from the inside. She went and touched a button on her overhead sun visor, it was the button to open the gate in front of the house, that lead to the garage. It started to open up slowly. So slowly that it was pure agony to sit and watch. Her hands that were griping the steering wheel only a few minutes ago, started to tap softly, and then worked themselves up to hard blows on the wheel.

"Come on. Come on. COME ON!" She started to raise her voice steady with each blow of the wheel until it turned into a downright scream.

Finally the gate door opened enough to where she could just barely get the car through. She hit the gas as the car drove up the driveway, until she heard a soft bang of metal that hit the car. She looked around, and then looked at her side rearview mirror—only to find that she no longer had a rearview side mirror. She hit the mirror on the gate as she drove up the driveway.

"Who the fuck cares?" she said out loud.

She pushed another button on her visor and saw the garage door open up. This door was also slow, but faster than the gate. She pulled into the garage and jumped out of the vehicle. She started to run into the house, but then stopped. She reached out for anyone's emotions that she could grab. She felt the King's calm and patient side that he always portrayed. But Matt's was still missing. She continued to outreach, and continued to fail to sense him. She marched into the house from the garage like she was about to whip a boy that had done something naughty.

She once again stopped short as realization dawned upon her: Tyler and his bitch were in her house—her house, and they were hiding somewhere in here. Maybe to try and kill her. In fact the chances of them trying to kill her is more than likely.

"Fuck you both if you think you are going to kill me." she said to herself, and resisted her urge, her need even, to storm through the house, and started to walk slowly and reaching out to feel emotions.

Moving slowly down the hallway, she still sensed her King, he was above her, and felt calm, almost peaceful. She hated it. It gave her almost nothing on what was truly on his mind. She came upon the home theater room and walked in. It was dark and devoid anyone that she could see or felt. She though she couldn't see or feel anything, she still turned on the lights and searched the room, she thought back to what she thought about earlier in the day; she was beyond taking chances. She gave the room a nice look over on any obvious hiding spots, like the small projector room that her and the King use for old time films, when they were both a few decades younger, liked to enjoy. She even checked in some not so obvious spots, like the vent shaft that was in the upper part of the projection booth just below the ceiling. There was no one in there. Well…at least in this part of the house. She moved on.

When she exited the home theater room, her eyes fell upon the door of the library. She thought about entering there next, but decided to circle back to it, once the rest of the floor was searched. She turned left, and made her way towards the bathroom and the kitchen. She only needed to glance into the bathroom to see that there wasn't anyone in there. The curtain to the bathtub was open and empty, and unless they could somehow fit themselves in the small cupboards of the sink, they weren't going to effectively hide in there. She moved on into the kitchen.

The lights were on. Empty kitchen but the lights were still on. She moved more slowly, looking at every crevice that was in the kitchen, hell she even looked at the oven and stove with suspicion. She kept looking around and around the room, thinking that someone was going to pop out. In fact, she hoped that was going to happen. Hoping they would pop out she she could grab them and kill them where they stood. Yet, there was no one around. At least no one that she could see at first glance.

Fuck this was stupid, just fucking stupid.

Why the fuck was she sneaking around in her own fucking house? Did she not own this house? Did she not have power to kill anyone that she saw fit? She was practically a fucking god for fucks sake.

She was so close to marching through her house and searching every room in a storm like fashion, claiming the lives of the two fucks that she knew were here. She wanted them dead. Dead. DEAD!

Then, sanity and reason grabbed her by the head. Brining with them, the memories of what those two have already done to her. This stopped her cold. She had to be smart about this. So far, what she was doing, was working. And if it was working so far, it could work the rest of the way, until those two were in fact, dead. These thoughts, were now her obsession.

"You're not getting me this time. Oh no."

She continued to move through the first floor of the house. Passing through the dining room, and the living room, giving them both a little time to check certain blindspots that could hide a person. She found no one so far, but she knew they were here. She knew that they were probably up on the third floor with her King, but she wasn't going to take any chances. Searching each of the rooms was the only way she wasn't going to be caught off guard.

She went to the library, the room she wanted to see the most next to the third floor. She had to see what had happened to the shitstain of a human being in the basement and why she couldn't sense him anymore. Before she entered the library, she stood at the foot of the stairs that was right before the second entrance. Looking up, and extended her ears, listening for the tiniest sound from up above. Listening to try and know what was going on up there. Hoping that her love was alright, despite betraying her. She needed him. She needed him to help her carry on her kind. For her father and her brother. Listening for sounds of pain, sounds of sobs even. If she heard those, she knew she would stop this search and dash straight up those stairs to save him. She stayed at the foot of the steps a little longer, trying to hear everything. She heard the tapping of the rain against the windows, the thunder that hit the ground and rumbled through the night miles away from here. She heard nothing from inside of the house. There were no sounds there other than her breathing and her rapping heartbeat that was as loud as the thunder outside. She never realized that she was scared. Never did it strike her that fear could grasp her like this. But never had some one potential gotten to her at her place of sanctuary like Mr. Green and his bitch had done.

There were no sounds. There was nothing.

She moved on into the library. As she opened the door, she was invaded by a instant smell that she was all too familiar with; gasoline. It hit her nostrils like hitting the aroma of a disgusting bathroom that had never been cleaned. It caused her to move her head back and wrinkle her face in disgust. Like fueling the cars it was meant to be used for, it fueled her anger. Those bastards are going to try and burn her house down. Burning her books and her house, and her King. Waiting for her, so she could go down with it. She turned her head and saw the pile of books and papers that were in the corner of the library. As she approached it, the smell of gasoline got stronger and stronger. She stopped short of the pile for a few feet.

"Think you are going to burn me, do you? If I burn, I will make you burn too. Every part that is you. From your body, to your souls. There will be nothing left of you. I will make sure of it." she made this promise to herself in a low voice, and moved on in the library.

It didn't take long to search the rest of the library, there were about eight shelves in the whole room that were filled with books and had limited hiding spots. In fact the closest hiding spot in the library, was the basement that had her hidden door. Once she was as satisfied as she could get about the library being empty of people, she went to the basement and opened the door. Overtime she opened the door to the basement, she was greeted by another smell of human waste and human blood that filled the air in the basement these days. That smell was still there, but not as strong. Before she turned on the light, she knew that Matt was gone. As she flipped the switch, it confirmed her suspicions.

The chains, the blood, the shit and the piss were all there. Dried out, but there nonetheless. But there was no Matt.

That's okay. You were on borrowed time anyways. Once I find you, you will be just as dead as your friends.

These thoughts calmed her down as she left the basement without taking a step through the door.

She made her way to the second floor, but she suspected that she wasn't going to find anyone there. They knew by now that the King couldn't leave the third floor as long as she willed him to stay there, and she willed him to stay there now. Still keeping him calm state about him. She checked the second floor anyways, telling herself not to be thrown off guard like she was in the past with these bozos. Like she suspected, there was no one. There was no one from the second floor, down. No one—

She had an idea. Why was she going to them? The King was on the third floor. This she knew for sure. And maybe…maybe…this was what they were expecting what would happen. There was still a big pile of gasoline soaked papers down in the library. What if she missed someone, what if Mr. Green was on the third floor, drawing her closer to him, while his little bitch came in and started the house on fire with that pile of books and papers. Could that be the plan?

Maybe. Maybe.

She had her foot on the stairs to take her up to the third floor, but then she lifted it up and receded it back onto the second floor. She wasn't going to do this. She wasn't going to play this game. She threw the maybe aside and thought that this was certainty. She moved over to the other set of the stairs that went back down to the library and started to make her way back there. As she did, she sent out a mental order to her beloved King: *Come to the library my love, and bring your friends with you.*

She felt two things as this order was made: She felt the King's presence move toward the third floor stairs preparing to make his decent, and fear in the King's emotions begin to rise.

"What is happening?" asked Tyler to Edward in a whisper.

"She has me going to the library. I can't not obey her commands, she has my soul."

"What the fuck should I do?"

"I-I don't know." Edward reached the stairs and started to decent. "Follow me with the gun on me. She wants to move the setting, I think. But as long as you threaten to take my life. Her emotions will still be unstable enough to be used against her. You need to take your shot then."

Tyler thought about this, and he didn't like it. Moving down to the library, when Tanya was going to move in and started the fire to the bomb was going to reveal their plan, flawed as it was, really fast. In fact, Anoaka probably figured it out already. She was supposed to wait fifteen minutes from the time that Anoaka arrived to make her way back into the house and light the fire in the library, so it could trigger the bomb, and have her leave right away in the car that was in the garage, with Matt sleeping in the truck. Edward told them to give him sleeping pills that were in the medicine cabinet so it would knock him out, and causing Anoaka to unable to sense where he was. They didn't know if that was going to work, but they had to try something. The whole plan was a series of Hail Mary's anyways, they figured that something had to work.

They were moving down the stairs and just touched the second floor when Tyler asked, "Do you have a lighter at all?"

"The only one that I had on me was the one that I gave to Tanya. Why? Thinking about starting the fire yourself?"

"Yes, but not anymore. I gave it to Tanya to use to start the fire. Unless there are any here on the second floor that I could use?" Edwards foot started making his way down to the first floor, when he turned and looked at Tyler with urgency, but kept his voice low.

"The second floor bathroom! There might be matches in the first drawer on the sink! Hurry!"

Tyler dashed to the bathroom that was about ten feet away from the stairs. He flipped the light on and saw the top drawer. He opened it and searched. The drawer was filled with all kinds toothpastes, ointments, toothbrushes still in plastic wraps, gels and Q-tips, but he could see any matches. He dug very briefly, then moved not the next drawer. The second drawer had only one thing in it: a hairdryer. He closed it shut thinking there were no matches, and depression sent in as he needed to make his way back toward Edward for the plan to happen, otherwise they were as good as dead.

There was one drawer left. He opened quickly, and saw something that made his heart race: scented candles—and a book of matches. He grabbed the matches and made his way back to Edward. As he got to the top of the stairs, he saw that Edward was only two steps away from the bottom, already turning his body to go into the library. Tyler jumped down the stairs, missing steps with each jump as he reached to bottom in four large bounds. He almost collided with the front door that was the opposite side of the stairs, from the momentum of his jumps. He made his way behind Edward, just as he entered the library.

Her King entered the library will a face that said he was calm, but his emotions were terrified. It relieved some of her anger as she felt the control come back her way. That was until, she saw the gun that was against, her King's head.

"Hello Anoaka." Tyler Green said as he entered the library, she saw that his face wrinkled for the smell of gasoline that was in the air. "Nice house. Must have costed a pretty buck."

"What the fuck do you think you are doing?" she said with the anger rising up again. Realizing that what ever ground she gained from moving the setting to the library, was only an illusion. A lie that she told herself. As long as that bastard had a gun on his beloved, there was no control.

"I'm putting an end to you. To this. You have gone on and destroyed too much. Killed too much."

"Any yet I haven't killed you, not yet anyways. That will change in a moment."

"We will see Anoaka."

Anger flared up in her voice. "DON'T YOU DARE CALL ME THAT! You are not worthy to say my true name. I can only guess," she turned her gazed, her wicked angrily gaze at Edward, her King. "that my King has told you my true name. Seems you have been telling them a lot since I have been making my way here. I think you are going to receive a bit of punishment for that my love."

Edward looked uneasy. Tyler could feel it. Even though The King knew that the only way for him to be free was to be killed by Tyler, he still didn't want to die. Just like the rest of humanity. But if death meant getting away from this psychotic bitch, he would welcome it. Even if uneasy about it. Edward spoke. "How long are we going to keep going? How long are *you* going to keep going my love?

"Life has to end sometime, and I plan on going tonight. Too many centuries I have lived, too many to where it doesn't feel like living anymore. Everyday is a chore, living in a prison with no bars, but still a prison nonetheless. You can dress up this house to fool the outside world, but as long as I am trapped here, I have no need for life."

"I gave you life, when death was sure to take you at the hands of your fucking uncle! We lived this long for the children that we long for—for centuries. That was what we have been living for. That is what *I* have been living for! And now when we are so close to getting what we want, you want this piece of shit to kill the both of us? Fuck you! Fuck you both!" Her face was as red with anger as her shirt. "You are not dying on my me today my love. But I am going to make you wish you were dead, more than you do now. Now get over here beside me while I kill this bastard and his bitch!"

Edward started to move toward Anoaka. "Now Tyler!" he yelled.

Tyler took the gun that was pointed against Edward V's head, and pulled the trigger. His head exploded on the opposite side as blood, bone, and brain matter sprayed the library wall, the door, and the floor beneath him. He collapsed with a heavy thud onto the ground as if he were nothing other than a sack of meat.

Anoaka screamed at the height of her lungs. Her anger, gone. Her will to kill, gone. She reached out to gather her husband of over five hundred years, but was stopped.

Tyler turned the gun that was pointed at her late husband, and pointed it at her. He pulled the trigger. Once, twice, thrice, till all four rounds made their way into Anoaka's body. Each shot pushed her body back as they hit her midsection, her shoulder, her breast, and finally, her heart.

"Tyler!"

Tyler looked around and saw Tanya looking through the other door on the other side of the library. "What happened to upstairs?"

"She changed the venue. Go now, I will catch up as I start the fire!" Tanya nodded and ran toward the garage.

Tyler took the matches and lit one of them after the second strike. He lit the whole matchbook on fire and made his way to the pile of papers and books. He threw the matchbook onto the pile, as it erupted on fire. He turned toward the door that Tanya peaked through—when he was stopped suddenly. He was turned around by the bare hand on the bare skin of his arm, and greeted with the face and bloody body of Anoaka.

"Leaving? I think not. You're not dead yet."

Chapter 27

Fire. Heat started to make its way up the pile of papers, books, and gasoline, fast and hateful. Anoaka grasp Tyler's throat and began to lift him up off the ground. All he could think of was her touch onto his bare, and sweaty skin.

She touched me.

I'm as good as dead.

"Getting hot in here, don't you think Tyler? Hot enough to make sure a body can never be found even. Interesting I think, to have your body show up hours away from the jailhouse that you were in this morning, only to be horribly burned to death." Tyler thought about the bomb that was in the fire. How any second it was going to go off, he waited for it while Anoaka kept talking. He was dead anyway.

"Your little bitch of a girlfriend will die too. I will find her. I always find them in the end. And I will kill your ex-wife just for sport. It still won't be enough for all the pain you just caused me! But for now, this moment your—."

She was going to say, "your death will satisfy me for now." when the bomb that Tyler had been waiting for so patiently, went off.

It threw both Anoaka and Tyler back, releasing her grip on his neck. Fire and debris shot out in all directions as the two of them flew across the library with the fire. Tyler hit hard against a book shelf, knocking the wind that was already dwindling out of his body from being choke, out of him completely. He didn't see where Anoaka was thrown, but he knew he needed to get moving and to get out of here before the fire and smoke made it impossible. He took in a breath, and found it filled with smoke. There was a burning pain on his arm and saw that it was on fire. While coughing in a fit to get fresh oxygen in his lungs, he rapidly hit his arm in an attempt to put the fire out. Once it was out, he crawled a little ways in front of him, trying to breath fresh air. He found some, enough to stop the coughing, but he knew that it was going to be completely gone in no time.

He thought about his gun, thinking he needed it to arm against Anoaka. Then he realized it was gone from his right hand. He should have realized it from when he put the fire out on his left. He looked around, trying to find it when his eyes landed on it of to his left, only a few feet away. He crawled over to it and picked it up, shoving it down the front of his pants. Trying to lift himself up, he continued to cough like crazy. Fire was spreading in the library, and it was spreading fast.

Fire breathed out in the shelves as it caught on the books. He looked at the ceiling where the pile of books that they used to bury the bomb was, and saw a pillar of fire as if it walked straight out of the bible. Heat radiated from the flames to the point that it was unbearable. He thought that if he survived he was going to have a hell of a suntan.

He finally got to his feet, but it hurt him to do so. He didn't know where in the library he was exactly, just that he had to find the door, and had to avoid Anoaka.

Suddenly, he felt pain throughout his entire body, o the point where it stopped him cold. Fear took over in his body. He knew what this was, it was Anoaka and she was pissed.

He began to move his legs involuntary away from the door, and toward a corner of the library. He got past some shelves that were teeming with flames to find Anoaka standing in the middle of the library. His feet started to move faster and faster toward her. She had her signature hateful smile upon her face. Even from all the blood that was pouring out of her, she looked terrifying. Her arm was outstretched as she waited to grasp her hands around his throat.

"I have nowhere to be. You already took my entire world." she said in a combination of anger and boastfulness.

Tyler decided not to fight it any longer. He moved his legs in force with her and almost charged himself into her hands. Once again lifting him off the ground. There were no more words, there were no more threats. There was now only death.

Tanya had the garage door open and the car started up, when the explosion rang through the house as if lightning outside had struck the house. She almost thought it did at first, until she remembered about the bomb. The Jaguar was silent when that bitch parked right next to her as she hid in the Jag about a half hour ago. She had a watch that she had gotten from Edward and waited the twenty minutes like she was suppose to do. Once that happened she got out of the car and went to the door to the library. Only she found that the confrontation that was supposed to take place on the third floor, was now in the library. She waited and hoped that everything was going to play out like they all hoped it would; with the bitch dead as a doornail. She waited until she heard the gunshots. All five of them. When she opened the door and saw that it was Tyler standing there, telling her to go to the car and he was going to be there soon. So she did, started the car and waited patiently—until the bomb went off. Once she heard the bomb go off, she leapt out of the car and started to make her way back into the house. She opened the door from the garage, and felt instant heat flood from the house. Smoke and fire started to leak from the doorway into the library down the hall. She made her way toward it when the fire started to grow from the doorway. It grew and grew, until it started to spread into the hallway itself. She stopped short a few feet away from the doorway, because that was as far as she could go with out getting toasted herself.

"TYLER! TYLER!" she yelled as hard as she could, but the rage of the fire drowned out any cries from Tyler. If there were any.

She took a few steps back from the heat, she had to do something. She wasn't about to leave her best friend, and maybe someday lover to a burning death. She refused to even consider that an option. But she couldn't go forward. What could she do? What could she do!?

She stood and considered for a moment. After thinking for a moment she went and turned back to the garage.

"Bye-bye." Anoaka said. She took her right hand, her free hand and held it at Tyler's chest. Orange light started to rise from his chest, only it was barely noticeable from the orange flames that surrounded them now. There was pain, oh yes there was pain. A wall of pain that couldn't be bypassed. It engulfed Tyler as he screamed with what little breath he had from the lack of oxygen. He looked down in the pain and saw a ghostly image coming from his body. It started to pull away from him, as it did he felt the pain that was in his body start to leave him. That lack of pain, that lack of feeling—it felt so good.

No.

There was a tiny voice of defiance that rang through his head. No. *No? What do you mean no?*

Not like this. Not by her.

Suddenly, he yearned for that pain. He wanted it. He needed it. After all, pain was what he knew best. Pain meant that he was alive, pain meant he was still here. He needed to be here. He needed to be here for Tanya, for Matt.

Now stop giving in and start fighting back.

He looked down and saw the ghostly image of himself moving away with his left arm. He tried to move it and saw that he couldn't. It was already gone. He looked to his right and saw that it was still there. He told it to reach up and saw that it was listening, at least for the time being. The ghostly image was making its way to separate from his right shoulder, as well as his head and right arm. He figured through his pain that if it reached his head, it was game over. His right arm shot out and grabbed Anoaka by the throat.

Her eyes widened. This had never happened before. No one ever reached out and grabbed at her when she made sure that they couldn't move. How was it happening now?

She didn't care. She kept going on in taking him. Taking him into the pain that was her hell. She saw the soul start to drive away from his right arm. She knew then that it would be too late for him. His grasp would release, and then fall to the side as he died. She saw it start to happen as the soul separated form his arm, his forearm, his wrist, now all that was left was his fingers. His weak, tiny little—

There was pain in her throat. Ungodly pain that she had never, NEVER felt before. It stopped her from breathing, what little breath was available. Worse, it spread through her chest, and up her face. When she looked down, she saw something that horrified her. Her soul was separating from her. It was small, but it started at her neck, right where the bastards hand was on her neck. It started to move away from her flesh along with his soul.

He was manipulating her soul with his! If this kept up, she would die.

Panic took hold of her at this thought and realized him. Released all of him back into his body. Her grasp let go of him, but his remained.

His hand on her throat tighten harder as he was released. The pain that was escaping him, slammed back and hard like train wreck. He felt terrible, and could barely breath, but he felt alive. He remembered the gun that was in his pants and pulled it out as fast as he could. He cocked the hammer back with one thumb and pointed the barrel right under Anoaka's chin. She saw this and started to wraith out on his right arm, the one that was around her throat. Once again there was a brief flash of orange, followed by an incredible pain throughout his forearm. He screamed out loud, but kept his gun underneath her chin, balancing it on top of his fleeing right hand. Then, he pulled the trigger.

There was a flash of blood popping out of the back of her head as she hit the ground with a thud not unlike the one her husband made only a minute or so ago. All her grips released when she collapsed, but the pain she inflicted in his arm did not abate.

He collapsed shortly after she did. Holding his arm and trying to catch his breath. The heat surrounding him and moving in to take him. He remembered shortly ago, thinking that pain made him know he was alive. The pain he felt now with the smoke entering his body and the pain on his arm, he now knew that he didn't want to be alive. Not anymore.

Fire was making its way toward him on the carpet, as he felt his skin burning. He played there and waited for death to take him, knowing that he did what he came here to do. Setting Matt free, and hoping that Tanya got away.

There was a loud crashing sound as Tyler played on the ground. He didn't realize that he closed his eyes, until he opened them up. He looked toward to sound of the crash and was flooded by cool moisturized air from the outside. The pain in his arm was still intense, but the fresh air filling his lungs, brought him back to coughing and delight. As he looked toward where the fresh air was, he was blinded by a lot of light and saw that the light was coming from a headlight from a car. A car had crashed through the outside wall and brought the air with it. He saw lots of stone rocks from the side of the house breaking their way int the burning library, but also saw that the car that broke in was blue. Only the one headlight survived the crash, and smashed the rest of the car with it.

The car then backed out of the hole that it had created and opened its driver door. Through the silhouette, Tyler could make out a woman's figure. Then she stepped into the light of the flames and could see that it was Tanya. She was running inside and rushed to grab his arm. "Get up! Get up, the fire is going to move in faster now that fresh air made its way in!" She was right the flames that were only a few feet away from him before, now made their way faster toward him. He started to move his legs toward the hole in the wall. He was slow at first, but then started to get the momentum going and started to get through despite the pain in his arm.

Once they got through, he started to go into the passenger side of the car. Suddenly he was pulled away from it by a pull of Tanya's arm. "Matt is in that one, we need to go over to the Jag!" Tyler responded to this with continuous coughing fits. H nodded and started to make his way over to the Jag that was on the street. "Get in!" Tanya screamed. He did.

He coughed for a while in the car. Trying to get it under control. "My arm. That bitch fucked up my arm!"

"Let me see it!" said Tanya as she started the Jag up again. "Let me see if I can rip my shirt of to stop the bleeding." She started to do so, until she saw the wound that was on Tyler's arm. Or lack there of.

There was no mark. Not even scratch marks that where surly going to be there from her claw attack in the end. There was nothing.

"There's nothing there Tyler. Theres no mark."

Tyler looked down. Shocked that there was nothing there. "Fuck! Who cares. We need to get to a hospital. Matt needs one. Hopefully he is still alive!"

"What about you?" Tanya asked worried.

"Another reason to go to the hospital. Let's go!"

Tanya put the Jag in gear, and started to drive. She looked in the rearview mirror and saw that the house was burning up all around now, despite the rain's efforts. It kept spreading and spreading for another twenty-five minutes, before a fire truck arrived to start to put it out. By then it was too late. All three floors collapsed onto itself by then, making the once beautiful prison that Edward had put it, into nothing more.

"Answer me this." Tanya said as she was starting to make the turns to make her way into town. "Is that bitch dead?"

Tyler hesitated as he tried to catch his breath to answer. "She better be."

Epilogue

"I'm fucking sick of wearing pants! It's fucking April and I want to wear shorts!"

"But it's freezing outside. You will catch a cold!" Tanya said.

"Then I will have one final runny nose before summer. So what? I will add it to the list of bad shit to happen to me this last year." Matt said. "Besides, I want to show off my legs in the wheelchair."

"What legs in the wheelchair?"

"Ha ha. You're a funny bitch!" Tanya knew that enough time had passed to where she was able to make this joke. Yeah Matt lost his legs, but he didn't have to feel down about it. Although the jokes didn't come overnight, but rarely anything did these days. Nightmares still plagued Matt, but no one could blame him. Being trapped in a basement for months on end, being tortured and starved, wasn't going to put you in for the soundest mind award anytime soon. He was still having a rough time getting use to prosthetics on his legs, but in the meantime, the wheelchair was more than suitable for him. At least he felt so. His physical therapist on the other hand, thought that he should make more of a go with them, all the time, everyday. Matt wasn't having that shit. Sure, pushing yourself helped you in the long run, but pushing yourself all the time, he felt just burned you out.

"Ty going to meet us there?" he asked.

"Yeah, he still has some shit to sort out with Sammy, but he said he would make it."

"What does he have to do with her now?"

"Well, with everything that went on," she still couldn't tell Matt Anorak's name without giving him a panic attack, so she often referred it to "everything that went on" to him. "She tried to put an acceleration on the divorce process and take all of his possessions while he was fleeing form everything. Seeing as how he looked so guilty that you were missing and all. But since Sgt. Gentle came forward and admitted seeing An—, I mean, the woman in the jailhouse, Tyler has been free and clear the charges. Putting the divorce process, 'back of the line' so to speak."

"Okay, that's great. What does that have to do with today?"

"Well today, everything gets finalized. Only he gets to have what he wants out of it"

"Oh." Matt paused at this. "Well, good then. Is he going to be alright?"

"Yeah I think so. Well, better than you anyways." she giggled at her own joke. She saw that Matt cracked a smile at this as well. "You hungry?"

"God I'm starving. My caretaker is vegan, and believes that all animals are sacred and shit. I just can't wait to sink my teeth into a nice fat brat, with everything on it."

"You're not going to put fucking coleslaw on it are you?"

"The coleslaw is the best part, Tanya!"

"Makes me want to puke overtime I see it."

There was a pause for a while. Tanya wheeled Matt up to a service van that had a built-in ramp for wheelchairs. Buckled him in, and then moved over to the drivers side to buckle herself in. When they started to get moving, Matt turned to Tanya and asked, "Does Samantha know about you and Ty?"

Tanya took in a deep breath. "I think so. If she doesn't, I would be a little surprised. After all we did spend months together on the run."

"Yeah, and you don't do something like that if you don't care for the guy." It was Matt's turn to lay down the jokes.

"Ha ha. You're a funny bitch, Matt."

"Whatever. If he didn't figure it out after all that you did for him, He would have hoped *I* didn't make it in the end, because I would have fucking killed him myself. You gave up everything for him, the least you deserve is his love."

Tanya blushed at this. "Thanks, Matt."

"But are things going okay between the two of you? Like how is his arm?"

"Things between us are okay, but his arm is strange. She left no marks behind, but it still hurts him all the time. Doctors have seen him and have even taken X-rays and MRI's, but they still don't know what is wrong with him. It got to the point where some of the doctor's think he is faking the pain. But who the fuck fakes arm pain from scratches?

"He had to go to the VA and get some medication form them for the pain. Nothing too strong, but something to take the edge off. Otherwise, he becomes really irritable. At least he was for the first few months, but he said that the pain has gotten better."

"Good. I'm glad to hear that. God knows how I would feel if I thought that bitch got the best of both of us."

"She didn't get the best of you Matt. Not really." They pulled into the park and started to drive toward the center where the Splash Pad and the miniature train where and saw the gathering of people.

"Is Don Gentle going to be here?"

"Yes, he wanted to express to you how bad he feels for treating you and Tyler so bad."

"Uh! I get it! You feel bad about it. I forgive you. Move on!"

"Well, if he didn't survive, Tyler and myself would be behind bars right now. Think about that."

"All I can think about is a brat right now. Help me get this chair out of this van, please."

"Ha ha. Yes sir!"

That was it. The papers were signed. Signed and notarized. Tyler felt like he knew he would feel like. Lousy.

"So there it is." He looked at Samantha square in the eyes. "Congratulations on your divorce. I would ask you if you got everything that you ever wanted from this process, but I still have my savings account, so I know the answer to that."

Samantha looked at him in disgust. "I never wanted your savings account. But if you were going to be in prison, I thought that someone should be able to have. Even if you wouldn't be able to."

"How thoughtful of you. Now have a nice life." He got up and started to exit for the door.

"Tell Tanya I said 'hi'." she called out to him. He gave her a wave back, without turning around. As he thought more and more about it, he was glad it was over. Glad it was over, and with something to hang on to. He thought about Tanya and what she was going to do tonight for supper. Or better yet, he might do something for her for supper. Yeah. That would be nice. Least he owed her he figured. He always told that to himself these days. Sort of like his own personal joke to himself. A joke, with screams of the truth in it.

Even though he felt lousy, he felt relief. Relief to know that almost a year ago from Samantha's proposal for divorce, that he could in fact trust, and love someone else again. That he wasn't as broken as he thought he was. Relief that he was alive. The pain in his arm told him that everyday. Although everyday, he didn't always feel like that. Somedays he felt like he wanted to take an axe to the arm and pray that the pain would go away, but something deep down inside of him told him that that wasn't going to happen.

He thought almost from the beginning that this pain was in the soul. In the end she damaged his soul and it was impossible to completely heal. Sometimes these thoughts made him sad, hell even angry. But then he would think about what it took for him to be alive here today and that made the pain seem more bearable.

He made his way to Marathon Park. Matt was having a barbecue with the police department in Wausau, sort of a going away gesture to him now that he couldn't chase bad guys with two prosthetic limbs. Hell, even Charlie's family was going to be there for him. They had a hard time since they found out he was murdered by Danny. Even if Tyler didn't feel that Danny was entirely responsible for that, it didn't matter, in the eyes of the law now, Danny murdered Charlie in his house. Tyler took some time to go over to his friend's house and talk to his wife Angie about what really happened. She didn't believe it at first. I think she even held Tyler a little responsible for what happened to her husband. Only these days he thought that these thoughts and ideas were slowly starting to make more and more sense to her. Causing Tyler to see more and more of her around these days. You couldn't talk to her about what happened, or what you think happened, but it was still nice to see her.

The best part of his days are the nights. Nights with Tanya that is. She started to make what happened to all of them seem not that bad, bringing in her kindness and her love to not only him, but to Matt as well. He looked forward to those nights. Nights like tonight. It made his days seem like the nights you had to sleep through to get to the mornings.

Samantha was not doing so well. Though she was free from Tyler, it wasn't in the most financial stable situation she wanted to be in; Max had to get hefty vet bills taken care of from the leg surgery that he had from jumping off a shallow dock; and Richard, her boyfriend was a worthless son-of-a-bitch that sat around and watched T.V. all day and waited for his unemployment check to come in every week. His unemployment was't even that much, a mind-blowing hundred-and-fifty dollars a week. Maybe enough for groceries if he gave a shit about groceries.

She was thinking that maybe this is a time for a change, yeah. After all, her divorce was now final. No more worrying about having to put on face for Tyler. Yeah. She was thinking she was going to drive home and kick Richard out of her apartment. It was her's now since he asked her to put her name on the lease instead of his, because he didn't have a job, and didn't want the landlord coming after him with everything tat he had, which wasn't much of anything.

She parked on the street and started to make her way into the apartment building. She entered the code to enter the building, when she felt light headed. She shook her head and waved the lightness away. She pressed enter on the keypad—and heard nothing afterward. She entered her code for the building again, hit enter, and once again heard nothing. She thought that maybe the buzzer was busted, maybe she should just pull on it to see if it would let her in. She reached for the door handle, when suddenly it turned into a nest of spiders that began to pour all over the door. They started to reach for her hands, some of them even jumping onto her hand and started to crawl up her arm to make their way to her face. She screamed as loud and as high as she could, trying to scramble to get the eight-legged fucker of her, but no matter how hard she hit herself, they would remain trying to get to her face. She ran away from the door, screaming and slapping herself to get rid of them, when she saw something far worse just across the street. It was Richard, dead and completely naked. Bugs and other creatures crawled and slithered up and down his decaying body. A creature that looked like a cross between a snail and a spider crawled around his penis. Roaches crawled on his arms and legs, and spider that looked like they came from the door, crawled onto of his head. He smiled at her. The smile made her go insane with terror. What was worse, he spoke to her.

"Come and get a piece of this Sammy! Come and get a piece of this, or I will make you have a piece of this! You don't want to make me give it to you, it's so much better if you *want* to have it!"

Right then she fainted.

"She is right where you said she would be." said the man talking in the cell phone, all dressed in green. "We will have her for him when he is ready. Yes. Yes. I am on my way."

Kolat hung up the phone, and put it in his pocket.

Author's Note & Acknowledgments

The Marathon County Police Department do not act in the way I have depicted in this novel. I wrote them the way that I did because I needed at least one of them to act like a self-centered asshole. Believe here and now when I say that they do not act like this in the real world. In my experience with them, they have carried themselves with the utmost form of professionalism and kindness where it is needed, even when it came to dealing with my heavy foot on a car pedal. I admit that as the story progressed that they became my whipping boy, which I realize was unfair and completely fiction. If anyone has been upset by this I sincerely apologize. You officers rock in my book!

There are a few ladies that I would like to thank: First off would be Samantha Beveridge for being my sister from another mother and another country for being there in support in the idea of this book and for everything else that had happened to the both of us for our time together since we met. To Courtney Hendricks who one of the strongest most intelligent women I have ever known, and has the personality to match it. Love you both!

As well As Vanessa Gray, Nichole Drew, and Sean Beveridge who have all read the book to help me with ideas, and input. You guys rock!

My wife who has supported me through all of my endeavors (this being the latest one) and not complained about them at all. Love you with all my heart sweetie!